Branches

THE LAMBERT AND FREEMAN FAMILIES
FROM 1934 TO 1965

SANDY LATKA

HERITAGE
Heart BOOKS

This book is primarily a work of fiction, although it draws on recollections of the author (Sandra), combined with extensive research into historical events of the time.

Several characters appearing in this work are entirely fictitious, and any resemblance to real persons, living or dead, is purely coincidental.

ISBN 978-0-9947991-0-4

Dedication

To Mike,
my first love and father of my two sons.
To George,
for being my everything.
To all of our children
and grandchildren and great grandchildren,
who make our lives complete.
Special thanks to:
Norma Hill, my ever patient editor,
whose encouragement inspires me.
Yasmin Thorpe, who shares her vast knowledge
of literacy with such generosity.
Dawn Renaud, who makes magic happen with print
and graphics.

The Branches: Descendants of Polly Freeman & Lance Lambert

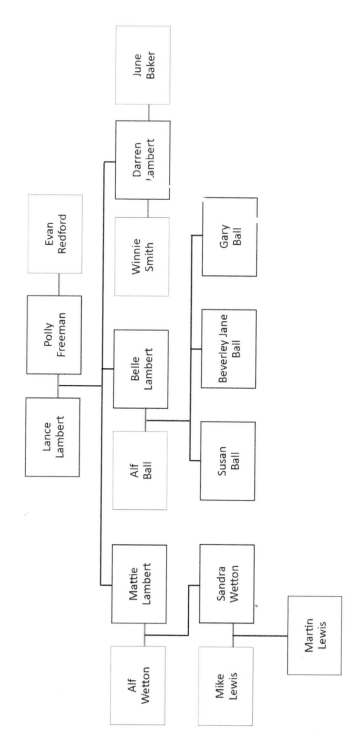

Introduction

Branches is the second book in a trilogy. The first book, *Twisted Trees*, follows the lives of the Lambert and Freeman families from 1861 to 1934. It is a love story, an inspirational story which tells how, in spite of sometimes insurmountable odds, good always triumphs over evil.

The families live in Derbyshire, England, and struggle through World War I, mining strikes and mill closures. Spencer Freeman loses his first wife in childbirth after their seventh child. He later marries a widow with seven children, and the games begin. Three sets of step-siblings intermarry. It is a very twisted tree.

The book ends with Polly winning the fight with her step-brother, Lance, who is also her husband, for custody of their three children.

Branches follows the life of Polly, and Evan Redford, who took her away from an unbearable existence and raised her three children as his own. The story begins in 1934, when Polly and Evan go to pick up the children, after court has granted custody, and it follows their lives up to 1965. Polly and Evan witness the Second World War and are again affected by tragedy.

The life of Mattie, the eldest child, is the main focus of book two. Mattie is the child of Lance, and in many ways she is his image. She is not a bad person, but dances to her own tune. Although her actions have consequences for all involved, there is no malice, just reckless pursuit of self-gratification. In rare moments of awareness, Mattie often regrets her compulsion to live so hedonistically. The moments soon pass and she is inevitably drawn back to the excitement of living for each moment.

The last part of book two introduces Sandra, daughter of Mattie and Alf, and traces her life through to her marriage to Mike and the birth of their son, Martin. At the end of the book, Sandra, Mike and Martin embark on a life changing journey.

One

A New Life Begins at Landrose ~ 1934

Cora knew her brother, Lance, had an evil temper, and even she was frightened of him. She had never wanted to house Lance and the children after his abusive marriage to Polly ended so violently. Lance was her brother though, and he had always dominated her. When Lance asked for shelter, she knew that the only possible answer was "Yes."

"We've got no choice, Spencer; we have to let them stay with us. Where else can they go? The bailiffs have locked his place up and put it up for sale already."

"What a bloody mess to be in, Cora. He's not done right by our Polly, but those kids have to have a roof over their heads until all this is over. I don't know how we can refuse." Spencer wasn't happy about Lance and his three children moving into their already cramped space. Both Spencer and his sister Polly had married their step siblings, and sometimes he thought that their marriages were cursed from the start.

Spencer and Cora had regretted their decision almost instantly. Lance was not a good house guest. They had witnessed his constant drinking and womanizing first hand. His outbursts of temper at the slightest provocation caused them both to walk on eggs in their own home.

Today Lance had lost his battle to keep the children. Polly had won and he was furious. Spencer and Cora dreaded having to face him.

Lance could not believe that he had lost custody of his children. "What judge in his right mind would give custody to a woman shacked up without benefit of marriage? She'll never be free to marry, I will see to that." Lance had a violent temper and was pacing the house like a caged animal. He had consumed far too much alcohol, and was now wound tighter than a tourniquet and ready to snap at any moment.

Spencer and Cora knew that the judge had made the right decision. Ever since their bitter break up, Polly had never stopped fighting to get her children back. She was a wonderful mother. She had left an impossible marriage where she had suffered verbal and physical abuse for years.

Cora looked at Mattie and Belle as they sat doing homework at the kitchen table. Darren was playing with some toy soldiers that Spencer had given him. They were all unaware of the day's events. She had seen how miserable they were without their mother, and knew that they would all be overjoyed to be reunited with her.

"When do you think Polly will be here to pick up the children, Spencer?" Cora asked quietly. The walls were like tissue paper, and she did not want to antagonise Lance any further.

"I don't know, Cora, but I know that I don't want to be around when she does. Get your coat on girl, and we'll get the hell out of here right now," Spencer whispered back.

"What about the children, Spencer? Is it safe to leave them with Lance in this mood?"

"They'll be fine, Cora. He's too busy feeling sorry for himself to think about them. Mattie will keep her eye on Belle and Darren. She's a smart girl, and I can bet our Polly will be here before we reach the end of the lane."

"Come on, Cora; let's go for a drive out to see Meg," Spencer said in a loud enough voice for Lance to hear. Cora was only too happy to go and visit her step sister Meg. She too was afraid of what might happen when Polly came to take her children away from Lance.

"Lance, we're off to see Meg," Cora called as she grabbed her coat from behind the door, and quickly closed it behind her. She had no desire to get into any arguments with him as he was now partially sober and in that morose mood that always followed his drinking.

Lance heard the door close and mumbled under his breath.

"Yes, that's it. Like rats leave the sinking ship. Well it's not over yet, nobody takes my children! A bunch of jumped up lawyers in fancy suits think they can decide my fate. Not bloody likely!"

Back at Landrose, Polly waited anxiously by the phone for a call from Jack to say that they could pick up the children. Jack was a wonderful lawyer and Polly knew how much she had to thank him for. He had fought fiercely and tirelessly to win back the custody of her children. Her children were her life, and when Lance took them away from her, part of her had died. When Jack promised Polly that she would be able to pick the children up and take them home to Landrose, it was as if he had given her back her life.

Polly grabbed the phone on the first ring, and listened to Jack's instructions. "Yes ... yes ... right away ... we're leaving right now." Polly hung up the phone and turned to Evan.

"He wants us to meet him at the police station in Wellington. I don't know why we have to waste time going there first, Evan. The court granted custody and he knows that he has to hand them over." Polly could not wait to hold them in her arms again, and even the twenty minute trip to Wellington would be torture for her.

"Now love, a few extra minutes won't hurt. We have the rest of our lives to enjoy with them. I am thinking that Jack has a reason for doing it this way. They'll be home with us before you know it." Evan wrapped his arms around her and led her out to the car. Polly knew he was right, but until the children were safely at Landrose, she found it impossible not to worry. Evan made it to Wellington in record time, and Jack and Sergeant Walker were waiting for them in the police station.

"Now Polly, we know of Lance's temper and his state of intoxication when we last saw him. We aren't going to take any chances of him doing something stupid. I want you and Evan to wait outside in the car, and we will go in and bring the children out to you." Jack was adamant and Polly could see that there was no use in arguing with him. She had never even thought of any danger, but now her heart raced as she, more than anyone, knew of Lance's unpredictable temper.

"He will never hurt the children," Polly wailed. "I am sure that he will not harm them. They are his flesh and blood and he could never hurt them."

"It's not the children, Mrs. Lambert, but he could very well try to hurt either you or Mr. Redford, and we don't need to risk that." Sergeant Walker had seen Lance on numerous occasions when he had been drinking, and knew of his violent temper.

Polly and Evan drove in their car behind Jack and Sergeant Walker out to Spencer's place. It seemed to take an eternity, but eventually they arrived. The place looked deserted, and Polly's heart raced as she thought that maybe Lance had taken the children away somewhere. They pulled up behind the police vehicle and Jack came over to tell them to stay put. "Polly, Evan, I need your word that you will stay here. No matter what you see or hear, I do not want you to move from this spot. The sergeant and I will handle this the way we know how. Don't worry, Polly, we have handled situations like this before and everything will be fine. You'll have your children back in no time." Jack gave Polly's arm a squeeze, and he gave her his most reassuring smile, but in his heart he knew that this was a very tricky situation.

Polly clung to Evan and never took her eyes off the house. She could hear her own heart beating, and every second seemed to be an eternity.

Lance was expecting to see Polly and Evan, not the sergeant and Jack, so he called for them to come in. The children were nowhere in sight, and Lance was sitting in a corner with just the light of a dim kerosene lamp, which was throwing shadows around the room. Sergeant Walker was one of the best trained men on the local constabulary, and even with the dim light, he scanned the room with razor like precision. Propped against the wall to Lance's right there was a 12 gauge double barrel shot gun. Quickly he leapt across the room and grabbed the gun. "You weren't thinking of doing anything stupid now, were you, Lance?" He checked the gun, and sure enough both barrels were loaded.

"Where are the children, Lance? Don't make this any more difficult than you have to. We are here to take the children back to their mother, and we don't want any more trouble." Jack's voice was calm and controlled. Sergeant Walker emptied the gun and, giving Lance a threatening look, he replaced the empty gun in the corner. "Now I wouldn't be doing any hunting tonight, Lance, in your state if I were you. I take it that you were planning on going out to bag a rabbit or two, right?" The two men were a team, and this was not their first domestic situation. They knew how quickly it could get out of hand, and it was important to diffuse the situation as quickly and nonviolently as possible.

Lance knew that he was beat, and staggering out of his chair, he led the way to the back kitchen where he had locked in the children. He knew when he was defeated and realized that he had lost the woman he loved and also his children. Much as he had abused her, she was the only woman he had ever truly loved. Lance knew that he could never have pulled the trigger on Polly, but Evan was a different story; he would have shot Evan without a second's thought, and to hell with the consequences. What did he have to live for now anyway?

Mattie knew what was happening, and was trying hard to keep from crying. She had bitten her bottom lip almost through. "Shut up the pair of you!" she said with a threatening look at Darren and Belle, who were both sobbing and clutching on to each other. Mattie was far more upset than she would ever let anyone know. Life at her aunt and uncle's had been miserable, and her father's temper and bouts of drunken stupidity unbearable to live through at times. It was the times when he was sober and ruffled her hair, calling her "a chip off the old block," that she would choose to remember. Jack unlocked the door, and Darren and Belle rushed towards him.

"Come on, my loves, your mom is waiting for you, and I know she wants to give you all a big hug," Jack said as he ushered the children out of the door. "Come on, Mattie, you're the big girl and I need you to show your brother and sister that everything is all right."

"All right?" thought Mattie. Nothing will ever be "all right" again. She looked back at her father, slumped in his seat, with his head in his hands, and all of the control drained from her little body. In a flash she pulled away from Jack and ran back to Lance.

Throwing her arms around him, she let the tears flow. "Don't worry, Dad. I'll always love you. You're my dad and I don't care what anyone says. I'm a chip off the old block." Lance put his arm around her as she wiped her tears away on his shirt before anyone else could see them. It was then that Lance broke down and roughly pushed Mattie away from him.

"Take her. Take them all, but they are all Lamberts and blood is a lot thicker than water. They'll all come back one day. It'll take a bigger man than Evan Redford to fill my shoes." Lance rose from his chair and slammed the door hard behind them all before he reached for the bottle of whisky. He needed to drink until his head was too confused to think, but he knew that when he sobered up nothing would change. His children were gone. No amount of alcohol could change his situation. With a blood curdling howl, he threw the bottle at the door and watched it shatter, along with all his hopes of any reconciliation.

As soon as Jack came out of the door with the children, Polly jumped out of the car and ran to hold them in her arms. Evan went over, picked up Belle and Darren, and placed them in the back seat of the car. Polly led Mattie back and helped her into the back seat. Darren and Belle were red-eyed, and tears ran down their cheeks as they looked confused and frightened by the whole affair. Mattie looked as if she were about to explode at any moment as she tried to hold back her mixed emotions.

In between tears, Polly hugged them all and tried to reassure them of her love. "You poor darlings, you must be so confused and frightened. Don't worry, my loves; things are going to be so different from now on. We are all going home to Landrose, and we will never be apart again. I need you to be a big girl, Mattie, and look after your brother and sister. They need you to be brave. Evan has made you a special bedroom of your own, Mattie, and it has a window that looks out over the fields."

Mattie was not convinced that anything was going to be better. Even though she had seen a different side of her father in the last several months, he was still her father. Evan was, in her mind, the cause of all the discord. She climbed into the back seat and glared at Darren and Belle. "Move over and stop snivelling; do you want the whole seat?" she said, as she sat down with a resigned look on her face.

The ride back to Landrose was made in silence, as both Darren and Belle knew that Mattie would not be afraid to give either of them a clip on the ear if they made a fuss. Polly clung to Evan's arm as he drove them along the country roads.

Mattie had only been at Landrose the one time when she had run away from Spencer and Cora's, but she could remember the cozy feel of the home. Everyone was tired, especially the two little ones, so Polly made them a bowl of warm cereal and then led them upstairs to their bedrooms. Mattie was the last of the children to go upstairs, and tired as she was, she could not help but notice how beautiful her room was. Polly had long anticipated the day she would bring her children home, and she had made sure everything was perfect. Evan had given the room a fresh coat of paint weeks ago, and Polly knew he was trying to stay positive for her sake. The bed was piled high with pillows and comforters, and there was a soft pink carpet under foot. "Goodnight, my little darling. Sleep tight, and in the morning we will go and explore all around the fields." Polly kissed her cheek, and by the time she had left the room, Mattie was asleep.

Polly went downstairs and smiled at Evan. "I thought that this day would never come, my love," she said as she put her arms around him. Evan turned her face up to his and kissed her lovingly.

"I knew it would come, Polly. The children are part of you, and you could not live without them just as I could not live without you." Arm in arm they climbed the stairs, knowing that although they had won the battle for the children, they would still have other obstacles to overcome.

Two
LIFE AT LANDROSE

Evan had spent almost his last dollar fighting the court case, and things would be tight financially. Polly knew that she could make money raising chickens and doing what she had done at Cranston Farm, so she persuaded Evan to buy her some chickens. Before long, Polly had increased her stock and was selling chickens and eggs to many of the people in the village. Evan was very good with anything mechanical, and he made extra money by working as a mechanic. If anything broke down, farm equipment or a lorry or a car, he could fix it. The days were long, but as night time came, they could sleep knowing that every day was a better day. Lucy and Meg became frequent visitors and never showed up empty handed. Meg was now pregnant with her first child, and Polly was as excited as if she herself was expecting. Lucy usually brought along Kitty and Frank, her two children, and the three sisters found comfort in each other's company, while the children played. Life sure had not been easy for any of them, but somehow they were able to put their troubles on hold when they were together.

Mattie, Belle, and Darren all went to Wellington School, and Polly saw to it that they were always dressed in good clothes and had shiny shoes. Lance never stopped trying to cause trouble for Polly. He bad mouthed Evan at every opportunity. One day Lance went to the school trying to cause trouble, and barged in to the headmaster's office. "I am Lance Lambert and my children are being kept at Evan Redford's place. I want to know if they are coming to school dressed properly. There'll be hell to pay if they are coming to school in rags!" Lance knew that Evan and Polly had been struggling to get back on their feet.

"Why Mr. Lambert, your children are amongst the best dressed children at school," the headmaster assured him. "They haven't missed a day of class and their grades are really good. You have nothing to worry about at all." Lance scowled, as he knew that somehow Polly and Evan must be getting ahead. He left the school dejected and knew his chances of taking the children away from Polly and Evan were hopeless.

He did not know that Evan had pinched and scraped, even down to mending his own shoes with old car tires, so that he could provide the necessities for Polly and her children. His only indulgence was his pipe, and he had now started to grow his own tobacco. It smelled awful, but Polly beamed as she saw him trying numerous times to get his pipe to light, knowing that he would not give up until he did. He had not quite perfected the drying process, so sometimes the damp leaves would not ignite. How could she complain about the smell, when she knew that this was just another sacrifice he had made for them all?

Polly loved life at Landrose and had started to make homemade wine from a variety of different plants and fruits and even vegetables. She always had a beautiful supper prepared, and the house was filled with appetizing aromas of home baked breads and hearty stews. One evening after supper, Evan and Polly were sitting quietly listening to the fire crackle in the hearth. Polly had at last started to relax and was less fearful of Lance and his threats. The children had gone to bed when suddenly there was a loud bang, followed closely by several more.

Polly jumped out of her seat and clung to Evan. "My God, Evan, it must be Lance." She was trembling like a leaf.

"Stay where you are, Polly. I will go and have a look. It's probably just kids fooling around," Evan said with much more conviction than he felt.

Polly sat nervously waiting for him to return, and then when she heard him laughing she finally relaxed. "By the heck, my girl, that must be one potent batch of wine you made," he said between fits of laughter. "You have six bottles that blew the corks off, and there is parsnip wine all over the pantry." He was brandishing a half empty bottle, and with a wink he said, "Fetch the glasses, love; I think we need a drink to steady our nerves."

Evan and Polly worked together, and every day was a day closer to regaining respect and acceptance within the community. Lance, on the other hand, slipped farther and farther into disrepute. Somehow he had managed to find employment within the electrical industry, and although his drinking and carousing carried on, he always made it to work on time. He was a hard worker and a good worker, especially when he was doing something that interested him. It was a life of potential gone to waste, as the more money he earned, the more he spent. Lance had few friends, and the ones that he did have were not a good influence on him. He flitted from one relationship to another, and his lady friends soon lost interest when his money ran out. Polly had been the love of his life, and he knew he would never find another love like the one he had lost. Even his brothers saw little of him anymore, and Harper in particular avoided him like the plague. Harper would never forgive Lance for involving him in the beatings of Polly and Evan. It was still difficult for Harper to accept that Polly had chosen Evan when she left Lance, as he had always loved his brother's wife. Now that Harper was a widower, he would have married Polly in a heartbeat if she would have had him. Polly had long since forgiven Harper for his actions that night at Landrose, when he had helped Lance to beat both her and Evan until they were left in a pool of blood on the floor. She knew how Lance was capable of manipulating his brother, and in her heart she knew Harper would despise Evan for taking her away. Polly had loved Harper as a brother and a friend, but had never given him any cause to believe their relationship could be anything else.

Polly loved Landrose and the fact it was nestled into the bottom of the lane. Unlike Cranston Farm, which stood at the top of bleak moorlands, Landrose was set amongst green fields and nearby woodlands. It was her joy to walk up the fields to the reservoirs and take lunch for Evan. Belle and Darren would often accompany her when they were not at school, and they would all have a picnic on the grassy banks. From the vantage point of the top reservoir you could see for miles. Life was almost too good, as Polly had never been used to such bliss. There were ups and downs as is the case in all families, but they were a family in every sense of the word. For the first time in her adult life, Polly did not have to face anything alone.

Mattie was the only one who steadfastly refused to accept Evan as a father. It did not matter what Evan did; he was not Lance, and all his kindness was lost on Mattie. Polly worried about Mattie more and more each day, as she was getting withdrawn and much quieter than was usual. Quiet and Mattie were two words seldom used in the same sentence, as Mattie was very vocal when things were not to her liking. The last several weeks Polly had noticed that Mattie was not eating much and she had lost some weight.

"What's the matter, Mattie? Are you feeling ill?" Polly asked one morning when Mattie was particularly slow to get ready for school.

"I've got a pain in my neck and I feel horrible," Mattie replied.

Polly looked at Mattie and she did look flushed "Come here, my love, let me have a look at you." Mattie quietly obeyed and pointed to her neck where the pain was.

Sure enough, there was a distinct lump on Mattie's neck and she was certainly feverish. "Evan! Come here and take a look at this. I think we need to get Mattie to a doctor."

Evan looked at Mattie's neck and was instantly concerned. He had seen something similar to this before, but did not want to worry Polly.

"I think we had better get her to the doctor and let him take a look, Polly," Evan said as he went outside to start the car.

Mattie did not even protest as Polly bundled her up and took her out to the car.

Once at the doctor's, Evan's fears were confirmed. Mattie had a tuberculosis gland in her neck. It was serious, and the doctor said that surgery was the only certain cure.

Polly was very frightened for Mattie. Tuberculosis was a terrible disease, and just the thought of Mattie suffering from it was devastating. Mattie listened to the adults talking and knew that whatever was wrong was not good. She really did feel awful, and hoped that now they knew what was wrong, it could be fixed.

Polly wrapped her arms around Mattie reassuringly, showing far more confidence than she felt. Trying to maintain her composure, she looked up at the doctor.

"Does that mean that she will be sent to a sanatorium, Doctor?" There was no way she wanted to be parted from Mattie again, even on a short term basis.

"Don't worry, Mrs. Lambert; we will get her scheduled for surgery as quickly as possible. She will not have to stay in a sanatorium, as I know that Landrose is just as good as anywhere for her to recuperate after surgery.

True to his word, the doctor scheduled surgery for the following week, and although Mattie was in hospital for two weeks, she was allowed home to Landrose to recover.

Fortunately it was a beautiful summer and Polly was able to move Mattie's bed to the window, which she could open and let Mattie benefit from the healing powers of the sunlight. The surgery was a success, and after another six weeks of bed rest, Mattie was allowed up at last. She had been miserable in bed, and missed her friends at school, especially her friend Olivia.

Olivia had suffered from polio and walked with a limp, but she never referred to it nor acknowledged she had any impediment. Mattie felt at her neck and cheek, and although she had not yet seen the scars, she knew that they were there. The first time that she saw the scars down her cheek and her neck, she was horrified. "I'm a freak," she cried. "I'm so ugly. No one will want to even look at me!"

"Now Mattie, do you feel that way about Liv, just because she has a limp?" Polly asked.

"No, of course not!" Mattie replied.

"Well then, why are you so concerned about a little scar?" Polly tried to make light of the situation, but in her heart she knew that Mattie would carry the scars for the rest of her life. A trail of deep scars created a path from Mattie's ear to the bottom of her neck. "They will get much better as time goes by, Mattie, and no one will ever notice them." Polly was happy that Mattie had made such a great recovery, and this was a small price to pay for having a healthy daughter again.

Evan had heard the conversation and he thought that he might know a way to bring Mattie out of her depression. He had saved money, and with it he now bought Mattie a bike, as Olivia had one and he had seen Mattie clinging desperately to the back of Olivia as she pedalled at break neck speed down Landrose Lane.

One night when Mattie came home from school, the bike was propped up by the side of the wall waiting for her. It was a shiny red Raleigh bike, and it had a big silver bell on the handle bars. She could not believe her eyes, and it was the first time she spontaneously gave Evan a hug. It had been a brief hug, but it meant the world to Evan as it was the first physical show of emotion he had received from Mattie.

"I'm off to see Liv. Tell Mom that I will be back before dark!" Mattie yelled, as she hopped on the bike, and ringing the bell all the way, headed towards Tibshelf.

"Be careful, Mattie!" Evan called after her, but it was no use; she had disappeared into the distance, bell still ringing. Evan smiled as he went back into the house and hoped that this might be the start of a thaw in Mattie's cold heart.

Mattie and Liv were a force unto themselves. They made their own rules and could find fun and excitement anywhere. "Hey Liv, come and see what Evan bought me!" Mattie shouted as she pulled in to Olivia's yard.

"I told you he was all right," Olivia said as she went to inspect the new bike.

Olivia liked Evan, and she wished Mattie would give him a chance. She had heard the stories of Lance and his mistresses and could not understand Mattie's ill feelings towards Evan, who in her mind was a far better man.

"He bought you a good one, Mattie; this is a beauty, and a bell on it too."

"He's not my dad and he never will be. It doesn't matter what he buys me," Mattie said with her chin in the air. She was conflicted as she really couldn't find anything to dislike about Evan, other than the fact that he wasn't Lance.

"Come on, Liv, let's go down to the rail tracks," Mattie said as she jumped back on her bike. Liv did not need any encouragement, as she was fascinated with trains and loved to sit by the tracks and watch them as they went past. Sometimes they would wave at the engineer and he would wave back. There were often some of the boys down at the tracks too, and they were far more fun to play with than the girls' siblings. Mattie was more interested in the boys than the trains, and especially one of the older boys named Sydney. He had hair the color of ripe corn and deep blue eyes. Sydney had missed Mattie for the last few weeks and knew that she had been isolated with tuberculosis. Sydney knew that T.B. could be a death sentence, and he had been worried about her. When the girls reached the tracks, Sydney was there with his friends, and Mattie instinctively put her hand over the scars and turned her other cheek towards him.

"Hey Legs! How are you doing?" Sydney called as he came towards her.

"I'm fine Syd," Mattie said as she tried to hide the scars. It was no use, as Sydney was looking directly at her. He reached out and took her hand away from her face. Mattie was close to tears, as this was the first time that he had ever touched her, and now he would see how disfigured she had become. Sydney saw no disfigurement, just the girl that made his heart race every time he saw her. He showed no surprise or pity, and tracing his finger gently down the line of scars, he changed the subject to her new bike. The awkwardness was over, and he probably never knew how much he had helped Mattie to overcome her self-consciousness that day.

Olivia was exceptionally bright and loved to write poetry. Very often the rhymes were quite risqué, and it was hard to believe they were penned by one so young. Mattie loved to listen to Liv's verses, and the two of them would sit and giggle as Liv would make up something about one of the lads by the tracks. Olivia had seen the attraction between Mattie and Sydney and had penned numerous verses about Sydney and his obvious crush on Mattie.

Time by the tracks went by quickly, and it was starting to be dusk.

"Oh damn! I have to get back or I will be in trouble again," Mattie said with a grin.

"What's new?" smiled Liv, "You are never out of trouble!"

It was to some extent true, as Mattie never could obey rules. "Clean your room" was usually accomplished a day or two after the request. Orders to stay away from the boys by the tracks fell on deaf ears. Mattie picked up her new bike, dusted off the sand and gravel, and waving goodbye to Liv, she pedalled as fast as her legs would go, all the way back to Landrose.

Her rush was not just the fact of being in trouble for arriving late, but the thoughts of Landrose Lane after nightfall. Even though the house itself was in an open clearing, the lane was narrow and flanked on either side by large hedges. Mattie would never forget the night she had run there close to five years ago, as a child of ten years old. She would always remember her fear that night, and it still sent shivers down her spine. Thank heavens she did not know at the time of the brutal murder that had happened only two farms away from Landrose House.

Since living at Landrose, she had heard about the murder of Lizzie Boot, at the farm she passed on her way home from school every day. It had happened years before, in 1896, but the murder was so brutal it had captured national headlines. William Pugh, an unemployed mine worker from the local Shirland Pit, had hacked Lizzie Boot to death with a billhook. He was apparently disgruntled because she had told her friend, Sarah Saunders, that he was a no-good good-for-nothing. William had tried to get Sarah to go out with him, and she had declined his attentions because of Lizzie's remarks. Lizzie was only 19 years old and had no idea of his intentions when he called at the farm that night. He lured her into the barn, under some pretence or other, and there he callously murdered her in cold blood. William was convicted of the murder and was hanged in Derby three months later in August 1896. He was just 21 years old.

The Boot family eventually moved and the farm sold, but the new occupants said that no matter how many times they whitewashed the barn, the blood stains still came through. Over the years the story had been embellished and had become even more brutal. People said the farm was haunted by Lizzie, and there had been numerous "ghost sightings."

Mattie quickened her pace and pedalled as fast as she could past Boot Farm.

Recent events had brought the story of Lizzie Boot's murder back to mind, as now there was another suspected murderer on the run. It was scarily similar to the Lizzie Boot murder, and this suspect was still at large. She had overheard her mother and Evan talking about Ronald Smedley, and the fact that he was on the run from the police. He was the main suspect in the murder of Jessie Ball, who was killed at the cottage where she lived in Matlock.

"They've not caught him yet," she overheard Evan say to Polly. "They think he is being helped by friends in this area, who are putting out food for him and sheltering him in barns and sheds around the neighbourhood."

"Well I know he is well liked and has never been in trouble before, Evan. Our Lucy said that if he did it, he must have done it in a fit of rage. He had good reason to lose his temper. He had been engaged to Jessie for two years and knew that she was pregnant; he planned to marry her in a couple of months. She was a really flighty girl according to everyone who knew her, and she was also seeing another fellow called Harry Ludlum. They think she told Smedley the baby might not be his, and he went crazy with rage."

"Until he is caught and stands trial, Polly, we will all have to wait and see what else comes out in court." Evan was never quick to pre-judge anyone, but at the same time he could not condone murder.

Evan and Mattie's mother had discussed the murder for the last week or so, and apparently several people who knew the couple had come to Smedley's defence.

Mattie had also seen pictures of Smedley in the paper and he looked like a really nice young man, but no matter what, he was a suspected murderer. For the past week there had been a full-fledged search and Mattie had heard the blood hounds trying to track him down. It was getting dark, and when Mattie saw Evan and her mother standing at the gate she let out a sigh of relief.

"Where have you been, my girl?" Polly questioned, trying not to let Mattie see how happy she was to see her.

"I've just been to show Liv my bike, Mom. We lost track of time, and it got dark so quickly." Mattie's heart was racing, but she would never admit how glad she was to see them. It did not matter if she was in trouble for being late, she was home and safe!

It was twelve days before Ronald Smedley was eventually found. He was fast asleep on top of a haystack in a field not far from Landrose. According to the news reports, he was remarkably fit, and his condition was attributed to the fact that he had been given food and clothes by sympathetic supporters. The papers were full of nothing else for the weeks leading up to the trial.

"They've got a petition started for the acquittal of Ronald Smedley," Polly told Evan one night over supper. "It sounds like they can't prove murder. He says they had an argument about the baby, and she picked up the poker from the fire and swung at him. He says that he grabbed the poker away from her and flung it at the fireplace before he took off in a temper. She followed him out, shouting after him, and he picked up a rock and threw it at her. His defence is that he left not knowing he had struck her in the head with the rock."

"Yes, I heard that he might get off with being charged with manslaughter, which means he won't hang." Evan hated violence of any sort, especially violence against a woman. He had witnessed it at first hand with Polly and Lance, and his feelings were mixed when the final verdict came through.

"Well, I am glad that it is all over," said Polly, "Now maybe everyone can get back to their own lives. There's been talk of nothing else for months."

Three

MATTIE STARTS WORK

Polly and Evan had settled into a comfortable routine at Landrose. Over time, Darren and Belle began to think of Evan as their father, and Mattie had accepted his existence.

It was hard to believe how quickly time was passing. Evan and Polly had finally overcome the gossip and become accepted in the community as man and wife. Polly's only heartache was that they were NOT man and wife, as Lance had steadfastly refused to EVER divorce Polly.

Olivia was a year older than Mattie, and at age sixteen, she had started working at Leashore Mills, so Mattie could not wait to finish school and go and join Liv at the mill.

"Mattie, you are too smart to work as a mill girl," Polly admonished. "Evan has said that he will pay for you to go to secretarial school and take a course in shorthand and typing."

"I don't want to be a secretary!" Mattie said, defiantly rejecting any suggestion she go to secretarial school. "I want to go to The Mill."

"Well Mattie, you are going to go and take the course anyway. That's final. We can talk about where you are going to work later. Maybe they will have a job for a secretary at the mill."

Mattie had heard the girls from the mill laughing and sharing stories of some of the fun that they had at work, and Mattie wanted to be part of it all.

"I don't want to be a secretary and sit in an office all day. I want to work on the mill floor with the rest of my friends. Liv says that she can get me a job in her department, and they have lots of work there." Mattie walked away, thinking that she would get her own way. Polly sighed, resigned to the fact that she was going to have a battle on her hands to convince Mattie to go to secretarial college.

At last Mattie completed her final year of school, and Liv wanted to go to Blackpool to celebrate. "How much money have you got, Mattie?" Liv asked "We are going to need enough for the train fare and some food. We can stay with my aunt Ruth, so we don't have to pay for a room or anything."

"My mam and Evan will never let me go overnight, Liv; they are so strict I still have to be in bed by ten every night. You would think I was ten years old!" Mattie grumbled.

"You don't have to tell them where we are going, Mattie. Just tell them you are staying with me. They will not mind that, and you don't have to tell them we are going to Blackpool." Liv knew that Polly and Evan were comfortable with the fact that Olivia came from a good home, and Mattie had slept over before. "Well then, how about money, what can you scrape together?"

Mattie looked crestfallen. She had never been able to save any of her allowance, and she knew the train would cost far more than she had. Suddenly she had a bright idea.

"Liv, I know how we can raise some money. Evan has a perfectly good set of false teeth he keeps in a drawer upstairs. He never wears them! They have some gold in them and I bet we can pawn them for enough money for the train fare." Mattie was like Lance; she would find an answer for anything.

Liv had a fit of giggles. "Mattie, you can't do that. What if he decides to wear them, and they are not where he left them?"

"He hasn't worn them for years. He has another set. I'll sneak them out tomorrow and we can take them into Alfreton." Mattie was already planning how she was going to accomplish her task.

The following day Liv and Mattie met up and set off for Alfreton. Mattie had wrapped the teeth in a clean napkin and put them in a tobacco box. They paced up and down outside the pawn shop, planning what they were going to say. When at last they went into the store they were met by an old bespectacled man, who surveyed the young girls over the top of his thick glasses.

"Well, young ladies, what can I do for you today?" he inquired.

"We want to know how much money we can get for these," Mattie said as she carefully unwrapped the teeth and showed them to the clerk.

He looked at the teeth and then back at the girls, with a quizzical look.

"Whose teeth are these?" he questioned.

"They're my dad's," Mattie answered.

The clerk gave her a stern look, "Does your dad know that you have them?"

Mattie thought of saying that her dad was dead, but then thought better of it, as she did not want to encourage the wrath of God. There was a difference between a white lie, and a big whopper, and that would definitely have been a big whopper.

"No," she answered, head down and feeling very uncomfortable under his scrutiny.

"Well I suggest you put them back where you found them before he misses them, young lady; I'm sorry I can't accept them without authorization from your father." The clerk did his best to keep from smiling as he watched them hurry from the store.

Liv and Mattie left the store resigned to the fact that the trip to Blackpool would have to wait for a few weeks. Mattie would try and save her allowance and earn a few extra shillings helping her mam with the chickens. She hated cleaning out the hen house, but when she was determined to do something, she would find a way to do it.

Polly and Evan insisted that Mattie go to secretarial school, and reluctantly Mattie agreed to give it a try. The first strike against the school from Mattie's perspective was that it was all girls. Other than Liv, Mattie had no close girlfriends. She was much happier in the company of boys. Most of the girls in her class were there because they wanted to be, but Mattie was there under duress. It was her nature to be number one at whatever she did, so even though she hated the class, she was soon a star pupil. This did nothing to endear her to her fellow students, as they thought she was stuck up and anti-social. In fact, Mattie could never see the point of fostering friendships with people with whom she had nothing in common. After six months at secretarial school, Mattie came away with a first class certificate and excellent shorthand and typing skills. She also came away with a loathing for secretarial work and a determination that she was going to work at the mill.

Mattie and Liv had still not managed to take their trip to Blackpool, even though Mattie had tried hard to save her allowance. Mattie wanted to start work at the mill as soon as possible. Sydney and Liv, her two best friends, were a big reason for her impatience. They were both full of stories of all of the fun they had at the mill.

Since she had finished at secretarial school, she had been assigned chores at home until she found work. Housework was even worse than office work, and Mattie knew that she had to find a job soon. One day when she was scrubbing the front step, she heard the mill girls laughing merrily on their way to work. That was all it took! Mattie flung the scrubbing brush as far as she could. "Sod it! I am going to tell mam that I am going to the mill and that's the end of it!"

Polly heard the pail and brush go crashing across the yard and knew that Mattie was about to issue an ultimatum. "Evan, it's no use, we are going to have to let Mattie start at the mill and just hope that she gets tired of sitting at a machine all day. She thinks it's all fun and games, but when she sees that it is hard tedious work, maybe she will change her mind."

Evan knew that Polly was right, but he had hoped she would take a job at Britannica Insurance, where he knew the manager. It was a good job with great prospects for a smart girl like Mattie. He had tried to broach the idea to Mattie, but his advice had fallen on deaf ears.

"Well, I think you are right as usual, love; she'll drive us both crazy if she doesn't get her own way." Evan's relationship with Mattie had improved somewhat with time, and he had to admire her determination. He laughed, "She's like a dog with a bone, that one. She'll never quit until she gets what she wants!" Polly saw so much of Lance in Mattie, and hoped that as time progressed she would not develop the same single mindedness. Thank heavens that Mattie had a much better sense of humour than Lance ever had, and she did not possess the same dark moody side as her father.

That night Polly and Evan decided to let Mattie try working at the mill. They both thought she would soon lose interest and want to find an easier job. They were wrong. Mattie loved the mill and was almost instantly one of the girls. The first day she was there, she wore a short skirt and a pair of high heel shoes that she had borrowed from a friend of Liv's. She left the house in her flat walking shoes and changed into the heels before going into the mill.

Mattie had great legs and she knew it. Even at fifteen, she loved to dress up and knew that she was captivating to the opposite sex. "Hey Legs! Welcome to the mill," Sydney shouted, and so her nickname was cast in stone for the rest of her life. She loved the attention from all the boys at the mill, especially Syd, who soon let all of the other fellows there know that she was his girl. Mattie did not mind being Syd's girl, but she did not believe that stopped her from being friends with all the boys. Maybe it was the scars that made her feel insecure of her looks, or just her nature, but she needed constant admiration. She basked in the limelight of being the center of attention; whether it was good or bad, it was all attention.

After a few weeks working at the mill, Mattie had managed to save enough money to buy a pair of high heel shoes of her own. They were black patent peep-toe shoes, with a white bow on the heel strap. She kept them in her bike bag and changed when she got to work, strutting into the mill like a diva. The shoes were not made for walking, but it mattered little as they sure lifted her spirits as well as her already five foot seven inch height. One night she came home late and forgot all about changing her shoes. Polly looked through the window and saw Mattie hobbling over the cobbles, perilously close to taking a tumble on the uneven stones.

"What on earth are you doing, my girl? You are asking for a broken ankle. Where did you get those shoes?"

"I bought them with my own money, mam, and I know how to walk in them! Aren't they lovely?" Mattie walked as carefully as she could into the house, then took them off and put on her flat slippers. She had no one to impress at home anyway.

That night when Mattie had gone to bed, Polly took the shoes to Evan. "Here love, see if you can cut a couple inches off these shoes our Mattie bought. They're nice enough shoes, but she'll break her neck on them." Evan dutifully took the shoes and very carefully sawed off about two inches, then re-heeled them. When he had finished they looked as good as new.

Next morning, Mattie, late as usual, raced downstairs, grabbed her lunch pail and her shoes, and threw them into her bike bag. Once at the mill she quickly took off her flats and put on her heels.

"What the blooming heck!" Mattie looked at her feet in dismay. Her toes were cocked in the air, and when she tried to walk it was like being on a roller coaster. Liv heard Mattie swearing and went to see what the problem was. When she saw Mattie's feet she burst into gales of laughter. "All you need is a red nose and an orange wig, Mattie, and you can earn a dollar or two at the fairground."

"They were my shoes bought with my money, and if I want to wear them and fall on my arse then it's my problem. They are ruined, and my mam and Evan can buy me a new pair!" The rest of the day Mattie had to wear her old flat cycling shoes, and she was in a foul mood when she got home. Eventually a compromise was reached, and Polly and Evan replaced the shoes with a new pair with a slightly lower heel. Peace reigned again for a while.

"Our Frank's going away on a job for a couple of weeks, Mattie, and he says he will give us a couple of quid to look after his parrot while he is gone." Liv knew Mattie would not be impressed to have to feed and water the parrot, but she also knew Mattie would go along with her to keep her company. Frank was living a few miles away from home. He was very frugal and had saved enough money for a down payment on a little stone cottage. Frank had bought the parrot a couple of years earlier, and had already taught it a limited vocabulary. "Kiss Frank" and "Bertie's a beauty" were its party pieces. Mattie decided the parrot needed to enhance its vocabulary, so by the end of the two weeks, Bertie was quite vociferous.

Frank came home and was pleased to see Bertie was still alive and looked none the worse for wear after being left in the care of Liv and Mattie. "Here you go, girls, you did a good job," Frank smiled as he gave the girls their payment.

Mattie and Liv thanked him and quickly took off, trying to stifle their laughter.

"Hello Bertie, kiss Frank. Bertie's a beauty," Frank crooned as he put his fingers to the cage to scratch Bertie's head.

"Bugger Frank, bugger Frank, piss off Frank, Bertie's a beauty," the parrot squawked.

Frank could not believe his ears, but it was too late. Bertie had been trained well, and his new vocabulary was now a part of his routine. Frank was a good natured lad though, and there was no doubt in his mind that Mattie had been the instigator. It was hard to stay mad with her for long as she had a way of charming herself out of most trouble. He had to see the funny side of it though, as it had taken him almost a year to train Bertie to talk, and it had only taken the girls two weeks.

Mattie and Liv were great pranksters and were often in trouble for causing a disruption, but they got away with a lot, thanks to Mattie's charm. Mattie was most often the instigator, but Liv needed little encouragement to follow her lead.

One day Billy Chisholm had been teasing them, and they put up with it for a while before deciding what they were going to do with him. They waited for him to go for his break, and then they both pounced on him. A slight lad with bright red hair, he was no match for the terrible two. Olivia pushed him into the elevator, and Mattie pushed the big clothes hamper in behind them both. They pressed the button, and before he knew it they had him in the hamper and had fastened the latch. At the next floor Mattie got out, and for the rest of the break they sent him up and down the elevator in the hamper. When they finally let him out, he was green and far too embarrassed to say what had happened, so they got away with it.

The only time they both came close to being fired was when they doctored the punch at the Christmas party. Mattie knew her mom had amassed quite a few bottles of her homemade wine in the pantry, and figured a couple of bottles would never be missed. "Mam and Evan are taking our Darren and Belle into town tomorrow, Liv, so I can sneak the wine out when they are gone. You had better come and keep watch while I put it into something we can take into the mill."

"Your mam will kill you if she catches you, Mattie," Liv exclaimed, as she was always a little afraid of what Mattie would get up to next, but at the same time she enjoyed the excitement of getting away with mischief. Mattie chose the bottles of clear wine, as she thought they would be easier to mix into the punch without detection. It was a particularly potent batch of parsnip wine, in fact probably closer to moonshine than wine. Mattie uncorked the first bottle and almost dropped it and its contents on the stone floor. Liv jumped as the cork shot out of the bottle like a rocket, and the loud pop was enough to wake the dead.

"Wow Mattie, that must be some good stuff," Liv giggled

"Quick, hold the jars, so that I can pour it in." Mattie wanted to get the job done as fast as possible.

She poured the wine into pickle jars and sealed it well. She had figured it would be easy to take into the party if she threw it in a basket with a couple of jars of her mom's pickled beets on top and covered the basket with a tea towel.

Before Polly and Evan returned, Mattie had made sure to spread out the remaining bottles of wine and hide any evidence of their theft. The basket was stashed behind one of the hedges on the lane, ready to pick up the next day. It was a very quiet lane and the girls had no doubts that it would still be there the following morning.

Liv and Mattie arrived at the party early and, uncharacteristically, volunteered to help with setting up the function. Liv set the beets on the table, and Mattie poured the brew into the punch. The two of them had already sampled the results before the rest of their work-mates arrived. The party was soon in full swing, and everyone was laughing and having a great time until the mill supervisor decided to sample the punch. He knew, at the first sip, that it had been doc-tored! Alcohol was strictly forbidden at the mill as it could be a very dangerous place to work. There were huge machines with numerous sharp needles, and accidents happened even in safe environments. He was responsible for the safety of his workers, and he had seen accidents happen before.

"Who did this?" he roared. "Own up now, or the party's over and everyone is docked two days' pay!" Mattie and Liv looked at each other and knew they could not be responsible for everyone losing pay. Together they put up their hands and accepted responsi-bility. "My office NOW!" he fixed them both with a stare that was as cold as ice. Mattie and Liv were suddenly stone cold sober and knew they were in big trouble. Much to the dismay of the party goers, the punch was quickly poured down the drain.

"Olivia Thraves, I am surprised at you. You know better than to bring alcohol on the premises. Mattie Lambert, I am guessing that you are the one behind this!" He fixed Mattie with a stare that sent shivers down her spine. "Do you realize that you could have caused someone to have an accident here with your stupidity? You could have lost me my job and caused the mill to be in trouble with the law!"

Olivia was not going to let Mattie take the blame alone. "I am just as much to blame as Mattie, sir. We thought it would be a laugh, and we did not think of the consequences."

"It was my mom's homemade wine, sir, and I brought it to the mill, not Olivia." Mattie was not going to risk losing Liv her job. If it meant Mattie was going to get fired, then so be it, but she would not let Liv share her fate.

"Well, what am I going to do with the pair of you? Olivia, you can take two days unpaid leave, and I am afraid there will be a reprimand on your file. I am sorry to do this as you are a good and reliable worker. If anything like this happens again, I will have no choice but to fire you.

"Mattie Lambert, you are new here and I will give some consideration of that fact. You were, however, the instigator, and so you are off work on unpaid leave for one week. You are on probation for the next three months and already start with a reprimand on file." The mill manager knew Polly Lambert, and he knew that Mattie would be in even more trouble when she had to explain to her mom why she was off work without pay.

"Get your coats and go home, both of you, before I change my mind and fire the pair of you now!"

He watched as the two girls, heads hanging, walked quickly out of his office. He understood that it had been a childish prank, and that they had not realized the seriousness of their stupidity. Olivia was a good worker and had never been in any real trouble before. Mattie, although new to her job, was a fantastic worker and had already been put on a very complicated linking machine that few people had the ability to work. It was a machine that needed exceptional eyesight and also keen precision; Mattie had both. He did not want to lose either of them, so he hoped his warnings had not fallen on deaf ears.

"What are you going to tell your mom, Mattie?" Olivia asked as they left the mill behind them.

"I guess I am going to have to own up and tell the truth, Liv. She has a way of finding out every time I do something, anyway." Mattie was not looking forward to having to tell her mom and Evan that she was on unpaid leave for a week. Since starting at the mill, Mattie had paid board, and she would not be able to pay next week. "What about you, Liv, what are you going to do?"

"I am going to blame it all on you, Mattie. My mom already thinks you are a bad influence anyway!"

Mattie laughed, as she knew Liv would not do that. She was a true friend.

Polly was furious when she found out what Mattie had done, and she thought the best punishment was to make sure that Mattie earned her keep for the next week by having to do the lion's share of the housework. There was no doubt this was the best possible chore to give her daughter, as she knew Mattie hated housework with a passion. "You can scrub that step, my girl, and clean all the window ledges before supper. Don't be thinking you are going out to see Olivia either. You are grounded for the next week!"

Mattie grudgingly took her punishment and counted the days until she was free again.

Things went back to normal at the mill, and although they still played jokes and had fun with their co-workers, it was innocent and harmless. Mattie became one of the best workers, and had soon risen to a better paying job. Syd had become less a friend and more a boyfriend. He waited for Mattie to finish her shift at the end of each day, and always cycled home along with her until she got to the end of Landrose Lane. It was a few miles out of his way home, but he loved spending time with her. She always stashed away the high heels before getting on the bike, and tucked her skirts into her pantie legs. Syd watched in total admiration. Her long legs and dark hair were a test of his restraint. He wanted nothing more than to feel her body next to his. He knew that he was older and that Mattie was still only sixteen, but damn it, he wanted her so bad.

One night as they cycled back to Landrose, Syd stopped his bike in front of Mattie.

"Come on Legs, give us a kiss," Syd pulled Mattie towards him, and almost off her bike.

Mattie pulled her bike away, and like a flash she was yards ahead of him. He knew her mom and Evan would be home at Landrose and thought better of trying to follow her.

"You have to be quicker than that, Sydney, if you want to catch me. Better luck next time!" Mattie laughed as she outdistanced him.

"That means there will be a next time, Legs. I take that as a promise."

Syd smiled as he turned around his bike and headed home. He was four years older than Mattie, and she was the first girl he had ever been interested in. She was different from any of the other mill girls. There was something mysterious about her that fascinated him. Her long slim legs and those flashing emerald eyes reminded him of the heroines he had seen grace the pages of magazines. *Yes*, thought Syd, *there will be a next time*. He was not one to give up, and he knew Mattie had eyes for him. In fact, most of the single girls at the mill had eyes for Syd. He was as nice natured as he was handsome, and it was very easy to like him. He was a mechanic and so worked on the machines when there was a break down. Sometimes the girls would deliberately jam a machine, just so Syd had to come and fix it. It was not Mattie's nature to chase after anybody, and if Syd wanted to be her boyfriend, he was the one who would have to do the chasing.

After several weeks of Syd's advances, Mattie finally agreed to go out with him. He arranged to take her to the Matlock Fair, and she was excited about going. It was always fun to go to the annual fair and stroll around the stalls and sideshows. Mattie spent a lot of time getting ready, including going to the sandpit in the yard, where she rubbed the damp sand all over her legs. Stockings were expensive, and even though she got a discount from the mill, she had to improvise when funds were low. The damp sand gave her long legs a nice tan sheen and she was pleased with the result. She decided against wearing anything too light coloured as she did not want the sand to stain her dress. The dark green dress with a tight bodice and waist and a full skirt that swayed as she walked was perfect. Mattie's flair for fashion was something else; she could make the plainest of clothes look sensational. She tied a white and yellow polka dot scarf at the neckline and sneaked a pair of Polly's white gloves into her purse. She would put them on once out of sight of Landrose.

Polly watched as Mattie got ready for the fair, and was not convinced she was going with Olivia.

"You are going to a lot of trouble just to go to Matlock Fair, Mattie. Are you sure it is Olivia you are going with? I don't want you hanging about with any of the boys from the mill." Polly gave Mattie a knowing look.

"Well of course there will be some of the lads from the mill there, Mam, but I am going with Liv," Mattie said. It was the truth, as both Liv and Mattie were going, but each was going to meet up with their date at the fair. Olivia had started to go out with Fred, a nice young man from the packing department, and they were a great match. He was mature for his age and came from a very good family. They balanced each other perfectly.

Mattie, on the other hand, was all about having fun, and she did not want to commit to any one boy—but there was something about Syd that was special. She had not gone to all this trouble for just anyone!

"Come on, Legs, let's have a ride on the Octopus," Syd called as he clasped her arm and set off towards a ride with buckets that spun in all directions. Liv and Fred were already ahead of them, the boys more enthusiastic than either Mattie or Liv. Not wanting to let the boys know they were scared, the girls each jumped into one of the still spinning buckets. Fred and Syd piled in after them, and Syd made sure that he was next to Mattie. The ride took off with a lurch, and as anticipated, the girls clung on to the boys for dear life. Syd chuckled, as his plan had worked. Mattie was stuck to him like glue, so close he could smell her freshly washed hair and the Evening in Paris perfume that would become her signature. Syd could have stayed on the ride all night, but Mattie wanted to explore the fairgrounds.

There was something about the fair that made Mattie reminisce about the gypsies that used to camp at Cranston Farm, and for a moment she was lost in her reverie. She still missed Lance, and often wondered where her father was. Blood is thicker than water she thought, as for all of Evan's kindness, he was not and never would be her father. The carnies, as they were called, were a vagabond lot of travellers that went from town to town, working for the fairgrounds. They were mostly dark skinned gypsies, and because of their hard physical work they were usually very muscular. Mattie thought of Tommy and Lyas and wondered where they were. She pictured what they might look like today; would she recognise them if she saw them? When Lance had spent time with the gypsy women who camped on their farm, Mattie had played with Lyas and Tommy. They were two rag tag gypsy boys who taught Mattie, amongst other things, how to cook and eat a hedgehog. Mattie understood her father's attraction to the gypsy way of life, as she too loved the colourful caravans and the free way of life the gypsies led. She had been too young to know of her father's womanizing, and saw no wrong in his nightly visits to the gypsy camp.

"Come on, Legs, let's go on the Big Wheel," Syd pulled her behind him and bought two tickets for the ride. He was hoping that the height might scare her a little, and who would she have to hold on to but him? He was wrong of course, as Mattie loved every minute of the ride and would have gladly gone on it again.

The evening was filled with fun. Syd and Mattie went on several rides and ate toffee apples and candy floss, and Syd showed his shooting skills on the rifle range. He was used to shooting live rabbits and was a crack shot, so shooting at plastic ducks was no challenge. After he had achieved a perfect score on round after round, the man behind the stall gave Mattie her choice of any of the trinkets behind the counter. "That's it for you, young fellow!" he said as he took the rifle away from Syd. "With that type of shooting you are going to put me out of business!"

Syd chuckled, and was glad that he had been able to show Mattie his skill with a rifle.

"So what are you going to choose, Mattie?" Syd said as he looked at the array of stuffed animals and dolls and glass ornaments.

Mattie had never been one for stuffed animals or for dolls, but there was a beautiful amethyst coloured glass sugar bowl with a lid that had a flower on top.

"That one," she said without hesitation. The stall owner gave her a disgruntled look, as she had chosen one of the best pieces in his stall. It had been with him at several fairs, as few people got perfect scores, and the ones that did usually chose one of the gaudy stuffed animals. He reached the glass bowl carefully from the top shelf and handed it grudgingly to Mattie.

"Thanks, Syd. It's perfect, and I will put it on my dresser and use it to put my best jewellery in."

"I somehow didn't think you were going to use it for sugar, Mattie," he said with a laugh. Somehow domesticity and Mattie were not synonymous.

When the night came to an end, Syd hated to say goodnight, but it had been a super time and he knew that Mattie had enjoyed it.

"Thanks, Syd, I really did have a great time, and I love the sugar bowl," she said with a smile.

"I had a great time, Mattie. You're a real corker, and tonight you look smashing."

Tonight was the first time that Syd had called her anything other than Legs, and the way that he said her name seemed to take their relationship from casual friends to a different level.

"Goodnight, Syd," Mattie smiled, and before he knew what had happened, she had kissed him. It was just a quick peck on the cheek, and he was too stunned to react before she had dodged away into the crowd.

"Come on, Liv. Let's make a break for it before they find us." Mattie was already a few yards ahead of Liv, whose limp slowed her down a bit. Liv was not sure she wanted to leave anyway, as she and Fred were having so much fun.

Syd touched his cheek where Mattie had kissed it, and decided against chasing her through the crowds. He knew she would come around in time, and he was not going to run after her. Mattie was the type of girl who would not appreciate a lap dog, and he knew that.

29

When Mattie got home, she carefully placed the amethyst sugar bowl on her dresser and thought of the fun she'd had that night. She had been very proud when Syd outshot all the other fairgoers. His open neck shirt and rolled up sleeves had shown his tanned and muscled physique. She certainly was not impervious to his charms.

"Maybe next time, I will let him kiss me," she thought to herself.

Mattie had not noticed Belle was still awake. The two girls now shared a room, as Darren had been given his own room now that he was getting older. "What's that you've got, Mattie?"

"Nothing for you to touch, Belle; it's glass and will break easily. Here, I'll show you," Mattie said, as she carefully carried the trinket over to the bed.

"It's beautiful, Mattie." Belle admired the sugar bowl, and now that Mattie was home, she turned over and promptly went to sleep.

Belle adored her big sister and did not have a jealous bone in her body. Mattie, on the other hand, had little time for Belle as the age difference gave them little in common to talk about. While Mattie was already working, Belle was still in school and playing with dolls. Belle was the one who had inherited her mother's love of domesticity. Even at her young age, she loved to spend time in the kitchen with Polly when she was cooking. Mattie enjoyed the meals but not the preparation. Mattie was all Lance, and Belle was all Polly. Darren also featured his father in his looks and his ways, but he was still the one who tugged at Polly's heart strings the most. Even Polly could not understand her strong emotions when it came to Darren. *Maybe it's because he is so much like Lance that I am protective of him*, she mused. Growing up in the image of his father would not be an easy path. Polly knew that Lance had been tortured by his own demons. She had on rare occasions seen how wonderful Lance could be, but far more frequently she had seen his outbursts of uncontrollable rage. She prayed that Darren would benefit from the stability and warmth of the home Evan had provided for them all. Evan was a wonderful role model for all the children. He never raised his voice in anger, or showed any special favour to any of them. When Polly and the children came to live with him, they became his life. Evan loved them all, and never for one second regretted opening his heart and his home to Polly and her children.

Mattie climbed into bed beside Belle, and wished she had a room all her own. It was a long time before she went to sleep, as the events of the evening were still flooding her mind. Sydney was indeed a great shot, and she had been very proud watching his precision as one by one he had popped off the plastic ducks. By the time he had finished there had been quite a crowd gathered, and it was obvious by the cheers that Syd was very well liked by his peers. Mattie remembered the quick peck on the cheek and the clean smell of his skin. Yes, maybe next time she would let Sydney kiss her. Eventually she drifted off into a deep sleep, and it wasn't until the rooster crowed that she awoke to a beautiful morning.

When Mattie came downstairs, Polly and Evan were deep in conversation.

"Things are not looking good, Polly," Evan said, as he helped himself to another slice of toast. "Hitler is posturing and heading us all towards another world war."

"Oh Evan, don't even think about it." Polly could not bear to think of going through another war. The last war had claimed the life of her beloved brother, Alfred, and she had seen so many lives devastated by the futility of war.

Seeing Mattie come into the room, they both quickly changed the subject. War was not something the children should have to worry their heads about. It did not matter though, as Mattie had already heard the rumours at work, and unlike Polly, she saw the romance of war. Some of the young fellows at the mill had already talked about the possibility of being called to do National Service. They were young and full of adventure, and the possibility of travelling overseas sounded like a huge adventure. None of them had witnessed the First World War and the devastating losses. She knew that Syd would be one of the first to sign up, as he was a leader in everything.

"There's already a bunch of the lads at the mill who are ready to go and fight. I think that they are almost hoping that we do have a war," Mattie said as she reached over and took the last slice of toast.

"That's only because they have no idea what they are talking about," Polly admonished. "There is never anything to be gained by conflict. If only women ruled the world, things would be a lot different."

Evan smiled at Polly, and pulling her towards him, gave her a quick kiss on the cheek.

"Well I'm off to work, my girl, before you start to rule the world as well as this household."

Polly smiled back and followed him to the door. She gave him a lunch box filled with fresh baked bread and his favourite bacon and egg sandwich, before reaching up to give him a lingering kiss.

"Lesson number one, Evan Redford: If a thing is worth doing, it is worth doing well." She winked as she closed the door behind him.

Four

SECOND WORLD WAR

When Hitler became the Chancellor of Germany in January 1933, he made a decision to use the Treaty of Versailles as a pretext for Germany to acquire land where German speaking people lived. He managed to successfully envelop Austria and Czechoslovakia, without even starting a war. It was Hitler's mission to become The Master Race, where only Aryans were valued. His racist theory was that only blue eyed blond Europeans were true Aryans. After experiencing the devastating losses of World War I, England and France had no desire to enter into a Second World War. It was only when Hitler threatened Poland that war became inevitable.

Neville Chamberlain was the Prime Minister, and the general feeling in Derbyshire, as in most of England, was that he was weak and gullible and the wrong man to be holding the fate of the country in the palm of his hand. He had flown to Germany in 1938 to meet with Hitler, first at his private mansion in Berchtesgaden, and then on two other occasions to try and negotiate a peaceful co-existence. He came back from the notorious Munich Conference in 1938 and jubilantly proclaimed, "I believe that it is Peace for our Time."

Chamberlain had been duped by Hitler. Winston Churchill, his strongest critic, stated that Chamberlain had been given a choice between war and dishonour, and Chamberlain had chosen dishonour but would have a war anyway.

At the beginning of September, war was inching closer by the hour. The order came for everyone to immediately use any and all measures to black out interior lights. The fear of a surprise night invasion was real and very frightening.

Polly did not want to cover the windows with tar or paint, as some people did, as this meant that day or night the house would be devoid of natural light. "Evan, give me a hand, love, to fasten these old blankets to a rod. If you make me a couple of brackets by the side of the window, I can hang them up at night and then take them down in the morning." Polly wanted to keep things as normal as possible when the children were around.

Evan set to work and made sets of wooden brackets for each window, and it became the nightly ritual to put the blackout curtains up before switching on any lights. Evan still had to carry on with his work, and often this meant driving out to a pump station at night. Now that the use of headlights was banned, his work was far more dangerous, as he had to negotiate the narrow winding roadways and steep hills in the dark. Polly always breathed a sigh of relief when she heard the rumble of the car in the driveway.

Churchill was indeed right when he said that there would be war. At 11:15 a.m. on 23rd September 1939, war was declared.

It was a beautiful Sunday September morning, and there was nothing that could have foretold the sudden chill that would befall the millions of listeners as they sat beside their wireless sets to listen to their Prime Minister speak. Polly and Evan sat by the side of the old "His Master's Voice" wireless and waited to hear Chamberlain's announcement. Against all threats of retaliation, Hitler had invaded Poland, and the reports of casualties were devastating. There was little doubt that the announcement would be a declaration of war. Polly clutched hold of Evan's hand and knew the impending speech would set their world in turmoil all over again.

"Oh Evan, not again. Isn't it enough that we have had to experience the horror of war; now our children have to go through this?"

"There is nothing we can do, Polly. This Hitler is a mad man and he has to be stopped." Evan spoke with much more confidence than he was feeling, as he seriously doubted Chamberlain's ability to lead a nation into such conflict. Evan believed that due to Chamberlain's incompetence, England had lost a huge advantage by waiting so long to challenge Hitler's actions.

The old wireless crackled and sputtered a little but the announcement came through loud and clear:

This morning the British Ambassador in Berlin handed the German Government a final note stating that, unless we heard from them by 11 o'clock that they were prepared at once to withdraw their troops from Poland, a state of war would exist between us. I have to tell you now that no such undertaking has been received, and that consequently this country is at war with Germany. You can imagine what a bitter blow it is to me that all my long struggle to win peace has failed. Yet I cannot believe that there is anything more or anything different that I could have done and that would have been more successful. Up to the very last it would have been quite possible to have arranged a peaceful and honourable settlement between Germany and Poland, but Hitler would not have it. He had evidently made up his mind to attack Poland whatever happened, and although he now says he put forward reasonable proposals which were rejected by the Poles, that is not a true statement. The proposals were never shown to the Poles, nor to us, and, although they were announced in a German broadcast on Thursday night, Hitler did not wait to hear comments on them, but ordered his troops to cross the Polish frontier. His action shows convincingly that there is no chance of expecting that this man will ever give up his practice of using force to gain his will. He can only be stopped by force.

We and France are today, in fulfilment of our obligations, going to the aid of Poland, who is so bravely resisting this wicked and unprovoked attack on her people. We have a clear conscience. We have done all that any country could do to establish peace. The situation in which no word given by Germany's ruler could be trusted and no people or country could feel themselves safe has become intolerable. And now that we have resolved to finish it, I know that you will all play your part with calmness and courage. At such a moment as this the assurances of support that we have received from the Empire are a source of profound encouragement to us. The Government have made plans under which it will be possible to carry on the work of the nation in the days of stress and strain that may be ahead. But these plans need your help. You may be taking your part in the fighting services or as a volunteer in one of the branches of Civil Defence. If so you will report for duty in accordance with the instructions you have received. You may be engaged in work essential to the prosecution of war for the maintenance of the life of the people - in factories, in transport, in public utility concerns, or in the supply of other necessaries of life. If so, it is of vital importance that you should carry on with your jobs.

Now may God bless you all. May He defend the right. It is the evil things that we shall be fighting against - brute force, bad faith, injustice, oppression and persecution - and against them I am certain that the right will prevail.

Evan switched off the wireless and put his arm around Polly. "Come on, lass, you and I have weathered storms in the past and we will be facing this together. We have to stay as calm as possible so the children don't pick anything up from our uncertainty."

"I knew it was coming, Evan, and I am not afraid for us, but oh! Those poor lads that will have to go to war. They have never seen the horrors of a war and have no idea of the hell that is about to be unleashed. Thank heavens Darren is not old enough to enlist, and hopefully this war will be short lived."

Evan had his doubts that this was going to be a quick victory. He knew that Hitler had been ramping up his army and his weapons in readiness for conflict. Polly was always Evan's first concern, and he was keeping his thoughts to himself. He knew that he had to be strong for her and the children. Darren and Belle were playing outside and had no idea of what was happening. Mattie was with Liv, and they were listening to the announcement along with Liv's brother and her Mom and Dad. The adults, who had experienced war, listened with dread and a strong sense of foreboding, but the announcement was exciting and energizing to Mattie and her peers. What did they know of war? It was something that was new to them, and therefore they had nothing to measure the news against. They would soon find out what war meant.

The factory became manned primarily by women, as all the eligible young men either signed up or were conscripted. Syd, as Mattie had predicted, was one of the first to sign up. He did not end up in the navy though, as he decided to follow his cousin Joe into the Royal Engineers Regiment. "We may as well let the bloody government give us an education while we fight this sodding war," Joe chuckled, and as Syd worshipped his older cousin, how could he argue.

In just a few short weeks the great austerity programs began. Everything was in short supply, from clothing to food. Factories began sewing uniforms and parachutes and essential items for times of war. Every household tried to do their bit, by donating all their old pots and pans and anything metal that could be re-fabricated and turned into weaponry. Secrecy was advocated and preached in schools and workshops alike. "Loose lips sink ships" became a national slogan. Spies were feared and suspected everywhere. There were several thousand potential enemy aliens living in England, and this was an immediate concern. Special tribunals were arranged, and all people of German and Austrian birth over the age of sixteen were subjected to categorization. If they fell into the "high risk" category, they were immediately interred. Herded together like cattle, they were sent to internment camps throughout Britain. Large manor houses, old school houses and racetracks, anywhere that could provide isolated and secure accommodation, was quickly commandeered and designated as an internment camp.

By mid-1940 the war was escalating to a point where even Mattie was fed up with the austerity and the general tension everywhere. Mattie received word of Syd from his sister who also worked at the mill, and apparently he and Joe were due to come home for leave. Preparations were in place for a big party, and Betty said Syd had especially asked her to see that Mattie was there to welcome him home. Mattie had thought of Syd often since he had left, and wondered how he would be changed by his experiences. She had blossomed into a stunning young woman, and at just eighteen years of age was mature beyond her years. During Syd's absence she had gone out with other boys, but there was no one in particular in her life. Mattie enjoyed the adulation of many, and loved the power of being just a little out of reach of all of them. Now she thought of Syd's impending return, and for the first time she was apprehensive and unsure of her charms. Would he still care for her, or had he met some cute little French girl while he was overseas? The last posting she had heard was that he was somewhere in France.

"When's he coming home then, Bet?" Mattie needed time to prepare what she was going to wear for the big day.

"Not sure yet, Mattie. You know what they are like, everything is top secret, but we think it will be in the next couple of weeks sometime. Joe's ma had a letter from him, and he thinks they will get picked up this month."

It was almost the end of May and everyone was looking forward to the grey rainy days ending. The weather had been as bleak as the news, and there seemed no end in sight to the war.

"Shall we go over to the B & B and see if they have anything new?" Liv was just as much into fashion as Mattie was, and the Bargain Barn was the only place they could afford. It was a second hand store to which everyone took the clothes that they no longer wanted, and often found different items to purchase. Liv knew that Mattie would be a willing companion, as she would certainly want to find something nice to wear when Syd got back.

"I've got a few things to take there, Liv, so I'll go home and throw them in a bag, and meet you there in an hour." Mattie went back to Landrose and sorted through her closet. Her taste had changed over the last couple of years, and she tossed all of the full skirted and brightly printed dresses she no longer favoured, into the bag. She knew just what she wanted for Syd's homecoming, and hoped she might be able to find something at B & B. When she arrived, Liv was already there and had found a couple of outfits that were perfect for her, and still in her budget. Liv was shorter than Mattie and had not developed the same bosom, so the two never competed for clothes.

"How about this one, Mattie?" Liv giggled as she held up a drab grey dress that looked as if it had come from a school ma'am.

"Thanks Liv, but I can do without your fashion advice, if that's the best you can do!"

Mattie browsed along the racks, finding little that caught her eye, but since working at Leashore Mill, she had learned a thing or two about alterations. Maybe there was something she would be able to sass up a little. She was just about to give up when a little green dress caught her eye. It looked shapeless, but the fabric was soft and would drape perfectly. The green would complement her eyes, and she knew that she could alter the dress to fit.

Liv looked at the dress, "Well Mattie, if you can make something out of that, I will be surprised. I like the material, but it's really frumpy." Liv did not have Mattie's vision, and wondered what had attracted her to that of all the dresses.

"Well, I know what I am going to do with it, and you just wait and see, Liv Thraves!" Mattie took the dress to the clerk and managed to badger him down to next to nothing. In fact he was glad to get rid of it, as it had been in the store for weeks and no one was interested in it. Mattie took her purchase home and draped it on a hanger, swathing the material this way and that until she finally approved of the results. She pinned and sewed the dress, and by the time she was finished it bore no resemblance to the one she had bargained for at the B & B.

When she tried on the dress it fit perfectly, but her trained eye told her it needed something extra to give it the designer touch she was looking for. She had darted the dress above and below the waist, which emphasised her hourglass figure, and she had cut off several inches from the hem. She took the discarded material and fashioned a belt that formed a diamond in the front. A little stiffening from Polly's sewing basket and *voila*! Perfection. She rummaged around in her cupboards for the right jewellery to wear, and decided that all it needed was a pair of earrings. The dress was stunning and under-stated, so she could go a little wild with the earrings. She chose a pair that she had bought at the fairground before the war. They were gold stars falling in a chandelier type grouping, and when she tried them on, they reflected the green of the dress. Looking in the mirror, she was well pleased with her night's work. She thought back to when Syd had taken her to the fair and the magic of that night. She had also worn a green dress then; although much different in style, she in-stinctively knew that Syd would like this one. For the next couple of weeks Mattie listened for any news of Syd's return.

Syd and Joe at last heard they were going to get picked up by the Lancastria. It was a converted White Star Liner that was being used as an evacuation ship during the war. "Come on Joe, get a wiggle on, we have to make it to Charpentier Roads to get the ship. It's sup-posed to be just outside Port Nazaire." Joe was every bit as anxious to go home for leave as Syd was, so took little coaxing to pack his kit and leave France and the hell of war. They had both looked death in the face and seen comrades blown to pieces in front of them. They had gone to war full of a sense of adventure and pride at doing their duty, but time had aged them both well beyond their years. Neither Syd nor Joe had shared their horror stories with family and friends back home. What was the point? How could anyone imagine the carnage unless they had lived it, as they and their comrades in arms had done?

At last they arrived at the dock and it was total chaos as several thousand soldiers and airmen all tried to embark. "Bloody hell, Syd, stick with me like glue or we'll get separated in all this bloody mess!" Syd tried his best to keep sight of Joe, but a big burly seaman pushed his way in between them, and before he knew it, a stream of airmen followed in his path.

"Joe, stay put and wait!" Syd tried to yell above the din, but he was unsure that Joe had heard. "Sod it!" Syd muttered under his breath, "I suppose I'll find him somewhere during the trip over the channel."

Joe looked around for Syd, but he was nowhere in sight. He pushed his way through the throng and finally found a corridor with a

bench that was rapidly filling with exhausted lads, all as eager and
excited as he was to be going home. "Shove up, boys, make room for
me and my coz. The silly bugger got stuck at the back of the line
somewhere." Everyone shuffled up a few inches and Joe threw his kit
on the seat beside him, leaving a space for Syd. They had stuck
together in the same unit and had been by each other's side through
most of their time in France. Although they were family and friends
in England, the bond they had developed overseas was something
altogether different.

The Lancastria sat at anchor waiting for the last of the troops to
finish loading. "Come on, let's get a move on. How many more can
they get on this bloody ship?" a soldier sitting next to him complained. In fact, the ship was way overloaded and now had over 6,000
people on board. Syd pushed his way through the crowds and
breathed a sigh of relief when he saw Joe and the empty seat beside
him. "You took your sweet time, our Syd. I bet if I were Mattie
Lambert you wouldn't have let me out of your sight!" Joe chuckled
and at last relaxed with his back against the ship wall. In spite of the
cramped conditions and the fact that the men were all physically and
mentally exhausted, there was a general air of jubilance.

It was around 1300 hours when they heard the sound of a German
JU88 bomber in the distance. The mood on board the Lancastria
changed instantly, as everyone was suddenly on high alert. The
Oronsay was at sea some distance away and appeared to be the target.
It was bombed but escaped a direct hit and managed to stay afloat.

"Jesus Christ, let's get a move on," Joe said, as he looked at the
dock and saw they were still loading troops. "Where are they going to
put them? We're jammed like bloody peas in a pod now."

"Them Jerry bastards are going to be back for sure; we're sitting
ducks here," said a young lad, who looked no older than sixteen.
Shivering with fear and cold, he clasped his coat around him and
covered his ears to shut out the sound of the bombings. The bomber
droned off into the distance, thinking it had scored a hit that would
sink the Oronsay.

"Come on, lad, we've made it this far. We'll be on our way before
they come back." Joe looked at the young fellow and realized that he
felt just the same fear and trepidation. The only difference was that
he had learned how to hide his feelings. With a loud booming voice,
someone started to sing "Roll out the Barrel," and one by one the

tired passengers joined in. It was almost two hours before the last of the passengers finally came on board. Syd figured there were somewhere between 7,000 and 8,000 passengers and crew.

It was almost 1600 hours when they spotted the German bombers returning. The red alert was sounded and people began to scramble for cover. The sound was deafening as the planes flew low overhead. Joe instinctively threw himself over Syd and pulled him down onto the deck. The first bomb hit the port side and ruptured a full fuel tank. Black clouds of smoke made it almost impossible to see, and as the ship began to roll perilously from port to starboard, the desperate passengers scrambled to jump overboard. Joe clutched at Syd and dragged him to the ship's rail. "This bugger's overcrowded anyway; come on lad, let's make a jump for it!" The last thing Syd saw was Joe's cheeky grin, and then there was a cataclysmic explosion and blackness.

The JU88 bomber had dropped a direct hit right down the funnel of the Lancastria. Joe and Syd were killed instantly as the explosion ripped apart the deck under their feet. In less than twenty minutes, the Lancastria was completely submerged and the sea was a churning mass of debris and bodies.

Churchill was reluctant to publish any news of the fate of the Lancastria. It was imperative morale remain high and news of casualties be minimized. This was the worst disaster in maritime history with over 3,000 lives lost. The true tally of the dead was impossible, but less than 2,500 escaped with their lives. The scope of the disaster was hid from the public for decades.

The Croft families waited for news of Syd and Joe's return, and had no idea of the fate of their loved ones. Mattie hung her dress in the closet, ready to wear when she saw Syd again for the first time since he had joined up. It was eight weeks after the disaster that Syd's mom and dad received a brief telegram: "Missing and presumed dead." Joe's mom and dad got the same telegram and the two families' lives were irrevocably changed. Rachel Croft refused to believe that the handsome son who had gone to war was not coming home. "It's a mistake, Ned, he'll be back, I know he will." She never cried, but her heart was broken and she clung to her faith in his return.

Betty Croft did not go to work for a week after the news, and when she did return she had big black circles under her eyes. She went to her work station and mechanically started to work on her day's allotment of garments. When break time came, she went to the canteen to find Mattie. Mattie and Liv were sitting surrounded by a group of lads from the maintenance division, laughing and joking, unaware of the news they were about to hear.

Mattie looked up and saw Betty's haggard look, but put it down to the fact that she had been off work sick. "You look like death warmed up, Betty. What was the matter? Are you well enough to come back? You'd better get some color back in your cheeks before your brother gets home. Where is he anyway? He's taking his time coming home." Mattie hoped that this did not mean that he had forgotten all about her and decided to stay in France with some pretty girl he had met over there. But then the old Lambert confidence kicked in and she smiled, knowing with great certainty that she was the girl he was coming home to.

Betty sank onto the bench beside Mattie. "He's not coming home, Mattie. Mam got a telegram last week. He's missing and presumed dead ... our Joe too." The canteen went deathly quiet and Betty clutched onto Mattie. Mattie pushed her away and ran out of the canteen as far from the mill as she could. When she finally stopped running, she fell in the grass and sobbed. She cried uncontrollably, but privately. Only Liv, who followed her out to the north field, saw her pain. "Come on, Mattie, they did say "presumed" — it's not certain," Liv said, trying to console Mattie.

"He's gone, Liv. I know it. I feel it." Syd was the only boy Mattie had felt a closeness with, and now all she felt was an emptiness.

"Let's get back to the mill before they come looking for us." Liv gave Mattie her hand to help her up. "You know Betty is in bits, and you ran out on her." Liv was by the far the more sensitive of the two and knew the pain Betty must be in. Betty and Syd were close in age and as close a brother and sister as could be. Mattie dusted off her dress and quietly walked back to the mill.

"Sorry Bet, I know you will miss Syd. I just had to get away for a few minutes." Betty had never been close to Mattie, but she did realize Syd had been very fond of her. By the reaction of Mattie to the news of Syd's death, she was sure Mattie felt the same way about her brother.

"It's all right, Mattie, we are all just gutted. Dad says he and Joe must have been together at the end, and that is something. At least he did not die all alone in a foreign land." Mattie felt a lump well up in her throat, and with a wan smile, she squeezed Betty's arm and walked back to her machine. No one guessed her inner anguish other than Liv, and that day Mattie sewed almost double her quota of work. Her dad had always said that work was the best cure for any ill. It was strange she thought of her father now, as she had put him to the back of her mind for the last eight years and had never even seen him. When the day was done, she went straight home to Landrose. Her pain was too great to share, even with Liv.

That night when Mattie went to bed, she sobbed into her pillow and vowed that she would never become so attached to anyone again. She had worshipped her father and he had not fought hard enough to keep her. The memory of Lance had blurred through the years, and somehow she had managed to filter out all of the bad, and now remembered only the good times. He had become larger than life to her, and she missed the closeness they had shared when she was young. *It's funny how there is such a fine line between love and hate*, she thought, as somewhere deep down she still loved her father very much. At ten years old, she had been old enough to realize that all the things that her mother and siblings had to go through were a result of Lance's intolerable ways. Mattie had gotten into many a fight at school when someone had taunted her because her mother was "living in sin" with Evan. Times had been hard, and she hated her father for not fighting hard enough to keep the family together.

Although Mattie had seen some of the arguments between Polly and Lance, she had no idea of the intense suffering Polly had endured. Lance's womanizing and constant drunken rages that almost always culminated in verbal and physical abuse had left Polly no choice other than to leave him. Polly loved her children intensely, and she always had their welfare as her first priority. The decision to leave Lance and live with Evan was monumental, as she knew what disrepute it would bring upon her. It had been the right decision though, as over time, people began to understand. Evan was a wonderful father to the children, and Polly and Evan were man and wife in every sense of the word. It was still a source of great pain for Polly that Lance steadfastly refused to give her a divorce and allow her to marry Evan.

Mattie would always feel that Lance had abandoned her, and now, the only boy she had ever cared for had left her. The next morning,

Mattie took the beautiful dress she had made and cut it into shreds. She would never wear it, and neither would anyone else. The dress had been for Syd, and now he would not see it. Before Polly and Evan were out of bed, Mattie threw it into the bin and covered it with some old rags. She never spoke of Syd again, and it was as if he had never even existed, but Mattie had his memory firmly locked in her heart.

Rachel Croft still refused to believe that Syd would not come home, and for months after the telegram had arrived, she still put his supper on the table and left the door unlocked every night. Betty went quietly about her work at the mill and life went on. They were not the only family affected by tragedy. As the war raged on, more and more people lost loved ones.

It was close to Christmas and everyone was making plans to celebrate. Rations were being saved, and friends and neighbours made plans for communal celebrations. Someone promised eggs and someone ham, and between them all there was anticipation of a few days respite from all thoughts of war. It was an uneasy rest however, as nightly bombing raids were still a threat to everyone.

Belle had just begun her thirteenth year and Darren was fifteen. Polly shielded them from her fears as much as possible. Mattie had already been exposed to the horror of war, and at eighteen she was mature beyond her years.

It was almost a full moon, and Polly doused the lights before peeking through the blackout curtains into the distance. She shivered as she thought of the consequences of a clear night. It was a perfect night for a bombing raid, and those German bastards never missed the opportunity to strike on a clear night.

The nightmare of the Blitz started on 7th September 1940, and London was the prime target. Hitler ordered his Luftwaffe to leave the military targets such as airfields and support installations, and concentrate on the densely populated areas of England. His aim was to destroy the morale of the British people.

His expectation proved wrong, as even though thousands of civilians, men, women and children, were killed, crippled, and left homeless, the resilience of the masses was even stronger. The bombing raids forced the people underground, to sleep in subways and warehouse basements when the raids were on. There was an air of camaraderie, and for a brief time in English history, all class barriers were blurred. As they huddled together, inevitably someone would start to sing, and strains of "There'll always be an England" could be heard most nights. Although Hitler failed to destroy British morale, he succeeded in wiping out large areas of London. He followed the bombing raids with incendiary bombs, and London burned for weeks.

Hitler was buoyed by his success at mass devastation, and expanded his bombing raids to all the major cities of England. Prime targets were cities with steel mills and factories that could produce arms and supplies for the war.

German planes now flew over central England, and in November they targeted Coventry with high explosive bombs and incendiaries. They destroyed fifty thousand buildings and set fire to the city.

Polly and Evan had learned the sound of the German planes, and knew when it was one of their own Lancasters or an enemy aircraft. The night was eerily quiet.

"It's a clear night, Evan, just the kind of night that brings trouble." Polly had an uneasy feeling in the pit of her stomach, as she saw the moon glinting off of the metal shed roof.

"Come to bed, my love," Evan gently took Polly by the shoulders and turned her to face him and away from the window. "Think about Christmas, Polly. We have a lot to be thankful for. There's a pig hanging in the cellar, and we've enough food to share with everyone." Polly smiled, and for a moment she forgot the war that was intensifying every day.

"Evan Redford, you're a good man, and I love you for it."

She linked her arm through his, and together they climbed the stairs. Polly checked on the children, and all were fast asleep. Mattie's dark head lay next to the golden curls of Belle. How different the two girls were, both in temperament and looks. Polly loved them both equally, even though Mattie was by far the most challenging of her offspring. Darren was wilful, and even at his young age he had developed a dominant disposition. He was asleep in his own room which was at the other end of the large hallway. Polly was always protective of him. He was, after all, her only son.

It was the 12th of December and only thirteen days left to make the final preparations for a family Christmas. Polly laid awake making tentative plans for a family Christmas, when as usual she would have the pantry full of special Christmas fare. It was not Christmas without a Christmas pudding with rum sauce and a trifle with half a bottle of sherry in it.

Evan turned out the light and opened the curtains to let the moonlight shine into the room. He climbed into bed by the side of Polly and instinctively wrapped her in his arms. Polly always smelled so good, and he nuzzled into her neck and felt her relax against him.

Suddenly Evan and Polly heard the sound at the same time. It was German war planes. There was no doubt.

Polly and Evan shot out of bed in an instant. Polly was shivering uncontrollably, and Evan quickly pulled her behind him as they gathered the children and went into the cellar. It was not the first time they'd had to take cover. Landrose was not a target, but the reservoirs were, and they were only two fields away. So far, they had been fortunate and no bombs had dropped close to home.

Belle and Darren were used to making trips to the cellar, and Polly had thought to equip it with a few non-perishable snacks and candles and books. They were too young to fully realize the danger they were in. Mattie was not really afraid of anything, and considered the trips to the cellar an inconvenience.

"Bloody Germans can't let anybody get a good night's sleep!" Mattie grumbled as she lugged her favourite pillow to the cellar.

"Watch your language, my girl!" Polly admonished. "You might work in a factory, but you don't have to use that language at home." Mattie just carried on with her grumbling, thinking she had probably used the mildest of her range of expletives. Under her breath she muttered her entire arsenal of foul language, and somehow felt much better for it.

The sound of the planes droning overhead could be heard in the cellar, and when eventually the sound faded into the distance, Evan ventured upstairs to see if it was "all clear."

Suddenly there were huge explosions and the distant sky was crimson. This was a major bombing raid and Evan was pretty sure the target was Sheffield.

Sheffield was a steel city with major factories like the Vickers Plant which made essential parts for Rolls Royce Merlin engines, used in Spitfire fighter planes. Hadfield's Steel Works also made ammunitions. Both of these factories, along with numerous other steel and iron works, would be key targets.

Polly and the children had followed Evan upstairs and heard the horrific boom and screech in the distance. "Oh my God, Evan. Oh those poor souls."

"I'm sure it's Sheffield, Polly. They have gone after the steel mills."

"But what about all the poor innocent souls that get killed in the process," Polly cried. "Are they going to beat us, Evan? How much more of this can we take?"

"They won't beat us, love," Evan said, with far more confidence that he was feeling. "We have never been beaten yet, and we're not going to start now."

The bombings continued and escalated until the 15th of December, and the loss of life was estimated to be close to a thousand people. Thousands more were injured, and over 78,000 homes were damaged or destroyed.

On the night of the fifteenth, Polly and Evan and the children were again in the cellar and could hear the planes droning overhead, followed by the bombs exploding. The raid lasted for what seemed like an eternity, and when at last the explosions stopped, they heard the German planes retreating. Suddenly there was a loud roar and the house shook, causing several dishes to clatter to the floor above them. "It's all right, Polly, I think that one of our lads is chasing them, and they have jettisoned a bomb in the rush to get away."

"It was too close for comfort, Evan," Polly whispered as she clutched Belle and Darren to her.

"It sounded like it fell in the bottom wood," Mattie said. Even she was a little shaken up by the frightening sound of a bomb so close to home.

The next day Evan was the first to get up and go to survey the scene. Thank the Lord that no human life was lost, but the sight was gruesome nonetheless as he approached the field near the wood. A bomb had landed in the field where the cows were, and there were pieces of cattle hanging in the trees and several dead cows torn apart in the field.

He walked back to the house and gave instructions to Polly to keep the youngsters inside.

"It's a mess, Polly. They did not damage any property, and the barn is still standing, but they killed at least six cows. I'll go and get Ted and Joe to round up some help and clean up this mess before anybody gets a chance to see it." For a moment Evan was upset about the loss of his cattle, but almost instantly he realized what a small cost it was compared with what all the poor souls in Sheffield had just gone through. He kept a brave face out to the world, and especially to Polly and the children, but inside he was as weary of this damned war as everyone else.

Five

MATTIE AND LIV LEAVE THE MILL

One day at work, Liv told Mattie of her plan to leave the mill and go to work for the railroad. Liv's dad worked for British Rail and had managed to get a job for Liv working on the signals. Liv was elated as she loved the railway and was happy to be able to work in a more rural environment.

"I can't turn it down, Mattie. It's a great opportunity and the pay's way better than the chicken feed they pay us here," Liv said, trying to justify her decision to leave.

"Well they can stuff my job too, Liv; I'm not staying on without you. I can go and work at Britannica Insurance and make use of all that secretarial stuff they made me learn." Mattie was determined to leave when Liv did, as they were a twosome against the world inside Leashore Mills. Mattie knew that when Liv left, things would be different. Somehow the two of them were always united and impervious to the petty differences always present in a large factory. Mattie had no wish to stand alone, as she had few friends amongst the girls, other than Liv, and since Syd had been killed she was fair game with all the lads at the mill. Now when one of the lads would call after her, "Hey Legs, what're you doing tonight?" she cringed.

"Sod off and leave me alone. You're all the same and I wouldn't give two pence for any of you!" She was being truthful, as since Syd she had lost all interest in the opposite sex.

The following week, both Mattie and Liv handed in their notice. Liv went to work at British Rail, and much to Polly's delight, Mattie got hired at Britannica Insurance. It was an easy interview. Mattie showed up wearing a short skirt, high heels and a new hairdo. She had seen the hairstyle of a Hollywood movie star in a magazine, and after a few practice runs, she had it perfected. Her dark hair was sleeked back, but draped a little to one side to hide the T.B. scars that she was ever conscious of. She had twisted it into a chignon at the back and pinned it with a pearl comb which used to belong to her grandmother, Star.

Don Riley, the manager, was the husband of one of the girls at the mill. He was several years older than Mattie, and very handsome. He eyed Mattie up and was instantly smitten by her charms. She looked several years older than her eighteen years and had an air of confidence that was intriguing. After a very quick test of her typing skills, she was offered a job. Don was impressed. "A looker and she can type as well." He thought it was his lucky day.

The insurance firm was close to the Drill Hall where the Officers' Mess was located. As the area was a prime target for German bombing raids, Mattie was trained as a fire warden. In case any incendiary bombs were dropped, Mattie had to learn how to extinguish the flames. Mattie and Liv still spent as much time as they could together after work, but their lives had gone in two distinctly different directions. Liv loved the quiet of being alone at the rail track, as it gave her precious time to work on her poetry and enjoy the beauty of the countryside. Mattie loved the excitement of working close to where all the action was, and it was not long before she became part of the after-hours crowd of fire wardens.

Don lusted after Mattie from the first time he met her, and he went out of his way to brush up close to her every chance he could. Mattie was flattered by the attention of a handsome older man, who was also the boss of the company. She had no intentions of a relationship, but was certainly not averse to a little fun.

Inevitably, one night when Mattie was the last to leave Don made his move. "When are you going to stop being a tease, Mattie, and give me a kiss?"

"You're a married man, Don Riley, and I know Josie from the mill. Go home and give her a kiss."

"You don't fool me, Mattie. You fancy me as much as I fancy you. I've seen the way you happen to bend over the filing cabinet when you know damned well I am looking!"

"You fancy yourself, Mr. Riley. Don't think I am going to dance to your tune."

Don reached across the desk and grasped Mattie's hand, pulling her towards him. It all happened in an instant, but before she knew it, she was in his arms. He towered over Mattie, who in her heels was about 5 feet 9 inches tall, and he had to bend to meet her lips with his own. For a moment Mattie revelled in the feeling of power she had over her boss, but just as quickly she pushed him away. She had enjoyed the kiss, but it was a game; there was no meaning in it for her.

Over the course of the next few months, Mattie played a cat and mouse game with her boss. When the mood struck her she would let him catch her and they would engage in some kissing and fondling, but Mattie was always the one to put a stop to things before they progressed into something more.

It all came to a sudden end when the lady from the Post Office happened to work late one night, and from her vantage point across the road witnessed what was happening between Mattie and her boss. Sissy Perkins was a nosy parker at the best of times, and made it her business to know everyone else's business in the village. She was a self-righteous spinster who was in her glory if she could preach the gospel and condemn a sinner. That evening she went home and penned a letter to the Regional Manager of Britannica, suggesting that he pay a visit to the Branch Office. Sissy went to great lengths to embellish the story and exaggerate the age difference and the marital status of Don Riley. He had refused to pay out an insurance claim for her a year ago, and boy, he was going to pay for it now.

Don was quietly transferred to another branch, and he and his wife Josie packed their possessions and moved to Chesterfield. Mattie did not give anyone a chance to discipline her; she found her next job as quickly as she had found this one.

Mattie's only regret was that now she would be further away from all of the excitement at the Drill Hall. She still had her bike, however, and although it was a little further to go back and forth to fire watch, she managed to do her duty. A big thrill was that she started to be invited to some of the dances at the mess, and there she met a lot of American officers. Mattie was a natural dancer, and although she had not taken any formal training, she glided across the dance floor like Ginger Rogers. It was all great fun for Mattie, who loved the chase, but she soon tired after the capture. She developed a pattern for playing one against the other, and was never short of cigarettes or silk stockings.

"You'll end up in trouble, Mattie, if you keep that up!" Liv chastised her one night when Mattie brandished a pair of new silk stockings like a trophy. Mattie could not take offence at Liv, though, as they were kindred souls and their friendship did not have room for discord.

"It's all right, Liv, I know what I am doing. It's all harmless fun, and this blooming war needs more of that. I'm living for today and sod tomorrow; who knows when and where the next blasted bomb will drop." Liv could not argue and smiled at Mattie.

"There's one thing for sure, Mattie Lambert; they would not dare drop a bomb near you. They'd have half the U.S. Army after them!"

Liv was still dating Fred and it looked very much as if a wedding might not be too far distant. Mattie had no intentions of being tied down to one man, and was quite happy with her life as it was. She had started to work at Rowell's, a family department store, and she loved the job. Working with fashion and being able to get staff discounts was far superior to working on insurance claims. Mr. Rowell was already quite old and crotchety, so no temptation there! He did take an instant liking to Mattie though, and was very impressed with her sales skills. Mattie liked the old man and she respected his knowledge of the business. She made it her mission to learn as much as possible from him. Mr. Rowell enjoyed his role as a mentor, especially as Mattie was so quick to learn new skills. Before long she had learned merchandizing skills and sales skills that were way beyond her years of experience, and she became a senior sales clerk before her nineteenth birthday.

$\mathscr{Six}$

ALF

Alf Wetton was the only son of Thomas and Julia Wetton, and lived in Riddings, a small village a few miles away from Wellington. He had enlisted as soon as the war broke out, but was soon discharged when a perforated eardrum put an end to his military career. He was angry that he could not fight alongside his friends, Billy and Tom Cope. The two brothers and Alf had been like the three musketeers. All throughout their childhood they had been inseparable. As they reached adulthood the bond became even stronger, and Alf thought of them every day they were away at war.

Prior to the war, Alf had worked at Granwood Floors, a company noted for its expertise in laying parquet flooring. When he was discharged, they were pleased to hire him back as he was a hard worker and could be relied upon to take any job, in the area or out of the county. Now that the war was on, not too many people were installing new floors, so work was short and he was not travelling out of the area as much.

The hard work had built strong muscles, and his large frame was well toned. He had inherited his grandfather's rusty brown curly hair and dark brown eyes. Six feet two inches tall, he towered above Tom and Billy who were both quite short and slight. Alf was never conscious of his appearance or his stature. He was comfortable in his own skin, and never felt he had to prove anything to anyone. Tom and Billy had both had a series of girlfriends, but Alf only had one. He met Gladys in his final year at school and knew she was the girl for him. Her outside beauty was equally matched with a sweet disposition and gentle nature.

"Well Mam, I've asked Gladys to marry me and she's said yes," Alf beamed one night when he came home from a night out with his girl. Money was short and he could not afford a ring, so Julia gave him a small gold ring with a pearl flanked by tiny zircons. It had belonged to Mrs. Gration, Julia's mother.

"Oh Mam, that's just perfect." Alf was touched by the gift and could not wait to surprise Gladys the next day. "We're not going to have a long courtship, Mam; things as they are, we want to be together as soon as we can."

Thomas and Julia were over the moon when Alf told them of his intentions to ask Gladys to marry him. She came from a very good family. Her quiet but congenial personality endeared her to all of the Wetton family. Julia was happy to help out with the plans wherever she could, and Tom enjoyed seeing his wife so distracted from the constant news about the war.

Gladys was busy sewing her own dress for the occasion and helping her mom make decorations for the Hall. The dress was white gossamer over a silk petticoat, and the delicate fabric suited Gladys perfectly. It was a busy few months, and Gladys, who was a petite, almost frail young lady, pushed herself to the limit to complete all the tasks on time. She had been so busy that she had not noticed how tired she felt until all the work was almost finished.

"I did not realize how much work goes in to planning a wedding," Gladys said as she put down the needle.

Noticing her daughter's pallid complexion and the dark circles under her eyes, Mrs. Wilde was concerned about her daughter. "You've been working too hard, our Gladys. I think you should go and see Dr. Lister and have him give you a tonic."

"I'm just a bit run down, mum. I'll be fine after a good night's sleep," Gladys brushed off her mother's concerns. She was feeling tired though, and she had been coughing steadily for a few days.

Maybe I will make an appointment to see the doctor, Gladys thought to herself when she caught sight of her reflection in the mirror. She wanted to look her best when she walked down the aisle with Alf. There had never been any other love for Gladys, and when she put her head on the pillow she soon drifted to sleep with happy thoughts of her upcoming wedding.

When Alf came to visit the next day, Gladys still looked tired and she was coughing much worse than the last time he had seen her. Alf insisted she delegate some of the work to her sisters and that she take a rest.

Grudgingly Gladys agreed, and passed along the harder tasks to her siblings. The cough did not go away and Gladys had to postpone the wedding plans.

"Alf, I am sorry, love, but I really would like to try and postpone the wedding for a few weeks, until I am over this cough. I don't want to look like this when I walk down the aisle."

"You can take all the time you want, pet. I can wait as long as I have to. You look beautiful to me just the way you are, but I know you want everything to be just right." Alf did not want to show his concern, but he had been worried that this cough was not going away.

She hid her symptoms as long as possible, but as the days progressed it was evident that this was more serious than just a bad cough. One night after Gladys had a particularly bad time breathing, the doctor was called. It took little time for him to confirm her fears: she had tuberculosis. Alf was sitting downstairs waiting for the doctor to come and tell him what the problem was. He was not at all prepared for the news. The prognosis was not good, and the doctor held out little hope she would recover.

"Prepare yourself, Alf; Gladys is in critical condition and her lungs are significantly damaged. I am afraid she is in a fight for her life at the moment." The doctor knew Alf, and how much Gladys meant to him. Sometimes he hated his job when he had to be the bearer of bad news.

Alf grabbed on to the edge of the table and looked incredulously at the doctor. "Surely there is something you can do. She is only twenty years old. We have all of our wedding plans made." Gladys had been his world for five years and he could not think of a life without her in it.

"We will do all we can, my boy, but the best thing you can do is to spend as much time with her as you can. At the moment she needs all the love and support she can get." The doctor picked up his hat and closed the door and the sorrow behind him. Sometimes he questioned why bad things happen to such good people.

Alf arranged to take time off work, and his boss was very understanding. He knew that Alf would work double time, if needed, once he came back.

"You take all the time you need, my boy. Look after that young lady of yours."

"Thanks, Mr. Upton, I wouldn't be any good at work anyway. I can't seem to think of anything else night or day. I have to be with her."

Alf sat by Gladys's bed and held her as she coughed up green sputum and eventually blood. She faded away in front of him, and there was nothing he could do other than to hold her and profess his love.

The doctors could not save her, and a few days short of her twenty-first birthday she quietly slipped away in her sleep. Alf was devastated. He felt as if his life ended when she died.

The wedding plans were set aside, and now a funeral was being planned. It was a small funeral, and Gladys was laid to rest in her wedding gown, wearing the ring that Alf would not take from her finger. Somehow, as she lay in the coffin, all traces of the pain she had endured were gone, and she was once again the beautiful young girl he had asked to marry him. Alf leaned into the coffin and gently kissed her for the last time. His tears unashamedly fell upon her cheeks.

His friends Tom and Billy Cope were both away at war, and other than his sister Vera and a few family members, he had no support to help him through the days ahead. He became reclusive, working all the hours he was able to get, then going home dog tired and falling into bed. Months passed and Alf refused to go out anywhere.

"Come on, love, you've got to get out and meet people one day," Julia pleaded. She hated to see her son so broken.

"I'm okay, Mam. I'll go out when I'm ready. Don't worry about me. Look at all the extra money I am making, Mam," Alf said in a weak attempt at humour.

Tom and Billy had heard the news of Gladys' death from a letter sent by their mom. Both felt sad for Alf and wished that they could have been there. Life was not good for them either at the moment. They were in different units but somehow managed to keep tabs on each other. Tom had narrowly escaped death when he was hit by shrapnel, but a few weeks in an army hospital and he was sent back to the front to fight again.

Tom was scheduled for leave, and he was anxious to go and see Alf as soon as he had spent time with his family. It was raining cats and dogs and the sky was grey and gloomy, but Tom set out on his bike for Riddings. This was a walk in the park compared to what he had faced in the trenches. He leaned his bike against the house wall and knocked on the old weathered door. Julia looked at the young man who stood before her. He had not escaped the ravages of war and had lost a lot of weight since she last saw him. Tom was not a big man to begin with, but now he looked small, old and tired. His eyes had lost their lustre and although his mouth smiled, his heart did not.

"Oh Tom, you have no idea how glad I am to see you. Alf has been living in a world of his own since Gladys died, and it seems like no one can get inside the wall he's built around himself."

Tom hugged Julia and looked up to see Alf coming down the stairs. The two men sized each other up, and just as Alf saw the suffering that Tom had been through, Tom saw the heartache Alf was feeling.

"We're a right bloody pair, mate!" Tom said as he gave Alf a big hug.

Alf smiled, and realized how true Tom's words were. When Tom had gone to war both of them had been full of fun and cockiness. Neither of them could have foretold the future, which was maybe a good thing.

"I'm only here for ten days, Alf, so I want it to count. There's a dance at the Alfreton Hall this weekend, and I need a bit of fun before I go back to kill a few more Gerry bastards." Tom said it light-heartedly, but it was a vain attempt to hide his dread of going back to the front. He did not relish the killing or the horror of seeing his comrades die. War was far from the glory he had anticipated when he so eagerly joined the forces. There was nothing glorious about wading through mud and swamps and diving in trenches to escape death.

Alf looked at his friend, and realized that no matter how much pain he was feeling, Tom's nightmare was not over. The least that he could do was accompany Tom on a night out. "All right Tom, I'll be ready Saturday night at 7:00," Alf promised. Gladys had not liked the smoky dance halls, and Alf was not one for crowds of people. In truth, he would have been happier if Tom had suggested a pint or two at the local pub.

Seven

MATTIE AND ALF ~ 1941

Alf dressed in his good slacks and put on a white shirt and tie. It was the first time in months he had dressed in anything other than work clothes. He had no desire to go out, and would not even be going tonight if Tom had not insisted.

He looked at his reflection in the mirror and cursed the fact that, as usual, he had to roll up the sleeves on his shirt. Unless he had tailor made shirts, it was impossible to get them with long enough sleeves to accommodate his 37 inch reach. There was no way his paycheque ran to buying tailor made clothes.

When Tom and Alf arrived at Alfreton Hall, the dance was already in progress. Tom eyed the floor for a likely partner, but Alf walked up to the bar and ordered a beer. He was not a dancer, and Gladys had not minded that. In summer they had often walked to a little country pub and sat outside in the garden. Gladys would sip on an iron brew, while Alf enjoyed a pint of bitter beer. It was no use thinking of those days, as he knew they were a thing of the past. Gladys was gone, and when she died a part of him died too. Alf glanced around and saw Tom had already found a willing partner and was whirling her around the floor to a Vera Lynn song. The sight of all of the happy couples clinging to the moment, unsure of what the war would bring, and the sound of the sad melody, did nothing to improve Alf's melancholy.

He turned back to his beer, thinking he would wait for Tom to come and join him in a pint of beer, and when he had a chance, he would slip away home early.

Mattie and Liv decided at the last minute to go to the dance and arrived halfway through the evening. Liv was always the first to be ready, and inevitably had to wait for Mattie to try on half a dozen outfits before she finally settled on "the one." Liv wore a cream skirt with a delicate peach coloured blouse, and her soft skin tones and beautiful curls gave her a very angelic appearance.

Mattie, on the other hand, had chosen her favourite color, green. It was a dress she had altered herself, and of course that made it one of a kind. Mattie smiled to herself as she slid the green dress carefully over her new hairstyle. She reinvented herself every few weeks with new hairstyles, new alterations to old clothes, and very often even a new persona. Tonight she had felt like Greta Garbo, and she had slipped shoulder pads into the dress and cut the back bodice almost to the waist. It was very daring, certainly not something that just anyone could wear. Mattie could and she knew it.

Green was her color, as it emphasized her amazing eyes. She was wearing a pair of silk stockings, courtesy of an American officer, who had also supplied the pack of cigarettes that she had in her purse. She opened the pack and slipped a cigarette into a long handled holder. It was partly for effect and partly to avoid nicotine stains on her fingers. She was proud of her long slender fingers and well-manicured nails.

Liv was already dancing with Fred, and Mattie surveyed the room to see who might be there. She was not interested in any of the lads from the mill or any of the local farm boys. She had gone to a lot of trouble for nothing: the stunning outfit and the sleeked back Garbo hairstyle were lost on the crowd here. She was dying to dance and show off her ballroom skills, and she wished she had gone to the Officers' Mess instead. She had more in common with the older U.S. officers than she did with this crowd. There were a few young lads home on leave from the army, but not one of them could hold a candle to Syd. She allowed herself a few moments of feeling sorry for herself and then the Lambert bravado kicked in.

"When one door closes, another one opens," had been a favourite saying of her father. Lance always had a positive affirmation for any given situation, and Mattie had inherited much of his tough veneer.

Mattie found her way through the crowd to the bar, and that is when she saw Alf. He took her breath away. There was something sad and mysterious about the way he was staring into a glass of beer. He didn't notice when she sat next to him, which was even more intriguing. Mattie was used to turning heads wherever she went. He had to be aware of her presence, as she was wearing just a hint of Evening in Paris, carefully dabbed behind each ear. It was her signature perfume, and it never failed to announce her arrival.

She studied his profile for a long time. He had a strong jaw line and thick curly hair, and although he kept his hair short, it was a little unruly. She could not see his eyes, as they were still staring into his glass of beer. He was half sitting on a bar stool with his long legs stretched out in front of him. His broad shoulders were rolled inward and he appeared to be trying to shut out his surroundings.

Mattie fished another cigarette out of her purse, and slipping it into the pearl and ebony holder, she pretended to rummage in her purse for a match.

"Hey stranger, do you have a light?" Mattie crooned in her sexiest voice.

Alf looked up from his beer and into the greenest eyes that he had ever seen. "Sure." He reached into his pocket and pulled out a box of matches. Alf rarely smoked, preferring to take "Top Mill" snuff, but tonight he had brought a pack of cigarettes to the dance.

"Where are you from? I haven't seen you here before," Mattie tried to make conversation.

"I'm from Riddings, and I'm here with my friend, Tom Cope. He is on leave at the moment."

"You look like you would rather be anywhere than here," Mattie responded.

Alf looked at Mattie, and although her beauty was not wasted on him, he was not ready for any entanglements. She looked like trouble: far too forward and painted for his taste.

"I guess I'm just not in the mood."

"Come on, dance with me, and I'll see if I can change your mood," Mattie grasped his hand to pull him on to the floor.

"Sorry Miss, I don't dance." Alf was truthful; he had never seen the point of shuffling around a crowded dance floor. Gladys had not been a dancer, and when he held her in his arms it had been in private and intimate. For a moment he was lost in his thoughts of Gladys, but Mattie was not easily brushed off.

"The name is Mattie Lambert, and if ever you decide you want to learn, I can teach you," Mattie persisted.

"Thanks, Mattie Lambert. Alf Wetton; pleased to make your acquaintance. Now, if you'll excuse me, I'd better go and see if my buddy is ready to leave." Alf pushed his large frame off the bar stool, and Mattie was even more impressed when she saw him tower above her.

She was about to try and forestall him, but he was already walking away. It was a blow to her ego, and a new experience. Mattie was not used to being ignored, but she was also never going to chase anyone, no matter how gorgeous they were. *He will be back*, she mused to herself, confident in her power of attraction.

Liv and Fred were coming her way, and Liv was surprised to see Mattie sitting alone at the bar. "What's up, Legs?" Fred said in his good natured way, "This crowd not classy enough for you?"

"Sod off, Fred! I'm not in the mood. Liv, I'm off home. I am just not in a dancing mood tonight."

Liv knew that it was no use trying to change Mattie's mind once she had made a decision.

"Okay, Mattie; are you going to take the bus back?"

"Yes, if I get a move on I'll catch the 10 o'clock."

The two girls hugged and Mattie did her best Garbo impression as she sauntered out of the hall. It did not matter how disappointed she was, she would never lose face and let anyone see she was sad.

Alf located Tom and saw he was already putting the moves on a pretty young dance partner. He gave Tom the wave, as he knew that tonight there was a good chance Tom would not be going back to Riddings with him anyway.

Tom waved back, and Alf left the hall. He walked up the highway to the bus stop, and just caught a glimpse of the green dress disappearing into a number 10 bus.

Must live somewhere near Wellington, he mused. Funny, she did not look like a girl from the countryside. He waited for his bus, and for some reason he could not get Mattie out of his mind. There was no doubt she was a stunner, but she knew it. She was so different from Gladys in every way. He thought of Gladys now. She would never have been so forward, and as for the backless dress, never in a million years. At last the bus came, and Alf was glad to get home and go to bed with his happy memories of Gladys.

When Mattie got home, Belle was still awake and wanted to hear all about the dance. She had seen Mattie getting ready and admired the beautiful dress and her stunning sister. In no mood to talk about the dance, Mattie shrugged off the questions, but she noticed her sister for the first time as a young woman.

Belle was now a teenager, and she was everything that Mattie wasn't. With her strawberry blonde curls and perfect oval face, she always had a ready smile which endeared her to all. Mattie was still trying to figure out why Alf had not fallen for her bait. Maybe he would be more attracted to a "girl next door" like Belle. Mattie touched her fingers to the scar that was always an imperfection she hated.

Well, Mr. Alf Wetton, Mattie mused, if you show up at the dance next week, you will have your little girl next door.

The next day Mattie met Liv after work and told her of her plan.

"I need your help, Liv; I want to dye my hair blonde. If I go and pick up the peroxide, will you help me dye it?"

"Oh, Mattie, don't do it. You have beautiful dark hair and it looks great on you." Liv had no desire to be part of this plan. She knew Polly would go berserk if Mattie coloured her hair.

"It's no use, Liv. I've made up my mind and, with or without you, I am coloring it! At least come with me to the chemist and help me to find the right stuff."

Resigned to the fact that Mattie would do what she wanted anyway, Liv accompanied her to the local chemist. After inspecting different strengths and brands, Mattie settled on a package that showed a pretty blonde on the cover, with hair a lot like Belle.

"I'm not helping you, Mattie. You are doing this on your own, and don't say I didn't try to warn you. Your mam will be mad as blazes with you."

"Well piss off home then, Liv, because I am going to do it tonight when Mom and Evan go to visit the Hoyles."

"See you tomorrow, Mattie," Liv said, feeling a little guilty that she wouldn't help her friend. "Come and show me the results tomorrow night."

"I'm on fire watch tomorrow night, so see you at The Mess at 8:00 p.m. I bet I get a couple of pairs of silk stockings when the boys see my new do," Mattie laughed, as she set off for home, package in hand.

Mattie was anxious for her mom and Evan to leave, and the minute they went out the door, she mixed the concoction. Locking herself in the bathroom, she mixed the ingredients together and carefully applied the solution to her hair. It was difficult to see the back, and she cursed Liv for not helping her. "How long do I have to leave this sodding stuff on?" She checked the package instructions and it said from 10 to 20 minutes. Thinking that 20 minutes would get the best results, she opted for 30 minutes, just to make sure. She placed the rubber cap over her head and sat on the toilet to wait.

"What are you doing in there, Mattie? I need to pee." It was Darren banging on the door.

"Go pee outside, I'm washing my hair," Mattie yelled.

It's dark out there, Mattie. Let me in. You've been in there forever."

Mattie wrapped a towel over her head and opened the door. "Be quick, you little pest. I need to rinse my hair."

Darren went into the bathroom and locked the door behind him. Mattie waited about five minutes, then banged on the door.

"If you don't come out right now I'm going to tell all your friends you're a scaredy-cat, afraid of the dark!" She knew that Darren did not like to admit to anyone that he was afraid of the dark.

At last Darren came out of the bathroom and Mattie quickly locked the door behind him.

She pulled off the rubber cap and put her head under the tap in the sink.

After rinsing off the solution, she was anxious to see the results. How would she look as a strawberry blonde? Would she look as sweet and innocent as Belle?

Mattie wiped the steam off the bathroom mirror and shrieked in horror at the image that was staring back at her. Her hair was the color of a chicken. It was bright yellow and looked like a matted mess of straw. "Oh shit! Oh shit! Oh crumb, what am I going to do?" Mattie could not believe the transformation. "I'm hideous! Everyone will laugh at me."

Belle and Darren heard the wails from the bathroom and waited with bated breath for Mattie to emerge. Belle saw her first, and tried to hide her shock at what she saw. Darren was not as tactful and started to laugh uncontrollably at the sight before him.

"It's all your fault, you little sod! If you hadn't locked me out of the bathroom I could have washed it off sooner." Mattie swatted him with the towel, and he ran as fast as his legs could carry him back to his room.

"Will it wash off, Mattie?" Belle inquired with a worried look.

"No Belle, it won't, and mam's going to have a fit when she sees it. How can I go to work looking like this?"

"It's not that bad, Mattie. You will be able to make it look all right when you put a few pins in it." Belle was not half as sure as her voice portrayed.

Mattie managed to get a comb through the tangled mess, and wrapped several lengths in metal rollers. Her confidence began to return—and what could she do about it tonight, anyway?

"I'm going to bed and will face the music when I get up tomorrow." Mattie had calmed down somewhat, and she would never let anyone see how devastated she was with her appearance.

There was little sleep for Mattie that night, and the next morning she climbed out of bed and looked into the dressing table mirror. No, it had not been a bad dream. She really did have hair like a yellow chicken!"

Well, my girl, she thought, *you have to do something with it.* Thank heavens turbans were all the rage, and she had a pretty lilac scarf. After 10 minutes in front of the mirror, she had managed to cover the worst of it, and she walked downstairs to face the music.

Thank heavens Darren was not up yet, as he would have been only too delighted to tattle on his sister. Polly was in the kitchen putting the finishing touches to breakfast, and Evan was sitting at the table reading his paper. Mattie fidgeted with the turban and sat down across from Evan. "Good morning, Mattie, you are up early this morning," Evan said as he looked up from his paper.

Their eyes met, and Evan tried his best to hide his shock at the sight of the yellow hair peeking out from under the turban. He quickly regained his composure when he saw the look on Mattie's face. He knew how sensitive she was about her appearance and thought she would have enough to deal with at work when she got there. "So what happened to our beautiful brunette? I expect you wanted a change, but you know Mattie, we all loved you just the way you were."

"My mam will play hell with me when she sees it. It wasn't supposed to turn out this color. Our Darren locked me out of the bathroom and I did not wash it off in time." Mattie looked so sad that Evan got up and put his arm around her.

"Come on, love, let's get it over with," Evan said as he called Polly out of the kitchen.

"Polly, come and have a look at our new blonde girl, before she changes her mind again and dyes her hair pink."

Polly took one look at Mattie and threw her hands in the air.

"What next, my girl; do you want to give me a heart attack? What have you done with your beautiful hair? Well, there's no work for you today: I will call in and let them know you are indisposed. I will take you to the chemist and we will find a way to tone it down a bit."

Polly reached out and pulled off the turban. It was too much; she could not help but laugh, and before long all three of them were holding their sides with laughter. Mattie was glad her mom was going to help her fix the mess, and so pleased she did not have to go to work looking that way.

After breakfast, true to her word, Polly and Evan drove Mattie to the chemist. She had readjusted the turban and was grateful that when they got there they were the only customers in the store. With the help of the chemist, Polly found what she was looking for, and they quickly set off back home to Landrose.

It took about two hours and some anxious moments as Mattie's hair changed through several stages of yellow and orange and at last ended up like a dark caramel. It was not as striking as her natural color, but in time it would grow out, and at least it was not hideous.

Liv could not wait to meet Mattie at the Mess, as she was dying to see Mattie's new hair and hear how Polly had reacted to the change. After work, she rode her bike to Landrose and arrived just as Mattie had finished styling her hair. Liv looked at Mattie and thought that it did not matter what her friend did, she would always be striking.

"It turned out good, Mattie," Liv said, relieved that she had managed all right without her help.

"No thanks to you, Liv. You should have seen the damn mess it was last night. It's taken me and my mam hours to get it this color. I did not go to work today so lost a day's pay to boot."

"Well, it looks good now, so come on, let's go for a ride down to the Mess."

Mattie thought that it might be a good idea to try out the new color on some of the army boys; after all they were just a distraction. She really did not care about trying to impress any of them. This hairdo was to impress the tall, dark and handsome stranger she had met at the dance. "Do you think that Alf Wetton fellow will be at the dance next week, Liv?"

"I don't know, Mattie, but I suspect that he might be. I knew this hair dye thing was for his benefit. He's the first guy that ever gave you the cold shoulder."

"No he didn't. He looked like he was upset about something. He was a million miles away, and I felt like he didn't even want to be there. I think his buddy, Tom, was the one who dragged him there that night."

It was turning dusk as they rode down the country lanes towards town. It was a picturesque area of Derbyshire with farmlands and bluebell woods. Other than the sound of their chatter and laughter, it was a quiet night. Then they both heard the sound at the same time. It seemed to come from nowhere but grew in intensity by the second.

"Oh shit! Oh god, Liv!" Mattie knocked Liv off of her bike and they both rolled into the ditch. It was the first time either of them had seen a German plane so close. "It's not one of ours, Liv. It's a Gerry." The plane was flying low and was heading straight for the town. They both lay in the ditch clutching each other and waiting for the sound of bombs.

Suddenly they heard the whoosh of a cluster of incendiary bombs being released, and then the plane gaining altitude as it sped away.

"Thank God it's incendiaries," Liv gasped.

"This time, but they will come back with bombs now that they have lit the way." Mattie knew what the pattern of attack was.

"Come on, Liv; let's get to the fire hall quick. We need to get the fires out as soon as we can." The girls jumped on their bikes and pedalled as fast as possible. When they rounded the last bend, they saw half the street was on fire. There was a general commotion and people running in all directions. Thank heavens the fire hall was close to where the worst of the flames were, and the crew on duty had already started to spray water on the fire. Mattie and Liv went to help a few of the locals who had buckets and pumps at the ready. In times of crisis everyone always banded together. Strangely, petty grievances were all forgotten, as one neighbour helped another to minimise the damage to their property.

It took a couple of hours to put out the fires, and thankfully there were no casualties or serious damage. In the distance they heard the sound of planes, but they were British planes. "It sounds like our lads have won this one, Liv!" Mattie and Liv were both covered in ash and soot, but feeling very exhilarated at being able to help by doing something useful at last. "Well, Mattie, it looks like you'll have to wash your hair again tonight," Liv laughed.

"You just take a look in a mirror at yourself, Liv." Mattie

couldn't keep her face straight, as Liv's blonde curls were now black and she looked like the golliwog doll that Belle was so fond of. The panic had passed, and Mattie and Liv stayed until the street was cleaned up before they left. It was now dark and the ride home was a little eerie at night with the black out. They both rode together until the fork in the road, and then each went her separate way home. Mattie knew that Polly and Evan would be waiting for her, as they must have heard the commotion even from Landrose.

"Thank goodness you're home, Mattie. You look like you've done a shift down the pit! Was there much damage? Was anyone hurt?" Polly was full of questions and Mattie was only too happy to tell of all the excitement.

Oh to be young, thought Polly, *when you are too naïve to understand the consequences of war.* The attack on Sheffield was still fresh in Polly's mind. The general morale was lower now than it had been at the start of the war. Rations were in short supply everywhere. Due to Evan's job they were more fortunate than most. The reservoirs and pumps were essential, so he was supplied with petrol for the car so he could tend to them. They also had a coal allowance and eggs and chickens, but Polly was ever conscious of the people who had to struggle to feed their families. So many homes were being run by women whose husbands were at war.

Evan put his arm around Polly and knew what she was thinking. He had an innate ability to know when she needed reassurance. "We're amongst the lucky ones, love. This war won't last forever, and I am sure that the fellow up above will see us all safely through this."

For the next two weeks Mattie never missed a dance, but each time she came home dejected. The tall dark stranger was nowhere in sight.

"Forget about him, Mattie. There's more fish in the sea," Liv tried to cheer up her friend.

"It's no use, Liv. I can't get him out of my mind. Every time I close my eyes I can see him. He looked so sad, and my god, he was handsome. I know that he is the one I want, Liv, and somehow one day we will be together."

"Well Mattie, you usually do get your own way, so who am I to argue? You know he said he didn't dance. Maybe he goes to the pub in Riddings."

"Liv, you are a star! Why didn't I think of that?" Mattie cheered up instantly. Now she had a game plan.

Mattie dragged Liv and Fred along to every pub in Leabrooks and Riddings, and finally one night they went to the Greenhill Hotel. The pub was packed and there was a group of men gathered around a dart board.

"Come on, Alf, double top!" a fellow cried out, and Mattie followed the call just in time to see Alf take aim and hit the target dead center. There was no mistaking his long, lean frame and his thick curly hair. It was obvious by the reaction of his friends that this was only what they had expected. He seemed to be more at ease than the last time that Mattie had seen him, as he reached out to take a sip of his beer from the nearby table.

Mattie was relieved to see he was with a bunch of men, and there did not appear to be any young women in the bar. In fact, Mattie and Liv had turned a few heads when they walked in with Fred. They would not have ventured into the pub alone, but with Fred as a chaperone they were quite at ease. He found a table and led the two girls over while he went to fetch them both drinks from the bar. Mattie's heart was racing; she wondered if he would recognise her. The last time they had met she was doing her best Garbo impression. Tonight she had decided to wear a tan skirt with a cream blouse, and no jewellery, just an orange neck scarf. Her hair, now almost back to its own color, was styled into a soft bob.

Tom was on his last night of leave before having to ship back to his unit, so he and Alf had gone out to have one last night together at the pub. Tom was the first to see Mattie.

"Well if it isn't the girl from the dance. You were wearing a green frock with no back in it. Almost gave me a heart attack, you did."

Mattie liked Tom. *Cheeky little bugger*, she thought, but he had such a nice smile and it was difficult to take offence at him.

"From what I remember, you were busy with that little redhead at the dance. I am surprised you even noticed me."

Tom gave an easy laugh. "I think that you get noticed wherever you go. My mate noticed you, but he was in no mood to socialize with anyone."

Just then Alf came sauntering over to the table. "Miss Mattie Lambert, isn't it?"

"Yes, I am surprised you remembered my name. You were in another world that night. I remember you though, the man who doesn't dance, Alf Wetton."

Alf looked at Mattie and smiled. She looked very different tonight than she had when he first saw her. In truth, he preferred the girl he was looking at now. He was not impressed with fancy clothes and lots of makeup.

Mattie had applied her makeup with care each time she and Liv had been out searching for him. It was very minimal, but artfully applied to accentuate her features and disguise the TB scars she was ever conscious of.

Just then Fred came back and sat down beside Liv. "Do you lads want to join us?" Fred said good-naturedly.

"We've got a darts tournament on the go, mate, but as soon as we have whipped the lads from the Pig and Whistle, we'll come and celebrate with you," Tom said as he headed back towards the darts alley.

Alf took a swig of his beer and gave Mattie a wink, before heading after Tom.

Mattie knew there was a spark that flew between them, and tonight she had Alf's full attention.

Alf and his mates from The Greenhill Hotel won the darts match easily, and there was a lot of cheering and back slapping when the game was over.

Tom joined them while Alf went to the bar to order them all a round of drinks. By the time the bartender shouted "last call," the group were all friends. Tom, never bashful, looked at Mattie and inquired, "So where is your escort tonight? Is there a boyfriend somewhere overseas? I'm sure that if he was around here he would not let you out on your own."

Mattie laughed, "You have a lot of questions. For your information, there is no boyfriend."

Tom noticed the sad look that came over Mattie's face and decided not to question her any further. Mattie had never had a boyfriend other than Syd, and she did not want to talk about him tonight.

"I'm back off to my unit tomorrow, Mattie, but my mate, Alf, will keep an eye on you for me while I'm gone."

Alf and Mattie exchanged glances, and this time his dark brown eyes burned right into her soul. For the first time in her life, Mattie lost her composure and actually blushed. She was furious with herself for such a display of emotion; it was totally out of character for her.

Maybe she isn't as cocky and confident as she likes to pretend, Alf thought to himself. He had not taken a girl out since Gladys had died, and this was the first time since then that he'd had any desire to see anyone else.

"What do you do when you aren't dancing, Mattie?" Alf asked.

"I work at Charley Rowell's, and I do fire watch duty a couple of nights a week."

"If you can get off early next Friday night, there's a group of us going to The Flying Horse. I can meet you after work if you want to join us .... You and Liv are welcome, too, Fred," Alf added, trying to establish the fact that this wasn't a date.

Mattie regained her composure. "We'll see, Alf. Thanks for the drinks."

They all said their goodbyes, and Tom gave Mattie a big hug. "Do you have a kiss for a soldier boy, Mattie? I won't see you until my next leave."

Mattie, who was a few inches taller than Tom, gave him a big kiss on his forehead. "Give them hell over there, Tom, and let's get this war over with."

Alf just squeezed her arm. "Next Friday night?" he asked as he turned to leave.

Mattie could feel her confidence returning. He was just as smitten as she was. This was destiny. There was no question about whether she would be waiting after work next Friday.

Eight

MATTIE AND ALF ~ 1941–1942

Over the next few months, the pair of them were inseparable. Each had compromised a little; Alf went to the occasional dance, and Mattie went to a few dart matches. Alf still steadfastly refused to learn to dance, but Mattie soon became quite a good dart player. They both loved the countryside and enjoyed bike rides and day trips to local beauty spots.

"I hear that you have been seeing a young man from Riddings, Mattie. When are you going to bring him home to introduce him to us?" Polly asked one evening, as she watched Mattie getting ready to go out. Polly was quite impressed with the change in Mattie since she had been seeing Alf. Mattie seemed to be more self-confident, and had lost a lot of her tough outer shell. There was a subtle change in her choice of wardrobe too. Mattie would always have a flare for the dramatic and latest fashions, but her recent choices had been slightly more modest. The dress she had chosen tonight was modest to the extreme. Mattie had chosen her outfit with particular care, as tonight she was going to meet Julia Wetton for the first time. Alf had invited her to his mom and dad's for supper.

"I'm going to see his mom and dad tonight, mom. I'll bring him home next week so you and Evan can give him the third degree!" Mattie grinned as she knew they would both have a million questions lined up to ask him.

Mattie had told Alf she would meet him at The Greenhill Hotel, and they would walk back to his parents' place. It was only three streets away and it would give her time to prepare for the scrutiny she was expecting.

The bus stopped right outside the hotel, and Alf was waiting.

His face lit up when he saw Mattie. Inside he was a bit nervous about the upcoming meeting. Alf knew his dad would accept Mattie and be his usual jovial self. He was more concerned about his mother's reaction. Julia had loved Gladys like a daughter, and it would be difficult for her to accept anyone else as a prospective daughter-in-law. Mattie was so different in every way; much more outspoken and liberated. Mattie smoked cigarettes and played darts with the boys, not to mention the fact she enjoyed a glass of sherry or a brandy and ginger. Mattie knew what she would be up against, and she had done her best to prepare for the meeting. The flat shoes and blue cotton dress did little to hide the long legs and shapely body. It did not matter what Mattie did, she would still be a knockout.

Alf smiled to himself, still remembering the green sensation she had worn the first time he saw her. He knew that Mattie had dressed to impress his mom and he was very relieved.

"Well come on, love. Let's get it over with. My mam comes on a bit strong, but her bark's worse than her bite," Alf joked.

It was the first time that Mattie had seen the big red brick semi-detached that Alf lived in. The house was at the top of a road that went to the Red Rec. There was a little garden in the front, and as they walked down the path, Mattie saw the lace curtains part just enough for someone to peek outside. She clutched on to Alf's hand and walked with her head high and her heart in her shoes to meet her inquisitors.

"Come on in, Mattie, and meet the folks," Alf said as he put a gentle arm around her and steered her towards the large kitchen.

Julia was just taking a big roast pan out of the oven and placing it on the hob. She wiped her hands on the big apron that she was wearing and went to greet Mattie.

Each of the women sized up the other.

A flighty young thing ... too forward and sure of herself ... and a smoker too! Julia smelled the faint aroma of a cigarette on Mattie. Even the Evening in Paris had not fooled Julia; she could detect cigarette smoke from a mile away. Tom was a smoker, and although she did not like him smoking, he was her husband. Women were supposed to be governed by different standards.

Julia was old fashioned and older than Mattie had envisioned, but even though she didn't have even a hint of makeup, she was still very striking. Her hair was pulled back into a chignon, and a very white apron covered an ankle length brown skirt, all giving the general impression of a school ma'am.

Tom was almost as tall as his son, but his back was stooped over a little from the years when he had worked at the colliery. He was now a station master at British Railways, and he was gradually losing some of his pallor.

"Hello lass, come and sit down next to me." Tom pulled out a chair from the kitchen table and made room for Mattie. Mattie instantly liked Tom; he had the same easy smile as his son, and his grey eyes twinkled as he watched his wife put the fresh buns on the table.

"There's nobody makes better bread than my Julia," he said with pride. "Tuck in lass, and we'll fatten you up in no time!"

Mattie smiled, "It all looks delicious," and the smell of fresh bread and stew was indeed very appetizing.

Julia had made a beef stew and it was plain but good. Mattie enjoyed it and complimented Julia on her meal. Julia had a thousand questions. She had known Gladys most of her young life, and she knew nothing about this new girl in Alf's life.

It never occurred to Mattie to help with the dishes; she was anxious to escape outside for a smoke and some fresh air. Even though the night had passed without any major catastrophe, Mattie had felt uncomfortable with all of the questions. Conversation had not been easy, and when Tom offered to show her his prize garden she was only too happy to follow him outside.

"I'll help my mom with the dishes, Mattie; I know my dad wants to brag about his garden." Alf knew his dad wanted an excuse to go outside for a smoke.

"Come on, lass. I'll show you my prize chrysanthemums." Tom was barely out of the door before he lit his first cigarette. Mattie was unsure whether she should have a smoke, even though she really needed one. Tom passed her his packet of Woodbines. "I expect you need a cigarette after my Julia's interrogation. She means well, lass. She is a good woman and she was very fond of Gladys. It was a real shock to all of us when she died. You've put the smile back on our Alf's face, my girl, and that's good enough for me."

Mattie took the offered cigarette, and Tom pulled out his old flint lighter and smiled as Mattie took a long drag on the cigarette. The two of them were very much at ease together, and Tom was justifiably proud of his beautiful garden. The flowers were beautiful and the grass was cut and weed-free. There was a tall hedge on one side that separated the house from the Red Rec beyond.

73

"I've got an allotment where I grow all the vegetables, Mattie, and maybe one day I'll take you there. It's one place I've never even taken my Julia. I have a little shed there and I can smoke in peace. It's a lovely little patch that catches the afternoon sun. Sometimes I even fall asleep sitting on my garden stool," Tom laughed.

The evening had not gone too badly, Mattie thought. Tom's warmth had made up for Julia's cool reception. The next introduction would be for Alf to meet her mom and Evan, but Mattie had no reservations about that. She could not see how anyone would not like Alf.

Mattie was right, as the following week when Polly and Evan invited Alf for supper, they both knew he was the man for Mattie. He was a gentle giant, comfortable in his own skin and very easy to be with. Polly was a little concerned with the age difference, as Alf was five years older than Mattie, but Mattie always appeared more mature than her years. Although Alf was considerably bigger than her brother Albert had been, Polly saw a lot of similarities. He had the same sense of humour and was so easy to be with.

Alf soon became a regular visitor at Landrose, and he loved the countryside around the house. Alf and Mattie spent hours walking up the fields and picnicking by the reservoirs. One day Alf showed up with a beautiful Golden Labrador puppy. He had always wanted a dog, but Julia had steadfastly refused to have a dog in the house. Landrose was the perfect place to raise a dog, and he thought it would be good company for Polly. He and Mattie would be able to take him with them on their walks.

"Alf, you can take that back. Cute as it is, I don't want a dog," Polly said firmly.

"Oh Mam, he's so lovely. Give him a chance. Alf's rescued him from the pound. If we don't take him, where's he going to go?" Mattie pleaded.

"We'll keep him for a couple of weeks, while you find another home for him, but if he's any trouble, he'll have to go."

Polly looked at the little bundle of gold fur and shook her head. Alf was hard to say no to, as he always meant so well.

"Come on, Tony," she said as she went into the kitchen to find some food and water for the puppy.

"So you've already found a name for him then?" Alf smiled.

"He looks like a Tony to me," was Polly's reply.

Tony had found a home and soon became Polly's shadow. He followed her everywhere and was an amazing dog. Polly had not realized how much happiness he would bring her. When Evan was working and she was home alone, it was a little lonely. With Tony by her side she was never lonely or afraid.

Alf knew that Mattie was the girl for him, and on 14th February, Valentine's Day 1942, he proposed. The wedding was something for everyone to look forward to as the ongoing war was really causing a general air of despondency; even the most optimistic were getting tired of it.

Julia had come to accept Mattie, but in her heart she still had reservations about the upcoming marriage. From what Julia could see, Mattie didn't have a domestic bone in her body. She was right. Mattie did love Alf very much though, and she certainly had the ability to make him smile again.

Tom and Mattie had become good friends, and he even took her to his allotment to help him pick peas one day.

"They're supposed to go in the bowl and not your mouth, Mattie," he laughed. It was impossible to stop Mattie doing anything she had set her mind on. Tom thought that Alf might have his hands full with this one, but at the same time she would certainly make life interesting. *Never a dull moment*, he mused to himself.

The wedding was set for 12 April 1942, and that did not give a lot of time for all of the preparations. Polly was a born organiser, and once the date was set, she started making plans. Everything was rationed and in short supply, but Polly had bartered all of her life. She was determined that Mattie would have a white wedding cake, and that meant securing some white sugar. Most wedding cakes were iced with chocolate during the war, but Polly was adamant that Mattie would have white icing. Trading eggs and chickens and even a few bottles of homemade wine, Polly was able to arrange the wedding she wanted for her daughter.

"Polly, you make sure Mattie has the wedding she dreams of. We've got enough money behind us now, love, and who better to spend it on?" Evan knew that it would mean a lot to Polly after so many years of struggling for acceptance in the community. It had taken a few years for Polly and Evan to live down the gossip of their relationship. There were still a few puritanical, self-righteous villagers who looked down their noses at people "living in sin," but this was the opportunity to show them what a strong family they were.

"Evan, you are a good man, and a good father. If our Mattie is as lucky as me in love, she will be all right." Polly put her arms around Evan and a tear trickled down her cheek. Evan had been a better father to her children than Lance had ever been. She would have loved to have had Evan's child, but it was not meant to be. They had both wanted a child, but at the back of her mind Polly knew that a child born of their union would be a bastard. Could they bring a child into the world knowing what he or she would have to face?

The next day Polly gave Mattie a bundle of notes. "Here you go, love. This is from Evan and me: make sure you find the nicest dresses you can. We want you to have a wedding to remember."

"Thanks Mom, and give Evan a kiss from me," Mattie said as she quickly put the money in her pocket. "I'm off to Liv's. She's going to come with me to Chesterfield Bridal."

Mattie and Liv had a ball shopping for a wedding dress, and dresses for the bridesmaids and flower girls. Mattie had the sales clerk bring out almost every dress in the store until she found the perfect one. Liv was surprised when Mattie selected a very simple, high necked gown. This was not something that Liv expected, as Mattie was usually far more flamboyant.

"Really, Mattie? You want to try that one on?" Liv wrinkled her nose.

"Yes, this is what I want to try on. You wait and see."

Mattie disappeared into the fitting room, and when she came out, both the clerk and Liv stood mouths agape at the transformation.

The dress was made of the softest white satin, overlaid with tulle and lace. It skimmed over her body and flowed softly to a gentle flare at the floor. The satin underlay stopped just above the bust, and the transparent lace carried on up to the neck and down the long narrow sleeves. It was nothing short of regal. When the clerk placed the floral coronet and long matching lace veil it was breathtaking.

"So what do you think now, Liv?" Mattie knew that she had found the perfect dress, as Liv was speechless.

Mattie had chosen purposely; she wanted the dress to be stunning, but demure enough to please her new mother-in-law.

"I think even Alf's mom is going to like this one," Mattie said with a smile. "She's hard to please, Liv, as she will always think that I am second best to Gladys. You can't compete with the memories of a dead girl. If she wasn't an angel before, she is now."

Liv took Mattie's hand and spun her around to see the dress from all angles.

"Well Mattie, if it's an angel you are planning on becoming, then I need to find a new best friend. Angels are no fun, and I love you just the way you are. Don't worry, Julia will come around, Mattie, once she gets to know you."

Liv was less sure of Julia's acceptance than she cared to admit, but she gave Mattie her most reassuring smile as she turned her attention back to the rack of clothes.

When Mattie selected the bridesmaids' dresses, Liv did not question her taste. Mattie chose the dresses from a sample rack, and arranged to have the girls come in and be fitted. "I want this dress, but I want it ordered in this color," Mattie instructed the clerk. It was the first time anyone had ordered antique gold satin for a wedding, but then there was a first time for everything. Most brides chose pink or lavender or pale blue pastels; this was a deep shade of gold.

Liv held the gold satin up to her face, and her eyes lit up when she saw how beautiful it looked. "Mattie, it's perfect."

Mattie chose pale gold shimmering tulle for the flower girls' dresses, knowing the whole effect would be exactly what she had been aiming for.

It had taken them all afternoon, and all of Evan's hard earned money to select the dresses. The two girls left the shop in high spirits. Even in the midst of war and uncertainty they had managed to forget the world around them and revel in the joy of the moment.

Nine

MATTIE AND ALF ~ 1942

Alf wrote to Tom to tell him of his engagement; however, the letter did not reach Tom until a few days before the wedding. Tom was happy for Alf, but it was hard for him to put all the atrocities of his surroundings out of his mind. The war was escalating and Tom had narrowly escaped a scathing attack. War changes people, and he hoped that when this was all over he would be able to regain his humanity. Death and dismemberment had become daily occurrences, and he knew in his heart that he had become desensitized to the horrors which surrounded him. His unit were tired and beaten down and surviving on meagre rations.

Tom's other close friend was another Alf. His name was Alf Ball, and he was enlisted in the British Royal Artillery 122 Field Regiment. On the day that Alf Wetton got engaged, Valentine's Day 1942, Alf Ball's unit had surrendered to the Japanese at Singapore. Word had reached Tom of both events simultaneously, and the irony of life was beyond his imagination. While one friend was celebrating his engagement, the other was heading for Changi Prison Camp and unimaginable hardship. Tom knew that Alf Wetton would have been in the war too if it had not been for his perforated eardrum. Funny, thought Tom, and even in the midst of his melancholy, he smiled: "There's Alf, a great big strapping bloke, and me a little shrimp like this, and who do the bloody army want? No wonder we are losing this war!"

Back in Wellington, Landrose House was abuzz with activity. The bridal party were all ready to go to church. Polly had splurged on a beautiful two piece cream silk outfit and Evan wore a dark navy tailored suit. Polly fussed with her hat until she had it at the perfect angle, and indeed the bridal party would not have looked out of place on the cover of "The Country Squire."

Julia and Tom, and Alf's sister Vera and her daughter Sylvia, were just as busy preparing for the event back home in Riddings. Vera wished that Joe could be there to see how beautiful Sylvia looked in her flower girl dress. Joe was fighting overseas and he had only been home on leave twice. She missed him terribly and prayed for his safety every night. Alf came downstairs dressed in his dark grey suit and white shirt, wearing a silver tie and the tie pin that his dad had loaned him.

"It's not too late to change your mind, lad," Tom said jokingly.

"No Dad, not much chance of that. She's my girl and I'm the lucky one."

Julia wished she could be as sure about that. Over the last few months she had got to know Mattie better, but she still had difficulty in accepting anyone after Gladys. Mattie was about as opposite to Gladys as was possible, and she hoped with all her heart that she would make Alf a good wife.

"You look grand, Alf. She's the lucky one. I just hope she realizes what a good man she is marrying." Julia could not help but feel a little trepidation at the marriage. But Julia had a good heart and she would try her best to welcome Mattie into the family.

It was hard to find a place to rent, and Julia and Tom offered to rent two rooms to the newlyweds while they looked for a place of their own. Riddings was not Mattie's favourite place, and she hoped it would be a short term solution. Julia had mixed feelings about the arrangement. It would give her a chance to get to know Mattie better; still, she was a little concerned about the day to day reality of living together.

"Come on, lad, get a move on. You're supposed to be the one waiting at the altar."

Just then the taxi came to pick them up and they all squished into the one car. Money was tight and Julia could not see any reason to hire two vehicles when one would do. They arrived at the church in plenty of time, and Alf was pleased to see so many of his friends had turned up to wish them well. The whole darts team was there and most of his mates from Granwood. Alf and Mattie had decided on a reception at the church hall where everyone would have snacks and drinks, followed by a more private, invitation-only, sit down supper to follow. Alf would have been happy without the sit down supper, but Polly insisted that as she and Evan were willing to pay the bill, Mattie would have a "proper" reception.

Alf stood at the front of the church for what seemed an eternity, before at last the strains of the wedding march could be heard. He turned around just in time to see Mattie coming down the aisle on Polly's arm. Mattie had refused to allow Evan to escort her. He was not Lance and that was all there was to it. She looked more beautiful than he had ever seen her. He loved the wild and carefree Mattie and the quirky dresser he had gotten used to, but this was a different girl walking towards him. It was as if she had grown into a woman over-night. His chest almost burst with pride as he saw the effect she had on the congregation.

Mattie looked at Alf and knew that he was who she wanted to spend the rest of her life with. He was everything she had lacked. Her father had let her down. Her only other love had been killed on the Lancastria, and she always felt that she had been abandoned. Evan was a great stepfather, but he was not blood, and hard as he tried he could never replace her real father. Alf was larger than life, and she had never felt safer than when she was in his arms. Today he stood tall and proud with his hand outstretched to pull her to his side at the altar.

Polly and Evan held hands in the first pew, and Polly said a prayer that Mattie and Alf would have the same love that she and Evan had. Where would they all have been without Evan's love?

Julia looked at Tom and was thinking identical thoughts. Julia was not a demonstrative lady, but Tom knew she loved him as much as he loved her. He smiled back at her and whispered, "By heck girl, you're just as pretty as the day I married you." Julia shushed him up, but was pleased with the compliment. She did not often have the opportunity or the money to dress "fancy." Today she was wearing a silver grey dress and jacket that she had hidden from Tom until now. She had hoped he would like her choice. His comments made her purchase so much more worthwhile.

After the service, everyone in the bridal party went outside for photographs, and Polly looked at her growing family with pride.

"I never thought that I could be this happy, Evan. I have you to thank for raising my three wonderful children, and now we have another 'son'."

Evan smiled as he put his arm around Polly. "Without you, Polly, none of this would have been possible."

"I guess we have done it together then, love. I hope Mattie and

Alf have the same happiness that I have with you. I couldn't wish anything better for them."

Six months later, winter arrived with a vengeance. The days were dreary and the nights were long. Mattie still loved Alf madly, but living in two rooms in the same house as her mother-in-law was not going well. Alf had been working on a big project in Blackpool, and that meant Mattie was alone quite a lot. She missed the fields of Landrose, and she missed Liv and the fun and laughter they always shared. Usually by the time she got home from Rowell's, there was little to do in Riddings, and it was not easy or cheap to get a bus to Wellington.

Mattie lived for the nights when she went to work as a fire warden, as then she got to spend time with Liv and have a laugh with the lads at the Mess. She usually went straight to the Mess after work and that way she saved on bus fare.

"I'm off, Julia," Mattie called as she left the house for work. "I'll be late tonight; it's fire duty again!"

Julia was not fooled by Mattie's nonchalance; she saw that on such days Mattie's bag was a little bulkier and that Mattie had gone to extra pains with her hair.

"I suppose you'll be home before we're all in bed. Our Alf wouldn't like you out roaming the streets at night."

"I'm just doing my bit for the war effort, like everyone else," Mattie called as she quickly closed the door behind her. *He's my husband,* thought Mattie, *not my sodding jailer.*

Julia worried about her son's marriage. She knew Mattie was bored with life in Riddings, and that fire watch was just an excuse for Mattie to meet up with her single friends and get up to who knows what. She knew Alf would not be happy if he knew how much time his wife spent hanging around the Officers' Mess.

In the bag, Mattie had a change of clothes and a pair of heels. After her shift at fire watch there was always time for a dance or two before the last bus left for Riddings. Liv would be there, and a few of the girls she knew from the factory. Mattie lived in a different world when she was dancing; all thoughts of war, or conflict of any kind, were a million miles away.

The day was over at last, and Mattie said goodbye to the last customer. Charlie Rowell knew the routine; Mattie would go into the washroom and come out ten minutes later, changed out of her work clothes and ready to party. He liked Mattie and she was one of his best clerks, but he was glad she wasn't his daughter-in-law. *She's not a bit like Polly*, he thought. *Funny how she's so different.* Charlie had never known Lance, or he would have known why there was such a difference. He had known Polly since she had lived at Landrose with Evan. *Now there's a lady*, he mused.

Liv was already at the Mess when Mattie arrived, and she could see Mattie was a bit down in the dumps.

"What's up, Mattie? Married life not what you expected?"

"He's so good to me, Liv. I know I probably drive him mad at times, but he puts up with my complaining and somehow always manages to make me feel better when he is around. It's just that he isn't always around. I think I'll go crazy if I have to spend much longer in Riddings. I wish we could find a little place of our own, but not much chance of that for a while yet."

Liv tried to cheer Mattie up. "Look on the bright side, Mattie; you don't have to do the housework and you have supper ready when you get home from work." Liv knew how Mattie hated housework of any kind.

Mattie had to smile as she thought of how true that was. Julia had long since given up on Mattie contributing in any way to the household chores, and for the sake of keeping peace, she had just taken on the extra task of picking up after Mattie.

Julia was used to looking after people. Her mother had died very young, and Julia had taken on the task of raising her siblings as a natural thing to do. Tom was just as much a family man, and he was never happier than when there were young folks around. His pay packet was not large, but Julia could always manage to stretch the money out to feed extra mouths. They had a good marriage, solid and comfortable. Like everyone, they had their ups and downs. The war was hard on everyone, tempers were often short, and it was usually the little things that started an argument. Julia was starting to feel the strain of the extra work, and frustration with having a prima donna daughter-in-law under foot every day.

Today Julia had gone to see the doctor for some test results. Not wanting to bother Tom, she had gone to see the doctor a couple of weeks ago, and had said nothing about her visit. *No use in upsetting anyone. I probably just need a good rest,* Julia had rationalized.

"Come in, Julia, sit down."

The look on Doctor Morgan's face was enough for her. There was something wrong.

"I'm sorry, Julia; you have sugar diabetes. It can be regulated by insulin, but you need to start immediately. I'm afraid your sugar levels are extremely high."

Julia was relieved it was something which could be treated. She had been carrying a huge weight on her shoulders for a few months now, thinking she had some terrible incurable disease.

"Thank heavens for that, Doctor," she said with a smile. "I thought you were going to give me some really bad news."

"It's not good news, Julia. Diabetes can be very serious if you don't regulate your sugar levels. You need to go on a strict diet and start a daily course of insulin injections. I will monitor your sugar levels, and we will adjust the dosage as indicated. Avoid stress and slow down. I'll give you a shot of insulin right now, and I'll send a nurse over tomorrow morning. You are going to need two shots per day until we get you regulated."

Easy for you to say, thought Julia, I've a family to feed and look after.

"Thanks, Dr. Morgan." Julia left the office knowing she could not keep her condition secret anymore. She knew that Tom would worry about her, but she had no way of explaining away the nurse's visits.

When Tom came home for his supper she was glad Mattie was at fire watch and Alf was still away at work. Julia waited until Tom finished supper and sat down by the fireplace to light a cigarette. He waited for Julia's usual "tsk tsk" as he knew how she hated him to smoke, but tonight she came to sit beside him. Tom knew instantly that there was something amiss. Julia never sat down until the dishes were cleared and the table put back to order, and she always waited until he had finished his cigarette before joining him.

"What's up, lass? It must be something pretty important for you to sit in this cloud of disgusting cigarette smoke," Tom said with a wink. "Is that young lass driving you round the bend?" He was not prepared for Julia's news.

"I've got diabetes, Tom. I went to the doctor's today and he says I have to start taking insulin twice a day. He says they can regulate it and keep it under control, but I will have to take it always. I suppose that explains why I have been feeling a bit under the weather these last few months." Julia tried not to cry, but she was not looking forward to a daily regimen of insulin injections.

"Come here, love, don't fret. We'll all chip in and help you out a bit more. You're a good strong lass, and it'll take more than diabetes to slow you down." Tom put his arms around her and blinked away his tears. He could not show her how concerned he was. Tom knew what diabetes could do to a body, and that the diagnosis was not good.

"Here, you sit by the fire and I'll clean up the dishes tonight."

Julia had to smile, as this was not an offer that Tom would normally make, but she was grateful for the offer anyway, and as Tom stubbed out his cigarette on the hearth, she relaxed back into the chair. Staring into the flames, Julia's thoughts were all over the place. Yes, she was scared of what the future held, but at the same time she was so grateful to have the love of a good man. There was no doubt Tom would be her anchor in the days and years ahead. They were a team and they would always face life's challenges together.

By the time that Mattie came home, Tom and Julia were at ease and saw no point in relaying the information to Mattie that night. She would find out soon enough when the nurse came to administer the insulin injections.

Mattie breezed in, not a care in the world, having had a great night at the Mess Hall. There had been one call out when an incendiary landed a few streets away, but the fire was soon out and there was no heavy bombing that night. Mattie was never short of dance partners as she was by far one of the most attractive girls there. It was all harmless fun to Mattie. Life was for living every moment, and squeezing every drop of enjoyment possible out of every second. She saw no problem with the fact that she was a married woman and still teased and flirted with all of the young officers at the mess. "It's all harmless fun, and life is so unpredictable." Mattie had lost her first love, Syd, and Alf had lost Gladys; who knew what the future held?

Kicking off her shoes at the door and throwing her coat on a chair, Mattie went to make a cup of tea before going to bed.

"Now young lady, you know where the closet is. Hang your coat up and put your shoes away," Tom said, in his usual soft voice, "and brew a cup of tea for mam and me while you're at it."

It was impossible to take offence at Alf's dad, as he was such a sweet person. It was, however, out of character for him to be con-

84

cerned with housekeeping. Mattie gave him a quizzical look as she complied with his request.

Tom did not respond, but went to the cupboard to get out the tea mugs. Mattie made the tea, something that she did do well. She warmed the pot and made sure that the kettle was at a full boil before steeping the tea. When she was sure it was the required shade of darkest brown, she poured out three mugs and added a good slurp of milk to each one, before sitting down to join her in-laws.

"By heck, lass, you can stand your teaspoon up in this. Just the way I like it."

Julia had little to say, and kept her thoughts to herself. Mattie knew Julia disapproved of her going dancing when Alf was away, but in truth she was never concerned with any public opinion. Tom kept the conversation neutral and asked about Liv and the fire watch. They chatted for a while, and Mattie finished her tea and went to bed. She could hear Tom and Julia talking late into the night, and finally fell asleep with her book still in her hands. An avid reader, Mattie loved to escape into a world of fiction. She loved romance novels and lived in the pages of many, living the part of the heroine in each one.

It was the following day when Mattie, having seen the nurse arrive to administer the insulin, found out Julia had diabetes. She knew now why Tom had been so concerned about his wife the night before.

"Sorry to hear about the needles, Julia, that must be horrible. Twice a day, you'll look like a pin cushion!"

"Thanks Mattie. I can always count on you to cheer me up," Julia responded. She knew full well that sympathy or empathy were just words in the dictionary to Mattie.

"I'll be home early tonight," Mattie called as she was leaving for work "Alf's coming home from Blackpool tonight."

She missed him so much when he was away, and although she had fun at the dances, it was Alf whom she wanted to have in her arms at bedtime. He was the rock she leaned on, and when he was home all was right in her world.

Alf was still working on the huge flooring project at Blackpool Tower Ballroom, and it had kept him away more than usual. This time Mattie had really missed him and was getting tired of spending so many nights alone. It was impossible for him to give up a good job though, as there were many people out of work, and they would give their right arm to have such a good job. Mattie's day dragged on and it seemed like it would never end. Normally the days flew by at Rowell's, as Mattie enjoyed every minute of her work. Much the same as at Leashore Mills, Mattie was still an instigator of fun and mayhem. She got away with a lot because of her phenomenal sales ability and a knack of getting rid of slow moving merchandise.

The other girls would often have to stifle giggles as she artfully held an oversized jacket to the back of the customer, while they viewed the front. The procedure was reversed as they looked at the back. She was so quick that it was seldom noticed, and the customer left with a jacket that never looked quite the same once they were out of the store. Mattie justified her antics by the fact she only did that with sales items which had already been reduced far below cost just to move them from stock. New merchandise was a different situation, and she made it her mission to know the stock in each department. She could put together a complete ensemble fit to grace the cover of any fashion catalogue. The repeat clientele asked for Mattie by name, as they knew she would send them away with a stylish purchase. Charlie Rowell put up with a lot from Mattie as he knew she was by far his best sales clerk. At last the day was over, and Mattie eagerly tidied up her counter and balanced her till.

Charlie poked his head out of his oak panelled office, "Mattie, come into my office when you are finished. I need to speak to you."

"Oh, tonight of all nights," Mattie mumbled under her breath. It was not a common occurrence for Charlie Rowell to summon someone to his office unless they were to be reprimanded. Try as she might, Mattie could not think of anything she had done to get herself into trouble, but she was sure it must be something dire.

Oh well, face the music and dance, she thought as she walked into his office with far more confidence than she was feeling.

"Mattie, I have had my eye on you for the past several months and I think that you are working below your capabilities."

Mattie's face dropped, as she had thought she had been giving her job one hundred percent of her effort.

"Now then, Mattie, that was not a criticism. You are my best sales clerk, but your skill is with merchandise. How would you like to be a buyer, and deal with the suppliers for me? Of course it will be a higher paying position as it carries a lot more responsibility, and you might still have to help out on the floor when we are busy."

Mattie's face lit up like a beacon and she almost jumped over the desk to give him a hug, but thought better of it, knowing his very conservative nature.

"When can I start?" was her only question. Mattie had the sense not to ask how much of a raise she would get, as she knew he was a fair man, and any pay raise would be very welcome. In fact, she would have taken the job without a pay raise, as she had often thought that some of the stock was already outdated when it came in.

"You can come with me to meet some of our suppliers, and work with me for a few weeks before you take over. I will pay you an extra ten percent of your salary until I feel that you can handle it on your own. Once you take over the position I will increase your salary by twenty percent."

Mattie could not believe her ears. She knew she could do the job, and the extra money would make it easier for her and Alf to save money for the time when they could move out of his mom and dad's place.

"Thank you, Mr. Rowell. I won't let you down," Mattie said as she looked across the big oak desk at him. He was short and a little stout, and his spectacles were always on the end of his nose. Tonight there was a little twinkle in his eye as he said, "I know you won't, Mattie. I have every confidence in you."

Mattie left the office with far more confidence than when she had entered it, and could not wait to get home and share her good news.

Alf came home, tired after a long bus ride back from Blackpool, but anxious to see Mattie, having anticipated holding her in his arms again after having spent the last week alone in a cold and barren hotel room. Unlike Mattie, he seldom went out alone when he was on a job. Sometimes he would have a pint of beer after work, but he never stopped to socialize. He hated the separation just as much as Mattie did, but the pay was good and he enjoyed working on the complicated flooring task at the famous Tower Ballroom. This floor was nothing short of spectacular, and he was justifiably proud of his work. There was a lot of pleasure in accomplishing a difficult job and receiving accolades for his endeavours.

Mattie was anxious to share the good news of her promotion, but it would have to wait until later than night when they were alone in bed. Tom and Julia had told Alf of Julia's diabetes, and he was sad to hear of the diagnosis but happy to hear that at least now it could be treated. After losing Gladys so suddenly to tuberculosis, he had been worried about his mother's ill health over the last several months.

"Well mam, I'm sorry to hear that you have to have insulin injections, but I'm glad they can keep it under control." Alf gave Julia a big hug, and she wiped away a tear as she hid her face in the comfort of his broad shoulders. Mattie was not the only one who missed him when he was away. There was just something about him that made everyone feel so much better when he was around.

There was very little privacy in the old house, despite its size. The front room where Alf and Mattie stayed was steps away from the main kitchen and living area, and the linoleum floor was bare other than a couple of throw rugs. Every sound carried. The only privacy they shared was if they went to bed before Julia and Tom, and could have a brief time of togetherness.

"Well I think we'll have an early night, mam. It was a long ride back from Blackpool," Alf said as he ushered Mattie in front of him towards the old wooden door that led to the steep staircase going upwards to the three bedrooms.

Tom gave Alf a wink and knowingly said, "I hope you're not too tired, my boy." Julia scowled at Tom as she caught the innuendo. It was no use, as Tom would be Tom, and he knew Julia was nowhere near as straight laced as she would have people believe.

Unlike Landrose, the bedrooms had no carpet and were very cold. The only heat came from the downstairs fireplace, and the thin curtains did little to shield the windows from the elements. Alf and Mattie both dove into bed quickly and pulled the quilts up around them. The cold was soon forgotten as they gave in to the pent up passions of their week apart. Lying in the comfort of Alf's arms, Mattie was at peace. They lay awake long into the night, and Mattie told Alf of her promotion and her hopes of one day being able to have a place of their own.

"Just be patient for a little while longer, Mattie. We will find somewhere, I promise you, but I don't want to move until I have a job where I am home every night. I would worry about you on your own. At least I know you are safe with mam and dad when I am away."

Alf had not told Mattie, but he had been checking out another job that paid much better and would be steady day shifts, with no out of town jobs. It was a hard job in an iron foundry, but Alf was never afraid of hard work. Aiton's Iron Works was booming, thanks to the ongoing war. They had a contract to make some very intricate pipes that were used by the navy. Alf had heard they were expanding, and he had already made enquiries about a job once the new division was opened. He would have to start at the bottom, but he was confident in his ability to advance quickly through the ranks.

Mattie had hoped to convince Alf to move out more quickly, but she knew he would not be persuaded until he was ready to do so. It was just good to have him at home, and she did not want to spoil the magic of their togetherness. They made love one more time before falling asleep, warm and comfortable in each other's arms.

Ten

AN EVENTFUL 1943

It was a cold February morning and Mattie was feeling more irritable than usual at having to awake in a cold bedroom. The water she had taken upstairs the night before was sitting ice cold on the old wash-stand. Tiptoeing over the frigid linoleum as fast as she could to the scant warmth of a small hooked rug, she quickly had a strip wash before reaching for the clothes she had laid out the night before. She missed Landrose and the warm carpets, but most of all she missed the feeling of home. Alf had still not found work at Aiton's, although he was on a call list. He had been gone for three days this time, and life in Riddings was not suiting Mattie at all.

"Come on, lass, sit down and have a bowl of porridge with me," Tom called as she emerged through the stair door into the kitchen. Julia was already clearing the table and getting ready for the nurse to arrive with her twice daily insulin injection.

Mattie managed a smile at Tom, as he did go out of his way to make her feel at home. There was a pot of glue-like porridge sitting on the hob, and Mattie spooned a clump of it into a bowl. Milk was in short supply, so it was oats and 90 percent water, and a very small amount of rationed sugar. "Ugh! This tastes horrible," Mattie said, but quickly regretted her quick remark as she saw Julia give her a resigned look. "Sorry Julia, I know it's not easy to make the rations stretch these days. Don't take any notice of me this morning. I'm just not feeling great. My stomach is already churning and I feel like I am going to be sick."

Julia and Tom gave each other knowing looks, and suddenly Mattie realized what they were thinking. She had been so busy at Rowell's learning the buyer's trade, and then still going to fire watch, she had not taken notice of the fact that she had not had her period for about eight weeks. Julia and Tom hoped their suspicions were right, as they both loved children and so far had only one grand-daughter, Sylvia, who they loved to pieces. Julia was secretly thinking this might be just the thing to slow Mattie down and keep her home at nights. She never quite believed Mattie needed to stay so long at fire watch, and suspected she was spending time with the soldiers when her shift was over.

Mattie had not thought about starting a family. She saw other young women pushing prams and trying to keep crying babies quiet. It had never appealed to her at all.

Well, I may as well find out for sure, Mattie said to herself. *It's no use worrying about something that might not happen.* The next day Mattie went to see the doctor, and sure enough, she was pregnant.

"Well Mattie, you can expect to have your baby sometime in late September. You are very healthy and I don't foresee any problems. I think it might be an idea for you to quit smoking though, young lady. Look at that as a benefit for your health as well as for your unborn child."

The doctor saw the crestfallen look on Mattie's face and did not know whether it was the smoking ban or the thoughts of a baby that caused Mattie to look so forlorn.

Mattie left his office feeling very confused. *I am not ready to be a mother. Already it starts—no smoking—and what next, swollen ankles and a stomach the size of the Hindenburg?* She knew her mom and Evan would be ecstatic, as there was nothing Polly loved more than children. Both Evan and Polly would have loved to have had children of their own, but it was not to be. Even though it would be another mouth to feed, Mattie was pretty sure Alf would welcome the news.

Why was she so lacking in maternal instincts? There was so much fun to be had going to dances and going out to the pub where you could forget the war and all the general gloom and doom of the austerity it brought with it. A baby? That would mean she would lose her figure, and the thought of that was enough to send her into a deep depression.

Then her father's words came to mind. "If there is not a way around the problem, you go right through it." Nothing was ever insurmountable to Lance, and Mattie was just as determined as he was. *Maybe it won't all be bad,* she thought. *Only seven months to go.* She reached into her purse and pulled out the packet of Woodbines, still almost full. She put one between her lips and lit it up, taking a long drag of what was to be her last cigarette for a long while. The taste was nauseating, and she laughed out loud as she thought that sometimes the Lord works in mysterious ways. If she didn't have the strength to quit on her own, then maybe she was getting a little help from above. Mattie threw the cigarette down and returned the pack to her purse to give to Tom later.

Mattie was not sure how Alf would take the news. A baby certainly had not been planned, or even discussed. There was a war going on, and they were still living in two rooms at Julia's house. This would certainly mean they would have to look for somewhere to live. *Well, there is a positive!* Thought Mattie, *We really will have to move when a baby comes along.*

When she broke the news to Alf, he was surprised but happy, and he put his arms around her. "So when is my son going to be born?" he questioned, a smile lighting up his face.

"Our daughter is due in September," she smiled back at him. Mattie was convinced she was going to have a girl. "Well, shall we break the news to your mam and dad, although I think they both knew before I did? Your mam doesn't miss a thing and she noticed I was a bit queasy a few days ago. I saw the look she gave your dad, and they both gave me the once over."

"Well love, I know they will be thrilled to bits to know they were right. There's nothing my mam will like more than a baby to fuss over."

"That's as may be, Alf, but we can't stay here after the baby is born. We need a place of our own where we can have the room to put a crib, and somewhere we can have our own lives at last. I feel like I am living in a goldfish bowl here. Your mam is good, and Tom's a treasure, but I feel as if they are both watching my every move and waiting for me to put a foot out of step."

"That's just how you feel, Mattie. It's taken mam a bit to get to know you. You can be a bit of a handful at times," Alf winked. "She knows I love you, and that is all she was ever bothered about. It took her a long while to get over Gladys's death, and I think she was afraid I would get hurt again. I hear what you say, though, about finding a place of our own, and we will as soon as I find something we can afford. We can't afford to bite off more than we can chew right now. There will only be one wage for a while, Mattie, once you have the baby."

"I know, Alf. Don't take any notice of me right now. I am still getting used to the fact that I am pregnant, and my hormones are all over the place. I love you and I know you will do the best you can for all of us." Mattie felt sorry for her complaints as she knew there was no one more hard working than Alf. He did overtime whenever he could, and picked up odd jobs whenever they were available. Because of his size and strength, he was capable of heavy work, and whenever help was needed he was usually the first one to be called.

"Let's go to Wellington and break the news to your mam and Evan. There will be some celebrating at Landrose when they find out." Alf could not wait to tell his mates at work, and of course Bill and Tom. He was more excited about the news than Mattie was. She was pleased to see his reaction though, and was starting to feel a little better about the whole thing. "Let's go out there on Saturday morning, Alf. We can call at Liv's at the same time. She will be surprised. Not a word to anyone though, Alf, until I have told my mam," Mattie said firmly. She knew Polly would be hurt if she found out from someone else.

Saturday morning they set off early for Landrose, and surprised Polly and Evan when they got there while Polly was still making breakfast. Mattie was the first to walk in, and the smell of the home cured bacon frying in the pan met her as she opened the door.

"Hello, my duck. What brings you two out so early in the morning?" Polly beamed, as it was a lovely surprise. She always loved to have her children visit. "Have you had your breakfasts? I can soon put a bit more bacon in the pan."

Mattie tried her best to stop from heaving, but it was no use. She ran outside quickly, as there was no way she could reach the upstairs bathroom in time. The smell of the bacon was just too much.

Polly heard the heaves, and with one look at Alf's happy face, she knew why she had been blessed with such an early morning visit.

"Well, Alf, are you going to make me a grandma sometime soon?" Polly went to give him a hug. "I guess it will only be one extra for bacon this morning?"

"Yes, Mam, we are expecting a baby at the end of September, so that gives you plenty of time to get your knitting needles dusted off." Alf could see Polly was overjoyed at the thoughts of a baby to fuss over.

"Congratulations, Alf," Evan smiled.

Mattie came back in looking a little pale, and seeing the look on all their faces, knew her secret was no more.

"Come on in, my love, and have a cup of tea. I will put a bit of camomile in it and that will settle your stomach a bit. Don't worry, love; the morning sickness will go away soon." Polly put her arms around her daughter and hoped that her prophecy was right, as she knew Mattie hated to be sick.

"I'm just going to take Tony for a walk, mam, while you three have breakfast. I need a little fresh air. I'll come back and have a cuppa in a bit." Mattie needed to walk in the Landrose fields and just be alone with all her mixed feelings. Maybe there she could make sense of what was happening with her emotions. Landrose was always a place of comfort and healing. She thought back to the time when she had been confined to her bed with tuberculosis, and she had spent weeks looking out over the fields. Tony ran on ahead of her, every few hundred feet turning back to check that she was following him. The walk did her good and she came back with colour in her cheeks and feeling much better. They stayed and visited for a while before leaving to go to Liv's and a few other friends. It turned out to be a good day, and Mattie smiled as she saw how proud Alf was to make the announcement at each stop.

Mattie still had to tell Mr. Rowell, and she knew he would be disappointed to lose her. They had really become a great team, and she enjoyed working with him. The next day Mattie decided to get it over with before the rest of the staff arrived. Charley and Mattie were always the first at work.

"Mr. Rowell. I have something I have to tell you." Mattie was not sure what his reaction would be, and hesitated before telling him. Charley looked at her over the top of his glasses, and instantly knew what the announcement would be. He smiled at her and got up from behind his desk.

"Is this a little good news and a little bad news, Mattie?"

"I'm pregnant, Mr. Rowell, and expecting a baby in late September. I really would like to work as long as I can, and as long as you will have me. We need the money, and I do like my job." Mattie hoped he would let her work for at least another five months. She would really try and save as much as she could before the baby arrived.

"Mattie, as long as you are healthy and able to work, your job is here. If you ever decide that you want to come back afterwards, there will be a job waiting for you. I am very happy for you, and I know that

Polly will be in her glory with a baby to fuss over." Charley knew Polly was a born mom, and somehow he also realized Mattie would need her help.

Mattie worked at Rowell's until the end of August, and never missed a day of work. The girls all threw a big farewell party after work on her last day. Each of them had either knit or crocheted or bought some item of baby clothing. Mattie was sad to clean out her cupboard and know she would not be coming back, at least for some time to come.

Mr. Rowell stayed in his office until they were all about to leave, and then called Mattie in to see him. Mattie was uncharacteristically emotional. She would really miss her crusty old employer. He had always been more than fair with her and she really did like him very much. Charley pushed his heavy old leather chair away and came out from behind his desk.

"Here you go, Mattie. I hope this helps a little. Use it to buy that little one whatever it needs."

Mattie looked at the envelope and could see that it contained several pounds. "Oh, Mr. Rowell, I never expected anything. You have been so good to me. I will miss you all so much." Mattie was now in tears.

Charley was at a loss. He was uncomfortable with emotion, so gave her a little pat on the arm. "Off you go then, girl, and don't forget to come in and see us some time."

When Mattie left his office he took off his spectacles and wiped a tear from his eye. He would miss Mattie's always upbeat personality, and he would certainly miss her as an employee. He knew she would get a surprise when she opened the envelope. He had paid her wages up until the end of the year.

He was right, as when Mattie got home and counted the money, she could not believe her eyes. He had no idea how much this would help them, or maybe he did. She could not wait to show Alf the generosity of her employer, and all the gifts she had received from her co-workers. It helped to elevate her mood, as getting towards the end of the eighth month, Mattie was feeling tired and uncomfortable. The doctor was pleased with her check-ups however, as although she felt she was the size of a house, she had stayed well within the guidelines for weight gain. Thanks to Julia and Polly, she had little to do when she came home from work, so she was well rested. "Pregnancy suits you," "You look a right picture," and other comments followed her wherever she went.

Pregnancy does NOT suit ME, thought Mattie. *It's easy for them to say, they can still go out dancing and have a smoke when they want one.* Even though her last cigarette had nauseated her, Mattie still missed her cigarettes fiercely, and when Tom lit up a Woodbine, it took a lot of control for her not to follow suit.

Eleven

SEPTEMBER 1943

The past eight months had gone slowly for Mattie, and she had hated being pregnant. Maternity clothes were horrible, and she felt like she was wearing a tent most of the time. Other than her expanding waist line and baby bump, Mattie had changed little during the whole pregnancy. Polly and Evan insisted that Mattie and Alf come and stay with them for the last couple of weeks.

"You need to be with your mom when the baby is born, Mattie. You can have the pink room, and Evan will see to it that the fire is turned on every day." Polly was far more excited about the baby than Mattie was, and she too was convinced it was going to be a girl. Mattie had only chosen girl's names. It was going to be Sandra Mary.

"Just think, Evan, the first child ever to be born at Landrose House," Polly said as she busied herself sorting out an array of baby clothes she had bought over the past few months.

Evan chuckled, "That little girl will have more clothes than a princess when she is born, but what if it is a boy, Polly? Poor little chap will not have a thing to wear; he'll be like a tiny urchin."

Polly smiled and went about her chores. *It will be a girl. I know,* she mused to herself.

Mattie had had an amazingly healthy pregnancy and had no difficulty working up until the last month. The extra money was going to be useful, as Alf had seen a house that might be up for rent, and they would have to pay a month's rent in advance as well as a damage deposit. Mattie had not seen the house as it was still occupied and would not be available until the middle of October. She knew where it was, and although nothing could ever compare to Landrose, it was in a convenient location in Ripley. She was anxious to have a place of their own, so it really did not matter that much as long as they could have their own space at last.

September was almost over, and no signs of labour. It looks like it will be October, thought Mattie forlornly. Another month in maternity clothes. Will this baby never be born?

It was a beautiful September morning and Mattie decided to go and pick blackberries from the top field. It had been a great year for all the berries, and Mattie craved one of her mam's blackberry and apple pies.

"Don't go too far, Mattie. Stay where I can see you. You never know when you are going to go into labour." Polly knew it was no good telling Mattie not to go, but she would certainly keep an eye on her through the kitchen window.

Mattie came home a couple hours later with a big pail full of juicy blackberries. Polly had already made pastry and chopped the apples while she was in the kitchen. She looked at Mattie and laughed, as her daughter was covered in blackberry juice, having obviously eaten a good share of the berries already.

"You go and wash up, love, while I get the pie in the oven. Alf should be home soon and you don't want to greet him looking like that."

Mattie was only too happy to go and clean up and put on a comfy robe. *Maybe I overdid it a bit with the blackberries*, she thought, as she was feeling a bit uncomfortable.

Supper was delicious, as always, with Polly taking such pride in seeing everyone clean their plates. Mattie did not manage to finish her supper and excused herself from the table.

"I think I'll go and have a lie down; I'm feeling a bit funny, mam."

Polly looked at Mattie and knew instantly that she had started in labour.

"I'll come upstairs with you, love. Alf and Evan, you can clean the dishes tonight. I think that Sandra Mary is on her way."

It was about 10:00 p.m. when Mattie's pains were coming regularly. "How much longer does this go on?" Mattie groaned. She tried desperately hard not to scream as each pain wracked her body. Polly tried to comfort her daughter. "It will all be over soon, love. You will forget all about the pain when you see your little baby. Now be a brave girl, and I will have Evan call the midwife right away."

Polly shouted down to Evan to ring for the midwife. Her number was right by the phone, and he quickly complied as he knew by the sounds from upstairs that the baby was well on its way.

"Polly, she wants me to stand at the end of the lane as she does not know where the house is, and with the blackout, she'll have no lights to see by."

"Get off with you then, love. I think this little one will be here soon."

Evan was used to driving the winding lane with no lights, as often during the war he was called out to fix a pump or solve an electrical issue. It was a different story for someone unfamiliar with the lane, and there was no way they needed the nurse to end up in a ditch tonight. He cranked the handle of the Ford, and it started with the first try. Evan gave the old Ford a thankful pat on the hood and set off at twice his normal speed.

Alf was eager to go upstairs and see Mattie, but Polly insisted it was no place for a man, and he should stay downstairs and boil water. He was not sure what he had to boil water for, but dutifully put a big pot of water on the hob. Mattie did not want anyone other than Polly with her. The pains were coming every couple of minutes now, and she was covered with sweat. Her long dark hair was matted down her neck and back. Mattie groaned in pain, but Polly was determined to keep her daughter focused on the task in hand. "It'll all be over soon, my love. It might be one of the worst pains you'll have, but it will be one of the quickest forgotten." Polly repeated her mantra, hoping that her words were going to prove true.

"Where are Evan and the midwife?" Mattie shouted. "The baby is coming! Where are they?"

"AAAAAHHH!" Mattie's scream coincided with the arrival of the midwife. Jennie Greaves was a big lady, and when she got to the top of the stairs she was puffing and panting harder than Mattie.

The birth was uncomplicated, and a few minutes after Jennie's arrival, Sandra Mary was born. It was 29th September 1943. Jennie regained her breath and efficiently took care of Mattie and the new baby.

"It's a beautiful little girl, Mattie, and she's got your green eyes and dark hair." Jennie wrapped the little bundle in the waiting blankets Polly had warmed by the fire.

Mattie looked at her baby daughter and saw she was perfect. It was hard to see who she looked like at this early stage. Mattie completed her inspection, and she wondered when she would feel that maternal instinct everyone told her would come with the baby's arrival. Sandra Mary was the daughter she had anticipated, but somehow she felt detached, as if the baby belonged to someone else. She was relieved it was all over and that Sandra had ten fingers and ten toes and a full head of dark hair.

"Go to sleep, love, and get your strength back. I'll look after Sandra while you have a rest." Polly could not wait to hold the newborn in her arms, and instantly felt the love and connection with her first grandchild. "You are a little beauty, and you are my first grandchild. Do you know how much I love you already?" Polly crooned to the newborn as she gently swayed from side to side, holding Sandra close to her chest.

Polly called Evan and Alf upstairs to see the new baby, as she proudly cradled Sandra in her arms. Alf looked at Mattie and knew she needed to sleep for a while, so after giving her a big hug, he turned his attention to his new daughter. He carefully took his new daughter from Polly's arms. She looked so tiny and delicate. He had secretly hoped for a son, but he was happy to see that his daughter was healthy, and as cute as a button.

"You've got your mom's eyes, little one—and a set of good lungs." Alf looked at a loss as to what to do with his daughter to stop her crying.

"Give her to me, Alf." Polly instinctively took the baby, and in seconds she had rocked the little one to sleep. Evan put his arm around Polly, and the two of them could not have been happier. "A child born at Landrose, Polly: our little Sandra Mary."

The next two weeks were heaven for Polly and Evan, who spent far more time with Sandra than either Mattie or Alf did. In truth, they were far more enamoured with the baby than either Mattie or Alf appeared to be.

Evan's gift to Mattie and Alf was a beautiful Silver Cross Pram that stood on high silver polished wheels. It was dark navy blue with gold scrolls on either side. Polly had made cozy blankets for the crisp fall air, and she wrapped Sandra up snugly and placed her in the pram to take her for a walk. It was a beautiful October Sunday morning, and Polly and Belle were looking forward to taking Sandra out for a walk down the lane. Belle was only sixteen years old, but she had all the maternal instinct Mattie lacked. Belle was now working at Rowell's and had spent her last two weeks' bonus money on baby clothes.

"Here mam, put this new little bonnet on her. It's a bit nippy outside." Belle handed Polly a cute cream bonnet with little pink rose-buds around the edge.

"That's where all your pay check goes, my girl," Polly admonished, but she had to smile as she saw how much Belle loved her little niece.

Suddenly there was a scream from upstairs.

"Mam! Mam! Come quick. It's our Mattie. Something is wrong. Oh my god, Mam, come quick!"

Darren had been in the bathroom shaving when he heard Mattie scream. He dropped his razor and ran to the bedroom, where Mattie was standing next to the window clutching her nightgown, which was covered in blood. Mattie's face was ashen grey and she looked frightened to death.

Polly ran upstairs as fast as her legs would carry her, and at the sight of Mattie she almost fainted. There was blood everywhere, and Mattie looked like death.

"It's all right, love. Don't be frightened. You've had a hemorrhage. Come on, let me get you back in bed." Polly could not let Mattie see how afraid she was. Mattie had lost an enormous amount of blood and she was still bleeding.

"Evan, get the doctor quick, Mattie has hemorrhaged." Evan needed no second bidding as he had heard the commotion and knew something must be terribly wrong. He ran out of the door and was thankful the car started with one crank of the handle.

Mattie had tried to open the old sash window, and in reaching up she must have strained too hard. "Why on earth did you want to open the window?" Polly questioned, tears streaming down her face. She packed towels tightly between Mattie's legs and raised her feet with pillows. Mattie was scared and had no idea what was happening, as she felt as if her life was slipping away from her.

"What's the matter, mam? Is our Mattie all right?" Belle knew that something must be very wrong.

"Belle, I need you to look after Sandra for a while. Stay downstairs and let the doctor in when he gets here. Everything will be all right." Polly was nowhere near as confident as she was trying to appear. She had to stay calm and not alarm Mattie any more than she was already.

Thank heavens for the good doctor, who left his surgery immediately and went back to Landrose with Evan. He knew Polly would not call for him unless it was a real emergency. When he saw Mattie, he knew this was certainly very serious.

"She's lost an awful lot of blood, Polly. I've done everything I can. You'll have to watch her very closely for the next few days. Total bed rest. No putting her feet out of bed. She's a strong girl, but if she hemorrhages again I don't know what else I can do."

Polly could not let Mattie see how afraid she was, but Mattie was drifting in and out of consciousness. Doctor Whittaker had given her some strong sedatives and insisted the best thing was to keep her warm and quiet and as still as possible. Alf was just coming back from taking Tony for a walk, and when he saw the doctor's car in the yard he knew something must be wrong.

He ran into the house and up the stairs two at a time, almost knocking Belle over on his way. One look at Mattie and his heart almost stopped. He had watched Gladys fade away before him, and now his full-of-life Mattie looked at death's door. The pile of blood stained clothes and sheets were still in a basket at the end of the bed, and Alf struggled hard to keep from retching. How could anyone lose that amount of blood and still be alive?

"Mattie, my darling, don't you dare leave me. I can't live without you. We all need you. Stay with us." Tears streamed down his cheeks. Polly wrapped her arms around her son-in-law, and gently pulled him out of the room.

"She needs lots of rest, Alf, and she will be okay. I know she will. Our Mattie's a fighter, and you know it." Polly had never seen Alf so emotional. He was the big strong man who everyone else turned to for support. She had seen him keep calm when others panicked, like the time Tony had a run in with a fox. Alf was the one who tended his wounds and calmed Belle, who had witnessed the fight. In the short time Alf had been a part of the family, everyone had grown to love him. He truly was a gentle giant, and until now, no one had seen him show any sign of inability to cope with any situation. His back stooped and his face drained of all colour, he firmly hugged Polly and just as firmly returned to Mattie's side. "My place is here, Polly, and I will stay here until I know that everything is going to be all right."

It was there that Alf stayed, fitfully falling asleep for a few minutes at a time on the chair at the side of the bed. Mattie was a fighter, and although it took many weeks before she regained her strength and was allowed out of bed, she eventually began to take short walks around the house. Polly and Belle both adored Sandra, and Mattie did not have to worry about taking care of her new baby. Polly and Evan thought of Sandra as their own. Since the day of her birth they had spent more time with their new granddaughter than Mattie had. Polly knew the day was coming when Mattie and Alf would return to Riddings, and she dreaded the thought of them taking Sandra Mary. Evan was just as troubled as Polly was, as the two of them had never been happier than when they were spending time with the new baby. Darren mostly ignored the baby; as far as he was concerned she was just something that needed constant attention, either feeding or changing or rocking to sleep. Belle, on the other hand, loved the new baby. Mattie was in no hurry to go back to Riddings, as she had so much help from Polly and Evan and Belle. She knew Alf would be busy for a few weeks, as the house on Moseley Street was going to be ready for possession, and he had to do some fixing up before they moved in. Alf did not want Mattie to see it until he had the chance to clean it up, and he had enlisted some help to wallpaper one of the rooms. It was an old house, and the old brick had let damp seep through which had caused the paper to peel off the walls. It certainly was no show home, but he would do the best he could to make it as comfortable as possible.

The project took longer than Alf and Mattie had anticipated, and they had moved back to Riddings, as it was easier for him to travel back and forth from there. Eventually an exhausted Alf came home, grinning from ear to ear.

"Well, Mrs. Wetton, your new home is ready for inspection," Alf beamed. "Mam, can you keep an eye on Sandra while I take Mattie to Ripley?"

Julia was tired, as the diabetes was taking a toll, and in truth, she mostly spent more time with Sandra than Mattie did anyway. She could see Alf was proud of his handiwork, and knowing him, she was sure he would have done an excellent job.

"Go on son; I can look after Sandra. She should be ready for a nap soon anyway," Julia said, hoping she was right. Julia planned to take Sandra with her upstairs and would try to have a nap beside the cot while the baby slept.

Alf had done the best he could with the money he had allotted, and the old terraced house was a far cry from what it had been when he first rented it. It was still an old house with a musty smell that was impossible to eradicate. The coat of paint had brightened it up, and he had enhanced the old fireplace with a smart tiled surround. Mattie tried to be enthusiastic about her new home.

"It's lovely, Alf," Mattie said, trying not to show her disappointment. "It will look altogether different once we get some furniture in here and hang a few pictures." Mattie thought of the comfort of Landrose and knew that no matter what they did here, it would never be Landrose.

With furniture donated from Polly and Evan, and Julia and Tom, together with a few bits and pieces from the second hand store, they moved into Moseley Street. It took less than six months for Mattie to realize that housework was hard work, and taking care of a young baby was even harder. Alf was working long hours and Mattie was alone with Sandra in a house that felt more like a jail cell. On one of Liv's infrequent visits, Mattie poured out her heart to the only person who truly understood her.

"It's not that I don't love Alf, Liv: he's an absolute saint. He puts up with my moods and helps with a few things around the house. I just feel so trapped. I long to go dancing and have fun, and he hates dancing. I miss the fun at the fire hall and the laughs with the lads. I never thought a baby would be so much trouble. What with feeding and changing and washing diapers, it takes up all my time. Maybe I am just not cut out to be a mother. It comes naturally to my mam; she adores Sandra and I am sure she would keep her if I left her there. Evan is just as soppy over her, and they spoil her rotten when they get a chance."

Liv listened and understood Mattie perfectly. Liv also had no desire for children, and Fred felt the same way.

"Well Mattie, you do have a daughter, and I suppose you have to make the best of it. She is a lovely little baby though. She has your eyes, and maybe if you are lucky, she might have Alf's disposition," Liv laughed.

The two friends chatted for hours and Mattie was reluctant to see her friend leave. Time had flown by, and for once Mattie had felt more like her old self. Sandra had actually slept through the visit and it had been like old times.

Money was short and there was never much left over for frivolity. Alf was hired at Aiton's, and in a very short time he proved himself at the new job. He was placed on a project making complicated bends for ships' pipes, and there were always deadlines to meet. Overtime was constant, but paid little. At the end of a shift, he came home tired and aching from working on his knees in damp sand for hours on end.

The nightly ritual became a bath in the old tin tub by the fire, and then when he was not too tired, a walk to the top of the street to The Red Lion for a pint with some of his fellow workers. The pub held no attraction for Mattie. Most of the men played darts or dominoes, and talked about their day at work. Mattie knew what she wanted to do, and damn it she was going to do it, come hell or high water. She had heard about a dance instructor by the name of Bill Taylor, and she desperately wanted to go dancing. She was sure that Alf would not object to her taking lessons. One night when he was about to leave for the pub, Mattie brought up the subject.

"Alf, I want to take dance lessons. There's a class every Wednesday night at the school gym. It doesn't start until 7:30 p.m., and Sandra will be asleep by then."

Alf was happy Mattie had found something she wanted to do. He was not blind and could see she was getting bored with playing house. He knew housework was not high on her list of exciting things to do.

"Go ahead, love. It will do you good to get out a bit." Alf had no idea what a Pandora's Box would be opened.

Twelve

GOLD MEDALS

From the first time Mattie sashayed in to the dance class, Bill Taylor knew that he had a star pupil. Her legs were long and lithe and her back as straight as an arrow. There was a look of Greta Garbo and Jane Russell melded into one. She had regal bearing, but there was something he could not quite put his finger on. He need not have felt badly, as very few people could define Mattie. Mattie was simply Mattie, with no excuses. She loved being the center of attraction and she shone in the spotlight. Bill guessed her height to be around 5feet 7 inches. She would be a perfect competition partner.

Bill was right about his assessment of Mattie. In no time at all she was ready for competition. He of course would be her partner. He was tall and slim with sleek black hair, and the two of them would make a stunning picture as they danced together. Mattie could not wait to tell Liv, and plan how she was going to come up with a dress to wear for the occasion. Alf was another matter, however, as he had become a little concerned about the amount of time Mattie was now spending at dance lessons. The Wednesday night classes were now Wednesday and Friday, and the competition would be on a Saturday.

In Mattie's usual way, she resolved the dilemma by simply erasing it from her mind, and consequently, problem solved. Sandra usually slept through the night now, so Mattie saw no harm in leaving her in her crib while she went dancing. That is how the pattern evolved: Alf went to the pub, Mattie went dancing, and Sandra was left alone in the old house.

Polly did not know what was happening in Ripley, and only saw Mattie's excitement at being chosen as Bill Taylor's dance partner in the next competition.

"Well love, Evan and I will buy you a dress for the event. You have to look as good as you can dance. I know you will be a winner." Polly closed her eyes and remembered when she had dressed for farmer's balls, and how she had loved the spectacle of so many beautiful dresses and all the men dressed in their finery. The moment quickly passed as she also remembered how often the night had ended in misery when Lance had drank too much and become belligerent and abusive. Alf was different entirely, and Polly knew she never had to fear he would ever lay a finger on Mattie. He liked his beer, but never drank hard liquor, and although he drank a few pints at a time, his large frame showed no signs of over-indulgence.

"Really Mam, I did not know what I was going to do. Liv and I were going to alter one of Fred's sister's dresses, but it was kind of plain."

"Plain will just not do for my girl. How about I have Evan run us into Chesterfield and we will see what we can find?"

Mattie was over the moon. Belle had volunteered to have Sandra for the day while Polly and Mattie went shopping.

"I'll love having her, Mattie. Ken and I will take her for a walk down the lane and she'll sleep like a little lamb after being in the fresh air." Belle loved children and was looking forward to spending time with her little niece. Ken was a quiet young man, and whatever Belle wanted to do was fine by him; he just enjoyed every minute with her.

There were two shops in Chesterfield that sold the type of competition gown that Mattie would like, but both were very expensive. Polly was prepared for the expense as she knew how much work went into their creations. Both stores had their own seamstresses, and although not entirely custom made, they were tweaked to the customer's specifications.

Mattie tried on several dresses, and in truth they all looked spectacular, but in her own mind Mattie had already pictured what she wanted. Finally the clerk came out with a dress that Mattie knew, even before trying it on, was the one. It was a stunning creation of shimmering tulle and satin, that changed color as it moved: one minute sea green and the next a deep azure blue. The bodice was figure hugging and studded with sequins, and the back was cut daringly low to the waist. The skirt was a crinoline with yards of net underskirts that emphasized her tiny waist, and Mattie knew that as she danced it would show just enough of her long legs. Mattie disappeared into the fitting room with a huge smile, and Polly knew that no matter what the cost, this was going to be the one.

When Mattie emerged, the clerk and Polly let out a collective gasp. The dress had looked amazing on the hanger, but on Mattie it was magic. The color emphasized her green eyes and the fit was perfect. There was nothing any seamstress could do to enhance it. It was, in a word, perfection.

"Oh mam this is the one." Mattie twirled around and the dress shimmered and changed color as it caught the light. The sequins sparkled like diamonds dancing on an ocean. Mattie could not wait to show Bill Taylor the dress she had chosen. He had a black tuxedo he wore for the competitions, and all he had to do was add a few adornments in a matching color to complement his partner's outfit.

That night Mattie tried the dress on to show Alf and was surprised at his reaction. "It's lovely Mattie, and you look as pretty as a picture." It was obvious that he liked the dress, but there was something sad in his expression that Mattie could not fathom.

Alf looked at his wife and thought he had never seen anything quite so beautiful, but somewhere in the back of his mind he was reminded of a butterfly and a saying, "If you love something, set it free. If it comes back it is yours, if not, then it never was." The last few months of Mattie's dance classes, she had been so wrapped up in the upcoming competition that he had been feeling a little left out of her world.

At last the night of the competition came around and Polly and Evan both went to watch. Alf did not go, as there was an important union meeting that night, and in truth, he really did not want to see his wife in someone else's arms. He knew Bill Taylor was just a dance partner, but nonetheless he was a man. How could any man hold her in his arms and not want her? He was wrong though, as Bill Taylor was all about the dance. On the dance floor he was all business. Mattie was an expert dancer, and her striking looks and figure were a bonus he knew would help to influence the judges. Tonight she had taken her hair back and twisted it into a chignon and pinned a simple silver comb in the back. The severity of the style merely enhanced her exotic looks and gave full emphasis to the stunning dress. Everything was taken into account. Dress, posture, hairstyle, and of course the intricacy of the dance steps. Bill was a master, and step perfect, and Mattie matched him step to step. One by one the couples were eliminated until only Mattie and Bill remained on the dance floor. It had been her first competition and she had won the first prize.

Polly and Evan were justifiably very proud, and the only thing that would have made the evening perfect was to have seen Alf there. *He must be watching our Sandra,* Evan mused. Neither of them had any idea that Sandra was frequently left alone in the house. Polly worried a little that Mattie was in some ways a little too much like her father, and hoped that she did not have the same hedonistic view of life.

Once Mattie had started on the competition circuit, it was impossible to stop. It was like a magnet that drew her into a world full of excitement and adulation. She was recognised as a gold medal dancer wherever she went. Bill, knowing the impact her outfits had, started to foot the bill for her gowns, which became more spectacular at each competition. There was a price to pay for her total absorption in dancing competitions, and that was that she and Alf had started to drift apart. Sandra was almost forgotten in the picture, as once 7:30 p.m. rolled around, she was packed off upstairs to bed, and then both Alf and Mattie went their separate ways. It was inevitable that cracks would develop in the relationship, and arguments were frequent. One night when Mattie had been unusually late, Alf had sat at home waiting and stewing about where she was and why she was so late. He knew the competition should have been over hours ago. Mattie had won again, and after the competition she had stayed to celebrate with some of her new friends. She was not a drinker, but just enjoyed the company and being the centre of attention.

That night she was surprised to see Eric there. He was Alf's cousin and had the same imposing build; however, the big difference was his sandy blonde hair and deep blue eyes.

He wandered over to Mattie with a lazy smile. "What's wrong with that cousin of mine? I wouldn't be letting you out of my sight if you belonged to me."

"I don't belong to anybody Eric," Mattie said defiantly.

"Well now that we have that established, sit down and let me buy you a drink."

"No thanks, Eric. I'm not much of a drinker, but I will sit down for a minute. I know it looks easy, but these shoes are killing me," Mattie said with a laugh.

Mattie lost all track of time and found Eric very easy to talk to. He was stunningly handsome, and she knew he could have chosen to sit with any of the dancers if he wished.

Suddenly Mattie realized how late it was and realized that Alf would be at home before her.

"It was fun tonight, Eric, but I have to go." Mattie got up to leave, and Eric put his arm around her as he pulled out the chair. It was a quick gesture, and although over in a second, neither of them was unaware of the electricity between them.

When Mattie got home, Alf was not happy. Sandra had been awake with an ear ache, and he had been trying to pacify her. When he had eventually got her off to sleep again, he sat watching the clock and waiting for Mattie.

"It's time you realize you have a daughter and a husband, Mattie, and come home at a reasonable hour," Alf complained.

"It's time YOU realized I am not your property, and I am my own person. No one tells me when to come and go!" Mattie stormed.

"Well, I am telling you, my girl. If you come home at this time next week the door will be locked, and you can stay out all night if that is what you want."

That night neither of them slept. Both were thinking their own thoughts and regretting the exchange. For Mattie, Alf was still the man she loved, but he lacked the excitement she needed in her life. Alf's thoughts were just the opposite. He loved Mattie more than she would ever know, but he wished she was a little domesticated and not so mercurial. He knew she missed the excitement of the days when she was single. It was obvious from the moment she gave birth that motherhood was not high on her list of great moments in life. Maybe, he thought, the terrible hemorrhage she'd had after Sandra was born could be part of the reason she was so detached from her daughter. For his part, he was a man, and men were not built to be caregivers to children, at least not in his world. He had seen his mother look after her family of nieces and nephews, and knew she was at her happiest when the house was full of children's laughter. His father was a kind and generous man and would often kick a ball around with the older boys, but he did not participate in any of the daily care of his children. It was just the way that things were. The men went to work and earned the money for food and clothing, and mostly the women stayed at home and cared for their families.

By the time the next dance competition came around, Mattie had forgotten all about Alf's threat to lock the door if she came home late. She was anticipating wearing a new gown for the competition. It was a coral coloured profusion of net and tulle, with a billowing skirt and the low cut back which had become her signature style. That night she took extra care with her hair and makeup. Her hair was styled to one side with a coral rose tucked behind one ear. She looked into the mirror and, pleased with the results, went upstairs to check that Sandra was asleep. Alf had already gone to the Red Lion. It was a darts tournament night, and she knew that he would be late home anyway.

Locking the door behind her, there was no thought of guilt in leaving her child at home alone. She was asleep; what harm could come to her? Her thoughts were more of Eric. Would he be there to watch her dance tonight? She knew that as a married woman she should not be thinking this way, but oh god, he was exciting and handsome. He made her feel like a desirable woman and not a housewife and mother.

Bill Taylor looked at his dance partner and knew how lucky he was to have her on his arm for this competition. Her skill at ballroom dancing was beyond question, and combined with her impact on the judges, gold medals were accumulating. This was great for his dance studio, and since Mattie had joined him, there was now a waiting list for students.

Tonight however, there was some stiff competition from a couple out of Nottingham. They were a husband and wife team who had danced together for several years. The competition was so close that when it came down to the final two couples on the floor, Bill and Mattie and the Nottingham contestants had to dance not one, but two dances, before the judges could decide. The last dance was a tango, and Mattie smiled confidently. She knew this sensual dance was one of their best. It was perfection, and Bill and Mattie danced as one, not missing a step.

Eric sat away from the front of the dance floor, but he had not missed a move, and when Mattie came off the floor, he was by her side.

"You really were amazing, Mattie." His blue eyes twinkled, and when he smiled his face was a study in contradictions. His blonde hair and blue eyes gave him a look of innocence, but his roguish smile and strong jaw line hinted at a much more rakish side to his character.

"Thanks, Eric. I did not know that you were such a fan of ballroom dancing," Mattie smiled.

"There are a lot of things that you don't know about me, Mattie Wetton. You think you are the only one who can dance." With that he pulled her back onto the dance floor, which was now open for everyone to dance. He circled his long arms around her tiny waist and there was no doubt who the leader was. He was no Fred Astaire, and not an accomplished dancer, but his sheer masculinity and confidence made Mattie unaware of any flaws in his performance. Mattie knew this was a dangerous liaison, and that she should end this association before it started. Eric was engaged to be married and she was married. But logic was never her strong suit, and it felt so good to be living in the moment. She was not Mattie Wetton, wife and mother; for the moment she was a femme fatale with a rakish admirer.

She was the heroine in the books that she devoured, and all caution to the wind, she agreed to meet him again the following week, but this time at a pub on the opposite side of town. Once outside of the dance hall, Eric pulled her into the shadows, and kissed her so fiercely and passionately that her legs almost buckled underneath her. Shocked by her reaction to his kiss, she quickly made an excuse to leave. She really did have to get home anyway, as she thought that by now Alf would surely have gotten home before her.

As soon as she tried the door, Mattie knew Alf was home, and true to his word, he had locked the door.

"Damn, Damn, Damn!" What now, she thought. "Well, as Dad would say, if there is not a way around it go through it!" She tried the old sash window, and sure enough, Alf had not locked it. The window was facing the street and was hard to open, as it was glued with several years of chipping and peeling paint. After several attempts she finally managed to get it open. Her next dilemma was the fact that she could never get through it wearing the huge dance dress with its many layers of net petticoats. A quick glance up and down the street, and as usual, at this time of night there was not a soul in sight. All of the house lights were out and there was just a street lamp further down the street which gave a little illumination. Without a second's hesitation, Mattie unzipped the gown and let it slip down to the pavement. Throwing the dress in ahead of her, she stood in her coral corselet and high heel shoes contemplating the best way to climb through the narrow window. Raising herself up, she would have to jump head first and then swing her feet in afterwards.

Hands braced on the window ledge, she was just about to jump, when a cold hand grabbed her shoulder. Mattie's heart was in her mouth. She had not seen a soul on the street.

"Now what do we have here?" a deep voice boomed in her ear. "Is this break and enter?"

Mattie almost screamed, but then recognised the voice. It was Sergeant Flannigan from the constabulary at the top of the street. He was a tough cop, but also a good cop, and he knew very well who Mattie was and could easily guess the scenario. He had been down the entry at the house across the street doing his nightly rounds of his beat, when he heard Mattie struggling with the window.

"Come on, girl, I'll give you a leg up. You'd better get inside before you catch your death dressed like that!" He chuckled, thinking about the story he would have to tell his friends later. He could not help thinking what a looker she was. Right down to her skivvies, he mused. *By the heck, she must be a handful*, he said to himself. *There is something to be said for having an average looking wife who stays home and bakes biscuits, like good wives should.* He gingerly put his huge arms around Mattie and hoisted her up and over the window ledge, trying hard not to look at the view of her cute derriere as he did.

Mattie, now over her initial fear, was giggling uncontrollably at the situation as she fell in a heap on top of the beautiful new dance dress. Miraculously Alf had slept through the whole commotion, and the next day he had no idea how Mattie had got into the house. He had bolted the door from the inside, and the only other door had two bolts that were never opened.

The next morning Mattie was a little concerned about what Alf would have to say about her failure to come home at a reasonable hour, but as always, she quickly dismissed her concerns. By the time she had gotten Sandra up and dressed, Alf was already gone to work. Mattie looked at her young daughter, and try as she might, all she could think about was how much work she was. Maybe today she would go and visit Julia and Tom, as she knew that Julia would be only too happy to dote on her granddaughter. She and Tom would go for a walk up his garden and have a smoke together. It would be good to get away from the cramped quarters of the tiny terraced house. Today she did not want to be alone with her thoughts.

What kind of a wife and mother am I? She silently questioned, afraid to admit even to herself that she felt trapped, like a caged animal. She knew that she was treading dangerous waters with Eric, but at the same time her pulse raced with anticipation. Alf was five years older than her and his cousin, and he was far more serious and reserved. In some ways, he was the stable father figure that she had never known, and she always felt incredibly safe with him. There was no doubt that she loved him, but was love ever enough for her?

Julia looked through the window and saw Mattie coming down the garden path, with Sandra in her arms.

"Tom, its Mattie and our Sandra." For some reason both sets of grandparents referred to Sandra as "our" Sandra. It was if they all realized that they were more a part of her life than her parents were. "Put the kettle on, love," Julia called over her shoulder to Tom, as she went to meet her daughter-in-law.

"What a lovely surprise," Julia smiled, genuinely delighted to see them both.

"Come here, give her to me," she said, with arms outstretched to take Sandra.

Mattie happily obliged, as Sandra was starting to get heavy and it had been a long walk up from the bus stop. Julia smiled, pleased by the fact that Sandra was always spotlessly clean and dressed. Julia had doubted Mattie's maternal instincts, but at least she obviously looked after the necessities. Sandra looked well fed and content, and that was some comfort. Over time, Julia had come to accept that Mattie was not Gladys and never would be. *I suppose everyone raises children differently*, she rationalized. She would have thought differently if she had known of Mattie's practice of leaving her daughter home alone so many nights.

Tom was his usual jovial self and just as happy to see his granddaughter. "Here love, you hold her a minute while I make a cup of tea." Julia passed a gurgling Sandra over to Tom.

Mattie was surprised to see that Julia looked much older than the last time she had seen her. The diabetes was taking a toll. She had started to limp, and Mattie noticed that she rubbed her thigh as if it ached. It was an automatic motion that Julia was unaware she was even doing. The twice a day insulin injections were riddling her body with needle marks and bruises. The nurse who came each day was kind and gentle, but she was running out of new sites for injections. It was not in Julia's nature to complain, but she was tired, and another frustrating side effect of the horrible disease was that she was losing her eyesight. Julia loved to knit and crochet, and now even that pleasure was denied her.

The time went quickly, and Julia was sorry to see them leave. Tom picked up his granddaughter, "Come on lass, I'll walk you to the bus. This little girl is no light weight." He smiled to himself, as he looked at the cherubic little face beneath the knitted bonnet. She had Mattie's green eyes, but not the chiselled features of her mother. Sandra had rosy round cheeks and a little button nose. At this age she featured neither of her parents, and was showing early indications of independence. *Good thing*, Tom thought, as he had noticed that Mattie had barely looked at her daughter since she arrived. Julia, on the other hand, had been in her element, feeding and changing her granddaughter. By the time Alf got home from work, Mattie had supper ready and Sandra ready for bed. It was not Alf's nature to hold on to an argument or disagreement, so he greeted Mattie with his usual hug and kiss, and the two of them sat down to supper of roe on toast. Rations were still meagre, even though there were signs that this long and devastating war was finally coming to end. People were very hesitant to celebrate prematurely, as they had learned from past experience with Chamberlain how they could easily be duped by the government propaganda.

Thirteen

1945

Sandra was now almost two years old, and Mattie had been having an affair with Eric for the past eight months. It was a torrid affair that transported Mattie away from her everyday existence at Moseley Street. For a few hours each week she was the heroine in a Harlequin Romance, not a wife and mother living in a damp and cramped house on a nondescript street. Eric was nothing more than an escape from reality, and she had no qualms about cheating on Alf, as she justified her affair by rationalizing that it meant nothing to her. Alf was the love of her life. It only became complicated when Eric wanted more than an affair: that was never an option and Mattie ended the relationship as quickly as she had begun it.

Alf never knew of the relationship, or if he suspected it, he never brought up the subject. He had three very handsome cousins, all close to the same age, and frequent visitors to the house. Mattie flirted with all of them, and they in turn flirted back. It did not take long for Mattie to replace Eric with a grenadier guard who used to frequent the dances, and when that affair ended, another cousin filled Mattie's insatiable need for adventure and attention.

In May the war finally ended, and there was jubilation and celebrations all over England. Alf was looking forward to seeing Tom and Bill Cope return from the war. Miraculously they had both survived unscathed, at least physically. They, like many of their comrades, would never recover from the sights they had seen. The constant smell of death and the sound of gunfire and explosions would live with them for ever.

Polly and Evan were ecstatic, as it had been a horrendous year for them both. Darren had been called up for National Service, and he had been stationed near London where the bombs were dropping continuously. Polly had dreaded Darren having to go, as she would never forget the loss of her brother, Alfred, in the First World War.

However, it turned out Darren was thoroughly enjoying his time away from Landrose. He was Lance's son. When he discovered how attractive a uniform made him to the opposite sex, he never missed an opportunity to bed a pretty girl. He never anticipated his actions would have consequences, until one particular girl informed him she was pregnant with his child. He was twenty years old and not ready to marry anyone, and certainly not ready to shoulder the responsibility of a child.

When Polly got the phone call from Darren, she was distraught. Darren insisted that he was not the father and that he knew she had been sleeping with other fellows in his unit. Polly, rightly or wrongly, believed him, and after talking to Evan they both agreed to travel to London and see the young woman. She was a pretty young nurse, and Polly's heart went out to her. It was obvious she was scared and confused, and although she admitted to having been involved in another relationship, she was convinced this baby was Darren's. She did not want to get married either, but she did intend to keep the baby and needed some financial support. There was no hesitation from either Polly or Evan; chance what it took, they would do what they could to provide some financial help. The heartbreaking part of it all was that Polly would have dearly loved to raise the child, and Evan had no objections to that either. "It's not my child! I want no part of it," Darren insisted. "She's just trying to blackmail me for money. You do what you want, but I never want to see her or the baby."

Darren was heartless, and Polly looked at her son with great sadness. He was quite happy to see his mother and Evan bail him out of a bad situation, and had little or no remorse for his part in the whole affair. An arrangement was made and agreed upon; Polly and Evan would pay a lump sum upon the birth of the child, and Darren would sign away all rights of relationship and have no further contact with either mother or child. Polly admired the young woman's strength and determination that she would raise the child alone.

Polly cried almost the whole way back to Landrose, and Evan knew there was no way even he could comfort her. He remembered what they had both gone through years past in order for her to regain custody of her children. To see her son so easily deny responsibility and be so detached from what, in most likelihood, was his own flesh and blood, was sheer anguish. Darren stayed in London with little contact with home until his period of National Service was finished, and when he did return home he never mentioned the incident again.

Belle was now eighteen, and to say she was beautiful would be an understatement. Her strawberry blonde hair curled naturally around her face and shoulders. The bluest of eyes twinkled from a face that almost always had a glow of contentment. She had been dating Ken for a couple of years and their platonic relationship was an easy, comfortable one. Ken was the same age as Belle, and they enjoyed the same books and movies. Belle was not the same disposition as her sister Mattie, and she loved life at Landrose. Polly and Evan both thought that eventually Belle and Ken would get married as they were so well suited.

"Well Evan, I think that we should throw a party to celebrate the end of this horrible war. We can invite some of Alf's friends who have been fighting for us, and some of the neighbours." Polly was already preparing the feast in her mind. She loved to cook, and what an occasion this was. To heck with rations; they had enough food for themselves and to barter for things they did not have.

"Belle, love, will you take a couple dozen eggs in to work today, and pick up a bag of flour from Jenny Burton?" Polly knew Belle would have no problem helping with the black-market trade that was so prevalent throughout the country. It was the way the world worked when neighbours helped neighbours.

That morning Belle was a little late for the bus, but the conductor, seeing her running towards the bus stop, patiently waited for her to arrive. He, like many others, was smitten with her natural and unassuming beauty.

"Come on, Belle. I can't hold this bus up for ever," he laughed.

"Sorry, Chuck. I should have worn my running shoes!" Belle smiled as she glanced at her little Louis heel pumps. She was wearing a cornflower blue dress with little navy pumps; the war was over and she felt jubilant and happy. Carefully stashing the eggs in the overhead rack, she sat down next to Mrs. Wragg from a neighbouring farm. The bus took off a little faster than usual, as it was already a few minutes behind schedule. Then it happened.

The bus went around a bend in the road and the eggs went splat into the aisle. Eggs and shells everywhere. Chuck knew very well who they belonged to, but he would have suffered hot coals and still not give Belle away. Mrs. Wragg merely gave Belle a knowing look, but also had no intentions of exposing the culprit. Belle was mortified as she knew her mom needed the flour for her baking, but at the same time she had to see the funny side of the situation. Thank heavens everyone was in a good mood that day, and nothing more was said. The mess was cleaned up before the next stop, and Chuck light-heartedly made some joke about liking his eggs scrambled anyway. Jenny came through and sent the flour back with Belle on the under-standing the eggs would be delivered the next day.

When Belle got home and told Polly the story, she was a little dismayed at the loss of a couple dozen eggs, but picturing the epi-sode, she too had to laugh.

Polly baked for a week before the party and Evan knew she was in her element catering to her family and friends. It was the end of a horrible year, and at last Polly was optimistic about the future. Alf and Mattie were the first to arrive, with Sandra running on ahead of them. She had started to walk at ten months old and now seldom went anywhere at anything slower than a full trot!

"Come here, my duck, and give your mama a big kiss." Polly in-stinctively held out her arms. Sandra needed no encouragement as she loved her grandma Polly more than anyone in the world. Polly had become "Mama" as soon as Sandra could talk, and it was one of the first words she uttered. Mama meant love and comfort and a soft chest to cuddle up to. She smelled of lavender and soap, and when she held Sandra in her arms it was heaven for the little girl. Polly unconsciously hummed a contented tune when she had Sandra in her arms, and it would be a memory that would remain with Sandra all her life. Mama was a constant in a very unstable family environment at Moseley Street. Even at the age of two, Sandra was aware of the indifference of her mother and the lack of any show of affection.

"Come here and I'll take you to pick some flowers for the table," Evan said as he gently held out his arms for his granddaughter. He came a very close second to Mama and was named Gramps. Polly handed over Sandra as she went to hug Mattie and Alf. She noticed that Mattie was a bit quiet, and Alf was not his usual jovial self. Polly was not blind and could see they had probably been arguing before they arrived. She worried about the way Mattie and Alf lived their lives. Polly now knew that Sandra was often left alone in her bed at night while they both followed their singular pursuits. Much as Alf was easy going, and Polly knew he was a kind and generous man, he was also very much master of his own home. Polly would never dare to interfere with either Mattie or Alf. She knew that would be the end of her relationship with both of them, and even more devastating, her precious time with Sandra.

Soon the house was full of people, and the atmosphere became more light and jovial. Bill and Tom told some of the few funny stories they had about the war, and everyone concentrated on the positive. Tom had heard that his other friend, Alf Ball, had finally been released from the Ban Pong POW camp in Thailand, and was now in a convalescent home back in England. He had heard about the atrocities, and knew Alf had been lucky to survive such a long time as a prisoner of war. When he had a chance to talk to Alf, they planned a trip to see Alf Ball the following week. It was not that easy, however, as when they arrived, after a long bus ride and quite a walk, they were informed he was not allowed visitors for another month. Dejected, they returned home resigned to the fact that they would have to wait.

Alf had indeed suffered immeasurable cruelty and indignity, and had barely survived all the atrocities. He had been starved, beaten, and almost lost his fingers when he was beaten with a rifle butt for trying to steal food. The reason he was denied visitors, even his parents, was that his emaciated body needed to recover almost as much as his mental state did. The doctors had to break his leg and reset it, as it had been hit with a crushing blow from a Japanese soldier. When he had left for war he weighed over 200 pounds. Now he weighed 98 pounds. At six feet two, he looked like a walking skeleton. His face was gaunt and yellow, and his dark circled eyes were sunk in his head. His eyes showed little expression and focused on nothing in particular, as if a light had been extinguished behind them.

The nurses at the convalescent home were marvellous and dedicated to helping all of these brave young men recover. It was a hard job, as they saw all kinds of heartbreak. Young men who came back to lost loves; young men who came back broken beyond repair; and then the ones who came back hard and calloused by their experiences. Alf was one of the latter. He had survived by his sheer grit and determination. He had never succumbed to subservience, and had suffered for it. He had spent more time in the "no good house" than most, and it was amazing his many rebellious and defiant acts had not resulted in his execution. A ten day stint in the "no good house," a cage the size of a small coffee table, almost killed him. He was fed only bananas and had to eat them skin and all to survive. He went temporarily blind and suffered a severe bout of dysentery. If it had not been for his comrades covering for him during his inability to work, he would surely have been shot. Once you were unable to work as a slave, you were of no further use to the Japanese.

He had witnessed many of his comrades shot before his eyes when they stumbled and fell, exhausted, on the trek from railroad camp to camp, often covering twenty miles per day. One day, close to falling himself, he had leaned for a moment on the handle of his pick, and had sustained the crushing blow to his leg. Throughout the rest of the day he had to work in intense pain, but dared not show any sign of weakness.

He stole food whenever he could, and he exercised at every chance. He needed to stay as healthy as possible in the filthy conditions. Monsoon season was the worst. His recurring nightmares were often of the time when monsoon rains destroyed the tent where he and twenty-four other prisoners were kept. Three of the twenty-five survived the night; the rest succumbed to cholera or just lost the will to fight the pain anymore. The following day, the bodies were piled with lumber and set ablaze. Flames of brilliant colours shot into the air, and the stench was unbearable. These were his comrades, and he could easily have been one of them.

Hard work was going to be his key to survival. He was useful to the Japanese, and therefore his chances of escaping a bullet or a bayonet were greatly increased. Until he was captured, he was full of life and bravado, always a bit of a daredevil, but full of fun. When he came back from the war he was harder and more cynical, but if anything an even greater daredevil. He was afraid of nothing. If he could endure the horrors of concentration camp, he was invincible.

Strangely enough, this hardened convalescent was taught how to do embroidery while he was recuperating, and it was a wonderful way to turn his mind away from the recent past. It helped that the occupational therapist was a busty young blonde, who leaned closely towards him to teach him the intricate stitching.

When Tom and Alf were finally allowed to see him, Alf had regained a little of his former weight, but was still a mere shadow of the man who had gone to war. It helped to break the ice and disguise their shock at his appearance, when they saw him holding a piece of embroidery.

"What the bloody hell? Did those Japs turn you into a Nelly while you were there?" Tom joked as he went over to hug his friend and comrade. As he felt Alf's frail body under the nightshirt, he tried hard not to step back in shock.

Alf had been working diligently on an antimacassar for the back of his mother's couch. It was a work of art: the coat of arms of his regiment in great detail and color. The time spent had actually worked wonders, helping to take Alf's mind off things that were too painful to remember. It worked during the daytime, but the nightmares came back almost every night.

"You'd be doing embroidery, too, if you saw the lass who is teaching me. She's got lovely bits and pieces that she rubs against me when she has to show me a new stitch!" Alf gave a feeble wink to Tom.

The visit had been a good one, even though Tom and Alf were both saddened by the vast change in Alf Ball's appearance.

"As soon as you get sprung from here, Alf, we will go and do some real celebrating," they reassured him as they waved farewell. Once outside of the convalescent home, Tom let the shock of Alf's appearance sink in.

"Bloody hell, Alf, I wouldn't have known him if not for his voice. He's just a skeleton. He weighed close to 200 pounds when he left. I'll be damned if he weighs more than 100 pounds now." Tom had been in the army and had suffered many hardships, but nothing compared with being a Japanese POW.

It was six months before Alf was allowed to go home. Convalescence had changed his outer appearance, but had done little for his mental anguish. The nightmares persisted, taking him back to the tent during the big monsoon, and there were few nights he did not wake up in a cold sweat.

Fourteen

BELLE

Polly was doing what she loved to do: preparing a feast for company. Alf had asked if he could bring Tom and Alf Ball out to spend a day at Landrose. Alf had been released from the convalescent home for a couple of months already, and although he was almost back to his pre-war weight, he was still looking a bit pale and gaunt.

"A day out in the country, and some of Polly's cooking, will soon put some colour back in his face," Alf told Tom.

It did not take a lot of convincing, as Alf Ball had felt himself a bit out of touch with everyone after coming home. Somehow, all the mindless chatter about things that don't mean much of anything, was irritating to him. He did not have anything in common with many of the old friends he had left behind. Tom was different, as he understood much of what Alf had been through. The two Alfs had become friends over the last few months of visits, and hearing about Mattie and her family, he already felt like he knew them.

Belle and Ken were helping Polly set the table, and Mattie was sitting outside in the sunshine on the lawn with Sandra when the trio arrived.

"Belle, get the door, love," Polly called, and Belle, placing the last napkin on the table, dutifully complied.

"Come on in, Alf," Belle called, as she ran to the door to hug her brother-in-law. Alf gave Belle his usual bear hug, and she turned her attention to Tom. "Hi Tom, good to see you." Tom gave her a big hug and a peck on the cheek. Alf Ball had been standing back watching the interactions, for a moment losing his usual composure.

My god, man, you still do have feelings, he said to himself, as for the first time in years he knew what it was to feel alive. Every part of his body was very alive, and he could not take his eyes off the vision in front of him.

"Well, don't I rate an introduction?" he said to Tom.

123

"Sorry mate. This is Belle, Mattie's sister."

Belle looked up and noticed Alf for the first time. He was tall, dark, and very handsome. Alf had slicked back jet black hair and a dashing moustache, and his overall appearance was one of bravado and devil may care. At eight years her senior, he was so much more a man of the world than Ken, who was the same age as Belle. The difference in the two was too great to measure.

Without a second's thought, Alf followed the lead of Tom and gave Belle a hug, but it was not a peck on the cheek. He pulled her towards him and kissed her cheek with such intensity that her knees went weak.

Belle was unfamiliar with what was happening to her body. Her heart was racing, and she felt as if scalding hot water was running through her veins. This was something she had never felt before, and it was confusing. Trying to hide her discomfort, she quickly pulled away from Alf and showed them all into the house. Belle did the introductions as Polly happily started to put the finishing touches to a great dinner.

Alf was not pleased to see there was a boyfriend in the picture, but it was of no consequence, because he had made up his mind there and then that Belle was going to be his.

Ken sensed the electricity between Belle and Alf throughout the evening, and when he left that night he was far from happy. Belle walked with him to the bus stop, and their kiss goodnight was, as always, something that made his heart skip a beat. He knew that Belle cared for him a whole lot, but he was never sure she really loved him the way he worshipped her. Belle was eighteen and Ken had been her only boyfriend. Until today, she had thought that her feelings for Ken were enough to base a relationship on; now she had just glimpsed a different type of love.

Walking back down the lane, Belle knew her life was about to change. She was going to have to tell Ken, and she knew it would break his heart.

Why can't I be more like Mattie? she questioned herself. *She would have no problem breaking a heart or two.* Belle hated the way Mattie cheated on Alf, especially as he was such a great husband. That night Belle tossed and turned fitfully, dreading the prospect of telling Ken their relationship was over. "The quicker I do it the better," she rationalized, as she knew for sure that she could never settle for a love without passion now. It would be terribly unfair to string Ken along with the hopes of something she knew could never be.

Polly and Evan were not blind, and had seen the sparks flying over dinner, as Alf was very brazen with his open flirtation. It certainly was not love at first sight for either Polly or Evan. Unlike Alf Wetton, whom they had taken to instantly, this other Alf was a different character altogether. After everyone else had gone to bed, Polly and Evan sat on the couch watching the last of the coals die down in the fireplace.

"He was a bit forward with our Belle, and he's far too sure of himself for his own good," Polly said as she gave Evan a worried look.

"I can't say that I am impressed with him either, love, but the lad's been through a lot in the POW camp, and we have to give him a chance to adjust to life back over here." Evan was always ready to give someone the benefit of doubt and slow to prejudge.

Polly looked at Evan, and tears came to her eyes as she thought of how their own love had come to be. Evan was night and day different to Alf, but she knew, from the first moment they met, it was destiny.

"Come on, love; tomorrow's another day, and things usually have a way of sorting themselves out." Evan wrapped his arm around Polly, and together they climbed the stairs to bed.

Alf and Mattie got back home to Moseley Street, and Sandra had already fallen asleep on the bus home. She was so tired she did not even wake up when they undressed her and put her to bed.

"I think Alf was pretty taken with your Belle," Alf smiled to Mattie.

Mattie thought about the evening and had certainly noticed what was happening.

"Well, he is pretty easy on the eye. Altogether different to Ken: I never could see that working out anyway. Ken's a nice lad, but he is no match for a dashing war hero."

Fifteen

BELLE AND ALF

To no one's surprise, Belle told a devastated Ken that although she would always care for him, she had fallen in love with Alf. Belle was not proud of letting Ken down, as she knew that his love for her was far deeper. She had agonised for almost two weeks before telling him. Lying awake in bed, her thoughts were all over the place, but the reality of it was always the same. There were different kinds of love and passion, and her body told her that even though Alf may not be the one for her, she could never settle for anything less.

Alf pursued Belle with ardour. Over the next few months, Alf became a regular visitor at Landrose, always carrying flowers or gifts. He was far too cocky for Polly's liking, and she thought he was a bad influence on Belle. It had not taken him long to find a job after the war was over. In his usual self-assured manner, he applied for and got a job as assistant manager of The Maypole Grocery Store. It was a good, well-paying job with great hours, which gave him lots of free time to spend with Belle. The store was in Matlock, and each year there was a beauty pageant sponsored by the local merchants. Unknown to Belle, Alf had submitted her photograph to his boss, and entered her into the contest. He would figure out how to tell her when and if she was short listed, but he already knew she would be. Belle was a natural beauty and her personality shone through.

Alf was a daredevil and loved the thrill of pushing the limits of anything. He had bought an old car, and tinkered with it until he had it as high performance as possible, but it was still not enough. One day he saw an ad for a Norton Motorbike, and could not wait to go and see it. That night after work he went straight to Alfreton to see the bike. It was perfect. Alf soon sized up the situation and the reason for the young man selling his motorbike. Standing in the doorway was a very pregnant young woman with a very determined look on her face. It was obvious the poor chap had no choice other than to sell the bike.

Alf started up the bike, and listened to the engine purr. It needed a good clean, but other than that it was in great condition.

"It needs a bit of work done on it," he lied. "It'll cost a few bob to fix this up."

The two haggled over price for a while, but Alf knew that he could wrangle a deal, and he did. The cash payment was a big incentive, and before the night was out, the bike was his. He could not wait to get it all polished up and go to Landrose to show Belle.

Alf polished the bike until it gleamed, and as he had thought, the engine was top notch. Friday morning he rode the bike to work, as he planned to go to Landrose after he had finished.

Alf was good at his job, and the customers seemed to like his cheeky banter. He was never at a loss for words and got away with a lot because of his Rhett Butler looks. He flirted outrageously with all of the old ladies and could sell coal to Newcastle, as the saying went. He was just stamping a slab of butter with the Maypole imprint, when his boss called him into the office.

"Alf, come in here, please. I have something to tell you."

Alf thought of what he might have done that could get him in trouble, and truth be known, there was quite a lot. He also knew he was good at what he did, and he doubted very much that the reason for his being summoned to the office could be serious.

"That young lass of yours is quite a corker. She was hands down the choice of everyone on the board. Tell her that we will sponsor her as the Maypole Candidate, and we will pay for a swimsuit and a dress for her. She will still need to meet the board, and then there is an elimination process before the three finalists are chosen at Matlock Hall Leys."

Alf did not tell his boss that as yet, Belle had no idea she had been entered into a contest.

"Yes, she's a corker all right, and I'm sure she'll be right chuffed to know."

Alf was nowhere near as sure as he sounded. Belle had no vanity and had never realized how stunning she was. It was not her nature to show off or be the center of attraction. She was not a bit like Mattie, who was very aware of her own charms.

After Alf had served the last customer, he eagerly went out to the back of the shop to collect his new motorbike. After being caged like an animal as a POW, the feeling of the wind in his hair and the free-

dom of the open moorland was euphoric. By the time he got to Landrose, he was confident he could convince Belle to represent The
Maypole. He was invincible.

"What on earth is that racket?" Polly looked at Evan, as she went
to the window. "Well, what next? It's Alf and he's riding some sort
of motorbike. He came into the yard at ninety miles an hour. Where's
our Tony? Does Alf ever think there might be a dog out there, or
worse yet, our Sandra could be in the yard."

"Tony's in the kitchen, Polly, and you know our Sandra won't be
here until tomorrow." Evan was just as unimpressed with Alf as
Polly was, but for Belle's sake, he kept his thoughts to himself.

Alf carefully parked his bike, and went in with his usual devil may
care bravado.

"Come on, Belle. I'll take you for a spin."

Belle looked at the motorbike and it really did look very exciting
and shiny.

"Don't you even think of it. It looks like a dangerous contraption
to me, and he's only just got it," Polly said as she gave Belle a very
stern look. "Alf Ball, you learn how to ride that thing at a sensible
speed, and when you do, then maybe you can take my daughter on it.
Not until!" Polly was adamant, and where her family were concerned, she was still the matriarch. Belle knew there was no arguing,
and even though she would have loved to go for a ride, she deferred
to Polly's reasoning.

"Well, at least come and have a look at it, Belle," Alf grumbled.
He thought Polly had far too much to say about Belle's life. Belle was
almost nineteen, and as far as he was concerned she was woman
enough to make her own decisions. He and Belle went outside, and
after proudly showing off his prize possession, Alf broke the news of
the upcoming competition. Belle was stunned.

"Alf, how could you? I'm not going to parade around in a swimsuit on Matlock Hall Leys for everyone to see."

"You're beautiful, Belle, and I know you can win. There is a prize
for the winner, and the Maypole will buy everything you need for the
competition." In his usual way, he won the argument and Belle
reluctantly agreed. The next hurdle was to tell Polly and Evan.

"Let me tell them, Alf, in my own time and my own way. I know
my mam's not going to be very happy about it, but if I let her help me
with the swimsuit and dress, she might be more agreeable." Belle

knew she could convince her mom to approve as long as she knew everything would be in good taste.

"Just don't let her cover up all your charms," Alf grinned, as he thought that no matter how Belle dressed, she would still be the "Belle of the Ball."

Belle did convince Polly as she knew she would, but she was still far from comfortable with the whole idea herself.

When the house was quiet and Polly and Evan lay in bed, it was their time to share the day's experiences. Polly loved the fact they shared everything, and never had any secrets from each other. She knew instinctively that Evan would be able to understand her concerns and be able to calm her fears.

"Now Polly, lass, what are you fretting over? Belle's a smart young lass and she's asked you to help her choose the outfits she's going to wear. What more can you ask for? With your help, she'll look like a princess, and there's no shame in that. I think she's probably more worried about this than you are. We just have to give her our support and make sure she wins this pageant thing." Evan put his arms around Polly "She is your daughter, love, and she can't help being beautiful, just like her mother."

As Polly reached to put out the light, she kissed Evan lovingly. "I only want for all my children to know this kind of love. Is that so wrong of me? I just can't take to Alf Ball. He's too old and worldly for our Belle. First he rides in the yard on that blasted bike like some damned daredevil, and then he convinces our Belle to parade around Matlock in a swimsuit."

"Don't worry, love. I know she'll make you proud, and she would never let you down." Evan pulled Polly towards him and held her in his arms until he felt her relax against him.

Polly smiled to herself as she thanked her lucky stars that this was Belle and not Mattie. Mattie would have no qualms walking down Main Street in one of those new swimsuits that came in two pieces, neither big enough to cover a postage stamp! She knew Belle would be far more conservative.

The following week, Polly and Belle went shopping and both came home happy with their purchases. Belle had chosen a modest but gorgeous swimsuit in aqua blue. It fit perfectly, and the front was draped to one side across her right breast and left hip. The back was cut just low enough to show her beautiful shoulder blades. The colour accentuated her amazing hair and flawless complexion. There was nothing risqué about it.

The dress had been a more difficult choice, but eventually they had both agreed on staying with a shade of blue. Just as green was Mattie's signature, blue was Belle's. Polly would have liked Belle to choose a long gown, but Belle was adamant that if she was getting a free dress, then she would be able to wear it again later. The final choice was powder blue and had a boat neckline edged with white daisies. The dress was fitted to the waist and had a full circular skirt, held out by a net petticoat. Polly had to admit it was the right choice, as it showed off her tiny waist and shapely legs. She looked young and naturally beautiful. Belle refused to show Alf her choices, and made him wait until the day of the pageant.

Mattie and Alf went to the pageant, as did Darren and his girl-friend, Winnie. Liv and Fred and some of the girls from Rowell's also attended, and altogether there was a big cheering section for Belle. She was by far the most captivating entry, and easily won the judges' votes.

Alf could not keep his eyes off Belle. He still had nightmares about his time in the prison camp, but he would never share those with anyone. Today he was in a different world and watching his sweetheart being crowned The Queen of the May. Life was good and he meant to live it to the full. No point in waiting—he would ask Polly and Evan's permission to marry Belle. That was the proper thing to do, but even if they said no, he knew that one way or another she would be his.

There was a lot of celebrating after the crowning, and although Mattie was pleased to see her sister win, she was feeling very miserable with life in general. The affair with Eric had run its course. The grenadier guard had returned to his home town, and she was in between lovers. Once the excitement of clandestine trysts became routine, it was time to move on. Her life was far different than what she had ever imagined. A small child was a constant reminder that she was a wife and mother, and although she was still extremely attractive, she was a housewife. She hated the word "housewife," but felt it described her predicament. She did feel as if she was married to the house, and she longed to be the center of attention again. Seeing Belle surrounded by admirers was just salt in her wounds. Mattie had always envied Belle's natural beauty. She knew her own exotic looks were admired, but there was always an underlying feeling she could never outshine Belle.

Polly and Evan left the young celebrants and went back to Landrose with Sandra, who was going to stay with them for a few days. Landrose was a second home to Sandra, as she spent almost as much time with her grandparents as she did with her mom and dad. Polly and Evan were always delighted to have her, and she was always happy to be with them.

"Well, Polly love, Belle did us proud, didn't she?" Evan smiled as he grasped Sandra's hand. "Come on, scamp. Let's go and see if Tony missed us." Sandra was like a limpet stuck to Tony when she was at her grandparents. She would hook her fingers in his collar and tag along wherever he went. He was the best natured dog and seemed to understand he was her best friend. It didn't take any more convincing to have Sandra skip ahead and jump into the car to head back to Wellington. Even at three years old, Sandra knew where she was happiest. The smell of the grass along the lane, the warm comfortable feeling of going through the door into a house that smelled of baking, and the thought of hot chocolate before bed were all wonderful. Moseley Street smelled of cigarette smoke and was cold and damp. There were no bedtime stories or hot chocolate, and more often than not, no parents to calm her fears when she awoke alone in her bed at night.

Sixteen

1947

Polly knew that she could not stand in the way of Belle's engage-ment, as Belle was madly in love with Alf. She had many misgivings about the pending marriage, but for the sake of Belle, she tried her best to be positive and be happy for her daughter. Alf was more often at Landrose than not, and most always roaring into the yard on his Norton, scarf flying in the wind and not a care in the world. There was no denying that he did cut a dashing figure, and it was easy to see why Belle was charmed by him.

It had taken a long while for Polly to relent and let Alf take Belle out on the motorbike, always with the caution that he ride slowly and be careful. Saturday night they had decided to go to the picture house in Alfreton, and as they left Landrose a few clouds were starting to form.

"I hope he rides sensibly with that girl on the back," Polly said as she watched them pull out of the yard, "It looks like we might get some rain."

It was a short ride to Alfreton, and when they went into the pic-ture house it was still not raining. After the show was over they came out to a downpour.

"Come on Belle, let's pop into The Flying Horse and have a drink until this blasted rain slows down."

"I don't know, Alf; you know what my mam says about drinking when you are riding the bike," Belle said half-heartedly, as she didn't relish the thought of riding home in this deluge.

"Just one pint, love, and then we'll be off. It should have slowed down by then."

True to his word, he did have just one pint, and Belle had a shandy, made with half lemonade and half beer.

They sat and watched the rain abate before going back outside to face the damp ride back to Landrose.

Alf took off his leather jacket and insisted Belle wear it as she was wearing just a cotton jacket that was already wet. He wrapped his scarf around his neck, and giving Belle a kiss, he revved up the bike to set off back to Landrose.

It was pitch dark, no moon or stars to be seen through the thick clouds, and the road was wet and slick with puddles of water in the numerous pot holes. Belle clutched on to Alf tightly and buried her head against his back to shield from the wet and cold. Thank heavens there was very little traffic that night and they had the road to themselves. The road was narrow and full of bends and curves which were not easy to negotiate in bad weather. Suddenly, almost out of nowhere, they heard the sound of tires screeching behind them. Instinctively, Alf swerved towards the ditch, as he knew the approaching vehicle must have taken the corner too fast and lost control. It would have been impossible to see the motorbike until it was too late for them to stop. The bike's tires skidded on the gravel and both Alf and Belle were thrown into the ditch. The car came to a halt just inches away from them.

"Bloody hell, I didn't see you, mate," a lanky young kid stammered as he got out of the vehicle. When he looked at Alf and Belle he began to shake like a leaf. They were both bleeding profusely, and Belle was crying out in pain. There were another couple of equally young lads scrambling out of the back seat with the same frightened look on their faces.

"Help me get her in the car; don't just stand there, you maniac!" Alf was cut down his face really badly, and his nose was almost split in half. He wiped the blood from his eyes and went over to Belle. She had slid along the gravel and her leg had been split open from her thigh to her calf. The blood was spurting out like a geyser. He knew that if he could not stop the bleeding she would die. He took off his scarf and wrapped it as tightly as he could around her leg. The young driver was still standing in shock watching the gruesome scene in front of him. "Are you deaf and dumb? Move!" Alf screamed at him.

"It's going to be okay, Belle," Alf tried to reassure her, but he was far from sure that it would be okay. "We're close to her mam's place. I'll drive." The young lad was too scared to argue.

Back at Landrose, Polly was pacing the floor. "I know there's something wrong, Evan. Our Belle would have phoned me if she knew she was going to be late."

"They're probably just waiting for the rain to stop, Polly. Don't get yourself in a state." But the words were hardly out of his mouth when they heard a car pull into the yard.

Polly and Evan both ran to the door at the same time, and saw Alf carrying Belle out of the car, blood streaming down his face. Belle's leg was wrapped in Alf's blood soaked scarf, and dangling at an odd angle.

"Oh my god." One look told Polly that Belle had to go to hospital immediately.

"Why in heavens name did you bring her here, Alf? She needs to go to hospital and see a doctor quickly. You and that damned bike. I just knew this would happen. Oh Belle, my love, what has he done?"

Belle tried her best to be brave and not cause Polly to panic any more than she was already.

"It's okay, mom. I'll be fine. It really wasn't Alf's fault, mam." Belle bit her lip almost through, trying to control the pain.

Evan, always the calming voice, had already taken charge of the situation. He started his car, and instructed Alf to place her as gently and flat as possible in the back seat.

"You young fellows get to the hospital as fast as you can and tell them to have a doctor standing by. You get in the back with her, Alf, and hold that scarf as tight as you can until we get to the hospital. Polly, get in the front with me, and don't waste your breath on Alf. It's our Belle we have to look after first. There'll be plenty of time for questions when Belle has been looked after."

Evan drove faster than he had ever driven, and for once Polly did not complain about his speed. When they got to the hospital there were two nurses waiting with a stretcher, and Belle was wheeled straight into the surgery. Polly and Evan were told to sit in the waiting room.

"They'll take good care of her, Polly. All we can do now is wait, and be here when she comes back out. She'll not want to see you crying, my love," Evan handed Polly his clean white handkerchief.

Polly was inconsolable and there was nothing anyone could say that gave her any comfort. All she could repeat was "That blasted bike. That blasted bike. Don't you ever bring that blasted bike into our yard again. I knew that it was trouble from day one." Tears were streaming down Polly's face in fear and anger.

Alf was sitting slumped in a chair with his hands holding a towel to his face. He could not look at Polly, and he was still bleeding badly. "Now Polly, before you start in on me, it wasn't my fault. The car came out of nowhere and ran us into the ditch. There was nothing I could do."

Another doctor came into the waiting room to take a look at Alf, whose injuries to this point in time no one had taken much notice of. "Come on, Mr. Ball, let's have a look at you now." The doctor gently removed the sodden towel and revealed the extent of Alf's facial lacerations.

Polly almost fainted and had to hold on to Evan for support. His face looked like raw meat, and Polly was not sure if his nose was completely severed or not. How he had driven back to Landrose she had no idea. He had not shown any sign of being in pain, but she knew he must be hurting badly. There was still little sympathy in her heart for Alf as she could not bring herself to absolve him of the blame.

"What about my daughter, doctor? When can I see her?" Polly felt sorry for Alf's injuries, but she was still not ready to believe that speed had not played a part in the accident. Belle had no control over her fate when she was on the back of his bike. In Polly's mind he was to blame for even taking her on it.

"She is still in surgery, Mrs. Lambert, but she has a good surgeon and we will take good care of her. Please try to be patient, and we will call you the minute she comes out."

The doctor ushered Alf into the next room where they did their best to clean out the embedded gravel and stitch up what was left of his nose. "This is going to hurt, Mr. Ball, but we have to make sure that there is no risk of infection," the doctor said as he poured a stream of antiseptic on Alf's wounds. Alf did not flinch. This was nothing compared to what he had suffered at the hands of the Japanese. He just wanted to see Belle and know she was going to be okay. It had been dark on the road, and he could not see the extent of her injuries. He knew her leg was really badly cut, but he did not know where else she might be injured. He took all of Polly's angry comments without retaliation, as he silently questioned himself. Was he driving too fast for the road conditions? Could he have avoided the accident? He should have gone straight to the hospital instead of Landrose. He knew he had made a grave error, and was angry with himself for panicking. Cool, calm Alf Ball had lost his ability to think clearly in the face of an emergency, and this was totally out of character for him. He loved Belle so much, and all he could think of was what had happened to her beautiful leg. It was only a few days before when she had worn a swimsuit and stunned everyone with her beauty. He knew beyond any doubt that her leg would be terribly scarred. It did not bother him about the scar as long as she was going to be all right, but he knew she would carry a reminder of that horrific accident for the rest of her life.

It seemed like hours before finally the surgeon emerged from the operating room.

"We've done the best we can, Mrs. Lambert, but this is going to be a long recovery. Belle has a broken leg and a very deep gash in her right leg. The gravel rash will clear up in a few days, but the leg will take a long while to heal. The scar will get better; however it will never go away. We can be grateful for the fact she was wearing a leather jacket, which protected her body, and miraculously she didn't injure her face like the young man did. We will bring her into recovery soon and you can go in and see her. She is still sleeping as the anesthetic will take some time to wear off. I want her to rest as much as possible, so please sit with her for as long as you want, but don't talk or try to wake her."

Polly and Evan sat through the night with Belle, each one afraid to close their eyes. Belle murmured in pain several times throughout the night, and the nurse came in and administered more medication. Alf was in a bed in the next room, and after they had finished stitching up his face, they found that although he did not have any broken bones, his body was bruised and cut badly. He had given his leather jacket to Belle, and his thin shirt had been no protection against the road. Alf insisted on being allowed to see Belle, and when he hobbled into the room he felt the coldness of the atmosphere. Polly could not even look at him. They had no idea how much he wished he could take back the night's events. He loved Belle so much and would never hurt her. Alf looked at her pale face and her beautiful golden hair all matted and wet with perspiration. Choking back unfamiliar tears, he gently touched her face and left the room.

The doctor had been right. Belle took months to heal, and was on crutches for almost a year. Alf's recovery was much quicker, and before long he had his motorbike fixed and was back riding to Landrose. The first time he rode into the yard, Polly was furious, but Alf continued to ride to see Belle. For Belle's sake, Polly kept her anger under control, and only Evan knew how much she hurt each time she saw the bike come down the driveway.

The wedding had to be delayed until Belle could walk down the aisle without crutches and Alf's face was healed. He was left with a nasty scar down his nose, but strangely it did not detract from his good looks. Both Belle and Alf had been fortunate that the young country doctors were good at their craft, and had done a great job at stitching them both up after the accident. Alf's scar was just left of his nose bridge and ran in a neat line from top to tip.

Belle's scar faded over time, as the doctors had promised, but there was a thick raised white scar which was impossible to disguise, running down the length of her right leg. Belle never did blame Alf for the accident. She loved him as much as he loved her, and the excitement of the wedding plans helped to ease the slow process of recovery.

Sandra had been spending a lot of time at Landrose, and Belle enjoyed spending time with her chatterbox niece. Sandra had been born tongue tied, and the family joke was always that the doctor had "untied" it a little too much! The prospect of being a flower girl and wearing a long white dress was cause for a lot of chatter. "Will I carry flowers? What sort? What colour? Am I the only flower girl? The questions never stopped, and Belle laughingly answered all of them.

Seventeen

WINDY RIDGE MATLOCK

Belle's wedding day was perfect. There was a lot to celebrate. Most of all, Belle was walking without crutches again, and today she was almost floating she was so happy. Polly had slowly accepted the fact that Alf was going to be her son in law, and she knew how much he loved Belle. Sandra was pirouetting all around the kitchen, eager for the cars to leave for the church. Mattie had put her hair in rags the night before and today she had a mass of shining nut brown ringlets which were tossing around as she twirled.

"Sandra Mary, will you sit still for five minutes! Your hair will be a total mess before you even get to church," Mattie admonished. Sandra knew she had better behave, as when she was called Sandra Mary that always meant trouble.

Mattie was the matron of honour and absolutely hated the dress she was wearing. It was bad enough that Belle was looking amazing, young and full of life and excitement. Mattie felt as if she really was a matron. How could time pass so quickly and life change so much? She was between lovers and that was always a depressing time. Now she was just a wife and a mother, and that was never enough. It would not have mattered what Mattie wore, as she would always look exotic. If only she could understand how unique she was, maybe the endless quest for acceptance and admiration would end.

At last it was time to leave, and Belle gave Sandra a bouquet to carry. It was a pretty little arrangement of anemones and baby's breath in pinks and purples. Sandra was not used to seeing bought flowers, but was very familiar with every flower that grew in the fields of Landrose. Cowslips and water gillivers, daisies and blue bells lined every window sill at Landrose, as she liked nothing better than to pick flowers for Polly.

"What are these?" she asked.

"They are anemones, my duck," Polly responded.

"I've never seen enemies before," Sandra chirped as she climbed into the car. "I like them, though." Everyone thought that was hilarious, and as they left for church, even Mattie was smiling.

Darren took Winnie with him. Her petite stature and blonde hair was an exact opposite of Darren's swarthy dark looks and solid frame. Everyone loved Winnie. What was there not to love? She was barely five feet, and very slim with tiny feet and hands. Polly thought back to Star, her mother, who had died so long ago. Star had the same tiny hands and feet, and was a lady in her bearing and manner. Polly took Evan's arm, and as they watched Darren and Winnie, Polly smiled happily.

"She's a lovely lass, Evan. I do hope that Darren realizes what a treasure she is. Since dating Winnie, he's been a different lad."

"She is a little treasure, Polly, and I am sure he knows that. Maybe we'll be planning another wedding before long." Evan silently hoped that Darren would be good to Winnie. He was much like Lance in his ways, and he already had a reputation for being a rake.

When Polly and Evan arrived at the church, almost everyone was seated. Belle and her attendants were coming in the next two cars. Evan showed Polly to a seat, and then went back to wait for Belle. He was beside himself with happiness, as today he would have the honour of walking Polly's daughter down the aisle. Mattie had insisted on Polly walking her down the aisle, as she could never accept the fact that Evan was her father. Evan thought of all of the children as his own, and he loved them equally, but it had brought a tear to his eye when Belle asked him to escort her to the altar.

Alf was standing at the altar with his brother, as best man, by his side. Even from the back, he was quite the sight. Polly thought she had never seen him look anything but immaculate. Even when he rode that damned motor bike he was dressed in a leather bomber jacket and good trousers. His motorcycle boots were shone until they gleamed. Now he was wearing a black tuxedo and his white collar was peeping out below his jet black hair.

The wedding march began to play, and Alf turned around to see Belle being escorted down the aisle by Evan. Evan walked tall and proud, and Belle gave his arm a little squeeze as they approached the altar. Alf held out his arm to Belle, and she smiled up at him proudly. The congregation were hushed, as they were witnessing a wedding dreams are made of. Alf and Belle looked so much as if they were meant to be together. He was everything male, and she was as beautiful and feminine as it was possible to be. His jet black hair and moustache was a striking contrast to her strawberry blonde curls, which she had left to fall naturally over her shoulders.

After the ceremony, there was a big celebration at the local hall before Barbara and Alf went to their new home in Matlock. Alf had found a couple of rooms to rent in a very nice house owned by Mrs. Caldwell. It was a beautiful stone built house in its own private gated gardens. Mrs. Caldwell was getting on in years, and Alf had met her when she was a customer at The Maypole. One day when she was complaining about looking after such a big house, he seized the opportunity to suggest that she take in lodgers, who could help with the chores. She travelled to see her children quite frequently, and this would also mean she would have live-in caretakers whilst she was away. Mrs. Caldwell had met Belle, and had known Alf since he started working at the Maypole, so after very little hesitation she agreed to rent to them.

Belle loved the house and the gardens and Mrs. Caldwell. It was a perfect arrangement, as Alf could walk to work and Belle was close enough to a bus stop to go to Rowell's. She could never wait to get home to the house at Windy Ridge.

The next few years passed by in the blink of an eye, with Sandra being a regular visitor to spend time with her Aunt Belle. Whenever Sandra did not go to Landrose for the weekend, she went to Windy Ridge, or to Riddings to spend time with her Grandma Julia.

It did not matter to Sandra where she was, as long as it was not at Moseley Street. Landrose would always be her first choice, as that had the added attraction of open fields and Tony, and the pink bedroom with a fireplace, and a bedtime story always read by Polly. Rupert books lined the bookshelves, and Polly always made sure that there was a new story to read.

Windy Ridge was a different type of weekend, but just as much fun. Belle loved to take Sandra to The Hall Leys where there was a bandstand and music every weekend. There was always a stop in at The Maypole, and that meant candy. Sandra loved the house at Windy Ridge, and Belle had to keep a close eye on her, as she liked nothing better than to wander through all the rooms admiring the artwork and the ornate furniture. "You must stay on this side, my darling. Mrs. Caldwell lives over there, and that side of the house is private." Belle was never harsh with her niece, as she realized Sandra was just very inquisitive. Sandra adored Belle and hated the weekends to end.

Riddings with Julia was another adventure. Julia and Tom were far more old fashioned, and neither of them had the energy required to entertain their granddaughter. The bedroom at Riddings was up a very steep flight of stairs, and at the top of the stairs was a picture of Jesus. As the only light to ascend the stairs was a candle, the flickering light gave the picture an eerie, almost lifelike appearance. Sandra was sure the eyes were following her, and tried to avoid looking at the picture as she went up the stairs. The bedroom was cold and had a linoleum floor, but Sandra knew that although it was not Landrose, neither was it Moseley Street. Tom and Julia would be there throughout the night, and when she awoke with a nightmare, someone would calm her fears. It was enough for Sandra that they loved her, which was obvious by the special meals Julia would cook. The best treat of all was when Julia made homemade taffy. Sandra would watch as Julia threw the taffy around a door knob and pulled it until it changed from dark brown to gold, when she would twist it into the shape of a walking stick. It was delicious. Julia and Tom lived right next door to The Red Rec, and when she stayed with them that was her favourite place to be.

Alf would always drop Sandra off and pick her up at his mother's, and he noticed how much weight his dad was losing.

"Mam, is Dad okay? He has lost a lot of weight. Is he eating all right?"

"No, he isn't. I can't get him to eat enough to keep a fly alive, and he won't go to the doctor's." Julia was just as concerned about Tom as her son was, but he steadfastly refused to see a doctor. Alf made a mental note to try and talk to his dad when the two of them were alone. He guessed that his dad did not want to worry Julia.

Eighteen

SANDRA AT MOSELEY STREET

Sandra had every reason to hate Moseley Street. It was not a happy home. If it was not for Mr. and Mrs. Storer, life in Ripley would have been even worse. Elsie and Joe Storer were a childless couple, resigned to the fact that their love would never produce the child they so wanted. They had a beautiful red setter dog which they doted on and had named Susan. It was because of Susan that Elsie first met Sandra.

At a little more than three years old, Sandra had wandered out the entry of number 44, and as soon as she saw Susan, off she toddled as fast as her little legs could carry her. Elsie looked at the little girl coming her way, and slowed her walk so that Sandra could catch up. "What's his name?" Sandra asked as she bent down to pet the dog.

"It's a lady dog, and her name is Susan," Elsie smiled. "And what is your name?"

"My name is Sandra Mary, but I only get called that when I am bad. When I am good it is just Sandra."

Elsie laughed at this precocious child, who seemed much older than her years.

That fateful day was the start of a wonderful relationship, providing Elsie and Joe with a child to love and care for, and Sandra with two people who loved her unconditionally. Elsie was a little concerned that Sandra had wandered up the street all by herself, and thought that she should take her back home. Taking hold of Sandra's hand, Elsie smiled, "Come on lovey, Susan and I will walk you back home. Your mummy must be wondering where you are."

"Oh that's all right, she does not worry about me. I play by myself all the time. I can even go down to the bottom of the street all by myself," Sandra said, very matter-of-factly.

Elsie was a little surprised to hear that such a small child had such liberty. Although she was not a mother herself, she had a natural motherly instinct. She looked at the little girl holding her hand, and knew that if this was her child she would never let her out of her sight for a moment. Sandra was a cherubic little girl with the greenest eyes Elsie had ever seen on one so young. Her hair was braided into two pigtails and she was dressed in a pretty little dress. There was no outward indication that she was not looked after well, but Elsie detected something sad about her new acquaintance.

Number 44 was a few doors farther down the street, and a much smaller house than the one that Elsie and Joe lived in. The Storers' house had a double sized entry way, and a much larger back garden where Joe raised his prize bantams and budgerigars. Elsie had never particularly noticed number 44 before, but when Sandra stopped in front of the entryway, Elsie thought how unloved it looked. The entry was long and narrow and devoid of any whitewash. It looked black and foreboding. The single small windows on the upper and lower floor looked as if they needed a good clean, and the paint was flaking off the old wooden sills.

"Bye, Sandra. I hope I see you again." Elsie really did hope she would.

"Can I come and take Susan for walks with you?" Sandra asked eagerly.

"Well, if your mommy says it is okay, of course you can. Susan and I would like that."

Sandra gave Susan a big hug and disappeared into the dark entry.

Elsie turned around and went back up the street. She stopped in front of her home and admired what Joe had done to renovate it. The double entry was whitewashed and clean. The old windows had been replaced with wider double pane windows which sparkled in the afternoon sun. The lace curtains framed a big bowl of daffodils that Elsie had arranged and put on a table below the window. Her heart was a little heavy having just had a glimpse of what she was missing by not having such a child as her own. When she walked into the bright living room, she knew how much she had to be thankful for: a husband who loved her and a home she loved.

When Joe came home from his work as a painter and decorator, Elsie was eager to tell him about her visit from Sandra.

"Joe, she's a little imp. You can just tell that she's full of mischief, but somehow she looked sad. She lives at number 44, and the house looks like no one really cares about it."

Joe knew the house and also had heard a few rumours about the occupants. He had not told Elsie, as he knew she would worry about the little girl who lived there. Joe knew the neighbours, and had heard that Sandra was often left alone in her room at night while her parents were out. Joe was an accomplished drummer with a big band which played for some of the dance competitions. He had seen Mattie at some of the competitions and knew she was an excellent ballroom dancer. She was an outrageous flirt, however, and although he never saw her pay particular attention to one person, she was always surrounded by admirers.

"Elsie, you know who her mam is. She is the young lass who does competition dancing. I am sure you must have noticed her at some of the medal events: kind of attractive in her own way." Joe smiled at Elsie who was just as opposite. He looked at his wife who was perfect in his eyes. "Not as beautiful as you, by far."

Elsie knew Joe meant his words. They had a very deep love, and it was not born of any superficial outer beauty, but of a connection of souls. Elsie was not much over five feet, and although not by any means fat, she was round and "cuddly" as Joe called her. They were exact opposites in stature, as Joe was over six feet and slim, with sandy coloured hair. Their only disappointment in life was that they had not been blessed with a child. Neither wanting the other to feel guilt at their inability to produce a child, they chose not to seek medical advice.

For a moment Joe was sad as he thought of how much Elsie would have loved a child, and he knew without a shadow of a doubt she would have been an excellent mother.

That night when Elsie went to bed, lying in the arms of Joe, she could not help but think of Sandra. "She loved our Susan, Joe. Maybe she will come to see her again."

"Maybe it was you she was drawn to, my love. I'm sure she'll be back up the street again."

Joe was right. The next morning Elsie went out to take Susan for a walk, and there was Sandra, sitting on the doorstep.

"What are you doing out at this time in the morning, lovey? Does your mommy know you have come to visit?"

"Yep. I told her that I was going to see Susan. It's all right. I can't speak to strangers, but you're not a stranger. You are Susan's mom." Sandra's speech was almost perfect for one so young, and Elsie smiled as she reached for her hand. The two walked down the street to Borker Fields. It was a short walk past the old row houses to a field that led down to a viaduct, and Susan loved to be let off her leash and run around the field.

There was a little seat against the stone wall surrounding the vicarage that backed onto the field, and there Sandra and Elsie became acquainted. For some reason, Sandra, normally articulate, found Mrs. Storer hard to say. After several attempts, Elsie smiled, "Why don't you just call me Auntie Elsie?" Sandra was delighted.

"I have two aunties, Auntie Belle and Auntie Vera. They don't live in Ripley, though." Sandra thought how wonderful it would be to have an auntie living so close by. "My Auntie Belle lives in Matlock, and Auntie Vera lives in Alfreton. I can only see them if we go on a bus."

"Well, my love, you can see me anytime you want," Elsie said, not realizing Sandra would take this literally and from that day forth would be a daily visitor.

The next day was a Saturday, and Mattie and Alf were in the habit of lying in a little longer on the weekends. Alf's job at Aiton's started at 6:30 a.m., and he was a bus ride away from work so he usually left home at 5:30 a.m. during the week. The weekends were a pleasant break from long days spent in horrible conditions in an iron foundry. Mattie enjoyed the mornings when she could wake up with Alf still by her side. No matter her many dalliances, there was only one man for her and that was Alf. She knew she did not deserve such a love as the one he gave to her. Often in the quiet of the night she truly wished that being a wife and a mother were enough, and that she could be content without her endless quest for excitement.

Sandra had not had a good night. Saturday night was the worst night of the week, as that was usually a competition night for Mattie, while Alf met his mates in the pub to celebrate the end of a work week. This meant Sandra was left alone in the house from around 7:30 p.m. until 11:00 p.m. Her bedroom faced onto the narrow street, and the old house was far from soundproof.

Seven p.m. was bed time, and that meant going upstairs to a very cold and damp bedroom with a cold linoleum floor, and a utility war time bed, which was made with slatted wood. The only furniture in the room was a chest of drawers that had seen better days. There were no pictures on the wall, nor any ornaments like at Landrose.

There was no Rupert story. Just a peck on the cheek and a closed door, with the command to stay in bed and go to sleep.

Sandra was used to the routine and lay awake long after she had heard the heavy wooden door close downstairs. She knew she was alone, with only the dim light of a gas mantle, which was set as low as it could be. The flickering light made eerie shadows around the room, and when an occasional car went down the road the headlights were like searchlights finding all the darkest corners. Her heart was pounding, hating every minute of knowing she was alone, and she silently counted from one to ten and back again, always thinking that by the time she reached ten that she would hear her parents return. It was only then that she could go to sleep. That night, she lay watching the familiar shadows when she heard a horrific noise. It sounded like the house was falling down around her. She shrieked and sat up in bed until the noise stopped, and then, shaking with fear, she cried until there were no more tears left.

On the street below her bedroom window, Evan and Polly could hear their granddaughter crying and had no way to enter the house and calm her fears.

"Oh Polly, what were we thinking? They've left that child alone again, and the poor love is frightened out of her mind. She must have heard the coal dropping into the cellar."

Polly and Evan had brought a couple sacks of coal for Mattie and Alf, as coal was still expensive and they had more than enough, thanks to Evan's job. They always delivered the coal during the week at night, away from the prying eyes of any neighbours, but this time they had missed their usual night.

"Evan, what can we do? Can you get into the house? Did they leave a key anywhere?"

Polly and Evan went down the entry and searched in the outside laundry shed and all around the door, but could find nothing. They did not know what to do. Alf was not a man to be questioned, and although they knew where he would be drinking, they knew that to confront him before his friends would be a disaster. Where Mattie was, neither of them had any idea.

"It wouldn't take much for me to knock that door down and take her back to Landrose, Polly." Evan was beside himself with anger.

"Oh Evan, if you do, they might not ever let us have her again. It breaks my heart to leave her there, but we have no choice. I'll try to speak to Mattie tomorrow when they come for dinner." Sunday afternoons were always Polly's joy, as she got to spend time with all of her children and Sandra.

"That poor child. I wish we could take her back with us and keep her at Landrose forever. Neither of them are fit to raise a child." Polly was inconsolable and could not believe any child of hers could be such an irresponsible parent. They tried not to let Sandra know they were there, as they knew she would not understand why they could not take her home with them.

"I should have thought before I dropped the coal in the cellar, Polly." Evan blamed himself and silently fumed at his inability to do anything for Sandra.

"It's not your fault, love. They never think of anyone but themselves," Polly said between sobs. Her heart ached to go and console her only grandchild, although she knew it was impossible. Polly looked back at the bedroom window as the car pulled away, and she cried all the way back to Landrose.

It was a long while after that when Sandra heard the door being opened and the sound of raised voices. Her mother and father were having one of their frequent, volatile, but brief arguments. She waited until she heard the argument abate and the sound of their footsteps on the stairs, then turned over and feigned sleep.

Mattie peered into Sandra's room, and seeing her daughter motionless in bed, turned off the gas light and crossed the narrow passage to her and Alf's bedroom, oblivious to her young daughter's terrifying night.

Sandra fell asleep at last, but it was a fitful sleep full of bad dreams. The next morning, while Mattie and Alf were still in bed, Sandra decided to go and visit Auntie Elsie. Pulling a coat over her nightdress, she left the house. She had seen her mother open the door of the front room with the key that was always left in the lock. It was not a door that was used very often, as it opened directly onto the street. The big back door was too hard to open as the lock was out of reach and the door was much heavier. Up the street she went as fast as her legs would carry her, and down the big wide entry to the back door. Joe was already up and feeding his bantams when he noticed the little girl standing at the back door. "Hello, you must be Sandra. What are you doing here so early in the morning?"

"I've come to see Auntie Elsie and Susan," Sandra said as her curiosity got the better of her, and she walked towards Joe and the bantams. Susan came running down to meet her, and Sandra threw her arms around the gentle dog, who appeared not to mind the enthusiastic greeting.

She chattered incessantly and asked a thousand questions, all of which Joe did his best to answer. He was just as drawn to this little girl as Elsie was. "How about you hold the basket for me to put the eggs in," Joe smiled, "and then we'll go and see if Auntie Elsie will make us some breakfast." Elsie was at the kitchen window and could not believe her eyes when she saw Joe coming down the garden path with Sandra by his side.

"Look who I have here, Elsie. This young lady came to see her Auntie Elsie for breakfast."

Elsie looked at Joe and knew instinctively that from now on he would be Uncle Joe. It was as if someone knew this little girl needed them as much as they needed her. Elsie took the eggs and brought out some fancy egg cups that looked like chickens. Joe helped to set the table and made toast while Elsie boiled the eggs. Sandra told them she had eggs at Mama Polly's, but the eggs were bigger. Joe explained that these were smaller birds called bantams and so they laid smaller eggs. Putting two cushions on the chair, Joe helped Sandra up and placed a plate in front of her. He had carefully cut the toast into fingers and sliced the top off the egg. Placing a finger of toast in her hand, she needed no coaxing to dip the "soldier" into the egg. Neither Joe nor Elsie ever remembered a breakfast they had enjoyed more, and they did not realize it was now close to ten o'clock and Sandra had been there for almost two hours.

"Oh my goodness, Joe, her mam must be worried sick wondering where she is."

"Somehow I doubt that," Joe replied, without thinking.

Elsie looked at him questioningly, but decided that this was not the time to voice her concerns.

"Come on, love. It's time to go home. Your mummy and daddy will be wondering where you are. Susan and I will walk you back home."

Sandra was in no hurry to leave, but throwing her arms around Susan, she followed Elsie through the door.

When they neared number 44, Mattie was just opening the front door. When they had got out of bed and noticed Sandra was missing,

Mattie had found the front door unlocked. "I bet she's gone up the street to see that dog she's taken a liking to," Mattie called to Alf at the same time as she saw Elsie and Sandra hand in hand with Susan at their heels.

"I hope you don't mind, Mrs. Wetton, but Sandra came to see Susan, and ended up staying for breakfast. We didn't notice how the time had flown past. I hope you weren't worried."

"No, I thought she might have gone to see your dog, as she's talked of nothing else all week. I hope she wasn't a nuisance." Mattie took Sandra's hand. "She misses Tony, her Mama Polly's dog, but we're going to see him today, right?" she said to Sandra.

"She wasn't a nuisance, and if you don't mind, she can come to visit Susan anytime. Joe and I quite like the company," Elsie said as she looked past Sandra into the bare front room. Mattie had obviously taken great pains with her own appearance, as every hair was in place and her dress was immaculate. Elsie felt a little drab in her presence, as she was wearing a plain day dress and her naturally curly hair had a mind of its own.

It's funny that someone who looks so neat and proper does not take such care of their home, Elsie thought to herself as she walked back up the street to the warm and cozy home she shared with Joe.

"Come here, Sandra. Sit still for five minutes," Mattie said impatiently, as she struggled to get Sandra's hair braided and ready to go to Landrose. Mattie was proud of Sandra's long shiny hair, and always took great pains to see that it looked especially nice when she was going to see Polly and Evan. She had dressed Sandra in a little cream dress with pink rosebuds embroidered on it. It was one Belle had bought from Rowell's, and Mattie knew Belle would like to see her wearing it. Mattie looked at her young daughter, who looked party perfect, and she knew that after an hour at Landrose she would be back to the dishevelled imp that was more the norm.

Polly and Evan were not looking forward to the visit, as they knew that they had to say something about the previous night, but had no idea how to broach the subject.

"When they get here, you take the men out to show them the new barn, Evan, and I'll try and get Mattie by herself so we can have a talk. It will only cause trouble if you say anything."

Belle and Alf were the first to arrive, and Darren left to fetch Winnie. Dinner was all in the oven and the table was set. There was still an hour or so before dinner, so Belle decided to go for a walk with Tony and Sandra. "Come on, Mattie. It's lovely outside, come with us," Belle tried to convince Mattie to go down to the bluebell wood with them.

"You go ahead. I might come later," Mattie responded. "We've just walked all the way from Ripley." Her feet were tired and she had no intentions of walking any further. The walk from Ripley was a long one, even taking the short cuts across the fields. Sandra walked as far as her legs would carry her, and then Alf hoisted her onto his shoulders and carried her the rest of the way. Sandra loved this, as from her high perch she could see for miles, and she was always the first one to see Crich Stand. It was a game that Alf always let his young daughter win. Crich Stand was a monument to The Sherwood Foresters who had been killed in World War One, and it stood high at the top of Crich Hill, on their way to Wellington.

Polly seized the opportunity to talk to Mattie alone. "Evan and I dropped you a couple bags of coal off last night, love. Where were you?"

Mattie looked at Polly's worried face, and knew she was in for a lecture. It was not the first time Polly had voiced her concerns about them leaving Sandra alone in the house. "We weren't gone for long, mam, and she was already asleep when we left and fast asleep when we got back." Mattie gave Polly a look that said "Keep out of this. It is not your business." But she said nothing, choosing to stop the conversation where it was. Polly was not going to be stopped this time, though.

"That's what you think, my girl. She was crying her socks off when Evan and I were there. It's not right to leave her on her own. She's not yet five years old. If you and Alf can't look after her, then maybe Evan and I should keep her at Landrose where she is wanted." One look at Mattie's face and Polly knew she had already said too much.

"Does she look like she is not looked after?" Mattie snapped back. "Have you ever seen her not looked after? It's a different story when she stays here: She looks like a ragamuffin when I pick her up."

In truth, when she was at Landrose Sandra spent most of her time outside, and Polly had long since given up trying to braid her unruly hair. Playing in the field with Tony, she was often dirty and dishevelled when Mattie and Alf came to pick her up. Polly bit her lip, knowing Sandra loved the freedom of the open fields, and she had no intention of restricting that freedom.

"A bit of good honest dirt never hurt anybody, Mattie. You seem to forget how you played with the gypsies and came home blacker than coal. It does hurt a child to be left alone in an empty house at four years old!" She was afraid if she said more she would run the risk of not having Sandra stay again.

Sandra ran ahead of Belle and burst through the door with an armful of bluebells and cowslips. "Mama, for you," Sandra said proudly as she held out her bouquet.

Polly had to smile, despite her recent altercation with Mattie. Belle was holding both of Sandra's ribbons, and the braids were now twirling freely around her shoulders. The cream dress was grass stained where she had sat in the grass and made a daisy chain, which Belle had made into a garland for Sandra's hair. Polly had to admit that Sandra looked happy and healthy. *Maybe I am worrying too much about nothing?* Polly thought.

"Give them here, my pet. I'll find a jug." Polly looked at the window ledge and thought of all the times it had been filled with glasses and cups of all sizes when Sandra came to stay with them. What would she ever do if those visits were stopped?

The family were all together at last and dinner was served. Alf sensed Mattie was quieter than usual, and soon after dinner she was eager to leave. Evan went to get the car to give them a ride home, as he usually did, but Mattie politely refused his offer, saying they would take the bus. One look at Polly told Evan not to argue, and so the evening ended.

That night Polly and Evan lay awake in bed and discussed the day's events, but neither of them could see any resolution to their worries about Sandra.

"All we can do is give her as much love as we can, and make sure that when she is with us she knows how much we love her," Evan tried to console Polly. "Mattie and Alf are both good people, Polly. They just aren't that good at being parents. Everybody doesn't have a natural instinct, and maybe they will learn as they go along."

"In the meantime that poor child is being left alone, and there is nothing we can do about it?" Polly questioned. It was a question with only one answer, for Polly knew as well as Evan that any interference on their part would be met with hostility.

151

On the bus ride home, Sandra was already fast asleep on Alf's knee, having tired herself out with all the fresh air at Landrose. Alf questioned Mattie as to the reason for her obvious bad mood. Mattie could not tell him as she did not know herself. Was it her own nagging conscience that disturbed her, or the fact that Polly had criticized her parenting? Whichever it was, she knew she could not tell Alf. He was the master of his own home, and for anyone to question either him or his wife was unthinkable. Mattie did not want to drive a wedge between Alf and her parents. She knew in her heart that they only wanted the best for all of their children. They had helped Mattie and Alf on many occasions when rationing was difficult. Polly and Evan brought eggs and ham, and what they would do without the coal, she did not know. Alf loved Polly, and he and Evan got along well, but he sometimes thought they had far too much influence over their children. He would have been furious to know Polly had questioned what they did in their own home.

"It's nothing, Alf. I just had a headache, and I thought the walk to the bus stop would blow the cobwebs away."

"And did it blow the cobwebs away?" Alf said as he wrapped his free arm around Mattie. He knew that there was more to the story than Mattie had admitted, but also knew that whatever it was, Mattie was not going to tell him.

That night Mattie did not go straight to sleep, but lay awake thinking of the words that had passed between her and her mother. *Am I really such a bad mother?* she questioned herself. In her mind she justified much by rationalizing that Sandra was always dressed in the best clothes their meagre income could afford. She was never hungry, and Mattie made sure she had a bath twice a week, and her hair was washed every week. The fact that Sandra was left alone many nights was something Mattie chose not to dwell on. "She is safe in bed, and what harm can come to her?" She truly had no idea of the trauma Sandra suffered on those nights.

Nineteen

SANDRA GETS ILL

Life went on at Moseley Street with few changes. There were some traumatic nights, like the time when Alf forgot to put money in the gas meter before he and Mattie left the house. Sandra lay in bed, her heart racing as it always did as shadows crept across the room. Sandra tried covering her head with the bed sheets, but that was even worse. Her vivid imagination was far worse than any reality. When she threw back the covers the room was in total darkness, and she screamed in panic. The scream was heard through the thin walls of number 44 to the adjoining home of Mr. and Mrs. Bexton. They knew Sandra was often left alone, but did not want any trouble, so never intervened.

"Ernie, you have to go over there and see what the matter is," Mrs. Bexton insisted. "The poor child sounds terrified."

"You know how they are, Phyllis. Alf will have a fit if I interfere." Ernie was a mild mannered man and half the size of Alf. He had no desire to get on the wrong side of his neighbour. "She'll quieten down in a bit, Phyllis," Ernie said, hoping he was right.

He was wrong. Sandra's sobs could be heard through the wall until Phyllis could take it no longer. "If you don't go over there, I will," she fumed. "There's something wrong for her to sob like that."

Against his better judgement, Ernie went next door and finally found a way to get into the house. The old sash window at the back was unlocked, and after a few tries he managed to get it open. He knew the problem as soon as he got in and tried to light the mantle. He rummaged around and found the meter and put a penny in the box. He lit the downstairs light and went upstairs to try and calm the frightened child.

Sandra was sitting up in bed and staring at the door. When she saw the shadowy figure of a man come into the room she screamed again.

"It's all right, lovey. It's Mr. Bexton. I've just come to light the mantle for you."

Sandra recognised his voice and her sobs gradually subsided to a low moan. "I'll get Mrs. Bexton, love, and she'll make you a warm cocoa." He wanted to put his arms around the frightened girl, but was afraid he would frighten her all the more. Ernie went downstairs and let Phyllis in.

"Well, we've done it now, Phyllis. Alf will go mad when he gets home. We may as well take the lass back home with us and make her some cocoa. She's scared out of her mind, poor thing."

The words were hardly out of his mouth when Alf came down the entry just as Phyllis and Ernie were taking Sandra back home with them.

"What the hell do you think you're doing?" Alf was furious when he saw the open window and knew Ernie had broken in.

"He's doing what you should be doing," Phyllis shouted. "You two aren't fit to raise a child!" Ernie saw the look on Alf's face and tried to defuse the situation.

"We heard her screaming, Alf, and could not leave her by herself. We did not know what the matter was. She could have fallen or anything. As it was, it was the gas light had gone out, and she must have been frightened. I lit the gas and we were just taking her back for some cocoa."

Alf grabbed Sandra by the hand and pushed Ernie through the gate to his house with such force that Ernie went head over heels on the cobbled yard.

"Never come in my yard again, either of you, or I'll call the cops on you. That is break and enter ... Come on, you. Back to bed, now."

Alf could not understand why Sandra was so frightened, and was furious her cries had got a neighbour involved in their affairs. Sandra jumped into bed and covered her head with the sheets. *I'm in big trouble now. I wish I didn't have to live here. I want my mama.* Sandra's little head was full of confused thoughts.

Mattie came home from the dance a short while later, and Alf was fuming. Sandra could hear their raised voices, and knew her mom would be mad with her for causing so much trouble. Lying in bed, frightened not only by the memory of the shadows in the dark, but of the consequences she would have to face in the morning, Sandra felt as if her whole world was dark. Was she really so bad for causing so much trouble? Did other children just go to sleep and not be afraid of the dark? She loved her dad, and he had never been mean to her, but he was a larger than life figure who never showed any open emotion. She really did feel as if she was unloved and unwanted.

The memory of that night would be etched on Sandra's heart and mind for ever. That night was when the bad dreams turned into nightmares, and nothing could stop them. At least two or three times a week Sandra awoke in a cold sweat, screaming as a dark shadow came into her room and stood by her bed. This did nothing to help the feeling that she was a lot of trouble for waking everyone up in the middle of the night. Now she was afraid to go to bed, and so started creeping downstairs after her parents had left the house, making sure to race up the stairs as soon as she heard their footsteps in the entry. This practice led to another nightmare experience.

One night just before Christmas, after her parents had left the house, Sandra tiptoed down the stairs. She had decided the safest place for her to sit was with her back to the big heavy door which led out to the backyard. From that vantage point she could see all the other doors: the door which led upstairs, the door which led in to the front room, and the door she feared most, the one that led into the black cellar. The cellar was used to store coal, and was dark and sooty and smelled damp and musty. A grate on the street above was the only way that coal was delivered to the house. *If it's big enough for a sack of coal, it's big enough for a bogey man*, Sandra thought.

She sat listening to every creak and groan of the old house, with her back pressed against the backdoor. There was a wind blowing that night, and it was particularly noisy. She sat transfixed on the cellar door when it swung open. There was a big white ghost coming straight for her. Her screams would have wakened the dead, but she knew that there would be no response this time. Shivering in fear, she finally had the courage to open her eyes and look more closely at the apparition. It was a big white goose which was hanging on a hook behind the cellar door. Mattie and Alf had hung it ready to prepare for Christmas dinner.

One, two, three, four, five, six, seven, eight, nine, ten, then over again; Sandra chanted it time after time, thinking each time that by the count of ten, her parents would be home. Eventually she heard the long awaited footsteps and ran upstairs as fast as she could and jumped into bed, just before she heard the door open.

I hate this house. I hate this house, were her thoughts, and she longed for Landrose. That night she ached all over her body and this made her even more miserable. Only the thought of going to see Mama and Grandpa at Landrose over Christmas gave her any comfort. She knew there would be treats, and more than anything else, there would be lots of love. Mama Polly was all about love. Grandpa Evan let her tag along with him wherever he went, and she and Tony were his shadows. Neither of them ever tired of her chatter, and actually laughed at some of her antics.

The next day her aches and pains were still there, and over the next several weeks Sandra complained incessantly.

"Don't think you can skip school, young lady. You are going. There is nothing wrong with you," Mattie admonished. Sandra had started school at four and a half years old and now just turned five, she loved it.

"I like school, mam. It's not that. My legs hurt," Sandra moaned.

"It's just growing pains. You will grow out of it. Last week it was a sore throat, then a sore elbow, what's next?"

As soon as Sandra started school, Mattie returned to work at Rowell's. After the first day, when Mattie escorted her to school, Sandra walked the mile and a half to school and back alone. Most often, Sandra stopped at Auntie Elsie and Uncle Joe's where there was always a warm welcome, and a glass of milk and a biscuit. Auntie Elsie had noticed Sandra was not her usual bubbly self. She had gone through a series of coughs and colds lately, so Elsie had taken it upon herself to buy a tonic.

"Come on, my pet. Just a spoonful of this and you'll be right in no time." Elsie held out a tablespoon of clear liquid.

"Ugh! It smells horrible," Sandra wrinkled her nose.

"Not half as horrible as it tastes!" Uncle Joe laughed.

"Just hold your nose, love, and swallow. It will make you feel better." Auntie Elsie was not going to take no for an answer. "I have a nice candy for you when it is all gone." This became a daily ritual, but the aches and pains did not go away.

"Joe, I think there is something seriously wrong with Sandra. She's never complained before, and she's got no color in her cheeks at all. I am going to have a word with her mam and see if they are going to take her to the doctor."

"Now Elsie, you know what they are if anyone interferes." Joe had heard of the trouble with Mr. Bexton, and knew both he and Elsie would be devastated if they were not allowed to see Sandra again.

"Well, I'll give it another week and if she's no better, I have to say something." Elsie was aware of the possible consequences, but cared more for Sandra's health than anything.

Saturday morning, Sandra was not banging on the door at her usual time.

"Joe, Sandra's late this morning," Elsie said as she was preparing the table. Joe had already been to feed the bantams and collected the eggs. "I'm just going to have a peek and see if she's coming up the street."

"Oh my goodness! Joe! Come here quick!" Elsie panicked as she saw Sandra clinging onto a windowsill and obviously unable to move.

Joe ran out, and picking Sandra up in his arms, he carried her back to the house.

Tears were streaming down her face as she cried, "My legs won't work. I can't make my legs work. My knees hurt really bad."

Elsie forgot all about the breakfast, as one look at Sandra told her there was something terribly wrong. She was wet through with sweat and as white as a sheet.

"There, my love, lie quiet on the sofa, and Uncle Joe will get Susan to come and sit with you." She knew Susan could always bring a smile to Sandra's face, and the gentle red setter was the best baby-sitter she could have.

"That's it, Joe. We can't sit here and do nothing. This girl has to get to a doctor right away. I am going to talk to her mam and dad, chance what happens."

"You are not going on your own, love. I will go with you, but let's give them an hour or so as they're probably still in bed. She's comfortable now and she might even have a nap. Poor lass looks exhausted."

Sandra did fall into a restless sleep, and Elsie voiced her worst fears. "Oh, please God, don't let it be polio."

Joe had the same thoughts but dare not let Elsie see his concern. Sandra slept for almost an hour, and when she awoke, Joe and Elsie took her, wrapped in the blanket, back to number 44. Elsie knocked timorously on the door, her heart in her mouth, not knowing what sort of reception she would get.

Mattie opened the door and a waft of cigarette smoke greeted them. Seeing Sandra wrapped in a blanket in Joe's arms, Mattie panicked.

"What's wrong? Has she fallen?" Alf came to the door and took his daughter out of Joe's arms.

"There is something wrong with Sandra, Mrs. Wetton. She could not walk up the street. We found her clutching onto a window ledge."

"Oh, it's just growing pains. She makes more of it than there is. She'll grow out of it," Mattie said with confidence.

Elsie was enraged. "This child needs to see a doctor, and soon. There is something very wrong. This is not normal."

"Since you don't have any children of your own, I suppose you are an expert?" Mattie said cruelly.

"If I did, I would take better care of them than you do." Elsie was beside herself with anger.

Alf had not said anything to this point, but he was not about to listen to someone tell him what to do. "I think you should both leave, and let us look after our own daughter," he said very firmly.

Elsie would not be calmed, and laying everything on the line, she stood her ground.

"I am not going anywhere until I have your word that this child will be at the doctor's on Monday morning. If she isn't, then I am calling the social services and they can deal with this. One way or another, this child is going to see a doctor."

Mattie looked at Sandra, and she did not look well at all. "Maybe we should get her to a doctor, Alf. There might be something wrong."

"Thank you for bringing her home, but now it is our business and we will look after it by ourselves," Alf said as he prepared to close the door on them.

"I'll be back to see how she is tomorrow," Elsie said defiantly as she took Joe's arm to leave.

Monday morning Mattie had to take time off work, which did not please her, but she did take Sandra to see Dr. Paddy Ryan. He was old and a bit crotchety, but one of the best doctors around. He did a series of preliminary tests and all confirmed his first diagnosis. Sandra had rheumatic fever. "How long as she been like this, Mrs. Wetton?" he questioned.

"She's been complaining of pains in her knees and legs for a while, but we thought it was just growing pains." Mattie was now really frightened as the doctor's expression let her know this was indeed very serious.

"She needs complete bed rest immediately. I don't know yet if her heart's affected, but it is entirely possible that it is. I have to do more tests and she has to go on penicillin right away. I'll call an ambulance to take her to the hospital for tests, and then we'll see where to go from there."

For the first time in her life, Mattie was truly terrified. "Oh God, please let her be all right. I'll be a better mom. I'll do anything, but don't let her die." Mattie's head was swimming with what ifs. She knew at this moment that she really did love her daughter and could not imagine life without her. Alf was called at work, and he met Mattie at the hospital. Neither of them had any idea Sandra had been seriously ill. Both sat head in hands waiting for the results, and both blamed themselves for their lack of action sooner.

Once at the hospital, Sandra was prodded and poked and subjected to a myriad of tests. She was too sick and tired to even complain. The diagnosis was confirmed. She had rheumatic fever, and would have to be wrapped in cotton wool and bandages and stay in bed for at least two months, probably more.

"What are we going to do, Alf? She can't stay by herself, and she can't go to my mam's as the nurse is going to come every day. If I quit work, they may not take me back again and we need the money."

"Don't worry, Mattie. We'll sort it out somehow. I'm going to go home and get the bed downstairs into the front room. That will be a start. I'll see if I can get an electric fire to put a bit of heat in there." Alf had done what he did best, remain calm in the face of a problem and just take charge.

Elsie was pacing like a caged tiger all morning, and looking through the curtains for Mattie to come back down the street. Eventually she saw a big white van drive slowly down the street and stop in front of the Wettons'. The hospital had discharged Sandra with two aides to help transfer her to a bed at home. The doors opened, and she watched as the two men carried Sandra on a stretcher out of the back. She looked like a little Egyptian mummy wrapped almost from head to foot in cotton wool and bandages. Elsie's heart nearly stopped, but she dare not go and face Sandra's parents right now.

The doctor said all they could do was make sure she did not get out of bed under any circumstances and that she lay as still and quiet as possible. A nurse would stop in twice a day to administer injections and check her heart rate.

Sandra was very confused. She felt horribly immobile and hot and uncomfortable, but was not used to all the love and attention she was getting from her mam and dad. She looked around the front room, and the wallpaper was actually steaming due to the gas fire drying out the damp. It was much warmer than her bedroom though, and she could actually see through the window when she was in bed.

"Alf, I have to go and see Elsie and Joe Storer. They will be worried sick. They might be interfering busybodies, but they do love our Sandra." Mattie was unusually considerate of their feelings. "If it hadn't been for them, Alf, I daren't think what could have happened."

Joe had just got home from work when Mattie arrived to tell them of Sandra's diagnosis. Elsie could not believe her ears when Mattie actually thanked them both for prodding Alf and her to take Sandra to a doctor. Joe and Elsie were somewhat relieved to find out it was not polio, but they also knew the dangers of rheumatic fever.

"What can we do, Mrs. Wetton?" Elsie asked. "Both Joe and I will do anything we can to help."

Mattie explained Sandra had to be kept in bed and carefully repositioned several times a day so she did not develop bed sores. "I'm going to have to take time off work and stay home with her. I don't know if they'll keep my job, but what else can I do?"

"You can let me come and stay with her during the day," Elsie said in a heartbeat. "I don't have to go to work and I'd love to spend time with her."

Mattie could not believe her luck. Elsie really was an angel, and she regretted all the times she had been unkind to her in the past.

"Is that all right with you, Mr. Storer?" Mattie asked, completely dumbfounded by Elsie's generous offer.

"I reckon my Elsie is the best nurse she could have. We both love that little tyke, and whatever either of us can do, we will."

Elsie was true to her word, and Sandra's convalescence lasted for just over three months. During that time Elsie had made her as comfortable as she could. If Sandra had not loved Elsie before, now there was an unconditional bond between the two. Sitting in the damp front room for weeks on end would not have been anyone's choice, but Elsie did all she could to make it better. Every day she had some treat for Sandra. Some days she had homemade broth, some days egg custard, but always something she thought might help Sandra recover. Elsie loved flowers, and when there were no flowers in bloom she picked various twigs and leaves, which somehow she always made into beautiful arrangements to take to cheer up the drab room. Flowers soon became a trigger for Sandra's endorphins and immediately lifted her spirits.

Eventually the day came when Sandra was allowed out of bed. The release from her prison came with restrictions. No running or exertion for some time to come, regular visits to the doctor for checkups, and worst of all, she had to wear long pants at all times until he gave the all clear.

"Boys wear pants. Girls wear dresses!" Sandra said with her head held down. "Everyone will laugh and call me names for wearing pants."

Doctor Ryan looked at Sandra and thought she could never look like a boy, even in pants. "I know your mommy will find you some nice pants that are made just for little girls."

He looked at Mattie's immaculate and stylish dress, and knew she would be able to find something to fit the need. Mattie had not spent much time with Sandra during her illness, at a loss as to what to do. She was not a natural care giver like Elsie was. One thing she had always done was to make sure Sandra was dressed in the best that her meagre housekeeping money could buy.

Mattie looked at her young daughter and put her arms around her, with a rare but genuine hug. She had worried about her more than anyone would know. Mattie thought of all the times she had chastised Sandra for her rambunctious behaviour, and how she had missed it when Sandra was confined to bed. "Thank you, Doctor." Mattie was genuinely appreciative of the great care that Paddy Ryan had given to Sandra. He had even made a few house visits himself, which was not his usual practice.

"Just make sure you follow my directions, Mrs. Wetton. Her heart has a slight murmur, and we don't want it to get any worse. If at any time you think she is having a relapse, she has to go straight back to bed until the fever passes."

Sandra wore the hated pants all through the fall and winter, and eventually the time came that she could wear a dress again. Elsie and Joe were delighted and happy to see that Sandra was back to herself.

"Joe, there's a pantomime playing in Nottingham. Do you think that Mr. and Mrs. Wetton will let us take Sandra? It would be a lovely treat for her, now that she can wear a dress again." Elsie already missed her days with Sandra.

"Well, there's no harm in asking, love. I bet Sandra would really enjoy it." Joe was just as much attached to Sandra as Elsie was. He had missed his shadow when he was feeding the bantams or caring for his budgies. Joe never minded answering Sandra's never ending questions and enjoyed telling her all about his prize birds.

Mattie and Alf readily agreed for Elsie and Joe to take Sandra to the pantomime, and Sandra was excited at the prospect of a trip to Nottingham. She was not sure what a pantomime was, but she really didn't care as long as she was with Auntie Elsie and Uncle Joe.

At last the day of the outing came, and Sandra arrived on the doorstep several hours before their intended departure. Mattie had dressed her in a pretty little dress with a matching coat, and her hair was intricately braided with a matching ribbon. Sandra's hair was always something Mattie took pains with, making sure it was clean and shiny. She would only use Silvikrin Shampoo on Sandra's long and very straight hair. Her employment at Rowell's was such a bonus, as she was able to buy the latest of fashions at a discount. Elsie and Joe were just as excited, and proud to take Sandra out with them. Joe wished with all his heart they had been blessed with a child of their own, but he figured that this was probably as close as they would get to being parents.

Sandra was mesmerized with the big theatre. It had ruby red velvet curtains with gold tassels, and there were box seats all around the walls, which had ornate gold coloured wood carvings. Joe had managed to get them front row seats, center stage, as this was an occasion both he and Elsie wanted Sandra to remember and enjoy.

The curtain rose at last and neither Joe nor Elsie had ever seen Sandra so quiet. They had expected her to be asking questions throughout the whole show, but she could not take her eyes off the stage. It was a great show, and the actors were good at interacting with the audience, especially the ones in the first few rows.

"Where is Widow Twanky?" cried out one of the actors.

"He's there! He's behind you!" Sandra giggled as she pointed out the pantomime figure standing behind him. At each question to the audience, Sandra was right there with an answer. Joe and Elsie were thrilled to see how much she was enjoying it.

The intermission came all too quickly, and the big red curtains were closed. While the scene was being set for the second act, a magician came out and started to do tricks.

"Is there anyone who wants to come and help me find my rabbit?" he questioned.

Sandra jumped out of her seat and shouted "ME! Me. I can help."

The audience applauded as Sandra acted like a real assistant: obviously not a bit shy and enjoying the limelight. At the end of his performance, he hoisted Sandra into the air and asked for more applause. This was Sandra's first introduction to the stage and she loved it.

"You've got a future star there, mommy," he said to Elsie, as he deposited Sandra back in her seat. "She has a look of Julie Andrews, and she's certainly at home on the stage." Elsie was smiling from ear to ear as she was so proud of Sandra, and also the fact that he had assumed Sandra was her daughter.

That trip to the pantomime was the first of many, and Sandra was always a willing participant anytime the opportunity arose. On one particular occasion, Sandra decided she did not like her braids and wanted curly hair like Auntie Elsie. Eager to please her young charge, Elsie decided to curl Sandra's hair with tongs. Elsie put the tongs in the fire to heat up and then proceeded to curl Sandra's straight hair. At first Sandra was a little apprehensive when she could smell the burning hair, but when she realized it was painless, she was quite happy to sit still and anticipate the results. Elsie had not realized how different Sandra's hair was to her own, and the result was a very curly mass of hair that took on a life of its own. Elsie's hair was naturally curly and quite coarse, where Sandra's was like fine silk, and although each strand was fine, she had a mass of hair.

Uncle Joe came into the room just as Elsie was trying her best to tame the unruly mop.

"What's this? Who do we have here? It looks like Little Orphan Annie." He could barely contain his laughter.

Elsie looked at him with a worried look. "Her mam will have a fit when she sees it, Joe. What am I going to do?" There was no time to wash and dry the hair before they went to the pantomime, so all Elsie could think of doing was to try and calm the mop down with a little of Joe's hair pomade. Sandra was delighted with the results and tossed her head back and forth watching the curls tumbling around her face.

When Elsie took Sandra home, Mattie almost had a fit. The hair she had looked after so carefully was dry and burnt on the ends. She managed to contain her anger until after Elsie had left, but Sandra was threatened within an inch of her life if ever she let anyone touch her hair again. It took several weeks for Sandra's hair to return to its natural state, and Elsie never offered to curl it again.

Alf was worried about his mam and dad. Julia was suffering terribly from all of the needles and the many side effects of diabetes. Tom was losing weight by the day, and his smoker's cough was getting worse. When Alf went to visit one day, Julia confided again that Tom was hardly eating anything and would not go to the doctor. She was worried about him.

"You know your dad, Alf. He always puts himself last. He worries more about me than himself, and he really should go to the doctor. Can you have a word with him? He might listen to you." Julia was frustrated as Tom kept insisting he would be better in a few days, but he never was. Alf had meant to have that talk months ago, but with all the worries about Sandra's rheumatism, he had completely forgotten.

"I'll have a word with him today, Mam. He does look under the weather."

It was easy to get his dad to himself, as Tom was always happy to show off his garden. As Alf and his dad strolled down the path, he decided to open the conversation.

"Dad, mam's worried about you. She says that you aren't eating enough to keep a fly alive. You need to go and see the doctor, dad, even if only to ease mam's mind." Alf knew his dad would be more inclined to listen if he thought he was worrying Julia.

Tom reluctantly agreed to make an appointment. He had been putting off the inevitable, as he already had an idea what his problem was. He had worked for years as a station master on the railroad. The platform was always smoky from the old steam engines, and he breathed in fumes all day. He was not about to blame it on his pack a day habit, though it did cross his mind that he had smoked cigarettes since he was about fourteen years old. The reason Tom was not eating very much was that it had become very difficult to swallow.

The doctor did not take long to confirm Tom's fears. "Mr. Wetton, you have throat cancer and it is very advanced. I am afraid all I can do is try and make you as comfortable as possible, but I cannot operate."

"How long have I got, Doctor?" Tom asked, resigned to his fate.

"I'm not God, Mr. Wetton, so I can't tell you. All I can tell you is that you need to put your affairs in order as soon as possible. You could have six weeks, you could have six months, but it is all in the hands of the Man above."

Tom lived for another three months, and his death was a huge blow to everyone. He was loved by so many people. Julia thought her world had ended. How could she go on living without him? She never wore her heart on her sleeve, and people could be forgiven for thinking that she was unsentimental. Nothing was further from the truth. Julia was just a very private person. Tom and Julia had an amazing deep love and never felt the need to be demonstrative in public. Julia could not bear to think of not having his arms around her in bed at night. He was her comfort and her security, but most of all, he was her one and only love.

Life has to go on, and somehow Julia adjusted to a life alone, but it was a lonely life. She missed him every second of every day.

Twenty

SANDRA MEETS HER GRANDFATHER LANCE

Sandra had often heard the stories about the fact that Evan was not her real grandfather, and that somewhere there was a "blood" grandfather. She was not sure what that meant, but as far as she was concerned, blood or no blood, Evan was her true grandfather. He was the one who spent hours making a swing on the apple tree for her, the one who took her everywhere with him. She would sit for hours watching him tinker with a car or a pump, and her endless questions were always met with an answer. She loved him unconditionally.

One day when Mattie was catching the bus to Alfreton, she saw a man walk down the aisle in front of her. She had not seen her father for fifteen years, but there was no doubt in her mind that this was him. She watched as he took a seat several rows in front of her, and the familiar set of his shoulders was undeniably Lance. Without a second's thought, Mattie got up and took the seat next to him. Lance looked over and saw the beautiful young woman next to him, but his face showed no sign of recognition. Mattie was hurt and furious, but she was absolutely sure this was Lance.

"I think you're my father," she said with great confidence.

Lance's face suddenly lit up. "Our Belle?" he said.

"No, Dad. It's Mattie." Again, she was perturbed that even then he did not recognise her. She would have known him anywhere, and she had been a child when last she saw him. She had carried a picture of him in her heart for all these years.

It was a short ride to Alfreton, and he was travelling on to Codnor, but before the trip ended they had arranged to meet the following weekend in a pub in Ilkeston. Mattie could not wait to tell Alf about her meeting.

"Can you believe, he did not even know me? He thought I was Belle."

"Well, love, you have changed your hair color a bit over the years,

166

and he probably remembers you being much darker."

Mattie was always ahead of the fashion, and changed her hair color almost as often as her underwear. This month she was honey brown.

Over the next several months, the weekend meetings at the pub became a regular occurrence. Sandra was now often given a choice on such occasions. Stay home alone, or go and sit in the kitchen of whatever pub they were visiting. There was only once choice for Sandra, who hated being alone. Before she was eight years old, she knew every pub kitchen in the vicinity. Sometimes there was some-one else in the kitchen, but often as not she was the only one. It was enough for her that she could hear the merriment in the next room and know she was just steps away from her parents. On one such night Sandra had a surprise visitor.

Mattie and Alf had decided it was time Sandra met her grandfa-ther. The meeting did not go well. Lance had been drinking all night, and when he entered the room, his trilby hat was cocked over to one side and his whole appearance was one of excess. Once a very hand-some man, his face now showed the ravages of a wasted life. His nose was red and bulbous and his eyes were deep set and a very faded shade of grey.

"This is your grandfather Lance, Sandra. Aren't you going to give him a kiss?"

Lance leaned toward her, and the smell of alcohol on his breath was too much for Sandra. Even at such a young age, Sandra knew what a drunk looked and smelled like.

"You're not my grandfather; Evan is. And you smell," Sandra said defiantly and went to sit as far away from him as she could.

"Sandra Mary, you apologise to your grandfather right now," Mattie said with a withering look that said, "You'll be in big trouble when you get home."

"It's all right, Mattie, she'll come around in time," Lance said confidently.

He was wrong. On the second occasion they met, Lance thought he had an ace in the hole, as he had learned that what Sandra dreamed of more than anything was a pony. Her friend Judith had a pony, and Sandra longed to be able to ride. It was yet another pub kitchen and the same inebriated Lance blustered into the room, full of confidence.

"I have heard that a certain young lady would like a pony, and guess what, I have found a little beauty for you," Lance slurred.

"Well, it's not me. I don't want a pony," Sandra lied. She wanted a pony with all her heart, but not if it came from this imposter. "You're not my grandfather, and I don't want your pony. My grandpa Evan is my grandpa and I don't want another." Sandra was adamant even though she was certain her outburst would result in a severe lecture when she got home. She was wrong, as they were barely out the door when the lecture started.

"You be nice to your grandfather, young lady. He is your grandpa, whatever you say or do."

"I don't want to go to the pub with you anymore if he's there," Sandra said defiantly.

"Well don't worry about that, my girl; with your attitude you're better staying at home!"

"Mattie, don't pressure her. It's a lot for her to take in. Evan's been a great granddad, and of course it's hard for her to accept another one. When she gets older she'll see things differently." Alf liked Lance as he was definitely a man's man. They both worked hard during the day and liked a drink at night. He actually related to Lance more than he did to Evan. Evan was far more gentle, and other than his shot of Johnny Walker Black Label every night before bed, he was not a drinker. Alf had to admit Evan had been a wonderful grandfather to Sandra, though, and it was easy to understand why she loved him.

Mattie had told Polly of her meeting with Lance and the fact they were now meeting on a regular basis. "Mam, he's a master electrician and has a good job and a nice house in Codnor."

"I don't care if he lives in a palace. Leopards don't change their spots. He never paid a penny towards your upkeep. Evan worked his fingers to the bone and went without decent shoes on his feet to see that you children all had the best of everything. I've seen him go to work in clothes like rags when his workmen were dressed better than him. You forget so easily, but I don't." Polly was almost in tears. She knew Evan would be upset to know that Mattie had developed a relationship with Lance. Evan could never forget the night Lance gave Polly and himself such a beating that they were unrecognisable. Lance was a cruel and callous man, and Evan despised him.

Mattie and Alf continued seeing Lance, and also introduced Belle and Alf to him. Darren steadfastly refused to see him, as his memories of Lance, although not vivid, were not good. Sandra could not be convinced to meet Lance again, and although she hated staying alone in the house at night, it was preferable to the alternative.

Since her rheumatic fever, Sandra had recurring, almost annual bouts of rheumatism. The first sign would always be her left knee, which would suddenly become painful and unstable. Each time she was confined to bed rest and unable to go to school. It became a cycle of playing catch up for all the school tests, as Sandra frequently missed at least a month of school every year. This year was particularly bad as Sandra had a really virulent bout of whooping cough, followed by the measles, and was generally run down. After several trips to the doctor's, it was decided Sandra's tonsils and adenoids should be removed. The surgery was a success and Sandra's health improved greatly. The best part was that recuperation meant Landrose, and joy of joys, the pink room with a fireplace.

Polly and Evan were just as happy to have their granddaughter stay with them, and before her arrival Evan always made sure the gas fire was turned on, while Polly fluffed the pillows and warmed the sheets with a beautiful copper warming pan.

Twenty- One

DARREN AND WINNIE ~ 1953

Polly and Evan loved life at Landrose, especially when they were surrounded by family. The house had been quiet lately, however, as most of the children were living busy lives of their own. Belle and Alf were in Matlock, and Mattie and Alf and Sandra were in Ripley. Darren had just delighted them with the news he had asked Winnie to marry him.

"Oh Darren, you couldn't find a lovelier girl anywhere," Polly enthused. "Evan and I both love her to bits."

"You've found a treasure there, boy. You'd better put a ring on her finger quick before she changes her mind," Evan laughed. He was half serious, as he thought Winnie would have her hands full with Darren. They were so opposite, and Evan hoped Darren would be a good husband. He had seen how Darren could quickly lose his temper if things were not exactly to his plan. Evan did not like the way Darren took advantage of his mother, and seldom showed gratitude for anything she did for him.

"Mam, I need a white shirt ironed for tonight!" Darren called as he ran upstairs to take a bath before going to Winnie's.

"Typical," thought Evan. There was never any please or thank you, just a command. Evan never interfered, as he knew how Polly loved Darren and was able to ignore all of his faults. Evan saw Lance each time he looked at Darren. He was almost a carbon copy of his father, in looks and in temperament.

Winnie came from a very humble home where there was love, but few tangible home comforts. It was a small, draughty farm house with little natural light. The low ceilings and dark walls did nothing to cheer the place up. Landrose was heaven for Winnie to be. Evan always thought Winnie had fallen in love with the home Polly had made of Landrose, before she fell in love with Darren.

Polly was in her element planning for another wedding. Winnie's mum, Ruth, was not in the best of health. She had a goiter which was so large it restricted her breathing. The large goiter hung below her neck, and made many everyday tasks twice as difficult. When Polly offered to take over the job of wedding planner, Ruth was very relieved.

The wedding was drawing near, and Polly and Winnie arranged to pick up Sandra and go on a shopping trip. Sandra was to be the only bridesmaid, and was excited at the prospect of another beautiful long dress. It was a long day, but a fun day.

Winnie was so tiny it was not easy to find a dress that did not overpower her. She had set her heart on a dress with a full skirt, and could not be persuaded to choose a slimmer cut, which Polly thought might suit her better. Sandra loved every dress that Winnie tried on, and oohed and ahhed each time Winnie emerged from the fitting room. Finally, after trying on many dresses, Winnie came out with a radiant smile. If she had not known before, she did now, as Sandra let out a big "YES!"

"Oh Polly. This is the one. I love it." Polly was stunned, as it was without a doubt "the one." The bodice was plain and dipped to a small V below the waist, and the skirt, although full, was more of a gradual A-line. Long sleeves came to a point at the middle finger and, other than the very delicate lace overlay, there were no other embellishments. The look on Polly's face told Winnie she had chosen the right dress.

There was a bridesmaid dress designed to complement the bride's gown, and it was perfect for Sandra, although a little more than they had budgeted for.

"Try it on anyway, love, and we'll see." Polly gave the dress to Sandra, who needed no encouragement to comply.

It was perfect, and Polly stretched the budget to buy it. The trio left the store with happy smiles, and arranged to go back the following week to pick up the dresses. Winnie's just needed a minor adjustment to tighten the waist and shorten the sleeves. Sandra's needed a little easing in the bodice, but the store kindly offered to do the alterations for free.

"Well I think a coffee ice-cream at Sainsbury's has your name on it, love." Polly put her arm around Sandra as the three of them crossed the road to Polly's favourite coffee shop. It was always a ritual when they made a trip to Chesterfield that Sandra had a dish of coffee ice-cream, and Polly had a cup of freshly brewed coffee and a lighter than air scone.

Sandra led two totally different lives. Time spent with Polly and Evan, Winnie, or Belle was how life should be—full of laughter and fun, where she actually felt wanted and loved. But life at Moseley Street had not improved. The nightmares were still constant, and now at ten years old, Sandra's life was even worse.

"You're ten years old, girl. Old enough not to be afraid of the dark. Don't be such a baby." She had heard it all, and knew very well she was ten years old. She got told each time she awoke the house with a nightmare. Sitting savouring every morsel of the delicious ice-cream, Sandra was hoping the day would never end, but knew it would soon be time for Mattie to pick her up to go home.

The night before Darren and Winnie got married, Mattie put Sandra's hair in the proverbial rags. It was a ritual each time there was an occasion: Sandra had ringlets. She hated them, especially the night before when it took at least two hours to wash and dry Sandra's mass of long hair. Mattie brushed it until it gleamed, and then wound the rags tightly to Sandra's head. Sleep was impossible, but the excitement of the big day made everything bearable.

The effort was worth it. Mattie looked at her daughter as she was ready to go to church, and was very proud of the results of her hard work. Winnie and Polly had indeed found the right dress, and Sandra looked like a princess. Mattie was her usual fashion plate chic, as she always managed to find a perfect ensemble that accentuated her stunning bone structure and great figure.

"My two girls look smashing today," Alf said proudly as he armed Mattie and Sandra into the waiting car. Alf and Belle had gone to pick them up in Alf's Ford Consul, of which he was very proud. The three girls squished into the back and the two Alfs sat up front.

Belle was wearing a suit with a matching hat, and Mattie took one look at the hat and started to laugh. "You look like Mrs. Khrushchev in that hat, Belle. Ditch the damn thing before we get to church."

Belle was crestfallen, as she had really liked the ensemble, and now at the side of Mattie she felt frumpy. Mattie had been right however, as when Belle removed the hat and let her beautiful hair tumble in natural curls, the whole effect was entirely different.

Polly and Evan were in their elements as they proudly watched all their children come into the church. Darren was standing at the altar, his military training evident in his confident posture. Winnie came down the aisle on the arm of her very proud father, and all eyes were on the petite vision before them. If ever there was an angel on earth, it was Winnie.

The event was a great success, and friends and neighbors all had an amazing time at the celebration. Darren had found a small cottage to rent just a few miles from Landrose, and he could not wait to take Winnie home. It was furnished with odds and ends from second hand stores and estate sales, but somehow it all went together very well. The only thing Winnie had brought from home was her piano. She had a beautiful voice and loved to play the piano. Darren had managed to find a place for it in the front room, close to a window that looked down the fields.

For the next year everything was wonderful, and Darren was a good and loving husband. Winnie was a perfect wife and was loved by all the family. Sandra loved nothing more than the days she was allowed to visit Winnie, as that meant she got to "play" the piano. Much as Sandra loved music, she had no talent when it came to the piano, but Winnie was ever patient and managed to teach her a few simple songs. The best part was listening to Winnie as she played everything from jaunty little ditties to amazing concertos. The cottage was not as grand as Landrose, but it had the same feel. It was warm and friendly with stunning views of the fields below. On one of Sandra's visits, Winnie was paler than usual, and their walk down the fields was cut short.

"I'm just a bit tired today, love. Maybe we'll go back to the house and I will have a rest. You can play me that song I taught you."

Over the next few visits, Winnie tried her best to hide her fatigue. She had never had a lot of color, but now her skin was almost translucent.

Twenty-Two
LEAVING LANDROSE

Polly was worried about Winnie as she had gone from petite to fragile, and she was trying so hard to hide her failing health.

"Winnie, my love, you should go and see the doctor. It's not natural for you to be so tired at your age. I'll go with you if you like." Polly put her arm around Winnie and was shocked at how much weight she had lost.

"It's all right, Polly, I have been and there is nothing they can do. Please don't tell Darren yet." Winnie let the tears flow. "I have cancer and it can't be cured."

Polly was devastated, and at a loss for words. A great believer and a Christian, she questioned how any God could inflict this on someone so young and so lovely. Winnie was the sweetest, kindest person she had ever known, always putting others before herself. "Why?" Polly silently screamed.

"Are you sure about that, love? Now is the time when you will need a husband to look after you. Don't you think you should tell Darren?"

"He's not very good with sickness, Polly. There is no point in telling him until I really have to."

Polly looked at Winnie and read more into the statement than Winnie had said. She knew Lance never had time for any sign of weakness, and Darren was no different.

Winnie would never tell Polly of her heartache. She loved Polly like her own mother, and knew she would be devastated to hear that since she had been ill, Darren had been staying away from home a lot. He had taken to going out on his motorbike, which he'd gotten almost as soon as he came out of the army, taking long rides when Winnie was not well enough to accompany him. It was no one moment that she knew, but a series of small clues led her to the conclusion he was having an affair. A shirt that smelled of a strange perfume, a ticket stub found in a coat pocket, a sudden attention to his attire: all were the signs she needed to confirm her suspicions.

Winnie was always ready to take the blame for Darren's behaviour. *It can't be much fun living with someone who is always sick*, she thought to herself. She did try to put on a brave face and to look her best when he came home at night, but he barely noticed her anymore. Darren was seeing a girl called June, and he revelled in the excitement of a clandestine affair.

It was not a good year for Polly. Her heart was breaking for Winnie, and Polly did not like the fact that Darren seemed heartless to his wife's failing health. Darren had just been to Landrose to hunt rabbits in the bottom wood, and had left a couple for Polly to cook. She wished she could say something, but knew from experience it would be like talking to a stone wall. Darren always pleased himself with what he did and would not take kindly to his mother interfering in his life. After he left, Polly turned to Evan with a look of sad resignation.

"Surely he can see that Winnie is not well, Evan, and yet he spends more time than ever either out on that bike or hunting rabbits. He's never at home anymore."

"You can't worry for all of them, pet. They're old enough to make their own lives, and none of them would thank you to say anything. On the other hand, I would say a big thank you for a rabbit pie for supper tonight," Evan tried to make light of the situation as he tugged on Polly's apron, and pulling her towards him, gave her a big kiss.

"I've been having a bit of trouble with that darned oven lately, so even that might not turn out right," Polly grumbled, not prepared to be placated so easily.

"All the cooking you do, my love, you deserve a new stove and kitchen counter."

Polly had managed for many years with the fireplace oven and knew all its failings, but somehow always managed to prepare perfect meals in it. The thoughts of a new oven were very tempting though.

A few weeks later the workmen showed up and replaced the counter, sink and draining board and put in the new oven. Polly could hardly wait to try it out. It was Monday and a wash day, so Polly had put a pot of stew on to cook and was busy hand washing Evan's socks in the new sink. She carefully washed and rinsed the socks and put them on the draining board. Suddenly she had a terrific pain that shot through the whole length of her arm and actually threw her to the ground. Evan heard the scream and ran into the kitchen.

"Polly, Oh my god, Polly! What is the matter?" Evan dropped to the floor by her side. Polly was shivering and semi-conscious. He gently put his arm underneath her and grabbed a tea towel from the rack and slipped it under her head.

"Where does it hurt, Polly? Is it your chest?" Evan was concerned she had suffered a heart attack.

"My arm, my shoulder, and my head," Polly managed to groan.

"I'm calling an ambulance, Polly. You might have had a heart attack." Evan was worried sick. "Lay still, love, and they'll be here in no time."

Evan called the ambulance and then he called Belle. Belle arrived a few minutes before the ambulance. One look at her mother and Belle knew this was serious. She went to the sink to get a cold cloth, as Polly seemed to be burning up.

"OW! What the heck. I just got a shock!" Belle cried. "Evan, Mom must have got a shock when she touched the metal draining board." Belle was wearing rubber soled shoes, and thankfully had not been exposed to as much electricity.

Once at the hospital, the doctors confirmed that Polly had indeed suffered an electrical shock of some magnitude. "There is not much we can do, Mr. Redford. Just take her home and make sure she stays in bed until she starts to feel better. It may take a while for her to fully get over it, but being at home with familiar surroundings and family around her is the best medicine I can prescribe."

Evan was just thankful that it was not a heart attack. and he knew that Polly was a fighter. "You'll be all right, my love. Our Belle is going to come and stay for a few days until you are up and around again. I am calling those damned electricians who put that stove in, to get this fixed right away."

Polly looked at Evan in a daze. She felt very confused, and only half of what he said was registering. She knew it was something to do with the stove, but did not quite comprehend what had happened.

It turned out there was a loose wire that had come into contact with the metal draining board, and they had not grounded the stove properly.

Belle stayed for almost two weeks, and Polly made a slow recovery. Both Belle and Evan were concerned that Polly appeared to have lost interest in everything. She had to be coaxed to eat, and all she wanted to do was to sleep. This was not Polly.

The next several months there was little improvement in Polly's health, and the doctor feared she had something akin to post-traumatic stress syndrome. It was a form of depression that some-times occurs after such an incident. It was no doubt compounded by the fact of her worries about Darren and Winnie. She had also spent a good part of that year nursing Sandra through another bout of rheu-matism and her recovery from the tonsil and adenoid removal. Evan always knew Polly took the weight of the world on her shoulders, and he loved her for it, but he worried that this time she had overdone it.

"Mam, I think it's time you had a rest and let us look after you for a while," Belle said one day when she was visiting. "Alf has found a Fish and Chip Shop for sale in Chesterfield, and he thinks it could be a little gold mine. Why don't you and Evan think about leaving Landrose and get into a place where there is more life? You need people around you, and to get away from the isolation here."

Polly looked through the window at Evan, whose family had been at Landrose for generations. He was out in the garden picking his home grown tobacco.

"I could never ask Evan to leave this place, and I love Landrose as much as he does. We've had a lot of happy times here, Belle, and this house is full of happy memories."

"Well, just think about it, Mam. Why don't you and Evan come and have a look at this place with us on the weekend, and then see what you think. It has great living quarters, big enough for all of us, and it's close to all the shops and theatres. It would be good for you to be around more people, rather than spending so much time alone."

Belle had her wish, and Polly and Evan went to see the Fish and Chip Shop on Sheffield Road in Chesterfield. It was a nice, well-kept shop in a perfect location. It was close to The Mazda Lamp Company and to a huge car dealership called Brocklehurst Motors. "It's on a main bus route, Polly, and it gets all the trade from the factory and the car dealership at noon." Alf was very excited as he wanted des-perately to get into a business of his own, but knew that without the financial input of Polly and Evan this was just a pipe dream.

Polly had very mixed feelings, as she had always felt safe and se-cure at Landrose. Evan loved his job and his garden and she could not see him wanting to move.

"If it's what you want, Polly, then let's do it," Evan said that night when they were in bed.

"I don't want anything that you don't, my love. I am happy wherever I am as long as we are together," Polly squeezed his arm.

"Well, we should let Alf check it out a bit more. He knows all about operating a store, and I am sure he wouldn't want to give up his job if he wasn't confident this is a good business." Evan had been worried about Polly since the electrocution, and he would do anything, even leave his beloved Landrose, if it meant she would get better. Landrose was stone and mortar; it was Polly who made it a home.

It took almost four months of haggling back and forth, but finally a price was agreed upon and the decision made. Evan handed in his resignation, much to the dismay of his employers. He, and his father before him, had been the most reliable and competent managers the company had ever had, and he would take a lot of replacing. They knew Polly had been ill of late, though, and as they all knew and loved her, they understood Evan's decision.

Mattie and Alf were surprised at the news, but Sandra was probably the most devastated of all. Landrose was not just stone and mortar to her. Landrose was love and stability and most of all an escape. She could not bear to think of a life without Landrose. But she knew her grandmother had not been well lately, and if this move was because it would be good for her, how could she argue? That night when she went to bed, she cried silently into her pillow.

"What am I going to do without Landrose? Chesterfield is so far away. I'll never get to stay there like I did at Landrose."

As the time drew near for the move, both Polly and Evan were secretly hoping this was the right decision. On the day they left, the sun was shining and gleaming from the copper beech by the back pantry window. Polly loved that tree, and she gently touched its leaves in a last farewell. Neither Polly nor Evan could look back as the car pulled away, and they rode in silence, both too emotional to speak.

It was a huge adjustment to move from miles of open fields and the only sounds those of cows and chickens, to a busy main road, where busses and lorries zoomed by all day and night. It was very different sharing the home with Alf and Belle, but Polly had to admit she really liked the everyday interaction with her customers. Evan missed Landrose with all his heart, but Polly would never know just how much. He would have done anything to see her recover from the electrocution, and this seemed to have worked.

Twenty-Three
NEW LIFE ~ 1953

Belle and Alf had been married for five years and had begun to accept the fact they probably would not have a child, when one morning Belle awoke feeling very nauseous. Belle and Polly were sitting at the breakfast table when Belle suddenly jumped up and ran to the bathroom. Polly had seen this enough times to know that her daughter was pregnant. Everyone was over the moon with happiness. Polly could not wait for another grandchild. It was obvious Mattie and Alf were not going to expand their family, and poor Winnie was dying. Everyone made preparations for the birth, and although it would mean the house would now be full to capacity, somehow Polly knew they would make everything work.

Belle had a difficult pregnancy and a difficult birth, but Susan was born a healthy seven pound blonde bundle. She was an amazing baby who hardly ever cried, and Belle was able to leave her in her pram by the passage door while she worked. She never lacked for attention, as Polly and Evan were there the second they had a chance to pick up their new grandchild.

"She's a lot different to our Sandra, love," Evan smiled "She'd have us all on our toes."

Polly had to agree as Sandra could never have been thought of as quiet.

"Oh, those times went much too fast though, Evan. I can't believe she is 10 years old already. Little madam or not, I'd love to have those days back again. She misses Landrose, Evan, and I still worry about her."

Sandra was studying for her eleven plus exam when she got another bout of rheumatism. She desperately wanted the opportunity to go to Swanwick Hall Grammar School, and tried to hide the fact she was in pain again. It was Auntie Elsie who first saw the telltale signs and sat down with Sandra to have a talk.

"It's no use pretending you are okay, love, when you aren't. You need to do what the doctor says, and rest. Lots of children grow out of this as they get older. Your health is the most important thing you have."

Sandra really did feel awful and was finding it hard to study anyway, so she gave in and took the required time off school. Needless to say, she missed too many of the pre-exam lessons and failed the exam. She was devastated. School had been good lately; ever since Miss Cynthia Stretton came to teach, Sandra had found her focus.

Miss Stretton was a breath of fresh air, and although loved by all her pupils, she was not accepted by any of the old school teachers. She taught theatre and art, which most teachers thought were frivolous subjects anyway. Her dress was colourful and flamboyant, and her hair, which was often piled high and held by a clip, was varying shades of bleached blonde. Sandra soon became a star pupil, and for the first time in her life had a passion for something. Maybe it was all the pantomimes that Auntie Elsie and Uncle Joe had taken her to, or just a natural affinity for the stage. She was certainly never shy or lost for words.

"Mom, I am taking elocution lessons, and Miss Stretton wants me to enter the Royal Conservatory Exams. She thinks I have a chance of winning."

Mattie was thrilled. She had always hated the Derbyshire dialect and had done her best to make sure Sandra did not use the colloquial slang. Sandra was happy her mother approved, and she studied hard for the upcoming exam. This was good all round, as her mother now actually seemed interested in her activities.

Miss Stretton took an interest in Sandra, and when she found out she had failed the eleven plus, she made it her job to fight for Sandra to be allowed to sit it again. An exception was made due to Sandra having missed so much of the course work due to sickness. It was six months of solid studying, but Sandra passed the all-important exam just prior to her twelfth birthday. It was not going to be easy, as she would enter Swanwick with the thirteen year olds, but would be a year behind the eleven plus entrants.

Twenty-Four
DARREN AND WINNIE ~ 1955

Nineteen fifty-five did not start out well. Winnie was in and out of hospital, and Darren now knew his wife was dying of cancer. She was amazingly strong for such a tiny little lady, and she clung to life for as long as she could. Polly visited her whenever she could get away from the store, but more often than not, Polly and Mrs. Smith were the only visitors.

One day when Polly went to visit, she saw a crumpled up piece of paper on the floor by Winnie's bed. She stooped to pick it up, and just as she was about to throw it into the garbage, she recognised Darren's handwriting. Winnie was sleeping in a drug induced respite, so Polly quickly slipped it into her purse. *Why would Darren write a letter?* she questioned herself. Polly sat by Winnie's bed until she finally awoke.

Polly leaned over to give her daughter-in-law a hug. "How are you feeling today, my love?"

"I'm just really tired, Polly. I am so sorry I am being so much trouble for everybody."

"You couldn't be trouble if you tried, pet. We all love you to pieces, and if there is anything we can do to make things easier, then we will."

"The only thing that will make things easier is if this ends quickly. I really want to go, Polly. I have no fight left anymore."

Polly looked at Winnie, and tears streamed down her face at how unjust this seemed. Her daughter-in-law was barely twenty-three years old, and wishing for death to take her.

"Don't cry, Polly. You and Evan have been like a second mom and dad to me, and I am lucky to have spent what time I have with you." Winnie drifted back off to sleep and Polly kissed her cheek and tiptoed out of the room.

The shop was closed and the nightly task of cleaning out all the fryers and washing the shop window and the street outside were all done. Polly had gradually come to enjoy the Fish and Chip Shop. She loved the customers, and before long they all knew and loved her too. She was fastidious about cleanliness, and the store soon gained a reputation for great fish and chips, which were always cooked in fresh lard. Evan was never much of a mixer, so he had volunteered from the start to be the behind the scenes help. He was amazing, standing for hours in the cold "rumbling house," rumbling the potatoes and putting them into vats of a mild ammonia hydroxide solution. The worst job of all was dipping his hands into the frigid water to remove any eyes or imperfections in the potatoes. His hands were in cold water for most of the day and night. On busy days, which were often, he carried pail after pail of them up from the basement to the store above to be chipped and fried. He went to the railway station daily and loaded box after box of fresh fish into the boot of his car and then unloaded them all for Polly to filet and fry. Belle was great in the store, and also helped Polly around the house. Alf was a bit of a skiver, and did as little as possible with as much pomp as he could muster. He was always at home taking the cash and doing the books. This was a totally cash business, and other than a little old ticker tape cash register, there was little track of sales. When they were very busy, some things slipped by the register and were not recorded. Even though Polly and Evan had contributed the lion's share of cash to the venture, Alf behaved as if he was the sole owner. Polly did not mind as she knew this was his personality, but it did bother Belle, who hated to see her parents taken advantage of.

"Come on love, up the apples." Evan put his arm around Polly. He looked tired, and Polly too was ready for bed. It had been a long day. Polly had forgotten about the letter until now, but once she remembered it she pulled the crumpled paper out of her purse.

"What's that, love? Another bus load?" Evan asked, thinking he would have to make an early start if it was. Their fish and chip shop had become a popular stop for tour busses, and they had developed a plan of leaving an order for so many fish chips and peas at a given hour the following day. This ensured their passengers were not kept waiting, and Polly was prepared for a sudden influx of 25 or 30 customers all at the same time.

Polly was reading the letter, and her face turned white as she put her head in her hands and started to sob.

"What is it, love?" Evan could tell that this was something very upsetting.

"Oh! How could he? What kind of a man can be so cruel? That poor girl. No wonder she wants to die."

Evan picked up the letter and read:

Dear Winnie,

I have tried to deal with your cancer and sickness over the past two years, and I am not able to do it anymore. I need to get on with my life and so I am asking you for a divorce.

Sorry for everything,

Darren

Evan was furious. This was pure Lance. It brought back all the unhappy memories of how Lance had treated Polly, and this was even worse. Winnie was no match for Polly in strength, especially now that she was so sick.

"We have to go and see him, Polly, and let him know we have seen this. If he leaves that girl now, I never want him to cross this doorstep again. He is no son of yours, my love, if he can do this."

Polly hung her head with shame. She had defended Darren on many occasions, but this was just too much. How could anyone be so cruel and callous? "I'll get Alf and Belle to watch the store tomorrow night, and we'll be waiting for him when he gets off work," Polly said.

When Darren got home and saw Evan's big black Triumph Gloria parked outside, he wondered what had happened. His first thought was that Winnie had passed away, but as soon as he saw their faces, he knew he was in trouble.

"What kind of a man can do this to a sweet young thing like Winnie as she lies in her death bed?" Polly waved the letter in front of him.

"She had no right to show you a private letter," Darren growled, very upset at being found out.

"Winnie has more class than that, my boy. She's got more backbone than you'll ever have." Evan had to control his anger, as he had never before interfered with Polly's children. This was too much, and for the first time in his life, Evan wanted so much to strike out at his stepson.

"You don't know everything. It's none of your business, and I'll do what I want," Darren stood his ground with a sullen look on his face.

"Very well, Darren. You have chosen your path. Just know that Evan and I will stand by Winnie for as long as the Lord sees fit to let her stay with us. If you're any kind of man at all, you will try and put this right so she can die in peace. I don't want to see you again until you have told Winnie this was all a mistake. You did it in a weak moment, or whatever you have to say, but tell her that you did not mean it."

Polly and Evan left with no promises from Darren, and not knowing what they could do to try and ease Winnie's heartache.

The phone call came just as they were opening shop for the evening trade. Winnie had passed away quietly in her sleep. Much to Alf's dismay, Polly hung a sign on the door: "Sorry, we are closed due to a death in the family."

"You don't have to close the shop, Polly. Belle and I can handle it tonight." Alf was reluctant to lose any revenue.

"You can't handle it by yourself, Alf, and I am not going to help you. Show some respect." Belle could not believe he was prepared to carry on as if nothing had happened.

Everyone loved Winnie and although they knew this day was inevitable, it did not make it any easier to bear.

No one else knew about the letter, as Polly and Evan were too ashamed of Darren to tell anyone. Polly knew without a doubt that Winnie would not have shared the letter with anyone either. It seemed so little time since the wedding, and Polly remembered how proud she was on that day. Winnie had experienced so little happiness in her twenty-three years on earth.

"All we can think, Polly, is that she is certainly in a better place and out of pain now. There's another angel in heaven. I think she was just too good for us here on earth." Evan knew that Polly's heart was heavy with Darren's guilt, and the loss of her beautiful daughter-in-law.

The funeral was attended by people from the surrounding villages who had known and loved Winnie, and somehow everyone managed to get through the day. Darren could not wait for the day to end, as his own feelings of guilt had finally caught up with him. He was the last to file past the open coffin, and when he saw Winnie lying there, as she had requested, in her wedding dress, her face free of pain again, he broke down and cried genuine tears of regret.

Mattie and Belle went to support their brother, not knowing of his terrible letter to Winnie just prior to her death. Polly could not tell anyone; the shame was too great. He was her son.

Evan made an excuse to take Polly home early, as he knew that trying to keep up this sham was more than anyone should have to cope with. Polly had made an amazing recovery from the last few dark months at Landrose after her electric shock, and he did not want anything to put her back into another depression.

Darren did not want to stay in the house after Winnie died, and asked Polly and Evan if he could come and live with them at the fish and chip shop. Polly could not say no to her son, although Evan had a lot of misgivings. "He's your boy, my love, and you do what you want. As long as he does not want to be waited on. I won't have him taking advantage of you ever again." There was an attic bedroom that Polly cleaned out and made available. Evan was right, he was her boy, and she loved him even when she was disappointed with him.

Darren was devious, as he was not moved in more than a couple of weeks when he went to his mother with another request. "Mam, June is pregnant and her folks have thrown her out. She has nowhere to go. I am going to bring her here until we find somewhere to live."

Polly was furious. "Winnie's not cold in the grave yet and you want to bring some floozy into my house. Where is your self-respect?"

"She's got nowhere to go, Mam; I have no choice."

"Well you had better find somewhere to live and quick, because I will let her stay here until you find somewhere, but this is by no means a permanent arrangement. I don't know what I am going to tell Evan. He is not going to like this at all." Polly wondered how she was going to break this news to him.

"He's no good, Polly. I'm sorry, love, you've given him so many chances and he throws them all back at you. How dare he want to bring that girl here? If he has no conscience that's his problem, but if you let him bring her here, don't expect me to welcome her."

Polly was surprised at Evan's adamant stance. He was such a mild mannered and kind person. It was the first time she had seen him so mad. Evan was just so fed up with Darren taking advantage of Polly and was concerned for her.

June moved in to the already crowded accommodation, and from the start she did little to help Polly. Mattie was furious, and she was always the one to say her mind. When Darren and June were still there several weeks later, she went to the store and took Darren to one side.

"You be out of here by next week, Darren, or I'll have you thrown out. Our mam's not your servant, and she's not going to fetch and carry for the pair of you. I mean it, Darren, you'll have me and Alf to deal with if you're not gone by next week. I will go and talk to your mam, June. She can't expect my mam to look after you. She will have to take you back." June was crying but Mattie took no notice of her tears.

Polly was in the shop, but she could hear the commotion and had a good idea what Mattie was doing. She hated conflict, and her stomach was churning. There were customers to serve and she could not leave. In her heart she knew Mattie was right, but Polly was so much more soft hearted and would have let them both stay, even at the risk of her own health. Evan was like Polly, and although he hated the situation, he would never have been so ruthless.

Darren had never won a battle with his older sister. When Mattie put her foot down, that was it. "It's no use, June. Once our Mattie has a bee in her bonnet, she will not let go. I'm going to go to your mam's tonight and have a talk with her."

Darren knew his sister, and she would be true to her word, so that night he went to June's parents and pleaded with them to take their daughter back while he found alternate accommodation.

Twenty-Five

MATTIE, ALF AND SANDRA

On one of the doctor's visits to see Sandra when she'd had the last bout of rheumatism, he called Mattie to one side.

"Mrs. Wetton, the damp in this house is not helping Sandra's health at all. Maybe you should think about trying to find somewhere that does not have this problem?"

"We have our name on a waiting list for one of those new council houses, Doctor, but they say it is a long list," Mattie said resignedly. She knew the damp was a problem, but there was nothing else they could do to improve the situation.

"Well, Mrs. Wetton, I have some good news for you. You have just gone to the top of the list. I will sign a form declaring your current accommodation is contributing to Sandra's recurring bouts of rheumatism." He pulled a form out of his bag and completed it on the spot.

Mattie could not believe that after months of being on a list that never seemed to get any shorter, they were now going to be given priority. It took less than a month for Mattie and Alf to receive a letter telling them that they had a council house. They were both really excited, as this was a brand new house in a new neighbourhood—a new start. Their daughter was going to Swanwick Hall Grammar, which pleased them both immensely, and there was a lot to do and plan. The only issue was that Sandra had recovered from the rheumatism much more slowly this time, and still did not seem back to her normal self.

Just prior to the big move, Sandra had three very important elocution exams and was also taking part in a production of Shakespeare's *Midsummer Night's Dream*. The exam was going to be based on theory, and also the recital of a long piece of prose which she had to memorise. It was not an effort on her part as she loved every minute of it. She knew she would pass the exams, but wanted to get an honours mark. She was thinking that because she enjoyed this so much, she might like to eventually work with people who were hearing impaired, or who had speech impediments.

One night as Sandra was sitting practicing her recital, she complained of pains in her back and torso. "It's not like rheumatism, mom," Sandra grimaced. "This is different. It's kind of itchy one minute and then hurts the next."

"Lift your blouse, and let me take a look." Mattie took one glance and realized this was not good. Sandra had a violent red rash that looked really very painful.

A trip to the doctor and Sandra was diagnosed. "Has she been under any stress recently, Mrs. Wetton?" The doctor asked that and numerous other questions before giving his verdict: "She has shingles, and the best thing I can prescribe is that she cut down on her academic activities for a while."

He saw Sandra's crestfallen face, and added. "It's just for a while, my dear. But I do think you have to make a choice. Concentrate on your new school and studies there, and cut out either your elocution or drama courses. Rome wasn't built in a day, my dear." He knew she was in considerable discomfort, and it would probably get worse before it got better.

Why does everything always have to go pear shaped? Sandra was more than disappointed, and knew that to drop out of the play at the last minute would really put a strain on the rest of the cast, and her understudy would really have to step up to the plate.

Auntie Elsie and Uncle Joe's was still a refuge, and Sandra spent the next few weeks as a constant visitor. It was not going to be easy moving to the other side of town and not being able to walk the few doors up the street to visit. Elsie and Joe were just as sad to hear of the move, but at the same time they were pleased for Sandra's health. Elsie hated to see Sandra staying in such a damp room when she was so sick. The day of the move came, and Sandra was feeling too sick to even notice the new surroundings. All she wanted to do was go to bed and hopefully fall asleep.

It took several more weeks for the shingles to finally get better. Fortunately, as it was a school break, Sandra had not missed any of her new school. The Swanwick Hall uniform was very smart, and Sandra loved it. The first day at her new school she felt very proud to wear the black skirt, white blouse with a black and red striped tie, and a cerise sweater. A black blazer, piped with red, and a red beret finished the ensemble. The only thing Sandra disliked was the red beret, but she soon found that the penalty for not wearing it was daunting. Uniform was to be worn to and from school and that meant from home to school and back, no exceptions. A few thousand lines later, Sandra still tried to get away with not wearing it, but inevitably got caught.

Swanwick Hall was an amazing building with a lot of history, which fascinated Sandra. It was built in 1690 by a wealthy industrialist by the name of John Turner. It was turned into a school in 1922, the year her mother was born. She felt very privileged to be able to study in such an amazing building, steeped in such history and intrigue.

There were many rumours of underground tunnels linking Swanwick Hall to Swanwick Hayes, which had been used for the internment of German and Italian POW's. During World War Two, a Luftwaffe officer by the name of Franz Von Werra had escaped from the Hayes, and who knows if he had spent time in those tunnels? For someone with a vivid imagination, the possibilities were endless. The architecture both inside and out was stunning. The exterior was mainly red brick with stone detailing, but a large portion of it was covered with ivy. The inside had a magnificent oak staircase which led to the principal's office. The path there was very well worn!

Sandra had now found a new interest: history. Swanwick was an escape for Sandra. Although it was just a few miles away from Ripley and the council estate, this was a lifetime away from her home life. Mattie was not dancing anymore and had settled down a little, but she was still far from maternal.

The job at Rowell's was good and the pay was adequate. Alf, always the master of his own home, never expected Mattie to use her pay for household upkeep. He gave her a housekeeping allowance each week, and what she earned was hers to spend as she pleased. Although Mattie did spend on clothes for herself and Sandra, she also managed to put a little away for the future. It had always been her dream to own a store of her own, but that really was a pipe dream. Each week she checked the papers for properties, but they were all well out of her means.

Mattie was the most senior and talented sales person the store had, and as such was exposed to all aspects of the "rag trade" as it was called. Mattie had done it all. She had accompanied Mr. Rowell on buying trips until he was comfortable in leaving most of the buying to her. Mattie had also developed a relationship with the representatives of all the big warehouses. Sometimes it was a business relationship and often it was a step beyond. What an opportunity to travel out of town, and have a legitimate reason to be wined and dined in the best hotels. She always engineered a great deal for her employer, however, and her keen eye for fashion ensured sales were great.

She did some modelling, some buying, and a lot of merchandising. Mattie had a knack of displaying merchandise in such a way that it drew customers into the store. Once they were in the store, they seldom left without a substantial purchase. Since the war had ended and rationing and frugality were over, there was an atmosphere of entitlement. Ladies liked to dress well and feel good about themselves, and their men folk were happy to see them looking so good. The only thing that bothered Mattie was that she still went to work by bus, and did not drive up in the big Bentley that her employer did each day. She was very confident that if she could help make him rich, she would be able to do this for herself.

Alf was still working at Aiton's Iron Foundry. The work was hard, especially on the back and the knees, as it involved hours of kneeling in wet sand. He never complained, and worked any extra shifts that came his way. Like most of his fellow workers, the reward was to gather in the pub at night to quench his thirst and have a game of darts. By now, Alf had almost as many medals for darts as Mattie had for her ballroom dancing. Sometimes Mattie went along with Alf, and sometimes she and her friend Maisie went to the pictures. Maisie was a local hairdresser, and the two had become friends over the years that she had styled Mattie's hair.

Mattie was just in the middle of serving a customer when she was summoned to Mr. Rowell's office. Mrs. Woolsey, the bookkeeper, looked quite serious as she came to fetch her. "Mattie, you're needed in the office."

"I'll be right there, Mrs. Woolsey, as soon as I've finished with my customer," Mattie continued helping the customer to try on an expensive coat.

"Joyce will take over, Mattie. You are needed right now."

Mattie was not happy to relinquish this client, as this would be a feather in her cap and some commission to make such a good sale. But the look on Mrs. Woolsey's face said this was not negotiable, so she reluctantly followed her to the office.

Charley Rowell stood up from behind his big desk and came over to Mattie with a very serious look on his face.

"Mattie, I'm afraid there has been an accident, and Alf has been taken to hospital. A chain fell from a crane and Alf was hit by it. He is in Derby Royal Infirmary, and if you get your coat, I will take you there right away."

It was as if Mattie's world had come to an end in an instant. Alf was invincible. He was her rock and her anchor, and for all of her flirtations and affairs, he was still the only man she loved.

She had always wondered what it would be like to ride in a Bentley, but strangely now, she did not even notice her surroundings. She was counting the traffic lights, and each second they were delayed on their way to Derby. Charley was getting to be an old man and his driving skills were significantly diminished. He erred on the side of caution, so to Mattie it felt as if she could have walked there faster.

Mr. Rowell dropped her off at the entrance to the hospital. "Mattie, phone me if there is anything that I can do."

Mattie ran as fast as her legs would carry her to the front reception desk, where she was directed to a curtained off cubicle. Alf was white as a ghost and had a huge lump on his head and bruising down the side of his face.

"It's all right, love. The doctor says I have a skull like an elephant, and there is no internal bleeding." Alf tried to smile, but his face told a different story. Mattie looked questioningly at the doctor who was assessing him.

"He's right, Mrs. Wetton. He is a very lucky man. A chain fell from a high crane and he was hit with three links. He has the bump on his head and two significant welts on his back. He was knocked unconscious, and even though he did come around quickly, we have to keep him in hospital overnight for observation and more tests and x-rays. It really is a wonder it did not smash his skull."

Mattie threw her arms around Alf, and he grimaced with pain. "Steady on, love, easy does it."

The hospital allowed Mattie to stay until after visiting hours were over and Alf had been through a battery of tests. The verdict was the same. There were no broken bones, but massive bruising. The concussion was still a concern, and much to Alf's dismay, they refused to let him leave that night.

The following morning he managed to get himself out of bed and was dressed and sitting on his bed when the doctor came to make his rounds. "And where do you think you are going, Mr. Wetton?" the doctor frowned.

"Other than a bloody headache the size of Ilkley Moor, I am fine. I'll be better off at home than here in this racket. It's like being in Piccadilly Station. There are bells and sirens and folks screaming. I want my own bed and some peace and quiet."

The doctor had to smile, as he often wondered how patients were expected to recover in such a frenetic environment. The old hospital was large and badly in need of some major renovations. Despite its size, it was always overcrowded. The worst area of all was that in which Alf had been kept overnight. It was little more than a wide corridor flanked by curtained off beds, and it was the main pathway to the emergency operating rooms.

After a thorough exam and a review of all of the x-rays and tests, he agreed to let Alf go home, as long as he assured the doctor there would be someone to pick him up, and someone to stay with him during his recovery.

For the next two weeks, Alf looked worse before he looked better. The bruising had turned every shade from green to yellow to purple and black. His friend Tom was a constant visitor, and did a lot to buck up Alf's spirits.

"You look like you've done a few rounds with Rocky Marciano," he laughed as he examined Alf's bruises.

Tom had talked to some of Alf's friends from Aiton's, and they said they thought he was dead when the chain fell. It was a huge chain that had not been hooked up correctly, and when the crane operator moved the boom, it jiggled free and crashed to the ground.

"If you weren't built like a brick shit house, Alf, you'd be a gonner."

"Thanks for that, Tom. You sure know how to make a chap feel better."

"They're saying you have a good chance to claim some compensation, Alf, as it was negligence, and the company will have to pay out."

"It was Jack Crawley driving the crane, Tom, and he has four kids to look after. I'm not going to drop him into it. I'll be right in a couple weeks, and if they pay me for my time off, then I'm not going to make any waves. The super has already been to see me, and they are worried they will lose their safety record if I make a report."

Alf kept his word and resumed work as soon as he was able. Mattie and Sandra had never seen Alf anything but big and strong, and even now he refused to be coddled at all. "Stop fussing over me. I stand a much better chance of getting better if you just leave me alone." It was just the way he dealt with recovery. Although he appreciated their concern, he knew this was something he had to work through alone. His back ached far more than he let anyone know, and he was afraid that if he didn't keep moving, it would fuse together in one spot. In the quiet of the bedroom he did every stretching exercise he could possibly manage. His efforts were rewarded, and the day finally came when he could move free of pain. He gave no thought to the "what ifs"—such as "What if it comes back when you get older?" He was just shy of his fortieth birthday, and he was invincible.

As soon as he was able, he decided to take Sandra with him to visit his mom. He knew how worried she had been, but due to her health she had not been able to visit him. Julia was now suffering with all the side effects of her years of diabetes. Her eye sight was now to a point where she was almost blind. Cataracts on both eyes made her feel as if she was looking through a thick fog, and she was scared of losing her sight altogether if she opted for surgery. The years of twice daily injections had left her arms, legs, and buttocks like pincushions. Walking was difficult and painful, and now, to make matters worse, she had started to lose her hearing. When she was unable to see to read, knit, or sew anymore, her joy was to listen to the radio. She especially loved the story hour.

When Alf and Sandra arrived, she did not hear the door open, and when they walked in she was sitting with her ear almost touching the little old battery radio. He was sad to see her this way. Since his dad had died, Julia spent hours alone. His sister Vera and her husband Joe visited when they could, and Alf tried to visit at least once or twice a month, but she still spent many days and nights alone.

Her face lit up when she saw them and she struggled to her feet to give them both a hug.

"Come here, let me have a look at you," Julia pulled Alf towards her, struggling to see a clear picture of him.

"I'm all right, mam. I'm back at work, and the doctor says I am one hundred percent recovered. How do you fancy some fish and chips, mam? I'll pop down to Greenhill Lane and get us a take out." He knew this was a treat for Julia. "Sandra, you set the table for your grandma and put the kettle on. I'll be back before it's boiled."

Sandra set the table, and kept Julia intrigued with all the tales of her new school, half of which Julia heard and half of which she only guessed at. It was lovely to have such life in the house again, and when Alf returned he was happy to see his mam enjoying the company of her granddaughter.

The visit was over far too soon for Julia, but the memory of it she would relive long after they had gone home. Julia was pleased to see Sandra was growing up to be a sensible young lady, and that she was not at all like Mattie in her ways. Other than her green eyes, Sandra had little of Mattie's features. Trying to find a likeness to either of her parents was difficult. Alf often used to say that when Sandra was born the mould was broken, as she was one of a kind. He was not far wrong. Julia missed Sandra's overnight visits, but knew that school work came first.

Before re-sitting her Swanwick Entrance Exam, Sandra had also been taking some extra tutoring on weekends, which did not leave her a lot of free time. Sandra's great aunt Kitty was a school teacher who lived at Stony Ford with her husband Billy, who farmed and also ran a pub. Kitty was Lucy Lambert's daughter, and just like her mother, she was a brilliant and hard-working woman. Somehow Kitty found time to teach, help around the farm, and work with struggling students. Sandra loved her and also the visits to the farm. It meant a bus ride to Langley Mill and then a long walk down a lonely lane to The Boat Inn. Kitty had a son called Russ, and Sandra thought he was really something. He was a big sandy haired boy about three or four years older than she was. He worked outside with his dad on the farm, so unlike the city boys he had a healthy rugged complexion. He was a bit of a handful and always into some scrape or other. None of his escapades were malicious, just the typical high jinks of a sixteen year old trying to be anything but a teacher's pet. Russ barely noticed the twelve year old leggy girl who came for lessons after school and on weekends. He was more interested in sneaking a pitcher of ale and hanging out with his friends down by the canal. Kitty enjoyed the tutoring, and was happy Sandra quickly picked up the subjects she had struggled with after missing so much school time throughout the preceding years.

Sandra did well at Swanwick, and life was starting to improve for her. No more Moseley Street, and now she could care less if her parents were home or not. She was still afraid of the dark, and the nightmares never went away, but she was starting to emerge as her own independent being.

.

Twenty-Six

SANDRA MEETS MIKE

Sports day was fast approaching at Swanwick, and Sandra was entered into several events. Her best events were hurdles and high jump, but she was scheduled to participate in a tumbling and pommel horse competition. The hockey uniform was very smart. It consisted of a very fashionable grey divided skirt and a white blouse and red jumper. The athletics uniform was navy knickers and white shirts. Sandra hated the knickers as they were usually a bit baggy, so Sandra along with some of the other girls had found a way of twisting a knot in one side to tighten them and make them look a little more chic.

The boys at Swanwick loved sports day as it was a chance for them to show off their ability and also to ogle the girls in their navy knickers! Sandra, Sylvia and Shelly, the "S List," were usually to be found together somewhere, and more often than not, they were up to some sort of high jinks. They had noticed a group of senior boys standing on the side lines and cheering. These boys were two grades ahead, and out of the short pants and into grey slacks and white shirts.

"Hey Sylv, I think that one with the red hair has his eye on you," Sandra giggled, as she saw a boy with a shock of bright orange-red hair looking in their direction.

Sylvia swatted Sandra across the backside, "He's got his eye on you. That good looking one with the dark hair is watching me."

Several days later Sandra was passed a note that said, "Please meet me in the rose garden." It was signed, "Mike Lewis." Sandra had no idea who Mike Lewis was, other than the fact that he was one of the senior boys.

"Who is this Mike Lewis?" she asked around her own grade. The answers left her even more confused. He was everything from short and fat to tall and slim, and the truth of the matter was that no one was sure who he was.

Sandra had never had a boyfriend, and although several of her friends had crushes on some of the seniors, as far as she knew, none were actually seeing each other.

As she was going between classes the next day, Shelly pointed out who she thought was Mike Lewis. He was average height and build, and his only distinguishing feature was that he had a very bad pock marked skin. Sandra looked at him and he smiled back, a really nice smile. Sandra thought he looked like a nice person, and she thought he must feel very self-conscious about his skin. She knew what it was like to feel the odd one out, as until Swanwick, she had never seemed to fit in anywhere.

Sandra found the "go between" and passed a note back to say she would meet him at break the following day.

"You are really going to meet him?" Shelly and Sylvia questioned.

"I'm only going to go and say hi to him. He looks like a nice enough person. I'm not going to say no, just because he isn't what you lot think of as handsome."

That morning Sandra second guessed her decision, but decided she would keep her word.

Break time came and Sandra walked out to the rose garden. It was a beautiful rectangle, planted with colourful and sweet smelling roses within the school grounds. She was there first and was sitting on one of the benches admiring the roses when she saw the most handsome boy walking towards her.

"Hi Sandra. I'm Mike Lewis."

That was all it took. Shelly had been wrong. The boy with the pock marked face was a friend of Mike.

Mike was close to his full height at around six feet. He had dark brown hair that was slicked back, but with a cute lock that hung over his forehead. His smile was contagious, and he had a little cleft in his chin.

Sandra liked him instantly and the break time passed far too quickly. He had asked her to meet him to request she go to the senior dance with him. Apparently he had noticed her for the first time at Sports Day, and as he confessed later, "It was love at first sight."

Sandra had no idea what she was going to wear for the dance, as it was the first school dance she had ever been asked to attend. The worst thing was that she would be one of the few juniors there. "It's the school dance next week, mom, and what shall I wear?" she asked Mattie.

Mattie looked at her daughter who was now turning into a young woman. She did not like the fact it made her feel old to have a daughter growing up so quickly. Sandra took after both of her grandmas in that she had well rounded breasts and a tiny waist and hips. She had inherited Mattie's long legs and green eyes. Mattie was pleased that Sandra up until now had shown no interest in boys. She seemed to be unaware of the fact her daughter was turning into a very attractive young lady.

"I'm going to Nottingham on a buying trip next week, and I'll find something for you," Mattie said as she looked up from her novel. Sandra would have much preferred to be able to choose her own outfit, but at least she thought her mom would find something nice in Nottingham.

Two days before the dance, Mattie came home with the dress. She pulled it out of the box with a big flourish. "Here, go and try it on. It should fit perfectly. I had the lady at the warehouse try it on for me. She was just about your size."

Sandra looked in horror at the bubble gum pink profusion of net. It was as far from what she would have chosen as possible. Her face fell and she did not know what to say. "It's very pink," was all she could muster.

"It's young and pretty, just like you," Mattie smiled.

A compliment from her mother was something that did not happen every day, so Sandra dutifully went upstairs to try it on. Mattie had been right, it did fit perfectly. She stood on her bed to take a better look in the dresser mirror.

I look like I should be set on the top of a Christmas tree, she thought with dismay. *Talk about the sugar plum fairy!* Sandra would have much preferred something in a more neutral tone and with far fewer layers of net.

When she went downstairs, Mattie was delighted with the result. "You look lovely, Sandra. It is perfect." Mattie saw what she wanted to see, a very young school girl attending her first dance.

They both had different views of the dress, and the truth was somewhere in the middle. It was a pretty dress and the huge skirt showed off Sandra's tiny waist. The overall result was far more pleasing than Sandra realized. Self-confidence did not come easy for her. After years of being an only child, and never feeling as if she fit in anywhere, the transition to confident independence did not come easy.

"I'm going to stay at Grandma Wetton's after the dance, Mam," Sandra said as she packed her things for school and the dance.

Mattie was pleased that Sandra was going to spend time with Julia, and did not suspect that Sandra had an ulterior motive. Mike lived in Leabrooks, which was right next door to Riddings, and it meant that the two could see each other during the weekend.

Mike was waiting at the entrance to the dance, and he had on a really nice pair of slacks and a sports jacket. His eyes lit up when he saw Sandra, and it would not have mattered if she was wearing a sack, he only had eyes for her. The hall was noisy and crowded, and trying to talk over the din was impossible.

"Let's go outside and get some fresh air," Mike smiled as he took Sandra's hand. They sat in the rose garden and talked until the dance was almost over. Sandra told him she was going to stay with her gran in Riddings, and he was happy to know he would be able to see her over the weekend. They decided they would take the bus back to Leabrooks, and then Mike would walk her home to Riddings.

Right from the first day they met, Mike was her big brother, confidante, and very best friend. He was very mature for his age, which may have had something to do with the fact that his only sibling, Josie, was seven years older. His mother had given birth to a son who had died shortly after birth, and when she was suffering depression, her doctor advised her to have another child. Along came Mike about eleven months after the death of his brother. His parents were good people and certainly made sure he grew up with good values and principles.

It was quite a walk from Leabrooks to Riddings, and Sandra was wearing her first pair of kitten heels, but she did not complain as it was wonderful to be walking hand in hand with someone she was so comfortable with. They finally arrived at the Red Rec, and not wanting the night to end, they sat on the swings and talked for another hour, before Sandra realized her gran would be wondering where she was. Mike walked her to the stile and gave her a gentle kiss on the cheek. He watched as she disappeared into her gran's, wishing he had maybe aimed for the lips, but it was early days. He did not want to do anything to risk jeopardising this new relationship.

Sandra and Mike became the best of friends, and from that time on were inseparable. Even though he was almost two years older than Sandra, she was his first girlfriend, and he had already made up his mind that she would be his only girl.

Julia was waiting up for Sandra and wanted to hear all about the dance and who she had danced with. Sandra was only too happy to relate the night's events, leaving out the fact that she had walked from Leabrooks and had her first kiss, even if it was on the cheek.

"I went with Mike Lewis from Leabrooks, Gran, and he is a really nice boy."

"Mike Lewis, is that Sid Lewis's boy?" Julia's eyes lit up.

"Yes Gran. His Mom and Dad live opposite the bus stop in Lea brooks."

"They're a nice family. Sid has worked for Leland for a long while, and everyone there seems to like him very much. His granddad used to be a bit of a rake, though, and your granddad Whiskers and him used to get into a few fights on a Saturday night." Julia laughed with the memory of the two larger than life figures coming out of the Greenhill Hotel after a few pints too many. Julia was always happy that Tom had never drunk more than the odd social drink. He was not one for going to the pub; he was happy with his cigarettes and a walk down his prized garden or a few hours in his allotment. She missed him so much, and her eyes misted over with the thoughts of him.

"Well, young lady. It's off to bed for both of us." Julia lit the candle and up the steep stairs they both went. Sandra noticed her gran was having more difficulty than usual with the stairs, and wished there was something that could make life easier for her gran.

Sandra and her gran slept in the same bed, and Sandra did not mind at all as Julia would often take the opportunity to talk about her life and what it was like as a child. Julia loved to have someone to talk to, and Sandra fell asleep with Julia still talking. It was so comforting to know that someone was there by your side when you fell asleep. Sandra rarely had a nightmare at Riddings.

Twenty-Seven

MURPHY'S LAW

Sandra could not believe how her life had turned around: A school where she had friends and enjoyed her lessons. A boyfriend who was everything that she had ever dreamed of—and she would have loved him even if he had not been handsome; he really was her knight in shining armour. When she was with him she felt totally safe, and most of all she felt loved. She still missed the drama classes, but had a great English teacher by the name of Mr. Holt. He recognised Sandra's passion for English and Theatre and gave her constant challenges in assignments.

Sandra's fifteenth birthday was fast approaching, and she had changed a lot over the last year. Her self-confidence was much improved, and she had developed her own sense of style. Once out of school uniform, it would have been quite easy to mistake her for being at least eighteen. She had inherited some of Mattie's flare for dress, and although not nearly as flamboyant as Mattie, it was just as stylish. The fact that Mattie worked at Rowell's and could get discounts on clothing allowed her to get good deals. Sandra preferred coordinating pieces in toning shades of the same color, but she would always add just one eye catching accessory. She'd had to grow up quickly at Moseley Street, fending for herself from an early age. At the time it was often very sad and lonely, but the experience was not altogether a loss. Sandra was perfectly at home talking to anyone, and her level of maturity was far greater than her chronological years.

It was Friday night, and Sandra came home from school swinging her beret in one hand and her satchel in the other. She had quite a bit of homework to do, but then on Saturday she was going to visit Julia and see Mike. Her mom and dad were sitting at the table with a pile of papers spread in front of them.

"It's a steal, Alf. Let's go and have a look it tomorrow. Someone is going to snap this up if we don't act fast." Mattie was looking at an

202

SANDY LATKA

ad in the local paper.

"It'll take just about all our savings, Mattie, and it would be a big move." Alf was not convinced that this was the right time to make such a change.

"What are you talking about?" Sandra had heard just enough of the conversation to realize they were discussing a potential move.

"Nothing for you to worry about, Sandra. Your dad and I are just doing a little dreaming."

Later that night when Mattie and Alf went out, Sandra looked at the papers and saw that an ad for a store had been circled. It was a corner shop on Peet Street in Derby.

"How can they even think about this?" Sandra was distraught as she knew this meant she would have to change schools, and she would be miles away from all of her friends and Mike. That night she had a fitful sleep and awoke with the usual nightmare.

Alf gave in to Mattie's wishes, and the two of them caught the early bus to Derby. Sandra took the bus in the opposite direction and went to Leabrooks. Mike had asked her to come and meet his parents, so she had taken a little extra time to get ready. She wished she was not so down the dumps about the prospect of moving.

Is it impossible for things to ever go smoothly? Sandra thought to herself as she passed by the familiar landmarks en route. She stared through the bus window as it passed Swanwick Hall School, and she could not bear to think of having to leave.

Mike was waiting at the bus stop in Leabrooks, and they walked hand in hand across the road to his mom and dad's. Annie was a quiet motherly type of lady and made Sandra feel at home instantly. Sid was suffering from emphysema, from years of driving poorly ventilated heavy lorries throughout the war. He had quite a dry sense of humour though, and Annie gave him a few raised eyebrows at some of his attempts to break the ice. The visit went well, but Mike could see there was something weighing on Sandra's mind. He had always been able to know instinctively if there was something wrong.

"What is it? I know that there is something bothering you," Mike asked as soon as they were alone.

Sandra was almost in tears. "They have gone to Derby to look at a shop, and my mom wants to move there."

"They can't move your school now when you are doing all the work for GCE's. What are they thinking?"

"That's the point, Mike. They aren't thinking of anything but themselves. I have no choice but to go wherever they decide to move. I will be the last person they think of." Sandra was feeling very sorry for herself. "How are we going to see each other if I move to Derby?"

"It does not matter where you move. Derby is not that far away, and the bus stops right across the road. I will not let them separate us." Mike was adamant he would find a way to continue seeing Sandra. "They haven't got the store yet anyway, and maybe they will decide not to move. Come on, cheer up. You look smashing. Let's go into Alfreton and look round the market." He knew that would cheer Sandra up, as she loved to browse through the market stalls. Marks and Spencer's rejected items were sold on the market at a great discount, and they had the most elegant lingerie.

After a few hours browsing the market, with a stop for tea and a scone, it was time for Sandra to catch the bus home. Mike had been right, and she was feeling much better when she finally got back to the house. Her feeling of relief did not last long, as shortly afterwards Mattie and Alf came back with the news they had leased the store; bought all the stock, fixtures and fittings; and would be taking over in sixty days.

"I will need your help, Sandra. There is a lot to do. We have to clear out all the old stock and bring in new. The place needs cleaning from top to bottom. It will be spring break at school, so the timing is perfect."

"How can you say that? What about Swanwick? You just expect me to change schools?"

Mattie had not given it much thought and had assumed that Sandra would be able to travel to Swanwick from Derby.

"We will sort all that out in the next few weeks. You will like Derby, and it is a great opportunity for us to have our own business."

It was not possible to commute from Derby to Swanwick. There was a rule that if you lived in the borough you had to go to school in the borough. Mattie met with the Derby School board, and the only option was an all-girls grammar school called Homelands. There was no choice; Sandra was 15 years old and had to move with her parents. The introductory meeting did not go well. The head mistress was a very stern looking matronly woman with her salt and pepper hair pulled back into a tight bun. She was devoid of any makeup, and her icy stare did not miss a thing about Mattie's appearance. Mattie was wearing a stylish coral suit with the new fashion peplum at the waist and a flip pleated bottom on the skirt. It was quite short, and Mattie wore cream high heeled shoes which accentuated her long slender legs. She had recently adopted a new hairstyle, which again was right up to the minute fashion. It was called a continental cut and was quite short with little curls that hugged her face. This week it was coloured a mixture of brown and gold. She was everything the headmistress wasn't, and it was obvious from the first moment that each mistrusted the other.

Sandra was not allowed to wear makeup, and other than a tube of lipstick, which she kept hidden and wore when out of sight of home, she was always au natural. The head mistress turned her attention to Sandra.

"I don't know what your uniform was at Swanwick, but this year you will still be required to wear a regulation gymslip and white shirt, with sensible black lace up shoes and white socks. You can come to school next week and be fitted with a gymslip."

Sandra was about to protest, but looking at the face before her, thought better of it. Once outside, Sandra vented her anger.

"How does she mean, a gymslip? I have never had to wear a gymslip at Swanwick. I'm not going to wear a stupid gymslip. Does she think I am ten years old?"

"She was a bit of a dragon, I admit," Mattie said "She sized me up and down and back again. Don't worry, Sandra, it's only for the rest of the year, and then you move into the higher form where they wear skirts."

Mattie knew this was going to be a big change, but thought Sandra would take it in stride. In truth, Sandra had not given them much trouble through her early teens. Mattie thought back to her own teen years, and thanked her stars Sandra was nowhere near as much trouble as she had been.

"Come on, Sandra, we have work to do." Sandra had not yet seen the store and they were about to move in.

It was a big store front on the corner of Peet Street with three large windows full of merchandise. Two windows were full of baby clothes, kitchen towels, and a mishmash of odds and ends. The third window, which was around the corner, was full of knitting wool and material. The windows all needed a thorough cleaning, and the shop floor was faded worn linoleum. Mattie did not see any of that, as she saw what it could be. Sandra walked through the store, and it really did not get any better. The store was lined with dusty shelves full of boxes, and the doorway which led from the store to the back of the property was hung with a dark and dusty curtain.

The next room was long and narrow with more shelving on one side and the shop window on the other. Walking through that there was a small living room and through that an even smaller kitchen with a bathroom off to one side of it. It was all one long corridor of rooms.

"Where are the bedrooms?" Sandra asked as she looked around in dismay.

"You can sleep in the room next to the shop, and Dad and I will have a sofa bed in the living room. We will make it work. When the store starts to do well we can look for somewhere close by to rent, but this will be it for the time being, and we just have to make the most of it."

"Can this get any worse?" Sandra mumbled under her breath.

That day their first customer came in as they were starting to clean out the shelves.

"I want a bobbin of cotton. Don't give me one out of the window either; they're all faded." Mattie smiled nicely and assured the customer she would give her some cotton out of the new stock.

"And you had better move that doll out of the window. It's been sitting there in the same clothes for two years as I know of!" the disgruntled customer complained. "It's a good job you're the only store in these parts."

Mattie was used to dealing with difficult customers, and was not at all fazed by the remarks. She knew there was no other store like this one for at least two miles, and that was another reason she had decided upon this one. Very few people in the area had cars, and they either relied on a bus or had to walk to the stores.

"Just tell your friends to watch the windows. All of the old stock is going and will be replaced with new stock. Everything in the store will be on sale this weekend."

It was a stroke of luck, as the customer was one of the factory girls who worked at a factory just down the street. Most of the girls had to pass the store on their way to work and back. That day Sandra and Mattie worked until it was late into the night. Their only customer had been the one for a bobbin of cotton. They had bought two cream buns and a bag of tea from the grocery store on the corner of the next block. It had cost more than their one sale.

Mattie was silently praying she had made the right decision. She would have lease payments to make and stock to buy very quickly. Her ace in the hole was that she had a very good "in" with a warehouse in Derby that knew her from her work at Rowell's. The company dealt with a lot of imported goods, and the prices were much cheaper than a lot of their competitors. Knowing her skill in sales, they had agreed to let her take the first shipment on consignment. Before the weekend, true to her word, Sandra and Mattie took all the old stock out of the three windows, cleaned everything until it gleamed, and then re-arranged everything in one window with a sign saying, "Everything must go. New stock arriving Monday." The two other windows were covered with brown paper and a sign saying, "Watch this Space."

Miraculously, everything went, even the doll, complete with the baby outfit it was modelling. "If the price is right you can sell anything," Mattie said with confidence.

The new stock was carefully chosen to suit the market place they were in. Factory girls needed nylon stockings, sanitary products, and pretty but inexpensive clothes. Rivlin could fill the bill on all of that, and the windows were now very artfully displayed with eye catching merchandise. Sales were great, and Mattie learned that many of the factory girls liked to knit and sew, so she devised a plan of sales that would ensure repeat business. She bought some up to the minute pattern books and paired them with great quality and reasonably priced wools. A big sign read, "Lay-by your wool and purchase as needed. Up to six weeks lay-by."

The knitting wool business alone was so good that Alf had to build a series of pigeon holes to store all the customers' wool. Sandra's room was more like a stockroom than a bedroom, and her single bed was pushed up against the boarded back of the shop window.

The following week Sandra went to try on the school regulation gymslip. It was dark navy with three inverted pleats that ran from the neck to the hem, and was fastened at the waist with a sash. It was certainly not designed for someone with Sandra's shape. The pleats all pulled out across the bust, and because of that the front of the skirt came up in a half moon shape at the front. Different sizes were tried and nothing fit. The head mistress reluctantly agreed to let Sandra wear her Swanwick skirt until a gymslip that fit could be ordered.

From the very first class it was obvious the standard of education was not nearly as high as Swanwick, and Sandra was ahead of the class she had been placed in. It did not help to make friends when you were seen to be smarter than your classmates. Even the teachers often ignored Sandra's outstretched hand with, "Put your hand down, Wetton. We know you know the answer."

What is all this with calling everyone by their surnames? It sounds as if we are in the army, Sandra thought to herself. She was totally miserable. The new gymslip had still not materialized, and at assembly the head mistress called Sandra out and inquired about the regulation uniform. Sandra was mortified when she was handed an old uniform that had been pulled from the lost and found.

"Put this on and wear it until you get the Homelands Uniform. I will not have you out of uniform any longer."

Sandra took the uniform, which smelled of stale perspiration, as she had no option but to wear it. It came to about six inches above her knees, and the pleats were stretched to capacity. Sandra said nothing, but walked out of the office, and out of the school.

I'm never going back. I hate this place. It's a damn jail. She caught the bus back to the store and walked in, ready for the fight of her life. Sandra was trembling with rage and also at the possibility of the consequences for what she had just done. There could be no negotiation on this. Maybe she had a little Lambert blood after all, when her back was against a wall? Mattie came into the store when she heard the shop bell ring, and was shocked to see Sandra there at 10:00 in the morning.

"What on earth are you wearing?" Mattie exclaimed.

Sandra had sat on the bus trying to pull the horrible gymslip over her knees, and had been sure everyone could smell the old rag. By the time she had walked from the bus stop, she was in an even worse temper. "It's coming off right now. It stinks, and she made me wear it. I'm not going back and no one can make me. I'll quit school altogether if they try and make me go back there. I hate it! I hate it!" Sandra was crying with frustration, embarrassment and anger.

If Sandra was mad, Mattie was even more irate. She was in Sandra's corner on this one. She knew Sandra was having a tough time fitting in, and when she saw the uniform she had been made to wear, she was furious. "You had to wear this on the way home? I'll call the school right away. This is disgusting, and not even sanitary."

"I don't care what they say. I am NOT going back. I hate the school and the teachers. I'm not learning anything, and I'll go back to a regular secondary school rather than stay there." Sandra was defiant.

"There's no need to get upset. You are not quitting Grammar School, but we will find another one more like Swanwick."

It took a visit from the head of the school board and a lot of Mattie's persuasive skills to come to a solution. There was only one co-educational school in the borough that was the same level of education as Swanwick, and that was Joseph Wright Art School. There was just one catch—Sandra would have to pass an art exam prior to being accepted. Sandra was not particularly worried about this, as art was one of her best subjects.

The meeting with Mr. Bull, the headmaster, was arranged, and Sandra liked him instantly. He was a big jolly looking man and had a nice smile. He handed Sandra a book, *The History of Art,* which contained several photographs of famous paintings. "Choose a painting and copy it as best you can, Sandra. You can use the desk by the window."

Sandra browsed through the book and chose a picture by Goya. It was entitled *Dona Isabel de Porcel,* and there was something about the beautiful lady that fired Sandra's imagination. Mr. Bull glanced over at the intent young girl several times, but she was lost in her work.

Eventually she looked up with a smile and handed Mr. Bull the finished sketch. It was far beyond his expectations, and he reached over and shook her hand.

"Welcome to Joseph Wright, Sandra. I am sure you will enjoy our school, and be a great addition to our student body."

Sandra loved the school from the first minute she walked in and saw the old building's interior. It was not as grand as Swanwick, but it was full of great paintings and history. The best thing of all was that the school uniform was amazingly flexible. The only stipulation with the girls' dresses was that they were made in the same color and fabric, which was a beautiful cornflower blue poplin. The girls were encouraged to design their own as long as they were of a certain length and had a modest neckline. One of the classes had design and drafting lessons, and Sandra soon teamed up with a fellow student to collaborate on a dress. Linda was great at drafting, and Sandra was very good at design, so between the two they came up with a very stylish dress. It was perfect for Sandra, as the empire waist allowed her to have a comfortable fit across the bosom and then a form fitting torso before it came to a gathered waist and full skirt. It was a year of many petticoats, and the skirt accommodated that perfectly.

Sandra missed the daily visits with Mike, and there was no telephone to keep in touch. It was not easy to maintain their friendship, but they did it. Either Mike caught a bus to Derby or Sandra caught a bus to Leabrooks. By now Mattie and Alf both knew about Mike and liked him. Mattie, remembering her own escapades, was very strict with Sandra, and discouraged her from having any male friends, but somehow she was always trusting of Mike. Her trust was not misplaced. He was a perfect gentleman and everyone in the family liked him.

Twenty-Eight

SPAIN

Sandra had fit into Joseph Wright perfectly and loved all of the classes. Everything centered on the arts in all of their forms— pottery, dress design, interior design, architecture and the study of the history of art. There was also plenty of emphasis on the core subjects, and the result was an amazingly well-rounded education. The only subject Sandra struggled with was pottery. Not that she did not like it, but it was a combination of where the class was held, and her failure to produce anything that survived the kiln. She made some amazing vases and bowls, all with intricate designs, which looked great before the kiln. For some reason they all shattered in the firing. Not one piece ever survived.

The pottery class was held in the basement of Derbyshire Art College, and it was very hot and stuffy down there. Each month Sandra had an awful time with her periods. It was impossible to disguise her agony as she had tremendous stomach cramps and uncontrollable vomiting. On one occasion she threw up all over the pottery teacher, and was transported home by ambulance after passing out on the floor. After that she dreaded the pottery classes.

It was no comfort being at home, as she was in the room next to the shop and the doorbell rang constantly. A cold draft would waft right through the room every time the door was opened. At least she could lie still with a hot water bottle and suffer without an audience.

That year the senior class were planning a trip to Spain and there was a lot of excitement. Sandra wished she could go, but it was only open to 16 year olds and she was not yet 16. Just a few weeks before the trip, an announcement was made that a student had to drop out of the trip and there was one place left open. It was offered to the next lower grade, and the first person to bring in the money for the trip would be allowed to go.

Sandra raced home as fast as she could and begged to have the chance to take the last ticket. She had been working in the shop quite a lot when Mattie and Alf were out, and had never expected any payment, and she hoped they would consider this when she asked for the money for the trip.

"I have to take the money in tomorrow, Mam, as it is the first one who pays that gets to go."

Mattie had not made a bank deposit and she knew there was enough money in the cash box to pay for the trip. The shop had been doing really well, so much so that they were in the process of leasing another store on the other side of town. Alf had decided to quit Aiton's and run the second store. He had often helped Mattie out on a weekend, and he was liked a lot by all the factory girls. They were not a bit shy going in to buy their toiletries and pantyhose. Alf had an easy way with customers and they all loved him. The new store was also close to a factory, and as there was not another store in the area, they knew it would do well.

"I'll have to ask your dad, but if he says yes, then you can go." Mattie thought this was a great opportunity for Sandra. Mattie would have loved to travel, but the furthest she had been was many years ago to Guernsey to spend time with her friend, Marjory Peel. She would always remember how much she had loved the trip. Alf agreed and the next day Sandra was at Mr. Bull's office before he was.

Sandra was now the same size as Mattie, so a wardrobe for the trip was comprised of an assortment of Mattie's clothes and Sandra's. Mike was a little concerned that Sandra was going so far away, and he was afraid she would meet someone else and forget about him. In his eyes she was perfection, and he could not imagine anyone not falling for her. Sandra had never seen herself that way, but Spain was to alter all of that.

It was only a two week vacation, but Sandra had never had such an awakening. It all started with the trip there, when she found herself the center of attention of several of the boys on the trip. The attention was very flattering, but in comparison to Mike there was no one she was even remotely attracted to. Once in Spain, they were all accommodated in a Pension near a large market square close to the Ramblers. Sandra shared a room with three other girls, and they were all excited about the adventure. They lay awake the first night telling stories and giggling until the early hours of the next day. Sandra was the first to get up, and threw back the slatted wooden shutters to greet the day. She almost caused a traffic jam, as the policeman standing on a podium outside the window looked up to see a scantily clad young lady standing just a few feet above him.

"Oh god!" she gasped, and ducked down to grab a housecoat. "There's a traffic cop standing right outside our window." Everyone was up in an instant and laughing hysterically as they all went to have a look at the handsome policeman.

The holiday was amazing and gave Sandra her first taste of travel and adventure. Until now vacations had been to Hunstanton, or Skegness, or some other seaside town along the coast of England. A bull fight, an optional excursion, was scheduled for the following week. It was not on Sandra's list of favourite things to do, as she hated any form of cruelty and had no desire to go and watch a bull be tormented. At breakfast that day there was a very handsome Spaniard sitting at a table nearby. Sandra had noticed him watching her throughout the week, and they had exchanged smiles and greetings in the morning.

When a waitress came to the table and passed Sandra a note, she had to smile. The note was written in poor English, but was understandable: "Senorita come for walk with me on my motorbike?" and there were three boxes: "Yes," "No," and "Maybe."

Sandra looked at the young man and ticked "Maybe." She would make it her business to find out more about him before she would make a commitment. It did sound like fun to go touring the area on a motorbike, however. It turned out he was the nephew of the lady who owned the Pension, and was apprenticing at a local leather smith's.

After everyone left for the bull fight, Sandra went for a "walk" on the motorbike. It was an amazing day, and she saw beautiful little villages and farms and lots of local people who all made her very welcome. They stopped at a small restaurant high on a hill, at which the owner had chained two large glass wine casks to a table outside. His attraction was that if anyone could lift both casks, they could drink all they wanted.

"Come on, pretty lady, let me see you drink," he laughed. Naturally he had no idea that this was a 15 year old school girl. Sandra was wearing one of Mattie's dresses that was pale blue and yellow and showed off her suntanned and toned body.

Sandra laughingly complied and tried to lift the casks. It was impossible and she was throwing up her arms in defeat, when two big arms wrapped around her and the owner raised both casks to her lips. She was drenched in red wine! Everyone thought it was great fun as they watched her trying to get out the wine stains with the water hose that had been left purposely by the post.

Thankfully the day was perfect, and the young Spaniard was a wonderful companion. Sandra had never given a thought to any danger she might have encountered in accepting a ride with a stranger in a strange country. When she got back, she still had a few wine stains and her hair was windblown from the ride. The lady from the Pension and Sandra had become friends quickly at the start of the vacation, when Sandra came to lunch wearing a sundress.

"No es bueno," she said, pointing to Sandra's bare shoulders. Sandra realized she had not conformed to the Spanish custom, so quickly retreated to her room and put on a shawl. "Es bueno?" she asked when she returned, and she was rewarded with a big smile and a new name, "Senorita muy simpatico."

The young man must have confided in his aunt, as she quickly escorted Sandra to the kitchen and removed the remaining telltale wine stains. Thankfully her escapade went unnoticed, and other than her roommates, no one knew of the fabulous day she had enjoyed.

There were many incidents during that two week vacation that opened Sandra's eyes to a whole new world. For the very first time in her life, she had an idea that she was not the awkward teenager she had seen herself as. She spent all of her pocket money buying gifts to take home—a beautiful black and gold shawl for her mother, an assortment of miniature bottles of liquor for her father, and a hand-tooled leather wallet for Mike. The other gifts were three Spanish fans, one for each gran and one for Auntie Elsie. On the way home, she realized she had no money left and would have to go hungry on the long journey. Thank heavens she had a bus ticket to get from the station back to the shop.

She arrived home hungry but happy, and certainly more confident about her future. What an experience and one she would never forget.

Twenty-Nine

THE CHIP SHOP

Polly and Evan, with Belle and Alf, had built up the business at the chip shop until it was providing a very good living for both families. The only issue was that now Susan was getting older and Belle was pregnant again, the living quarters were bursting at the seams. Polly loved the trade and was most certainly the best asset the company had. She could filet a fish in the time that you could bat an eye. Her always effervescent personality endeared her to her customers. She knew them all, and their children and grandchildren, and took a genuine interest in their welfare. Her reputation for cleanliness and always using fresh fat in the fryers was a guarantee of steady business from all of the bus companies.

Belle was ecstatic about being pregnant and Alf suggested taking her and Susan for a few days holiday to celebrate.

"I don't like leaving Mam and Evan by themselves to run the shop, Alf. It is a big job for two people," Belle reluctantly declined the offer.

"I've talked to Mrs. Pierce, who used to work here before we bought the place, and she will come in and help while we are away. I've talked to Mam and Evan, and they both agree they can handle it. They don't have to do any books while we are gone, as I will handle it all when we come back." Alf had put all of his ducks in a row before even suggesting a vacation. Belle still felt a little unsure leaving everything to Polly and Evan, but the thoughts of a few days away by the seaside were very tempting. They made plans to go to Yarmouth, a quaint little seaside town, where Alf had found a Bed and Breakfast that was right on the seafront.

Mrs. Pierce came in to meet Polly, and the two women got along instantly. Mrs. Pierce could see Polly knew her way around the shop, and liked the fact she treated her as an equal rather than an employee. Polly liked the quick tongued but humorous Mrs. P., as she soon became. Mrs. P was very thin and bony, with long narrow feet, which due to bunions were always encased in a pair of oversized multicolour canvas slippers. Evan quickly dubbed her Olive Oyle, and Polly had to admit she did bear a strong resemblance to Popeye's love interest. She was a hard worker, and all their joking aside, they knew how lucky they were to have Mrs. P. working with them.

Belle and Alf had been gone for almost a week, and one night before bed Evan decided to straighten out the cash box. "I'll just straighten the bills and count it out, Polly. It will save Alf some work when he gets back.''

"I'll put the kettle on then, love, and we'll have a cuppa before we go to bed." Polly disappeared into the kitchen, and Evan set to work. He emptied the cash onto the table and began to count. He counted once and then twice, and then with a puzzled look he re-added the neat piles of bills. "Polly, come here, love, and count this again for me. There has to be something wrong."

Polly brought in the tea and sat down at the table. There was really no need to count. Even a quick look at the piles of money told her that the take was better than they had ever had.

"We only got one bus load this week, Evan. How can we have taken that much?"

Evan looked at Polly with a sad look. "Polly, it doesn't take a lot of thinking. What is the only difference this week?"

"Oh no! I can't believe that Alf would steal from his own family." Polly was devastated. It was not a small amount, and to think this had probably been going on for months was a terrible shock.

"We are going to have to face him with it, Polly. He can't go on thinking we are stupid."

Evan knew Polly hated conflict, especially as Belle would be in the middle. There was never any question that Belle knew about this, as she would sooner give than take. Belle never had money of her own other than the housekeeping that Alf gave to her.

Each night afterwards until Alf and Belle returned, Evan counted the take and bundled it with a tally on the top. He looked through the account ledger and saw the recorded deposits, all of which were significantly lower than anything he had counted during their absence. Alf and Belle came back looking relaxed and happy after their vacation, but Alf's face soon changed when he went to balance the cash box.

"Come on, love, I'll help you unpack and you can tell me all about Yarmouth." Polly picked up Susan and ushered Belle upstairs.

Downstairs Alf prepared to face the music. He had a thousand excuses ready, but never used one. Evan was adamant, and this was not the mild mannered man Alf thought he knew. Evan thought of all of the hard work Polly had done day after day. Barely hiding his fury, Evan confronted Alf with the discrepancy.

"I am not going to cause a scene, Alf. You know what has been going on here, and now Polly and I know as well. Make plans to find a job, and move out as soon as possible. It will kill our Belle if she knows what you have been up to. You need a bigger place anyway, so it's a good reason to move. Polly and I will have this place appraised and we will give you your share of the price. Not that you deserve it, but for Belle's sake."

"I expect my full share of the business. I'm not walking out of here empty handed. You can't prove anything. There are no paper records," Alf stood his ground.

"You will get exactly what is due to you, and not a penny more or less. You know what you have been doing, and you know it is not going to go on. Polly and I want you out of here as soon as possible. From now on, keep your hands out of the till." Evan took the cash box and locked it in the dresser drawer.

When Evan was alone with Polly he confessed, "Alf's right, you know, love. I don't have any proof, and much as I am sure I am right about this, there is nothing we can do if he refuses to leave."

"It doesn't matter, Evan. Right or wrong, they need a place of their own now. I'm sure our Belle will jump at the chance to have more room now with another baby on the way." Polly would miss Belle and Susan, but she knew it was the best answer to their problems.

Belle sensed that there was something wrong as there was a definite tension between Alf and her mam and Evan. Alf explained it by saying he had told them he wanted to be bought out of the business. "We need a bigger place, Belle, and now they have Mrs. Pierce they can handle it by themselves. Wouldn't you like to have a place of our own again?"

Belle was excited at the prospect of a move, and when her mam and Evan did not seem to mind, she began to look forward to a change. It did not take Alf long to find a job as a store manager in

217

Hasland, which was a quiet little community not far from Chester-field. Belle liked it instantly, as it included a nice house attached to the store, and there was a large back yard which was really private. She was thinking this would be a great place to put the new baby in his or her pram.

The store was valued and Alf was paid out. Belle never did suspect any other reason for the move. Polly and Evan were civil to Alf, but would never trust him again. The store flourished, and although it was very hard work, the rewards were great. Polly and Evan closed the store one day per week, and that was their day to go for a ride into the country. Evan had an old car that was getting rather unreliable, but he managed to keep it going with a lot of tinkering. One day Polly was all dressed up and ready to go for a ride, when Evan came in covered with grease. "Sorry love. The old girl's leaking oil; I'm going to have to go and pick up a new seal. No trip out today."

Polly was disappointed as she loved their days out, very often a trip to Chatsworth or Matlock, and sometimes a picnic. "Never mind, love. There's always next week." Polly knew that Evan was as disappointed as she was, and there was no point in making him feel worse.

Since the episode with Alf, Polly had very astutely put money aside each week. In actual fact, she had hidden it under the treads and risers of the stair carpet. Unknown to Evan, she paid a trip to the local car dealership and bought a Standard Vanguard, to be delivered for the following week. Polly knew nothing of cars, other than she liked the color of this one and it was a big solid looking vehicle. The salesman thought he had hit the jackpot when Polly opened her shopping bag and pulled out the full purchase price in cash.

"I want it delivered to the front of our shop next Wednesday morning. Just give me a set of keys and leave the other set in the glove compartment."

The salesman was happy to comply, and asked no questions. The following Wednesday Evan got up early and went to work on the old car.

"I don't think the car's going to be fixed in time for a trip today, Polly. I still have a bit of work to do on it." Evan was not prepared to take it on a long drive until he knew everything was roadworthy.

Polly smiled and dangled a set of keys in front of Evan. "Go and check out the street in front of the shop," she said with a big smile. "We are going out today and we are going out in style."

Evan went and looked at the two tone green Standard Vanguard and all he could stammer was, "I'm not really keen on Vanguards, Polly." But when he saw her crestfallen look, he smiled and said, "Well, there's a first time for everything. Come on, let's take it for a spin and see what she can do." It was the first of many outings in the Vanguard, and Evan never complained about it again.

Thirty

BEVERLEY JANE

Beverly Jane finally came into the world after a long and arduous labour, and Belle could not wait to hold her. Something was very wrong, however, as the minute she was born, she was whisked off out of the ward.

"What's the matter? Why can't I hold my baby?" Belle was sweating profusely and exhausted from the struggle to give birth to her daughter.

"It's all right, Mrs. Ball. There is a little discoloration we need to check out, but we will take good care of her."

Alf was sitting in the waiting room, and when he saw the nurse carrying the baby quickly out of the delivery room he jumped up to see his new offspring. He just had a quick glimpse of his daughter, but could see that she was a ghastly shade of blue.

The doctor came over to speak to him. "Mr. Ball, I am afraid that your daughter is what we call a blue baby. We have no prognosis at this time, but we will do all we can for her." Alf had never expected anything but perfection, and this was very hard to take.

He went in to see Belle, who had been sedated but was partially aware of what was happening around her. "It's going to be all right," Alf tried to reassure Belle, but he was far from sure himself. After several hours, the nurse came in carrying Beverly Jane, and Belle was ecstatic. She was now getting some color and she was beautiful. The nurses had dressed her in the baby outfit Polly had bought for her, a cute little white layette set, with a matching bonnet. Her eyes were a deep blue, and she had the tiniest rosebud mouth and a little button nose.

"Here, my pet, let your momma have a look at you." Before the nurse could stop her, Belle pulled off the bonnet and almost shrieked. The bonnet was hiding a very large domed head that was obviously misshapen. It was "hydrocephalus," which is a word taken from the

Greek language, and literally translated, means water head. The doctor came in and gave Belle the prognosis, and it was not good, such severe cases stood very little chance of survival.

The next six months were a nightmare. Belle was back and forth to the hospital with Beverly Jane, and each time there was no encouraging news.

Belle had little or no sleep as the baby had constant seizures and screamed in pain. There was nothing Belle could do to soothe her daughter. Even taking Beverly out in her pram was a constant stress, as everyone wanted to see the new baby. There was no way to hide the large head that was now swollen way out of proportion, and the looks of shock and sympathy cut right through to Belle's heart. Alf somehow was able to distance himself from his daughter, and never wanted to hold her or be seen with her. It all fell on Belle, and she was becoming more and more depressed. Polly and Evan were devastated, as they knew how much Belle had looked forward to the birth. Polly offered to pay for a specialist to examine her granddaughter and see if there was anything more that could be done. Polly was able to look past the swollen head and see the beautiful child that Beverly was, but she hated to see the amount of pain this tiny baby had to suffer.

Polly and Belle took Beverly to see the specialist, but he did not offer a lot of encouragement. He explained different forms of possible treatments, but due to the fact that Beverly had spina bifida and hydrocephalus, even the technique of a shunt might not be successful. It was a lot to contemplate, as it was major surgery and Beverly was already very weak. "Mrs. Ball, I am sorry to say that even after surgery, I have no guarantees for you. Even if Beverly survived the operation, she might be brain damaged and continue to have seizures for the rest of her life."

Belle hugged her daughter close to her chest, and cried all the pent up tears she had been holding inside. Polly did not know how to comfort her. The two women walked out of the specialist's office. Evan was waiting to take them home, and one look at their faces and he knew this was not a good prognosis.

"Mam, there is nothing we can do except love her and try and enjoy every precious minute we have with her. I'm not going to put her through surgery that has no guarantees."

Mercifully, Beverly lived only a few days after the visit to the specialist. Belle had to rush her to hospital one night when she had a particularly bad seizure. This time she did not survive the trauma to her frail little body.

"How can I be so sad and so relieved all at the same time?" Belle felt as if a huge weight had been lifted from her shoulders, but at the same time she felt an enormous loss. Beverly would always be a part of her life, and she would never ever forget the loss of her daughter.

Everyone rallied around and tried to ease Belle's pain. There was nothing but time that would gradually soften but never erase the memory. Alf and Belle were going through a tough time in their marriage after the death of Beverly. Alf had resented the fact that Belle spent so much time with the sick child, and Belle resented the fact that he didn't. People deal with death in their own way, and the loss of his daughter was harder on Alf then anyone knew. During his time as a prisoner of war, he had faced death and seen death every day, but it in no way made it any easier. It was just easier to hide his own feelings, and he had become an expert at that. Belle did not realize how much his daughter's death had affected him, and thought he was being callous and unthinking when he carried on life as normal.

Life did go on though, and Belle's next pregnancy, although not easy, produced a healthy and handsome little boy. Gary was adored by everyone from the minute he was born. When Polly first saw her grandson, she cried tears of joy. "He is just perfect, Belle, love. God is good. I have prayed every night for this moment."

"Me too, Mam." Belle was exhausted with the birth, but happier than she had been for months.

Thirty-One

MIKE AND SANDY

In her senior year at Joseph Wright Art College, Sandra had many friends and interests: school was another world outside of the Corner Store. The living conditions there were far from ideal, especially as Sandra now often had to share the pull down bed with her mother. Mattie had decided Alf's snoring meant he now had to sleep in the room next to the store. The cramped quarters afforded no privacy, and even doing homework was difficult.

Mike was still the only boy Sandra was interested in, but he was a bus ride away and she could only see him on weekends. He had graduated from Swanwick Hall, and although he had the academic requirements to go to Loughborough College, his parents did not have the means to send him. At Swanwick he had been the County Discus and Javelin Champion and excelled at all sports. He wanted to be a Physical Education Teacher and knew he would make a good one, but it was not to be. His alternative was to try and get an apprenticeship at the local colliery. If he was accepted, then he would be given the opportunity to work while at the same time having day release to go to college to sit the required exams.

He had an interview and was hired on the spot as a trainee mining mechanical engineer. It was not an easy or pleasant job, as he was going to be working underground and doing shift work. But there were limited opportunities in the area, so to be accepted was quite an accomplishment.

For a few weeks after Sandra returned from Spain she remained friends with some of her fellow travellers. They were all a grade higher, and because Sandra was more comfortable with the older students, she enjoyed their company. Mike was not very happy she had started going to a jazz club some weekends, since he was not at all interested in jazz or dancing. He also had a lot of studying to do as there were constant exams. There were lots of boys who wanted to

223

take Sandra out, and she even considered saying yes sometimes. She never did, though; as much as she tried not to, she compared them all with Mike. None measured up.

By Sandra's sixteenth birthday she and Mike had become inseparable. Life at Peet Street was far from ideal. Mattie and Alf were both working long hours in the two shops and then spending their evenings and weekends out. Sandra was alone again most nights when she did not go to Chesterfield or Riddings. Auntie Elsie and Uncle Joe had also moved to a new house, and it was now far more difficult to go and visit them. She had a strict curfew of 11:00 p.m. and was expected to be home, even if there was no one else there when she arrived. The last bus from Leabrooks gave her just enough time to rush all the way from the bus stop and be home in time.

Sandra did not like walking home from the bus stop, as she had to pass through a particularly rough area of town that was very poorly lit. Once she reached the area where the street lights were, she always breathed a big sigh of relief.

One night there was a really bad fog that caused all the busses to be late, and she did not get into Derby until after 11:30 p.m. She stepped off the bus into a thick pea soup fog that swallowed her up, and all she could see were shadows. Instantly she was back in the room in Moseley Street, and the hair stood up on the back of her neck. For a few moments her feet were glued to the ground and she could not even move. When at last she found her feet, she ran at break neck speed, tripping over the cobbles and her heart racing, until she reached the bottom of Drewry Lane, which led to Peet Street. The fog swirled around her, as she tried to stay calm and focus through the greyness. All at once she saw a huge figure walking quickly towards her and she let out an involuntary scream.

"Is that you, our Sandra?" It was her dad. He knew she would be late because of the fog and had decided to go and meet her. Sandra was never so pleased to see anyone in her life. "What's a matter? You're shaking like a leaf!" Alf gave her a quick hug and grabbed her hand to walk back up the street.

"I was late and knew you would be mad, and then I could not see in the fog. I suppose I was a bit frightened," she admitted.

"There is not much you can do when the busses are late, love. Your mam and me were just worried you had missed the last bus."

It was a good feeling to know they cared, and it was certainly good to be holding on to her dad's hand. It would have been difficult for anyone to be frightened in his presence.

Mike gradually became a constant, and it was never discussed but always assumed that they would get married one day. Sandra's happiest times were when she spent them with Mike. There was not a lot of money to do anything special, but simple trips to the pictures and days going to the market were all special in their own way. She was really proud of the way that he was acing all his exams, and he had changed so much since he left school. He had always been far more mature than many of his peers, but now he was a man.

Sandra was also sitting final exams, and it was a decision time for her too. If she wanted to further her education, it meant sitting A Level's to go to university. Her initial ambition of working with the hearing impaired had long since faded when she had to quit her elocution exams. Other options she explored were being an almoner, working with hospital patients doing the little things necessary to relieve their stress when they were unable to take care of things at home; or working in the newspaper business as a reporter. She decided university was not an option, as she had no desire to be reliant upon her parents for any longer than she had to. She also did not want to go out of town and farther away from Mike.

Work was not easy to find and a good job even harder. There were lots of jobs as factory workers or shop assistants, but neither held any fascination for Sandra. One day Alf came home with the evening paper, and it had an ad for a Cost Clerk at British Railways. The pay was great and the benefits were much better than most companies were offering. Not even sure what a cost clerk was, Sandra decided to apply. There was an interview and an exam that determined if you were going to be hired as a cost clerk or maybe at a lower position as a runner.

Sandra was granted an interview and she carefully dressed in her best outfit. It was a grey pencil skirt with a silver blouse, and a cobalt blue jacket with a silver fur collar. Looking in the mirror, she was pleased with the results. Her shoulder length hair was loosely curled, and she chose just a touch of lipstick and blush. She was always grateful she had been blessed with great skin and never did suffer the normal plagues of teenage acne.

The interviewer was a man probably in his late twenties, and he was impressed with the young applicant before him. He explained that the job was one of costing out the price of a steam engine. It entailed a lot of simple math, adding up columns of figures to achieve the end result of the entire cost. The test was easy, and Sandra passed with flying colors to start as a Cost Clerk.

Mattie was disappointed Sandra had decided not to go to university. She had always wanted her daughter to have a "career," but British Railways was a great employer. If she was determined to start work, it was as good an employer as possible.

The first day was an intimidating experience, as she was the youngest at a desk of about twenty people. She looked around at the other people seated around her. There was an older man with a pink shirt, which she found a little unusual, another lady who was probably in her late fifties and looked very much like a spinster, a few young married women, and some who looked around her mom's age. They all had eyes on Sandra. The older spinster lady was obviously the most senior, and she was the one who came to give Sandra her instructions.

She pointed to a huge Burroughs's adding machine which sat in the center of the large table. "If you REALLY can't balance then you are allowed to use the adding machine." Sandra looked up and saw the young woman opposite raise her eyebrows and shake her head. Obviously this was not something that anyone would want to do— only a last resort. At break time she met some of her fellow workers and found out how fortunate she was to start as a cost clerk.

"Most new girls have to be runners before they get promoted. I had to be a runner for a year before they let me have a desk job," the tall skinny girl said.

"What is a runner, and why is it so bad?" Sandra asked naively.

"Just what it sounds like, you have to run all over the bloody place taking papers and picking up papers and being sent on dumb errands. They sent me for a long weight, and I was daft enough to stand outside the machine shop for half an hour before I realized that they had sent me for a long WAIT. Anyway, my name is Brenda, and welcome to the desk."

Sandra did not escape all of the ribbing that goes with being the new girl, and they all had a lot of laughs when she asked questions about various engine parts. She was quite sure that male and female bolts were another attempt at long weight humour. She learned a lot in a very short time, and only once had to use the Burroughs's adding machine. The pay was good and the job was a lot of fun. Eventually Sandra was promoted to payroll clerk and that was an even better paying job. The best part of it was that once a week she had to put up all the cash envelopes. This was a very responsible job, in which all the payroll clerks were actually locked in a huge room and waited for the cash to be delivered by armoured truck. Once in receipt of the cash, it was your responsibility to put the correct amount in each see-through pay packet. It had to be placed in such a way that the recipient could check the amount before the packet was opened. No one was allowed out of the building until everything was balanced to the penny.

It became a challenge to be the first to finish, and then you helped a slower person to balance their cash. Once everything was accounted for, you were allowed to leave and did not have to come back to work until after lunch. It was great as Sandra's team were all good, and they often had two hour lunches on such days.

Sandra had been given the choice of whether she wanted to pay room and board, or keep her pay cheque and pay all her own expenses. She chose the latter, and was very proud when she managed to save a percentage of her pay cheque each week and was still able to buy nice clothes and a few treats. Now Mike and Sandra were both earning fairly good pay cheques and had started to discuss whether or not they would be able to save enough to get married when Sandra turned eighteen. There had never been anyone else for either of them, and it was not a giddy decision based on infatuation, but rather a feeling of destiny. Sandra had never felt so loved or safe in her life, and to think of spending the rest of her life with Mike by her side would be a dream come true.

Mike also worked hard and saved hard. His apprenticeship was going well and he was passing all of his exams with flying colors. He did not particularly like working down the pit, but it was a means to an end. The coal board were paying for his education, and maybe one day he might be able to utilize his training in a different area of the workforce. He had been saving furiously and at last had enough money to buy a modest ring.

That weekend he went to ask Mattie and Alf if he could ask Sandra to marry him. They were both expecting this, but not so soon, and although they were pleased, they hoped it would be a long engagement.

Sandra knew Mike was up to something, as he was obviously struggling with putting into words what he wanted to say. Eventually he threw all caution to the wind, and holding Sandra's hand in his, he asked her to be his wife. It was not entirely unexpected, but Sandra was still stunned by the proposal.

"Of course I will marry you. There is a lot to think of, though. It really is a big step."

"We will take it together, Sandra. We are both earning our own money, and I am still paying board. With both our wages, I am sure that we can find somewhere to rent and still have enough money left to live on. I've saved enough for a ring," Mike said with a smile. "I think we should go shopping."

What a day this has turned out to be, Sandra thought as they gazed in the window at a beautiful blue zircon surrounded with tiny diamonds. It was an antique store and the ring was second hand, but just perfect. Both of them saw the ring and liked it at the same time. They went into the store and the old clerk liked the two youngsters instantly. The ring was a perfect fit and did not need any alterations.

"Oh Mike, it's absolutely perfect. I love it." Sandra watched as the diamonds flashed in the bright lights each time she moved her hand. The delighted jeweller gave them a great deal on the ring, and smiled happily as they walked out of the store hand in hand with Sandra proudly holding up her left hand in admiration.

Everything happened at break neck speed after that. First of all, Sandra saw a job advertised as a payroll clerk for The Territorial Army. It was much higher paying than her already well-paying job, and was also closer to home. She applied for and got the job. The next thing that fell into place was that the people who were renting the flat above her family's corner store gave their notice to leave. The rent was cheap, as it was up three flights of steep stairs and was very much in need of redecorating. The stairs were of no consequence as they were both young and fit, and it was an opportunity to decorate the place to their own taste.

Sandra enjoyed her job at The Territorial Army and as she was again the youngest employee, she was treated very well by her fellow workers. Many of the male management were retired army personnel, so there were colonels and majors and captains. They were all extremely smart and very military in their bearing. At first Sandra was a little intimidated, but she soon learned that they were great people to work with. It was her job to calculate the money required to put up the cash pay envelopes for the different military units, and request the money from the bank. It had to be in specific denominations. So many pound notes, so many five pound notes, right down to the shillings and pence. Sandra had to go to the bank and pick up the money each week. It was quite a walk from Phoenix Street over the Derwent Bridge and into town. Sandra was always aware she was carrying a large sum of money, and she held the cash bag tightly to her body at all times.

One day Sandra was in the bank and noticed a young man watching her very closely. She did not think too much of it until she left the bank and started to walk back across the bridge. She was admiring the beautiful day and the sun glancing on the river below, when out of the corner of her eye she saw the same young man just a few paces behind her. There was no one else in sight on the bridge, other than the cars passing by, and she picked up her pace as fast as the high heels allowed her to. She made it back to the office out of breath and more than a little unnerved.

"I think I've been followed from the bank," she stammered to Captain Cooling.

"What? Are you sure? Where is he now?" Captain Cooling ran out of the office and looked down the street. Whoever it was had disappeared. After Sandra had been questioned, there were a few jokes, such as "Maybe he was just following a pretty girl." It was, however, taken more seriously than they intended to show her. From that day forth, Major Harding took Sandra back and forth to the bank in a company vehicle. There were no more incidents, and Sandra was very happy knowing her employers had quickly made arrangements for her future safety.

Mike often wished he had a vehicle, as the cost of bus fare was always going up and the bus schedule never seemed to fit his needs. He doubted very much if he would be able to afford a car for several years to come.

Opposite the corner store, there was a scrap yard of old vehicles which was owned by a local stock car racing celebrity, Jack Minion. Mike often visited Jack, as he was always interested in cars and engines. One day Mike saw a 1948 Ford 8 Van, which was badly in need of some tender loving care. It was sitting in the corner of the yard with a sign, "Make an Offer."

229

"How much do you want for that, Jack?" Mike asked as he opened the bonnet and checked out the engine. Jack liked Mike and Sandra, and knew the two had just gotten engaged.

"For you, lad, I'll give you a deal." Jack low balled the price to far less than the van was worth. Mike knew Jack's offer was a good one, and he had almost enough in his savings account. With a small loan from his parents, which he knew he could count on, he shook hands on the deal.

"Thanks, Jack. I'll probably need a bit of help fixing it up. Can I keep it in the yard until it's done?" Mike was already planning what needed to be fixed.

"Of course you can, lad. I'll give you a hand whenever I can. The motor's good, but you'll need to check the brakes and get a set of new tires." Jack could see that Mike was calculating how much all of this was going to cost.

"We'll look her over this weekend, and make a list of what has to be done. I'll order the parts at cost, and you can pay me when you can. I know you are not going to run away," Jack smiled.

Mike could not wait to tell Sandra the good news.

"Well, I will pay half of it," Sandra insisted, as she had been able to save a little nest egg with her new job.

"Let's toss for it. Heads you buy the van, tails you pay for the road tax." Sandra agreed, and they both laughed when the road tax came out to a few pennies more than the cost of the vehicle.

By Sandra's birthday in late September, they had set a date of December 26th for their wedding. The date was determined by the fact that most of the family were in business, and December 26th would be a day when they were all closed. Polly was in her elements when she heard of the upcoming wedding. "I'll buy your dress, my duck. You choose whatever you want. It's your day and I want it to be perfect." Polly was adamant Sandra go to The Bridal House in Leeds, which was famous for bridal couture. She knew Sandra would need to have it styled to fit, as at eighteen she had a figure that denied convention, being two sizes larger in the bust than she was in the waist and hips. Therefore her wardrobe mostly consisted of sweaters and skirts, other than a few dresses she had designed herself and had made by a local seamstress.

Polly's only regret in life was that Lance stood firm on his threat of never giving her a divorce. She loved Evan more than life itself, and so wished she could legally use his name. Each time a census taker came, Polly would try to avoid filling out the information. As far as she was concerned, she was Mrs. Redford.

"Funny how things work." She could not believe her eyes when she received a letter from Lance's lawyer, asking for a divorce. The letter arrived very shortly after Sandra's wedding announcement. "I can't believe it, Evan. After all these years." Polly was staring at the letter incredulously. "I wonder why now, of all times?"

"I don't care why, all I want to know is how fast we can get this over with, Polly. I have waited over thirty years for this moment. Maybe I can make an honest woman of you before our Sandra gets married. Wouldn't that be something if we got married first?" Evan chuckled.

Polly signed the papers, and as there was nothing to contest or dispute, the divorce was settled very quickly.

Evan needed to go shopping, not something he was accustomed to, but he needed to do this alone. One day when he was going into town to pick up the fish order, he made a little side trip. He knew Polly's birthstone was a sapphire, and he thought the blue stone would be perfect for an engagement ring. He went to the best jeweler in Chesterfield and bought a beautiful sapphire and diamond on a plain gold band, with a matching gold wedding ring. He would keep this as a surprise until their wedding day.

"I don't want any fuss, Evan. I want to keep this as quiet as we can. I'm not even telling the children until we are married." Polly hoped he understood her need to keep their marriage a secret. Most people thought they were already married, and would be shocked to know they had cohabited for so many years without the benefit of legality.

"Whatever you want, my love. If you want to go to the registrar in Sheffield, we can do that. Just set up a time and date and I'm your man. See when we can get an appointment and book as soon as we can. Just give yourself time to go and buy a new outfit and a nice hat. Something special for my special girl." Evan always loved to see Polly in a hat. She wore them well and had matching hats for most of her special outfits.

Polly did not need any further encouragement. "All right, pet. You help Mrs. Pierce and I'll take an hour or two off today and pop into the city."

The shopping trip went well, and Polly bought a beautiful cream suit with a silk blouse and a coffee and cream matching hat. She was very pleased with her selections as she had a pair of shoes and a purse that would go with it very well.

The day came at last, and Polly and Evan set off on their secret mission. Mrs. Pierce came in to watch the shop, and seeing them both dressed to the nines, didn't know how close to the truth she was when she exclaimed, "Where are you two off to? You look like you are going to a wedding."

Neither Polly nor Evan answered the remark, but quickly said their goodbyes and departed. They dared not look at each other for fear of showing their emotions.

The wedding was a very quiet registry office affair, and the witnesses were staff from the office. As Evan looked at Polly, he thought that she was more beautiful now than the day he first saw her. She was a vision then, but now he knew she was very real, and what he saw on the outside was only a hint of the beauty within her. Polly clutched Evan's hand, and thought of all the wonderful things he had done for her and her children over the years. She owed him her life. He had saved her from an abusive marriage and brought up her three children as his own. Above all, he had made every day a blessing.

They left the office hand in hand, both of their hearts bursting with the emotion of finally having the blessing of the sanctity of marriage. "Come on, Polly. I'm going to take you to the best restaurant in town and we are going to celebrate."

Off they went and had a long and leisurely lunch before heading back to the store. When they arrived, Mrs. Pierce had handled the lunch trade and locked up for the afternoon break. The store was not due to open again until 5:00 p.m. for the supper trade. Polly and Evan were pleased they did not have to face any more questions on their return. Polly was the first one to enter the living quarters, and she let out a shriek when she saw water everywhere. "Oh Evan, what on earth has happened?" Polly ran to the bottom of the stairs where the water appeared to be coming from. Evan took one look and guessed what had happened. The hot water tank was upstairs in the bathroom, and it must have leaked.

"Never mind, love. It's only water. It could be worse," he said as Polly went rushing past him. "Hey, don't get all your lovely clothes messed up. I'll see to it."

"You don't understand, Evan. Look under the carpet! Oh my goodness." Polly bent down and pulled out a wad of wet through money.

Evan started to laugh. "So that's where you do your banking, is it? I think it's time you started to trust the banks, Polly. If had been a fire, you would have lost it all."

Polly went to change, and the two of them spent the rest of the afternoon collecting the soggy paper money and putting it to dry out between towels on the bedroom floor. Nothing could dampen their spirits though. "Well for sure we will remember the day," Polly laughed.

"There is no way that I could ever forget, Mrs. Redford. It's a new beginning, and if the next thirty years are as wonderful, what more could anyone ask?"

"It's only water, and that carpet was ready for replacing anyway. Call the insurance and I'll put the kettle on. I'm dying for a cuppa."

The insurance took care of the restoration work, and Polly ended up with a nice new stair carpet, which she never used as a bank again. They had achieved their goal of getting married before Sandra. Now they were looking forward to sharing their news with the children.

The following Sunday, they invited all of the children over for supper, and would not take "No" for an answer from any of them. Polly was the one to share the news, "Evan and I have something to tell you all." She began, "Lance finally gave me a divorce, and Evan and I got married last week." Evan's face was full of emotion as he put his arms around Polly, and for the first time, in front of the children, gave her a loving kiss. Evan had never thought of Polly as anything but his wife, but he knew that society would think differently, had they known that they had not had the benefit of a marriage certificate until now.

"Mam, I am so happy for you both, but why on earth didn't you tell us? We would have been there with you," Belle exclaimed.

Mattie looked at Belle and Darren, and shrugged her shoulders, as if to say, "Are you totally stupid?" Instead she hugged Polly and turning to Evan, said, "I know Mam would want this to be as quiet as possible, with no fuss. It was just a bit of paper that for some stupid reason, seems to make a difference." Over the years, Mattie had finally come to realize that Evan and her mother shared a love that transcended any legal propriety. She still did not recognise him as her father, and never would, but there was no denying his love for her mother.

Mike and Sandra spent hours working to fix up the old van. They sanded out the rust spots and brush-painted the van a shade of dark blue. Sandra's Auntie Vera gave them some old furniture covers that were no longer needed, and they recovered the very well-worn seats.

Mike and Jack worked together to tune up the van and get it into reasonable running order. It was still temperamental, and sometimes it went at the first crank of the handle, but other times it needed a push to get started. No matter all its idiosyncrasies, they were very proud of it. They laughed through the many challenges. When it rained, there was a leak just above the passenger seat and it was necessary to carry a cup to catch the leak. The windshield wipers worked on a vacuum system, so when you were going uphill, they could barely cope with the rain; then as soon as you came downhill, they swished back and forth like crazy.

It was decided the van was in good enough shape to make the trip to Leeds for a fitting for the wedding gown. Mike and Sandra took Susan and Denise, the two small flower girls, with them in order to purchase their outfits at the same time.

"Oh no!" Sandra woke up on the day that Mike was due to come and pick them all up to go to Leeds, and she was in so much pain and discomfort. All of the excitement had started her period almost a week early.

"Bugger it! I have to go. We have an appointment and it's the last chance we will have to go this month." Sandra went into the bathroom and threw up. "I am going to be fine," she told herself, but with little conviction.

Mike knew she was not well the minute he arrived, but she insisted they could not cancel. It was a trip from hell. Mike had to stop along the busy highway at regular intervals for Sandra to throw up. The two little girls were both bored with the long journey and many stops. Mike had to negotiate the unfamiliar and busy roads while at the same time trying to concentrate in the midst of so much chaos. By the time they reached Leeds they were all exhausted, and then they had to locate The Bridal House.

Sandra felt terrible, and wished she could have the chance to wash up and lie down for a bit, but that was impossible. Mike reluctantly left the girls at the store and went to park and wait for them to return.

"Are you sure you don't want me to come in with you? Will you be okay?"

"You can't come in. You don't get to see the dress until the day. It's bad luck." Sandra gave a weak smile as she kissed him goodbye. "We'll be all right, won't we, girls?"

Sandra walked into the store with Susan and Denise and was met with a very snooty sales clerk. It was a high class store and obviously used to serving the "upper class." Although well dressed and well spoken, Sandra's stressful trip had left its mark, and she was pale and dishevelled.

"How can I help you?" the sales clerk looked down her nose at the trio in front of her.

Sandra had a definite idea of what she wanted, and had already designed the dress she had in mind. It was a December wedding, so she had chosen white velvet and a very simple form fitting dress with a mandarin collar and long sleeves. It was going to be complemented with a white fur muff and a little pill box hat. It looked sensational on paper, and Sandra knew the cut would be classic. The little flower girls were going to be attired in the same velvet, but with the addition of coloured sashes and capes.

"This is what I am looking for," Sandra handed the sketches to the sales girl.

"We don't work like that here. If you want something like that, you will have to go to a private seamstress. Here you choose from our catalogue, and when you find something you like we will bring it out to show you. We then tailor the dress to fit." She handed Sandra two thick catalogues, but there was nothing close to what she wanted.

Halfway through the first catalogue, Sandra had to ask to be excused and just made it to the bathroom in time to throw up. The sales clerk gave her a knowing look when she came back, and said very sarcastically, "How soon is the wedding?" It was obvious she had put Sandra's appearance down to her being pregnant. Nothing could have been farther from the truth, as Sandra was still a virgin and intended to be until after she was married.

The result of the day was that Sandra chose the first and only dress she tried on. It was the exact opposite of what she would have chosen. It had to be altered across the bust, but other than that, it fit perfectly. It was all Nottingham Lace, and had a boat neckline at the front which dipped to a V at the back. The waist was tiny and fitted, also going to a V just below the waist, before exploding into a crinoline lace skirt. There was a deep frill of net that surrounded the bottom of the dress and then wrapped upwards to meet at the back waist with a white rose.

"Oooohhh, you look like a real princess," the two girls oohed and aahed. "It's beautiful." Even the snooty sales girl appeared to admire the result.

"It's fine. I'll take it." Sandra could not wait to take it off, as the weight of it was making her feel even worse. The two flower girls ended up with similar style dresses in pale blue, with little matching shawls.

How she made it through the fitting and then the long journey home, Sandra did not know. The old Ford made the trip, and the two youngsters fell asleep on the way home. It had not been the wonderful time Sandra had anticipated, but Mike had certainly been the hero of the day. He had miraculously negotiated heavy traffic and strange roads, while at the same time making unscheduled stops for Sandra to throw up.

By the time the dress arrived six weeks later, Sandra had totally forgotten what it looked like. The only way to get into it was to have assistance to step into the huge crinoline. Sandra counted seventeen different layers of net underskirts and then extra hip peplums. Although it had not been her original choice, somehow it worked, and the result was truly stunning. She hoped that her mama, Polly, would approve of her choice.

There was still so much to do before the wedding. The flat had to be decorated and some old furniture had to be refinished. Mattie and Alf had ordered new teak furniture, and agreed to give Sandra and Mike their old heavy oak dining set. Somehow this had to be carried up the three flights of stairs and then polished back into some of its former glory.

The bedroom was the first task, and it was transformed from a dirty white walled room with equally dirty windows, into a beautiful bright floral oasis. Sandra chose lavender and yellow floral wallpaper to cover the uneven walls, and managed to find the exact matching lavender for drapes. Mike sanded and painted an old chest of drawers that he had brought from home. He was a bit unsure of Sandra's choice of deep yellow with white knobs, but was pleasantly surprised with the end result. They could not afford to change the flooring, so the grey battleship linoleum had to stay. The kitchen was a mismatch of eclectic furnishings, and the dining area was dwarfed with the big old dining set. Sandra and Mike polished the deeply carved roses and all of the intricate woodwork until it came back to life.

The floor plan was exactly the same as each floor below, so you basically had to walk through each room to get to the next. Entering through the kitchen/living room, you then walked through to the bedroom. The bathroom was at the top of the stairs, and the only access was by going across the landing on the exterior of the flat. Not very convenient in the middle of the night! They thought it was just perfect anyway. It was theirs and they would be together as man and wife.

The day of the wedding, the street was lined with many of the customers from the store, who knew of the wedding and wanted to catch a glimpse of the bride on her way to church. Sandra stepped outside to cheers and into the waiting wedding car. The dress was so big her father had to get into the front seat with the driver as there was no room in the back with Sandra. It was a short ride to church, and as was the custom, Sandra still had the veil over her face, not to be removed until after the ceremony. Once at the church, there was another crowd waiting outside and more cheers and well wishes.

It was bitterly cold and trying to snow, and Sandra had to clutch hold of the veil, which blew every which way in the wind. Alf was wearing a top hat and tails, and looked very handsome and very proud as he armed his young daughter into the church.

Sandra was totally unprepared for the amazing décor that greeted her. All of the Christmas decorations were still in place. The magnificent old stone church was resplendent with all of the beautiful white chrysanthemums that had been placed in every single niche along the stone walls. The altar was lit with large brass candles, and the red and gold altar cloth was also adorned with vases of chrysanthemums. The ornate stained glass windows of St. Peter's Church twinkled in the candle light. It was a long walk down the aisle and Mike watched in awe and admiration as Sandra took each step towards him.

It was the beginning of a new life for both of them, and the wedding and reception at The Coppice Hotel were very grand. Most of the guests were family and friends of Alf and Mattie, other than a few very close friends of Sandra and Mike. It was just the way things were. The number of invited guests was determined by Mattie and

Alf, as they paid for the lion's share of the wedding. Names were penciled in and numbers tallied, leaving the number of guests that Sandra and Mike could invite. After the wedding luncheon, everyone was invited to The Gibson, Mattie and Alf's favourite pub, where they both felt more comfortable than at the fancy Coppice Hotel.

After a respectable time of mingling with guests and saying all the thank you's, Sandra and Mike bid all farewell and left the party to go home and change. They had a short time to catch the bus to Blackpool, where they had booked a brief honeymoon. Mike changed out of his tuxedo and put on a new suit, bought for the occasion. It was the latest style with a short jacket and high buttons. He looked amazing. Sandra had chosen a soft peach coloured suit with a matching pill box hat. When they arrived at the bus stop, there was no disguising the fact that they were newlyweds, as they both glowed with happiness. It was also easy to see they were on a tight budget, as they were starting out their new adventure by travelling four or five hours half way across England on a draughty bus. The van was not an option, as at that time of year the road conditions were uncertain and the temperamental old jalopy could not be relied upon for such a long journey.

It was late at night when they arrived at their destination, a very modest Bed and Breakfast that was a few streets away from the beach. Their first night as man and wife was bliss. Neither knew what to expect. It was the first time for both of them. Long after their timid love-making, Sandra lay awake thinking she had never felt so cherished.

Blackpool was freezing cold, and even the foam along the edge of the sea was frozen. Neither had taken enough warm clothes, and the biting wind and cold cut through them when they walked along the promenade. It did not matter how cold it was. They were together, and Sandra had someone who loved her unconditionally and completely. Mike had his girl, and he knew he would always be there for her. Things did not start out smoothly, however, as when they unpacked, Mike's bank book was missing from the suitcase. He thought that someone might have removed it as a wedding prank, but whatever the case, they had only the small amount of cash they had taken with them. They had purchased a return ticket on the bus, but the terrible weather continued, and their bus was cancelled as the road across the Snake Pass was closed due to snow.

"What are we going to do now, Mike? Will they give us a refund?" Sandra looked at Mike with a worried expression.

"There's only one way to find out. Let's go and see the ticket agent." Mike was not at all sure their money would be refunded, but it was certainly worth a try.

After some discussion, the bus depot refunded part of their fare, and they managed to scrape up enough money to pay for two train tickets home.

It was freezing on the train, and they had only a few shillings left, just enough to buy a cup of tea and a packet of biscuits at the next station. It would take more than a few obstacles to dampen the young lovers' spirits. They laughed as the canteen lady lined up the tea cups and poured a row of strong looking tea in a continuous stream over the cups and the counter.

"Well, Mrs. Lewis, what do you think about married life so far?" Mike grinned.

"It's perfect." Sandra snuggled up to him to keep warm, and thought that truly she had never felt so loved and so safe.

Thirty-Two

MARRIED LIFE

The first year of married life did not come without its share of ups and downs, but always they were taken in stride and overcome together. Mike never knew how violent and frequent Sandra's constant nightmares were until after they were married. The first time she awoke screaming and in a cold sweat, it must have been an awful shock.

"No! No! Help! Help!" Sandra screamed, as she dove beneath the covers. Her heart was beating as if it would jump out of her chest.

"What the heck?" Mike awoke from a deep sleep wondering what on earth the matter was. It was the first time he had witnessed Sandra having a nightmare. Once he was wide awake, he realized what had happened. She had told him about her nightmares, but he had no idea how frightening they were until now.

"It's all right, darling. I am here. There is nothing to worry about. You're safe. No one will ever harm you while I am here." He wrapped his arms around her and held her tight until she fell back to sleep.

Over time he got used to being wakened by screams, and never once did he complain. It was always the same routine. He would hold her safely in his arms whispering calming words until she fell back to sleep. Sandra hated the fact that she disturbed his sleep so often, especially as he worked shifts, and she knew how little sleep he got anyway. "I'm so sorry, love. I awoke you again last night. When will these nightmares ever end? I know it must be awful to be startled in the middle of the night, with your wife screaming like a banshee," Sandra said as she handed him his lunch pail to take to work the next morning.

"Give us a kiss before I go. I'm more worried about the van starting this morning than anything. The darned thing has been tough to start the last few days."

Sandra reached up and gave him a long lingering kiss. She knew how lucky she was to have such a good husband.

The van was always parked outside on the opposite side of the road and facing downhill. Sandra watched through the window as Mike cranked the handle to start it. Some mornings it started, and other mornings he had to run alongside it pushing it downhill and jumping in at the last minute when the engine finally fired. This morning his fears were confirmed, when after several cranks of the handle, it would not start.

"Damn it!" he exclaimed. *Of all mornings, there is safety meeting before work this morning. I'll never get there on time,* he thought to himself.

Sandra could see his frustration as he looked up to the window above, and throwing his hands in the air, he went to once more give the van a push. As he walked to the side of the van, he saw the local rookie cop standing with his hands on his hips watching the whole scene. He had a big grin on his face and obviously thought this was very funny. Mike was already frustrated, and at the sight of the cop just standing there, he lost his usual composure.

"Don't just stand there, like a nelly. Get your finger out and give me a push!"

The bobby was too surprised to do anything different, and as Mike jumped back in, the bobby gave it a big push. The van spluttered a few times before it finally chugged away down the street. Sandra watched as the van disappeared in a cloud of smoke, and chuckled to herself as she saw the young bobby brushing off the dirt from his uniform. His cheeky grin was gone.

Sandra went into the ice cold bathroom and got ready for work. She usually left home about an hour after Mike, so she had time to make the bed and tidy up before leaving. The flat was by no means fancy, but together they had turned it into a home. It was a sense of pride for Sandra to close the door behind her, knowing that when they both got home from work, they would open the door to a welcoming atmosphere. Sandra never lost her love of flowers, and Mike saw to it that his paycheque always stretched to a bunch of daffodils or tulips, which she would arrange and place on the kitchen table.

Money was managed very carefully, yet there was seldom anything left over for savings. Their income stretched from pay packet to pay packet and very little further. The tenants in the flat below were a strange couple, and their constant fights and then make up sessions could be clearly heard in the flat above. One day the lady from the flat below gave Sandra a key, and asked her to let the plumber into the washroom as he would be there before she got home from work. Sandra arrived home from work at 5:00 p.m., and shortly afterwards there was a knock on the door.

"I'm here to fix the tank over the toilet in number 210. Can you let me in?"

Sandra followed him downstairs and opened the door into the bathroom. "Oh my god," she gasped as she opened the door into a terrible stench and filth everywhere. The bathtub was filled with coal, and obviously no one had bathed in there for a long while. There was a coal shed in the yard below, but obviously the tenants were too lazy to climb up and downstairs to fetch the coal when needed. The toilet was unflushed and the floor was piled high with dirty clothing. Sandra had never been so embarrassed.

"Oh, I'm so sorry. I've never been in here. I had no idea it was like this. I'll leave you to it, but please come and let me know when you have finished so I can lock the door again."

Sandra was mortified, thinking he would suppose her flat was in the same filthy state. He had to come back, so she could ask him to look at her bathroom, and he would see it was not the same. When he came upstairs, she made some pretence for him to check a tap, and he followed her in to a shiny clean bathroom with pretty curtains and clean towels arranged nicely on the brightly painted shelving. The plumber checked the tap, and was not fooled by Sandra's ruse to show him the difference in the two flats.

"It's all right, love. Not a thing wrong with it. Amazing how different folks look after their property, isn't it?" Sandra thanked him and took back the key, making sure he got a peek inside the main door of the bright and clean flat she and Mike lived in.

The flat had been a good first home, but the constant noise from the tenants below and the inconvenience of the stairs was far from perfect. Mike and Sandra heard about a house that was going to be for sale in Leabrooks. It was closer to Mike's job, and although it would be a bus ride for Sandra, she did not work shifts like Mike did. The only way they could buy it was if they could get a loan from Annie and Sid. It was Annie who first heard about the house, and she encouraged Mike to make some enquiries. Sandra and Mike heard the old gentleman was sick, and his wife wanted them to move closer to their daughter. It was a brick built detached house on a large lot, and although in need of repair and a lot of upgrades, it had potential.

"Mam says that we can go and see the house this weekend, Sandra. I think she would really like it if we lived closer, and both mam and dad are happy to give us a loan if we do decide to buy it." Mike was as excited as Sandra at the prospect of moving.

"I can't say I will be sorry to say goodbye to the neighbours," Sandra smiled, as the recent occurrence at the flat below was still imprinted on her brain.

"Let's go bright and early Saturday, then. Mam's asked us to stop there for a late breakfast," Mike said, knowing he would get no objections from his wife.

They arrived at Annie's just as she was putting the finishing touches to a great breakfast. They enjoyed the meal, but both were eager to go and check out the house. Annie convinced them to have another cup of tea, as she thought the elderly couple might not be ready for visitors so early. By the time they left to walk up the street, it was afternoon.

"Come in, you two. Annie said you wanted to see my place. Come and see Arthur before I show you around." Sandra thought maybe Arthur was not feeling well, and followed blindly into the front room. There on the table was a coffin with Arthur dead as a doornail. As Sandra stared in horror at the waxy body, Arthur expelled his last nasal fluids.

Mike caught hold of his wife, and politely suggested they take a look around the rest of the house. Sandra was in so much shock that she barely remembered a thing about it other than the coffin and Arthur.

"Well, that went well," Mike said as they walked away. He was trying hard to keep a straight face. "You look like you just saw a ghost."

"Did you see what happened? Was he really dead?" Sandra could not believe what she saw.

Mike explained that sometimes shortly after death the body can still expel bodily fluids.

Arthur had obviously been dead for a very short time. But his wife went about the house showing as if there was nothing at all unusual about her husband's dead body being in the front room.

Back at Sid and Annie's they told the story of their house viewing, and the fact that although it needed a lot of work, the price was very reasonable. Mike's mom and dad agreed to give them a loan, and the following day they made an offer which was accepted instantly.

"Can you believe it: a house of our own, with a garden front and back? I love the fact that it is detached and it stands well back of the street. I am not sure I fancy going outside to the bathroom, but who knows, maybe we can find a way to add on to the place later." Sandra was full of ideas already as to what she wanted to do with the place.

"We'll have to do things as we can afford them, love. I want to pay mam and dad back before we incur any major expenses." Mike and Sandra had never had a debt until now, and neither of them liked the feeling of owing money.

"We have to tell Uncle Joe and Auntie Elsie. They will be chuffed to bits to know that we are moving closer to Ripley." Sandra was looking forward to breaking the news to them. Since living in Derby, they had not seen as much of them.

Mike loved them as much as Sandra did, as he knew how invaluable they had been in her childhood. "We'll go and see them tomorrow and tell them our news. As soon as we get possession, we can bring them to take a look." Mike would value Joe's advice on some ideas he had for renovating. Mike and Sandra had agreed they would have to stretch the budget to replace the old wallpaper, and strip the many layers of paint from the doors and windows and give them a fresh coat of paint.

Uncle Joe and Auntie Elsie were delighted with the news, and they were the first people to see the house once it was empty. Joe had painted and papered many old houses, and this one was no worse than others he had seen before. He saw beyond the years of grime to what it could be.

"It needs a bit of fixing up, love, but your Auntie Elsie and I will come and help you get it ship shape." Joe put his arms around Elsie, knowing she would be by his side in this as she was in everything.

Uncle Joe volunteered to do all of the painting and decorating, and also to get the materials for them at his cost. It was the best gift anyone could have given them, and Sandra could not believe how they had yet again come to her rescue. Mike and Sandra would never have been able to accomplish what they did without Uncle Joe and Aunt Elsie's help.

The next three months went by in a whirlwind of preparations. They had to give notice on the flat, and then they had a mountain of work to do on the house before they could move in. Most of the initial work was scrubbing and cleaning, and taking down the numerous nails that were hammered into the walls. Sandra had noticed when she first saw the place that there was an assortment of family photos hanging in all of the rooms. Mike suggested they remove the wall from the hidden staircase and open up the room by exposing the stairs and putting up a nice railing.

"It is mostly labour, and I can do all of that by myself. The railings won't cost a fortune, but I know it will make a big difference."

Sandra did not need any convincing. It was a great idea and really made the room so much larger and brighter. She chose a very modern "paint splash" wallpaper with small pale green and terra cotta splashes on a white background. The ceiling was terribly stained with years of resident smokers and coal fires. Uncle Joe cleaned it all off and papered it with a heavy embossed Lyncruster wallpaper, which Sandra insisted be painted in a matching pale terra cotta. Much to everyone's surprise, the result was very eye catching and modern.

Each room was tackled and transformed systematically until the old house bore no resemblance to its former self. It was a little show home that Mike and Sandra were justifiably proud of. Sandra had not told her Riddings gran as she wanted to keep it a surprise until they had it all finished. She knew how happy Julia would be to have them both living so close by.

It was almost time to move in, and Sandra came home from work eager to carry on packing the last of their belongings. Mattie was at the door of the shop as Sandra came home, and it was obvious something was wrong.

"It's your grandma Julia; she died last night. The doctor thinks it may have been a diabetic coma." Mattie knew Julia's health had been deteriorating rapidly, and the news of her death, although sad, was not unexpected. Sandra had seen her gran sick for many years, but somehow never thought she was so seriously ill. The news was a terrible shock to Sandra, and the impending move became second to the terrible sorrow of Julia's death.

Alf and his sister Vera took charge of all of the arrangements, and a small funeral was planned at the church in Riddings. Julia was going to be buried in the same grave as her beloved husband Tom, at the top corner of St. James Church yard. The day of the funeral, Sandra watched as the men from the funeral home tilted the coffin on one side to get it through the narrow doorway. It was too much. She could not believe that they treated the body of her grandmother with such disrespect. Once they had left, Sandra ran up the garden path and cried, heartbroken, thinking of her gran dying all alone and of how she wished she had told her of their upcoming move, and of all the times she had not said, "I love you."

The weight of Julia's death was not eased when Sandra later found out it was the nurse who had found Julia when she came to give her the morning injection of insulin. There was no phone in the house, and obviously Julia had been too weak to walk next door for help. She had been dead for some time, and was sitting fully dressed in her best clothes. It was obvious Julia must have known she was dying. She was a very proud lady, and would never have been seen unbathed and undressed. To think of her gran's last lonely hours, knowing she was dying, brought Sandra to tears for many months afterwards. Loneliness was a terrible thing, and Sandra knew that more than anyone as she had lived most of her young life that way.

Thirty-Three

LEABROOKS

Neither Mike nor Sandra were sad to leave the flat on Peet Street, and both were very excited to actually become home owners. They would have a vested interest in all the renovations, and their efforts would build equity in their investment. It was not perfect, as it was an old brick built house that suffered the same problem with damp as most of the houses in the area. There was one coal fire in the house, and it had to heat all five rooms. To the young couple, though, it was still a massive accomplishment to have their own home at such a young age.

Little by little, as they could afford it, they made upgrades wherever they could. Now that Mike was earning more money, they could think of starting a family. Both of them loved children and wanted to start their family while they were young. Sid was the one who really questioned why he had not yet been presented with a grandchild.

"What are you waiting for? It's time there was the patter of tiny feet around this old house again," he teased his son and daughter-in-law constantly, until one day Sandra could tell him she was indeed pregnant.

"I think we can put your dad out of his misery, Mike. I'm just a few days late, but I know I am pregnant. You are going to be a dad, Mr. Lewis." Sandra was beaming from ear to ear, even though almost from the day of conception she was constantly nauseous.

Mike was beside himself with joy. "Are you sure? Don't you need to go to the doctor to find out?"

"I'll make an appointment to go as soon as he can see me, but yes, I am sure. I feel different and I just know I am expecting. We won't tell anyone until the doctor confirms it, though." Sandra was dying to see the look on Sid and Annie's faces when she broke the news. She knew they would be over the moon with happiness for them. She was a little unsure as to what her own mother's reaction would be. Mattie had never particularly enjoyed motherhood, and there was little reason to believe that she would enjoy being a grandmother.

Bobbie Ryan had now taken over his father's practice, and when Sandra visited him the following week, he confirmed her suspicions.

"Congratulations, Mrs. Lewis. You are indeed pregnant, and you can expect to deliver sometime around the 3rd of June." He could see that his words were what she had been waiting to hear.

Sandra and Mike went that night to break the news to Sid and Annie, and they were both thrilled to bits at the thoughts of another little grandchild. They doted on Denise, the daughter of Mike's sister, Josie.

From the start it was a difficult pregnancy. Sandra did not just have morning sickness. It was morning, noon and night sickness. Just the smell of fresh bread or the taste of milk caused her to heave. The only thing that sometimes helped with the nausea was sour apples.

On one occasion, late at night, Mike actually climbed over the fence and got apples from the neighbour's tree. Sandra continued working at the Territorial Army for as long as she could, and carried a plastic bag with her on the bus, which she often had to use to throw up in. It became increasingly difficult to work with the unpredictable bouts of nausea. Reluctantly she handed in her notice to finish work. The company was wonderful, and had a big farewell party, plus lots of gifts and cards from all of the management and staff.

Sandra appeared to be having more difficulty with the pregnancy than was normal. The baby seemed to be pushing her body out at each side, and sleeping was almost impossible. Her ankles were swollen and uncomfortable, and the nausea continued. One night when Mike came home from work, Sandra was sitting on the couch in tears.

"I feel so rotten, Mike. It's not supposed to be like this, I am sure. I'm so tired and my stomach feels like it can't stretch any further."

"Come on, love, let's go and get you a check-up," Mike insisted.

Doctor Ryan took one look at Sandra and was concerned she might have high blood pressure. Her face was flushed and her ankles were swollen to twice their size. He took her blood pressure and gave her a full examination. His grave expression told her there was something very wrong. He very strongly suspected the baby was lying in an awkward breech position and this was causing a lot of Sandra's discomfort. It was her first child and he knew this was not going to be easy.

"What is it, Doctor? Is my baby all right?" Sandra remembered Beverly Jane, and her heart stood still waiting for his response.

"Sandra, we have to do a scan and see if we can find a reason for all of this," the doctor said as he finished his exam. "We will get it done right away, but in the meantime, don't worry. This little one has a very strong heartbeat. I don't want to give you any medication if we can help it. The best thing you can do is take life easy. Put your feet up as often as you can and do not over exert yourself."

Mike could see the minute Sandra came out of the office that there was something wrong, and when she told him about the scan his face fell

"He's going to be fine, love. I know it. I've felt that little guy kick, and he is a fighter for sure." Mike could not let Sandra see how worried he was.

The scan results came back worse than Dr. Ryan had expected. He called Sandra in to tell her the bad news. Mike insisted on going to the appointment with her. He did not want her to be alone if there was a problem.

Bobbie Ryan had often seen his father exhausted after a long day in the surgery, but had never had any doubts he wanted to follow in his father's footsteps. He loved being a doctor, especially when he could help to improve someone's life. Being the bearer of bad news was a part of the job he would never get used to, however.

"I'm sorry, Sandra, but the baby is breech and you need to go and see a specialist." The doctor was concerned, as it was a very difficult transverse breech. He did not explain the seriousness of the situation, but both Mike and Sandra could see the concern on his face.

Sandra made the trip to see the specialist and he explained in detail, showing a picture of the growing baby, what the issue was. The baby was lying back down across Sandra's stomach and had one arm raised above its head and the other arm straight out in front of it.

"We'll give it another couple of weeks, and if there is no movement, then we will try and reposition the baby to the head down position. See my secretary on the way out and make an appointment to come back in a fortnight." The specialist was quite matter of fact and tried not to alarm the young expectant mother.

The two weeks passed and Sandra was still feeling far from well. By the time she arrived at the specialist, her blood pressure was way above normal.

After examining Sandra and trying to reposition the baby, the specialist looked very grave. "I'm afraid the baby has not moved, and I am unable to turn it due to the position it is in. Sometimes as the pregnancy progresses the baby may turn by itself."

"How serious is this, Doctor? Will my baby be all right?" Sandra was in tears, both with the discomfort of the doctor's manipulations and the fear of the unknown.

"You are under my care as of now, and I will monitor the baby and you every two weeks until your due date. We will make arrangements for you to go to Derby City Hospital, which is equipped to deal with difficult births. We will take very good care of you and your baby."

Sandra told her parents and her gran, and Polly immediately offered to pay for a private hospital. "I'm coming with you on your next visit to the specialist, love. I don't want you to have to go to the City Hospital where you have no guarantee of a specialist being on call."

Mama Polly kept her word, and on the next visit she inquired about a private hospital bed and the attention of the specialist.

"I'm sorry, Mrs. Redford, I'm afraid I will be out of the country on Sandra's due date. You can request a private room, but there is no guarantee there will be a specialist available for the delivery. All of our personnel are well trained, and there should be no problems. If it is a private room that you would like, I can certainly arrange that."

Sandra could see no point in that. "I'll be fine, mama. If I am at Derby City, there are bound to be good nurses and doctors on staff all the time." Polly was still not convinced, but Sandra insisted.

The due date arrived and still the baby had not moved position. Sandra's blood pressure was now so high the doctor feared toxemia.

"We are going to admit you to the hospital for a few days and make sure you have some rest before this little one decides to be born," the doctor said as he looked at Sandra's swollen ankles and feet. Sandra was still a few months shy of her twenty-first birthday, and it had been a very difficult nine months. Although she did not want to go to hospital, she was too tired and uncomfortable to disagree.

Almost two weeks after the due date, there was still no sign of labour, and the baby was still very much a transverse breech. Rightly or wrongly, the specialist had made a decision that, although it was a big baby, Sandra was young and able to deliver without him performing a caesarian operation. He had decided that if necessary they would use forceps to deliver the baby. He had done this many times, and still preferred this rather than cutting open a young mother.

The young doctor came into the room and gave Sandra a brief examination. "Sandra, we are going to induce labour and this will encourage the baby to be born rather than wait for it to take its own time," he said, as he instructed the nurse to put a needle in to Sandra's arm and start a drip.

Sandra looked forlornly into the doctor's eyes. "The specialist will be here for the delivery won't he?"

"I'm afraid not Sandra. He is still away on vacation, but don't you worry, I will take good care of you." He could see she was feeling very scared and wanted to reassure her that all was well.

Nothing happened for about three hours and then Sandra felt the first of a series of excruciating pains. Mike sat by her side as he watched, unable to do anything to help. He was exhausted just watching the ordeal. The procedure had started Sandra into three minute labour and it continued for a total of thirty six hours. He sat by the bed and held her hand, and kept putting cold cloths on her forehead. Beads of perspiration mixed with silent tears streamed down her face. She tried not to cry out, but sometimes the pains were so intense, she moaned in pain. During the labour she was wheeled in and out of the operating room several times, each time with the assurance that the next one would be "the" time. The only pain killer she was given was an occasional whiff of something called gas and air. Mike felt every pain along with her, and wondered how much longer she could go through this.

Finally, when Sandra thought she could take this no longer, after the most arduous and painful time in the surgery, her son was born. "He's not crying. Why isn't he crying? What's wrong?" Sandra tried to raise herself up to look at her son.

"You are not the only one who has had a difficult time, young lady. This little fellow has been fighting to be born for a long while. We had to use forceps to deliver him, so he needs to be cleaned up. We are going to put him to sleep in an incubator for a while and let him get some rest." The baby was quickly rushed to an incubator, because despite his weight of nine pounds one ounce, he was exhausted with the long and difficult birth. Sandra was desperate to see her newborn son, but was told that until he had been assessed and stabilized, she could not see him.

It was a long and arduous night and Sandra was still in a lot of pain. The nurses came in and out of the room throughout the night, as they had kept her in a special unit overnight to monitor her recovery. She drifted in and out of fitful sleep, and could occasionally hear the nurses talking.

"They left it too late for a C-section. That was a close call," she heard one nurse say.

"It was a big baby, and to deliver it breech was just awful. Poor lass, it was her first, and now probably the last, as I doubt she will want any more after this one."

The next morning when the doctor came on his rounds, he explained her son was doing very well, and he should be allowed out of the incubator later that day.

"We were hoping he would reposition during the birthing process, but I am afraid he was unable to turn. There was a danger of him being strangled with the umbilical cord and we had to use forceps to assist in the delivery. Your son has some bruising that will fade in a few days. Transverse breech babies are very rare, and often do not have such good results. Breech presentation is a problem primarily because the presenting part is a poor dilating wedge, which can cause the head, which follows, to be trapped during delivery, often compressing the umbilical cord. Your little boy saved his own life, by having a hand over his head when he was delivered. You have a healthy son and we don't anticipate any problems. Having said that, I am sorry to say we had to give you a lot of stitches which will take time to heal. You will have to sit on a rubber inner tube for several weeks, I am afraid."

Sandra listened to all of his words, but the only thing she focused on was that she had a healthy son and she would be able to see him later that day.

Derby City Hospital was a huge hospital, and the room Sandra was sent to the following morning had about twelve beds in it. In each bed there were women in various stages of labour, or mothers recovering after difficult births. The noise was deafening, as there were babies crying and women moaning in pain. Derby was a very cosmopolitan city, and thus there were many different ethnicities and they all dealt with pain differently. Screaming was not uncommon.

Mike had been at the hospital for most of the night, and was eventually allowed to go and visit his wife and his new son. When the nurse brought in their baby boy, they both cried tears of relief. He was perfect. He was much larger than most of the babies on the ward, and as he had not been born head first, he had a beautifully shaped head. He was the image of Mike, which pleased them both. "He's definitely a Martin Karl," Sandra said. That was the name they had both chosen for a boy. A little girl would have been Sarah. After letting Sandra hold her son for a few minutes, the nurse bundled him up and put him in a cot by her bed. Mike and Sandra never took their eyes off him as he lay quietly by their side. "Shouldn't he be crying or something?" Mike questioned. Sandra looked around, and most of the other babies were making noise. "I don't know. Wiggle his crib." Mike rocked the crib, and still no movement. "Nurse!" Sandra shouted. "Please come and check my baby."

The nurse came over and looked at the sleeping baby. "You'll be glad of a little peace and quiet in a few days, young lady. He's just sleeping very peacefully." She did not know how many times her words would come back to haunt the young couple.

Mike left the hospital after visiting hours were over, eager to share the news of his new son with the rest of the family. His first stop was at Polly and Evan's, and Polly cried with relief to know that everything had turned out well. She had lost many night's sleep worrying about Sandra's difficult pregnancy. "God is good," she exclaimed. "Give them both big hugs from us both, and we will see them as soon as we can."

On his way back to Leabrooks, he stopped at Ripley to tell Mattie and Alf, and was not at all surprised to see that they were not home. He knew where he could find them, and made his way to the Gibson, where they were sitting drinking with friends. Mattie was relieved to know that it was over for her daughter, and that the baby was healthy, but she was less than happy when Mike addressed her as "grandma."

"I am not grandma," she said very clearly, "He can call me nana." As far as she was concerned, at forty-two years of age she was far too young to be anyone's grandma.

The reception at Leabrooks was far more jubilant. Sid was just as happy as Annie about the birth, and especially as it was a boy. Sid slapped his son on the back and went to pour a drink. "This is cause for celebration, lad." Mike looked at the dusty bottle of Apricot

Brandy and thought, *It must be, that bottle's never been touched for a while!*

If the birth had been difficult, the next nine months were even more so. Sandra had a slow recovery from the traumatic birthing ordeal, and Martin was almost impossible to placate. It was important to Sandra to breast feed, but she had difficulty from the start. She had watched as other mothers, far less well endowed, had to express milk because they had so much. She found it painful, and was never sure Martin had been fed enough. He cried when he had been fed, when he had been changed, and always the minute he was placed in his crib. *How come he always wants something?* Sandra thought. *He could give me a few minutes peace.* She loved her new son with all her heart, but was afraid she might be doing something wrong.

"What can I do?" Sandra cried in despair. "He has been fed; he has a clean diaper." A visit to the doctor did not give a lot of encouragement.

"He is just colicky. Some babies are. Do you give him gripe water? He is a big baby and maybe you need to supplement your breast feeding with a bottle and some Pablum."

"I have tried gripe water, and I feed him on demand, which is at least every three hours; sometimes it is only two hours," Sandra said forlornly. "I will try the bottle and Pablum though, if it might help."

Once Sandra increased the amount of Martin's milk and introduced Pablum, by way of cutting a larger hole in the plastic teat on his bottle, things started to improve slowly. Now that she breast fed him and then gave him a bottle, the nightly feedings lasted at least an hour. After each feed, Sandra fell into an exhausted sleep, only to wake up thinking she had fallen asleep with him in her arms. She would wake up in panic, thinking she had suffocated him.

Sid thought he was perfect. "He's just got a mind of his own. He lets you know if he wants something," Sid would say when Martin was being difficult.

"Trouble is, he always wants something," Sandra said as she smiled at Martin, who was being a perfect sweetheart for Grandpa Sid. The truth was that as he was such big baby, he probably hadn't been getting enough to eat; now that he was having the Pablum, he was far more content.

Mike was still working shifts and this did not help the situation, as when he worked on the night shift Sandra was still afraid of the dark, and feared waking up with a nightmare. Mike and Betty Bagshaw were friends of Sandra and Mike, and knew all about Sandra's fear of the dark. Mike Bagshaw was the local constable and patrolled the area on his bicycle at night. He made it his duty to ring his bell as he passed by Sandra's when Mike was working. It was comforting to know he was on duty and patrolling the neighbourhood. Mike was almost finished his apprenticeship, and the old blue van was replaced with a Ford Prefect that was much more reliable. Martin eventually outgrew his colic and Sandra could deal with a healthy, but rambunctious child. Life was good.

Thirty-Four

THE YEAR OF CHANGE

Polly and Evan were making an excellent living in the fish and chip shop, but the hard work was taking a toll on them both. It was especially hard on Evan working all day and evening in the cold rumbling house. He never complained, but Polly hated to see him standing with his hands in ice water all day. She knew he would never complain, but she had to find a way to open a discussion about their future.

"I don't know how much longer we can carry on doing this, love," Polly said one night when they had finally closed the store. She had just come inside from washing off the pavement, and her feet ached from standing behind the counter all night. She knew Evan would be far more likely to consider a move if he thought it was what she wanted.

Evan rubbed his cold hands back and forth, trying to get a little feeling back into his fingers.

"Tomorrow's another day, love, and we'll both feel different after a good night's sleep." He hated to complain as he knew Polly loved the business. "I'll do the lock up tomorrow night, love. I know it's a big job to clean up after you've been on your feet all day." He made a mental note to try and help out more, but the truth was he too was exhausted at the end of each day.

Mattie and Alf were both doing well in the clothing stores. Thanks to Mattie's talents at buying, their profit margins were fantastic. One day Mattie heard from one of her suppliers that another store was coming up for sale. "It's a bargain, Mattie. They are not good operators and are struggling to make their payments. They owe us for the last two shipments, and I've checked with other suppliers. We'll all be lucky if we get paid. It's in a good location, but it needs cleaning and a good owner who knows how to make a go of it. I bet you could pick it up for a song."

Mattie thought about the news all day, and then called up her mam and Evan.

"Mam, there's a store in Derby that's coming up for sale. Why don't you and Evan come and take a look at it? We could operate all three separately, but I can buy for all three at once, which will give us a lot more discounts and save us all money."

"I don't know, my duck. Its hard work here, but I know the business and I love my customers. What do I know about the clothing trade?" Polly thought what a big decision it was.

"I can teach you anything you need to know. You are a great knitter and embroiderer, mom; you could stock knitting wool and patterns and embroidery silks. You would be able to help customers with their choices. The rest you will pick up as you go along."

Mattie convinced Polly and Evan to go and have a look. The store was in a nice location, with big old houses on the opposite side of the street. The store had very nice living accommodation, although very much in need of a good clean. Polly could see beyond the mess and dirt, and envision the place when she had it put in shape. Evan was impressed with the large conservatory at the back of the property. It was a beautiful glass addition that looked out onto the large garden and lawn. His thoughts immediately went to having a few plant pots and growing some tomatoes and a few herbs. He missed his garden at Landrose more than he had ever admitted to anyone.

"There's a lot to think about, Evan. We have a good living at the fish and chip shop, I know, but this would certainly be a nice place to live." They both gave the move a lot of thought, but in the end they decided to make an offer on the property subject to the sale of the fish and chip shop. Polly and Evan did not even have to advertise the shop, as when they told Mrs. Pierce they were going to sell, she knew a buyer. She knew the money the store was making, and if she could have afforded to buy it herself she would have done so. Polly and Evan set a price, and sold for the asking price. It was all done and settled in less than sixty days.

The day of the move was a day of mixed feelings. They had enjoyed their time in Chesterfield, and also the brisk trade of the fish and chip business. "I hope we are making the right move, Evan," Polly said as she looked back at the store for the last time.

It did not take long for Polly and Evan to get their new business and living accommodation into pristine order. Polly looked proudly around at the results and waited for the first customer. It was a very different business, and it took a while to get used to the slower trade.

In the fish and chip shop, the sales were much smaller, but there was a steady stream of customers. The profits they made from one customer in the clothing business were equal to a bus load of hungry customers at the fish shop. Thanks to Mattie's efforts with the stock, profits were high, and the end result was that the shop did very well. Polly gradually became used to the clothing business, and especially excelled in the sale of materials and wool and threads. Evan did what he did best. He was the everywhere man. If an order needed to be picked up or a special delivery made, he was there. If new shelving was needed or renovations of any sort, he was the man. Everything was going wonderfully, and when Mattie came to visit one day, Polly had no idea of the announcement she was about to make.

"Mam, Alf and I have seen a pub for lease in Stanton, Burton on Trent area, and we have been to have a look at it. Alf is going to apply for tenancy."

"What? Why on earth are you going to sell the stores now? Everything is doing so well." Polly could not believe her ears.

"Alf has always wanted a pub, Mam, and this is a great location on a bus tour route. It's called The White Horse Inn, and it has a football pitch and cricket grounds attached to it."

Polly was less than convinced that this would be a good move. Alf and Mattie had both been so busy with the dress stores that they had seemed to be more content and less inclined to pursue different interests. She had been very pleased to see them both spending more time together these days. She thought at last Mattie had settled down.

"It's a big move, Mattie. Are you sure you want to give up the two stores and make such a big move? We've only just moved to Derby, and now you're going to take off and leave us." Polly knew that in the long run, Mattie would end up doing whatever she wanted to do. Mattie would give but a second's thought to any impact their decision would have on anyone else. "All I ask is that you don't do anything rash. Think about it for a few days before you rush into anything. What about our Sandra and Mike and the baby? You'll never get to see them all those miles away."

"I've thought about it, Mam, and Alf's done what I have wanted for the last few years, and this is his chance to do what he wants. If he is accepted, then we are moving." Mattie was just as excited about the prospect as Alf. The store had become routine, and she was bored with life at Peet Street.

Alf had to undergo a very thorough interview and investigation, but he was accepted without question. Both of the stores sold for a good profit, as they were in far better shape when Alf and Mattie left than when they had arrived. Unlike Polly and Evan's store, the premises were just leased, so basically all that was sold was the stock and the goodwill. Polly was very disappointed, as it meant that now they had moved to Derby, she would not be close to any of her children. Alf and Belle had moved to Bromley in Kent, where Alf had a bigger store. Polly hardly ever saw them anymore. Darren and June were now living in Tansley area and their visits were few and far between. Now Mattie and Alf were moving miles away. Sandra and Mike visited with Martin when they were able, but Polly missed her family around her. Her children and their children were her greatest joy.

Alf and Mattie were embarking on a big move. Mattie loved the "rag trade" but it was starting to lose its charm. The store's customers were mostly the factory girls, and the biggest sales by far were for knitting wools, nylon stockings, and personal items. There was no challenge in selling such mundane things. She certainly missed the excitement of dealing with higher priced fashionable merchandise. "You have to cater to the market that you have," was something she had learned early, and her business savvy had certainly helped to make the current business a success.

"Are you going to miss the shop, Mattie?" Alf enquired one night, when they were busy packing up the last of their belongings.

"No, Alf. It has had its day. It was good while it lasted, but I am ready for a change." Mattie was in fact looking forward to the new adventure.

"It's going to mean long hours, Mattie, and a big change for you." Alf was concerned that Mattie would have difficulty adapting to the different lifestyle. He had no idea how wrong he would be. Mattie was in her elements from day one, when she first walked into the pub as the manageress.

"Cor blimey, mate, would you take a look at that?" a stunned patron said to the fellow leaning next to him at the bar. "By the heck, it looks as if things are looking up at The White Horse."

"I might be buying a few pints here, now the scenery has improved," drawled the tall blonde young man, as he eyed Mattie up and down with an approving, if somewhat brazen leer.

Mattie knew all eyes were upon her, and as most of the patrons were male, their looks of approval outnumbered a few sour looks from the women in the bar.

She was wearing an emerald green sheath dress, which clung to every curve and accentuated her long slim legs. Her hair was now a shade of dark auburn, and she had chosen to wear it up in a very classy chignon. The gold earrings and bangle reflected the pub lighting. She had rings on three fingers of each hand.

"She's hardly dressed for changing barrels," a plainly dressed middle aged lady commented.

"I'll volunteer to go into the cellar and help her," her husband piped up.

"You just get your pint down you, and be thankful she's not your problem. I bet he's got his hands full with that one," his wife snorted.

Alf looked at the stir Mattie had caused as she walked in, but he was used to that by now, and it did not bother him. He was by far the most self-assured person in the pub. He was the landlord, and that in itself commanded respect. Everyone liked Alf the minute he took over the management. His easy and ever ready smile welcomed all that entered. Alf's tall and muscular build was noticed as much by the women as Mattie's charms were by the men. Unlike Mattie, Alf was always unaware of his effect on the opposite sex.

"A moment of your time, ladies and gentlemen," Alf said, as he rang the big brass bell on the counter. "I'm Alf Wetton, your new landlord, and this is my wife, Mattie. I'm sure that in the next few weeks we will get to know you all. Anyway, sup up, and your next drink is on Mattie and me."

Mattie soon found her best job in the pub was picking up empty glasses and cleaning tables. It was easy work, and she had the opportunity to flirt with all the male customers. Sales were great, as the young lads from the soccer club and the cricket club liked nothing better than to have a few pints in the pub after their games on the adjoining field. They made it a game to see if they could guess what Mattie would be wearing next. Very often it would be a short, tight skirt that showed off her best attributes as she bent to clean the tables.

The blonde young man at the bar became a regular, and he never took his eyes off Mattie. Sometimes he had a pretty young lady with him, but often he was alone. There was something about him that intrigued Mattie. There was an air of danger about him. His hair was dirty blonde and always tousled, as if he had just got out of bed, and maybe he had. He had very muscular arms and a permanent tan. Mattie guessed that whatever he did for a living, it must be an outdoor job. It was just a matter of time before he made his move on Mattie. The sparks had flown from the first minute their eyes met.

Mattie felt alive again. She had missed the excitement and the danger of an affair. Jack was a regular at the pub, and their open flirting was not unnoticed. Alf thought it was just harmless fun, and Mattie being Mattie. He was wrong. It did not take Mattie long to devise ways in which she could meet Jack.

"I'm going to the licensee meeting," or "I am going to pick up supplies," were just a couple of the reasons she would give to be absent for a few stolen hours. Alf had never taken his driving test, as he never wanted to drink and drive. His reasoning had always been that when he went out, he had a drink, and busses were there when he needed one. Mattie had taken her test, and after three or four attempts finally passed, and what freedom that gave her. They purchased a van, which Mattie used for pickups and deliveries and clandestine meetings.

Jack was by far the most dangerous liaison that Mattie had ever had. He was always one step ahead of the law, for some petty crime or other. He was quick tempered, and very hot headed with a short fuse. In the beginning the relationship was mercurial. Mattie loved to play with fire, and she was particularly in her elements when she could play one against another. Bob, who started out as a friend of Jack, also had his eyes on Mattie, and Mattie was attracted to both of them. All it took was for Mattie to pay a little more attention to Bob, and the fight was on.

"Alf, I've seen this little caravan in Market Bosworth, and it's being leased for a song," Mattie said as she looked up from the local paper. "We really need a place to get away, where we can have some relaxation away from the pub."

"And when do you think we can do that, Mattie? Right now I can't leave this place, without a manager in it. It takes time to train good staff who are reliable enough to trust with this business." Alf saw no sense in leasing a caravan, no matter how cheap.

"Let's just go and drive out there and take a look before we open on Sunday," Mattie cajoled.

"Well just a look." Alf did not mind a drive out to the country, and it would be one of the few times they would be alone together.

It was a beautiful day, and when they arrived at Market Bosworth the sun was shining on the little trout pond that was beside the amazing stand of trees lining the driveway to the big estate. The caravan was being leased by the owner of the estate, and it came with use of the trout pond. Alf was sold on the idea as soon as he saw the beautiful location, and all his previous reservations were gone by the wayside. It was a little patch of heaven, and the thought of being able to fish in the pond, no matter how infrequent, was very enticing. Before they left, they had signed a year's lease on the caravan.

As the weeks turned into months, it became harder and harder for Mattie to hide her affairs, as by now she was also having an affair with Bob. The caravan had become, as she had intended, a love nest for Mattie and her two lovers. It was perfect as it was in an isolated location on a large estate, and the owner had his own private access on the opposite side of the acreage. In all the times she had been to the caravan, she had never seen him.

Mattie was playing a dangerous game, and even she did not realize how dangerous it was until it was almost too late. She had tired of the affair with Jack as he was becoming more and more demanding of her time. He thought he could treat her the same way as he had all the other women who had been in his life. Mattie would never let any man dominate her. She had witnessed Lance treating her mother with indifference, and she would never tolerate that. Bob was different; he was young and exciting, just as Jack was, but he was a hard worker, with a good job. He treated Mattie like a princess, and never put any demands upon her. Mattie struggled with her conscience almost daily, but she could always come up with some justification for her behaviour. There was never any doubt she loved Alf. He was her one true love. *It's the Lambert curse,* she thought to herself. *I hated when my dad treated my mam so badly, and here I am doing the same thing.* The periods of remorse were brief and soon forgotten, however, when the opportunity for excitement arose.

Jack had been particularly troublesome in the pub, and had gotten into fights with some of the locals. Alf had threatened to bar him, and put him on probation for a couple of weeks.

"Jack, you're a good customer, but you are costing me business with your damn foolish fighting. I won't have it in my pub. Nobody wants to come for a night out and get beer thrown all over them. If you want to fight, take it outside and off my property."

Jack knew Alf meant what he said, and despite all the men he had fought, he would never risk getting into a fight with Alf. Alf had a 37 inch reach, which had won many bets in the pub, as he could outreach any man there. There were many occasions when Alf had to throw out an obnoxious customer, or step in to separate a fight. Jack had never seen him afraid of anyone.

"I have to put an end to this," Mattie thought, "and quickly."

Before Jack left that night, Mattie found the opportunity to speak to him and arrange to pick him up to go to the caravan the next day. Jack smirked; he thought he was still the winner.

Mattie picked Jack up as arranged, and they left for the caravan. Jack was all smiles and full of self-confidence. Mattie did not say anything as he put his arms around her and pulled her roughly towards him. She would wait until they were away from Stanton.

Mattie had no intentions of going to the caravan that day. She headed for Market Bosworth, but stopped short of the caravan and parked the van in a secluded lay-by.

"What's going on, Mattie? Is there a problem with the van?" Jack looked at Mattie's face, and knew this was something more serious.

"It's over, Jack. I can't do this anymore. You'll push Alf too far one day, and I don't want to be the cause of it. You think you are invincible, but you are really treading on dangerous grounds. If he ever finds out, he'll kill you."

"You seemed to like my dangerous grounds at one time, Mattie. What's changed? Is it Bob you want now? Are you just getting tired of me and think you can throw me over?" Jack growled, his face purple with rage. He was not used to any woman finishing with him. He was the one who said when an affair was over, and this was not over as far as he was concerned.

"I don't need any excuses, Jack. This is over. I'm going back to the pub." Mattie started the engine and turned the van around.

Jack grabbed the steering wheel and pushed Mattie roughly to the other side of the seat.

"Turn this van around now, Mattie, and head for the caravan, or I will drive us into the next vehicle that comes along the road."

Mattie managed to regain control of the van, as Jack did not drive. "You blithering idiot! Let go of the wheel or you'll kill us both." Mattie was white with fear, but determined that she was heading back to the pub.

Just then a big lorry came towards them, and Jack grabbed the wheel again and started to turn towards the oncoming vehicle.

"Stop! Stop. I'll go back and we can talk. Please Jack, if you care for me, don't do this." Mattie was now getting very scared. The caravan was way off the beaten track and she was very afraid to go there with him in this mood, but what choice did she have? When they reached the caravan, Jack pushed her out of the car, and grabbing her arm, dragged her up the steps.

"Jack, please," Mattie begged "See some sense. This is over, and there is nothing you can do about it."

"Oh yes, well that's what you think, Miss High and Mighty." Jack pulled her towards him and started to pull off her sweater. Mattie tried to fight back, but he hit her hard enough to send her flying over the coffee table and onto the couch. He was three times her size and weight, and she had no way of stopping his advances. Eventually, when he had satiated his need for sex and power, he let her go. "Now you can go because I say so. There's plenty more where you came from."

Mattie sobbed, not knowing how she was going to explain all the bruises and bites he had made on her body. She had to go back to the pub and pretend like nothing had happened. She was lucky to have escaped with her life that night, as Jack was certainly way out of control. Mattie went into the small, poorly lit washroom, and managed to clean herself up as much as possible.

"You're a big man, Jack, to hit a woman. I only have to tell Alf and you're a dead man walking," Mattie bluffed as she knew there was no way she could ever tell Alf what had happened that night. There was no doubt in her mind that Alf would indeed kill Jack if he knew what he had done. She also knew that would be the end of her marriage.

They drove back in silence, and after she dropped Jack off, she drove around for a while thinking what she could do. She decided to wait until the pub would be busy and slip in through the back door, hoping she could wash and change before she was seen. As far as anyone would ever know, she had slipped and banged her head on the side of the van. She tiptoed upstairs and did the best she could to minimize the bruises with makeup. The bites which she could not hide, she covered with a high necked sweater and a scarf.

An hour later she breezed into the pub as if she did not have a care in the world. It might look that way, but underneath, Mattie was shaken to the core. She needed to get away for a few days, so she told Alf she was going to go and see Polly and Evan, and visit Sandra and Mike and Martin. It had been months since she had visited them, and Alf was pleased to see her make an effort.

"It'll do you good, love, to go and see your mam and Evan, and it's about time you spent some time with your grandson."

Mattie did go and visit Polly and Evan, where she stayed for a few minutes before saying she had some errands to run. She had phoned Bob and asked him to meet her in Derby. She needed to talk to someone, and had few friends left whom she could confide in. They met in a hotel, and after spending a few hours together, Mattie made her excuses to go back to Polly's. "If Alf phones up, Bob, I have to be there. I can see you again tomorrow, but I have to stay at mam's overnight."

Bob was far more understanding than Jack, and reluctantly agreed to say goodnight.

"I'll meet you back at the hotel in the morning," Bob said, hating to see her go.

The next day Mattie had to make the planned trip to see Sandra and Martin. It was about ten a.m., and Sandra glanced out the window to see her mother walking up the driveway. Mattie was wearing a very short, tight skirt, with a high necked sweater that stopped an inch short of the skirt's hem. She was negotiating the cobbled driveway in a pair of stiletto heels. Sandra looked at her mom and thought she looked like a hooker with her heavy makeup and large earrings. Their relationship had not improved with the birth of Martin. Mattie had made no effort to visit her grandson since his birth.

"Hello, Sandra. I am on my way to Chesterfield to pick up some supplies, so I thought I would pop in and see Martin." Mattie peered into the playpen where he was, for once, quietly playing with his toys.

"Well, this is a surprise. I will put the kettle on and make a cup of tea," Sandra said as she walked past Mattie into the small kitchen.

"Don't bother for me. I can't stay," Mattie called after her.

"You could at least stay for half an hour and visit for a while."

Sandra looked at her mom and saw the telltale bruises, and the turtle neck sweater had not completely concealed the bites on her neck.

It was too much for Sandra, as she had heard the rumours that her mom was having affairs, and now here was the proof. She obviously had a reason for coming, and Sandra realized she was just providing an alibi for Mattie. Sandra walked over to the window and looked down the street. Sure enough, Mattie had parked a block down the street, and there was a definite outline of a man sitting waiting in the passenger seat.

"Mam, you look like a common hooker, and you're covered in bites and bruises. What kind of a mother comes to visit her daughter like that? Don't ever use me as an alibi for your shabby affairs. This is the first time you've been to see your grandson since he was born, and now you can't spare the time to pick him up and give him a cuddle?"

It had been a hectic week as Martin had been fussy all week and Sandra had managed little sleep. It had rained for the best part of the week, and the nappies could not be dried outside. Sandra had to arrange them on a clothes horse in front of the fire and keep rotating them to dry. She was tired and cranky, and Mattie got the full force of her frustrations. It was hard to see all the other grandmas proudly cooing over their grandchildren and taking them for walks. She would have loved to just have a few hours to herself occasionally. Annie had her hands full with Sid, whose health was deteriorating daily, and although she loved her grandson, had precious little time to spare. Mike was a great dad, but he worked shifts, and it was hard for him to be there when he was needed.

"Don't you speak to me like that, my girl! I'm still your mother, and you need to show some respect."

"You have to earn respect, and right now you just make me disgusted!" Sandra could not control her anger and disappointment.

Mattie picked up her coat and stormed out of the house. "It'll be a long while before you see me again," she shouted as she left.

"Good!" Sandra shouted back equally loudly.

She watched as her mother negotiated the cobbles, and then she sat down and cried until no more tears were left. It was out of character for her to have been so blunt and out of control. At that moment, Sandra just wanted to be a million miles away from her parents. She loved her father, but he had always been fairly distant. He was what everyone referred to as a man's man. If that meant he found it difficult to show open affection, then they were right. Sandra thought back over the years and could not remember a time when he had spontaneously given her a hug or a kiss. On the few occasions when Sandra had made any negative comments about her mother, he had always quickly and firmly advised her that it was none of her business. It was frustrating, as it seemed everyone knew of Mattie's affairs and felt quite at liberty to discuss them. Alf chose to turn a blind eye, and for the life of her, Sandra could not see why. Sandra was ashamed of her mother's blatant disregard for any moral values, and hoped people knew she had vastly different principles.

When Mike came home from work that night, he knew immediately something was wrong.

"What's the matter, love? Has that young fellow been giving you a rough time today?" he said, as he went to pick Martin up and give him a hug. "Have you tired your mom out today, little man?"

"It wasn't him. It was my mam. She came here covered in bruises and love bites, and just came to use us as an alibi. She had some fellow in the van waiting for her, and she wasn't here for five minutes. I'm so sick of being in the middle of it, Mike. She's making a fool of my dad, and he either can't see it, or doesn't want to see it." Sandra was close to tears again, and Mike put his arms around her. "I told her not to come again, Mike. I feel awful. She is my mam, but I can't just pretend everything is all right when it isn't."

"Don't let it upset you, love. You know what your mam is like, and she's not about to change. It's her life, and if your dad doesn't seem to bother about it, what can we do?" Mike had long since stopped worrying about Mattie's way of life.

Thirty-Five

BIG DECISIONS ~ 1965

Mattie was true to her word, and did not visit again. Sandra heard stories of what was going on in Stanton, and realized nothing had changed. She made no effort to contact either of her parents. Mike and Martin were her world, and everything in that world was fine. Martin was slowly outgrowing his colic, but was still a bit of a handful. He was a typical Gemini, and needed constant stimulation. Mike's shift work and Sandra's sleepless nights were hard on her. She worried about Mike working down the mine. There were accidents on a frequent basis, and some of them left the victims either disabled or dead. It all came to a head when Mike came home early one day with his hand in bandages. Thankfully it had been a very minor accident, but it could have been much worse. A piece of roof had dislodged and smashed his hand. It required several stitches, but would heal.

"Mike, what next? I worry every day you go to work. What would we ever do without you?"

"I'm getting pretty fed up with it myself, love. There's a lot of talk about them closing some of the pits down, and there's nothing much else to do around here. I think it's time I made a change. I have all my papers, and I am pretty sure that I can get a job in any company that needs a machinist millwright. How would you feel about leaving Leabrooks?"

Sandra was surprised and pleased Mike was thinking the same way she was.

"Are you really serious? Do you mean it?" Sandra hugged him. "Oh please, Mike, let's do it. Let's make a big move."

"How big are you thinking?" Mike had an idea what she was talking about. The past few months there had been many ads in the *News of the World* newspaper. Australia and Canada were both in the middle of huge campaigns to attract skilled workers to emigrate.

They had both looked at the ads and wondered what it would be like to start all over again in a new country.

"Right now, I would love to start a new life in a new country, as long as it is with you and Martin. You are all I need. Just think, Mike: No being in the middle of conflicts, just our own little family. Can we check it out, Mike? Please?" Sandra saw the smile on Mike's face and knew he had been thinking the same thing.

"Do you really think you could leave everyone behind, love?"

"The hardest of all will be grandma and granddad, and Auntie Elsie and Uncle Joe. Of course I will miss your mam and dad, and I suppose I might miss mine, but we can write, and if we do well, we can come back and visit. What about you, Mike? Do you think that you can leave everyone behind?"

"I have thought about it for a few weeks now, and yes, I can. I am ready for a fresh start, and as long as you are okay with this, let's start making some enquiries."

It did not take long for Sandra to do some research and book an appointment at Leeds immigration office.

"Let's keep it quiet until we know for sure if this is what we want, and if we get accepted," Mike said, as he was a little concerned that if any of the family knew, they would try and convince them both to stay. He was particularly concerned about his dad, as Sid had not been doing well of late. His emphysema was progressing quickly, and there were times when he rushed to the door, gasping for air. Sid loved Martin and would really miss him. Martin was just what Sid had hoped for in a grandson. He was a little rascal and had a mind of his own. Even as a baby he showed signs of being strong and independent. Sid's failing health had slowed him down somewhat, but he was always the patriarch.

The day arrived at last for the interview in Leeds. Polly and Evan had agreed to babysit Martin, and were only too happy to have him. They did not question what the reason was, so thankfully Sandra did not have to explain. The interview was long, and this was only the preliminary interview. The first session was really to determine where the prospective immigrants wanted to go. There were two films: one on Canada and one on Australia. Sandra and Mike watched them both in awe, seeing lifestyles they had only dreamed about. Like most things, Sandra and Mike were in agreement that Canada was their first choice. One of the reasons for choosing Canada was that it was closer in proximity to England, so it would be easier to travel between the two countries. The rocky mountain landscape had mesmerized them both with its beauty. The interviewer took an instant liking to the young couple and was impressed with Mike's qualifications.

"You are just what Canada is looking for, Mike. There is a real shortage of skilled trades people, and with your papers, I am sure that you can pretty much walk into any job you choose. Now, if you want to go to Quebec and work in a mine, I can also arrange to have your fare paid. All you will have to do is sign a two year contract with the mine. Of course you will be living in a work camp until the contract is completed. At the end of two years, you are then free to send for your wife and work wherever you please."

Mike and Sandra looked at each other in disbelief. How could he possibly think that they would be willing to separate for two years? The interviewer smiled as he saw their exchange.

"If you choose to go somewhere else in Canada, you will have to pay your own fare. The good news is that, if you are accepted, we will give you a three year interest free loan to pay your fare. I think it looks like that is the option you would choose."

"Yes, whatever decision we make, it will be a choice for the three of us. One of the reasons we want to emigrate is that we want to move away from a mining area. We are looking for a good place to bring up children; somewhere where there is clean air, open spaces and pine trees. We have been doing a little research of our own, and we do like the looks of British Columbia."

"Well, I have just come back from a tour of Canada, and one of the places that impressed me very much was Kamloops in B.C." The interviewer pulled out an album with some of his personal pictures inside. "It was beautiful, and I am sure this little town is going to grow. It is on a main route to Vancouver, and it is already attracting some new industry."

"It is beautiful. I've never seen sky so blue," Sandra said in admiration. Mike was sold the moment he saw the rolling hills on either side of the river, and all of the surrounding lakes. He had always loved the outdoors, and the thoughts of having all that within a few miles of the town was almost too good to be true.

"We still have to do some more paperwork, and there will be medicals and such to complete before we can actually give you immigration papers. My personal feeling is that you will have no problem in being accepted. Go home, discuss it all again between yourselves, and if you are both sure you want to go to Canada, start making some preliminary plans."

Once outside, it was hard for them both to contain their excitement. "How are we going to keep quiet about this?" Mike said. "I am sure that one look at us and everyone will know that something is up." Sandra put the big file of maps and papers that they had been given, in the back of the car, and was anxious to get home and look through them.

It was late when they arrived at Polly and Evan's to pick up Martin. He was supposed to be asleep, but typical Martin, he had other ideas. Each time Polly had taken him to the foot of the stairs, he had started to complain loudly. The only way they had kept him amused was by singing "Mairzy Doats." It was a song that had come out the year Sandra was born, and Polly had sung it many times to her when she was a baby.

Polly was holding one hand and Evan the other as they circled Martin around, singing:

Mairzy doats and dozy doats and liddle lamzy divey
A kiddley divey too, wouldn't you?
Yes! Mairzy doats and dozy doats and liddle lamzy divey
A kiddley divey too, wouldn't you?

They both looked ready to drop at any minute, and Martin was just as wide awake now as when his parents had left.

"You little monkey, come here," Sandra held out her arms. Martin was not used to being left with anyone, and quickly let go of Polly and Evan and ran to his mom.

"He just wouldn't settle, love. We tried everything." Polly had never had trouble with children, and could not believe she was unable to get Martin to sleep.

"Don't worry, Mama. He will be asleep in five minutes once we get him into the car." Sandra remembered all the times they had loaded him into the car late at night, and had driven around the streets until he fell asleep. The only issue then was getting him out of the car and into bed before he woke up again. Mike and Sandra were both grateful for the diversion, and an excuse to leave for home before they had to answer any questions about their day.

Sure enough, Martin was asleep before they had even reached the end of the road, and Sandra and Mike each had a million dreams in their heads about what the future might hold.

The next day Mike was on day shift, and when he came home from work, they spread out all the immigration information on the floor and looked at maps and statistics on population and economy and industry. The more they saw, the more they knew they were making the right decision.

"We have to enter this with a one way ticket, love," Mike said. "If we are going to make a commitment, then it can't have an escape route. I am sure that it won't all be easy, but it will never work if we have a feeling it is just an adventure. This is for real."

"I know it is what I want, and I am just as convinced as you are that we have to make a go of it. That means selling all our possessions, other than what we can take with us. I don't want to have anything to come back to." Sandra reached for his hand. "If we have each other and Martin, we have all we need."

Just then the door swung open, and in came Maurice. He had a habit of not knocking on the door. Martin and Maurice had been friends for many years, living in adjacent streets for all their lives. Maurice was more "family" than friend, and usually came in by the back door, helping himself to any baking that was on the kitchen counter as he came in.

"Damn," said Mike as Maurice walked in.

"That's a fine greeting," Maurice said as he walked over to the pile of papers. "So what are you two up to? You look like you're planning to rob a bank or something." It was too late to try and hide what they were looking at.

"Maurice, you have to promise to keep this quiet. We haven't been accepted yet, and we don't want anyone to know until we are sure we are in fact going," Mike swore Maurice to secrecy.

Maurice sat on the floor with them both, and they were shocked to learn that he had also been looking at the immigration ads. "I've been looking at this as well, but Evelyn won't go. She is afraid to leave everyone behind. She says we don't know anybody over there, and she'll have no friends. If I tell her you are going, she might change her mind. If she does, can we come with you?"

Evelyn was a shy young lady, barely five feet tall, and very lacking in self-confidence. She did not mix with many people, but was always comfortable with Mike and Sandy.

Maurice sat and went over all the papers with them, getting more interested by the minute.

"You can tell Evelyn. If she wants to go, then you have to get hold of the immigration people quickly, but as I said, this is not for general knowledge." Maurice was not much taller than Evelyn, but his cocky mannerisms made up for whatever he lacked in height. He walked out of the door feeling ten feet tall. He was sure Evelyn would rethink her decision if she knew Mike and Sandra were going to go to Canada. It took a little convincing, but Maurice managed to talk Evelyn into going to look at the information. He was actually surprised when she agreed to set up an interview.

Everything moved so quickly, it was just three weeks later when Sandra and Mike got their approval. Maurice and Evelyn were approved shortly afterwards, and now all they had to decide was how they wanted to go, and when they wanted to go. The fare was not much different if they went by sea or air, and they all agreed they would go by sea. They wanted the experience of going by sea, and then travelling the breadth of Canada by train.

"Wow, can you imagine all of the countryside we will see? It will take three days and nights just to cross Canada from coast to coast. We have to tell everyone now," Sandra said, dreading having to tell her grandparents, and especially Auntie Elsie and Uncle Joe. They had always thought of her as their own, and she could anticipate their dismay when they heard the news.

"I know," said Mike, equally concerned about breaking the news to his parents and his sister. Mike and his sister were not overly close, as there was a big gap in age, but she was his sister and he loved her. "Well, we'd best get it over with right away."

Polly and Evan were both very upset to hear the news, but they loved Mike and had every confidence he would look after his family wherever they might be.

"Oh, love. Are you really sure?" Polly asked.

"Yes Mama. Mike and I have given it a lot of thought, and we both think we have a better future in Canada than we have here. It sounds like a great place to raise a family, and Mike will be out of the mines, Mama."

Evan looked downcast. He and Polly had spent more time with Sandra than her parents had. He would have loved to have had a child with Polly, but it was not to be. Sandra was as close as he had ever come to having a child of his own. Sandra did her best to assure them they would always stay in touch, and that they would plan on coming back for visits as soon as they could afford it.

The same scenario played out at Auntie Elsie and Uncle Joe's, and it was even harder in a sense, as Sandra knew they were both devastated by the news.

Elsie and Joe watched them walk away, and Joe put his arms around his wife. "It doesn't matter how far they go, Elsie. I know our Sandra will never forget us."

"I know we will never forget her, Joe," Elsie said as she sank into the chair.

Sandra and Mike went to Stanton and told Alf and Mattie, who were surprised at the news, but took the announcement much more calmly than anyone else. Mattie looked at the young couple and envied their youth and enthusiasm. Alf had a great respect for Mike, and he knew Sandra would always be taken care of as long as Mike lived. At the back of his mind, he knew Sandra and her mom had become very distant, and he knew the reason why. Alf was not a demonstrative person, but he put his arms around his daughter, and as he hugged her, he hid a tear.

"Good luck to you both. I think you are old enough to know what you are doing, and there's not much future in the mines in England at the moment." It was a difficult visit, as Sandra thought how many times in the past she would have given anything for a hug like that. Now that she was going so far away, her father finally showed some open emotion. Sandra looked at her mother and wished with all her heart that things could have been different between them. Since having Martin and becoming a mother herself, she realized it was not always easy, but how she wished for any show of emotion. Mattie was more troubled by the announcement than she would ever tell anyone. There was no question she loved her daughter and her family. Many nights she had tossed and turned, rethinking the past and wishing she could have been a different type of mother.

"Look after them, Mike," she exclaimed, and giving them all a very brief hug, she disappeared into the back kitchen, where she sat and cried for all the lost years.

Mike told his mom and dad, and as expected, Sid was very upset. Annie took it more in stride, but then she never showed her feelings very much. It was not that she didn't have feelings, but rather that she was a very private person. That night, she lay awake for hours and hid her tears in the pillow. She had lost one son shortly after his birth, and now twenty four years later she was losing another one to a foreign country thousands of miles away.

Sid rushed to the door and gasped for air. His emphysema was always worse when he was stressed. "God be good and let me see them all again," he prayed, but he had little hopes of his prayers coming true. He was far sicker than anyone knew, and had serious doubts he would ever see them all again. Annie went to pull him back inside and closed the door.

"Come on, Sid. Let's get to bed. It's no use worrying. They have made their decision, and you can't blame our Mike for wanting to get away from the mines."

Once everyone had been told and it was all out in the open, things happened quickly. The first thing that had to be done was to book the passage. There was the house to sell, and the two cars to sell, the Ford Consul Mike had worked on, and the Volkswagen they had recently purchased; all had to be advertised as quickly as possible. There was a house full of old but good furniture to get rid of. Mike had to give his notice at the colliery.

Looking at prospective dates for sailing out of Southampton, the cheapest passage was on a Cunard Liner, called The Franconia, which was due to sail on 25th October 1965. Both of them being very naïve, they never equated the cheap fare with the fact that a late winter sailing of the Atlantic would be far from pleasant.

An estate agent came to view the small detached house, and was pleasantly surprised by the updated interior. "You will have no trouble getting your price for this. It is a little gem," he beamed, as he could see this would be an easy and quick commission. Sure enough, within the first week of listing they had a prospective buyer. He and his wife liked the house, but it was not big enough for their needs. "If you are selling that Volkswagen in the driveway, I would be interested in buying it, mate," he said to Mike.

"It's for sale, and I have all the records of the repair and maintenance on it." Mike loved the car and had no qualms in testifying to its reliability. Before they left, they had agreed upon a price and the buyer had paid a deposit. Not only that, but he was agreeable to Mike using it until the time of their departure to Canada.

"Wow, what a stroke of luck was that?" Mike beamed as they

went back indoors. The following week the agent brought another prospect. It was a quiet young man who came to view the house with his mother, who did most of the talking. He was obviously in love with the house, and was already talking of how he was going to furnish it. His mother looked at him sternly and said, "We'll give it some more thought before we make an offer. That stone wall needs to be finished, and we will have to do some yard work. It all takes money, you know." After they had left, the agent assured Mike and Sandra they would be placing an offer. "She's just trying to wheedle down the price, but he is determined to buy it. I can tell a buyer when I see one."

He was right, and Sandra and Mike accepted the offer. "Whew, I never thought it would sell so fast. I can't believe how lucky we have been so far," Mike breathed a sigh of relief.

Maurice and Evelyn were going through all the same motions, and they too had good luck with everything. "It's as if everything is meant to happen for the best," Sandra said. "I think we were destined to make this move."

The buyer wanted a quick possession, so Sandra did her best to sell or give away furniture and possessions not destined to go to Canada with them. She was busy packing boxes when there was a knock on the door. It was early morning, and Sandra was not used to company at that time. When she opened the door it was the young man's mother.

"Hello. What can I do for you?" Sandra asked, thinking to herself that the deal was signed and sealed, so it could not be to haggle about price.

"I am sorry, Mrs. Lewis, but the sale is off."

"What? Your son has paid his deposit, and the papers are signed. We leave for Canada in seven weeks." Sandra was incredulous, and her tone was less than polite.

At that the woman burst in to tears. "My son is dead. He had a massive brain hemorrhage and died last night."

"Come in. I am so sorry." Sandra instantly regretted her terse comments a few moments ago. "I'll put the kettle on. Please sit down and tell me what happened."

His mother explained that he had been so looking forward to moving in, and she had never seen him so happy. In between sobs, she told Sandra what had happened.

"He spent half the night drawing up plans of what he was going to do with the yard and how he was going to add a conservatory onto the back. I had to tell him to put his papers away and get to bed. It was nearly midnight before he went. About two in the morning, me and my Ted heard him cry out. It was an awful cry and we both jumped out of bed right away. It was already too late; he was lying in a pool of blood and was choking. We called the doctor right away, but he said there was nothing we could have done. So, you see that I am sorry for your inconvenience, but we have worse things to fret about."

"I'll call the agent right away, Mrs. Morton, and let them know. I am sure they will be able to return the deposit. We would not think of keeping it under the circumstances. Please forgive me for my first response." Sandra did not know what to say. Of course she was upset the deal had fallen through so closely to their intended departure, but she could not imagine the grief his family were going through at this time.

After Mrs. Morton had left, Sandra went to call the agent and tell him the news. He was not happy the sale had fallen through, and even less happy that his commission would not be paid out as quickly as he had hoped.

"I'll put another ad in the paper, Sandra. Don't worry. I know it will sell again." True to his word, he quickly placed another ad, and again there was a fast response. He set up a viewing for the following week, and as Sandra and Mike saw the young couple walk up the driveway, they both had a feeling that the faces were familiar. It was a couple of students who had studied at Swanwick with them both several years ago. They loved the house at first sight and wrote up an offer that very night. It was slightly less than the first deal, but both Sandra and Mike were happy to sell to them. They loved the way the house had been decorated, and even made a deal on the oddments of furniture that were still left.

Everything was falling into place, and the last few weeks were full of goodbyes, as one by one, friends and family came to wish them both well. Mike and Sandra spent the last two weeks with Annie and Sid, as their house was now empty and everything already shipped ahead of them. Mike had helped his mom bring the bed downstairs into the front room, as Sid was now having difficulty in climbing the stairs. His emphysema was playing havoc with his breathing. It was hard to see the sadness in both of their faces as they seemed to try and hold every last memory of them all in a mental photograph, which they could pull out at a later date when they were so many thousand miles away. One particular snap shot Sid would remember with a chuckle.

"What the heck! It's the first time I have ever seen anyone take a bath in the kitchen sink!" Sid was bent over double laughing, as he walked into the kitchen late at night. Sandra had thought that Annie and Sid were both fast asleep, and was having a strip wash in the kitchen before going upstairs to bed. She was balanced precariously on one foot with the other foot in the high kitchen sink.

"Sid, what are you doing up at this time? I thought you were fast asleep." Sandra pulled the towel around her as quickly as possible.

"Eeh, lass. I wish I could still cock my leg that high! I just got up for a glass of water."

"Go back to bed, Sid. I'll bring you one in a couple of minutes." Sandra smiled, a little embarrassed at being caught in such an awkward moment.

The weather was awful, and it had rained for days when they went to bed in Leabrooks for the last time. The forecast for the next day was fog, and Mike and Sandra had booked a cab to take them all to the train station. The train was due to leave at 7:00 p.m., and they had allowed enough time for any delays in getting there on time. Sid and Annie both decided that it would be too difficult for them to say goodbyes at the station, so were glad of the time together before the night of their departure. Sid was very emotional, and Annie tried her best to hide her sorrow in seeing them go. "Don't forget your mam and dad, lad. We're always here, and you've always a home to come back to." Mike and Sandra knew they meant what they said.

"The cab is already half an hour late. The fog must be bad all over. We'll not have any time to waste at the station," Mike said as he looked through the curtains into the bleak evening.

"Maybe it stopped to pick up Maurice and Evelyn first," Sandra said hopefully. At last there was the faint distant glimmer of head lights, and he could see the cab sign on top. "It's here, Sandy. This is it." Mike looked through the window and could just see the outline of the passengers in the back. Maurice and Evelyn were already in the cab and the driver came out to help with the luggage.

"Cor blimey, mate! You sure don't pack light!" he said as he hefted the heavy suitcases, and with great difficulty packed them into the boot along with those of Maurice and Evelyn. Mike and Sandra watched the cases disappear into the boot, and walked back to the door where Sid and Annie were standing, arms around each other, each looking very sad. "Bye, Annie and Sid. Thank you both for everything. We love you," Sandra said through tears. "Martin, give grandma and grandpa a big hug and a kiss." Martin dutifully complied. He loved his grandparents, and he and Sid were definitely cut from the same cloth. Sid hugged Martin as he tried to hide his own tears. Mike hugged his mom and could feel her body shaking with emotion.

"Love you, mom and dad, and don't worry about us." He knew this was an impossibility, as they would always worry about their son and his family.

The cab driver honked his horn, and Mike and Sandra took one last look around before waving a tearful last farewell. "Oh Mike, I hope we are doing the right thing," Sandra said as the cab pulled away from the curb. "Your dad looked like all the life had drained out of him. Are we being really selfish? It's not going to be easy for either of them when we are gone." They had both been caught up in all of the excitement of planning a new life, and now that it was time to go, the magnitude of their decision really hit them.

"We can't think that way, love. We have to go with the determination that this IS the right decision and that we are going to make a new and better life in Canada. Once we have made our fortune, we will come back and see them all every year." Mike put his arms around Sandra and Martin, not letting either of them see his own emotions. It had been really difficult to say the last goodbye, and he was more worried about his dad than he had let anyone know. He knew in his heart that with the pit closures and the lack of any decent employment opportunities in the area, they had made the right choice. The money from the sale of the house and the two vehicles was a huge comfort, as they were setting off to a new country with no job lined up, and no home to go to. The plan was that an immigration consultant would meet them at their final destination, Kamloops, and he would take them to a motel where they would stay until they could find accommodation. It was up to Mike to do his own job search, but he was young and confident in his own abilities.

The cab was moving at a snail's pace, and it was almost impossible to see the edge of the road. *It's like we are disappearing into the fog, never to come out the other side,* Sandra thought to herself, but tried very hard to smile and stay positive.

"Bloody hell, I could walk faster than I can drive," the cab driver complained as he tried opening his side window and peering through the pea soup fog. Thankfully there was very little traffic on the road, as only people with no option were out in such weather. "I've been driving a cab for twenty years, and I've never seen a night like this."

"Just our luck." Mike was glad to hear that the cabby was an experienced driver. He would need to have his wits about him on such a drive. "Are we going to make it to the station on time?"

"Don't you worry, lad. I'll have you there with time to spare. I checked with the station before I left, and your train's due in late. Nothing will be moving very fast tonight."

Martin had fallen asleep the minute the cab pulled away from Leabrooks, and Sandra cuddled him in her arms and smiled as she thought how cute he looked in his new outfit. She had been told that the Canadian winters were very cold, and to take lots of warm clothing. On a shopping trip to Derby, Sandra had fallen in love with a little brown tweed jacket that had a matching hat with ear flaps. It fit Martin perfectly, and he looked just like a little lumberjack. At fifteen months old he was all boy, and the outfit looked like it was made for him. Sandra had chosen to wear a wool suit, and had splurged on a beautiful brown velvet hat that was trimmed with fur. She loved hats and this one really suited her. Mike was wearing his overcoat, and looked very young and handsome. Maurice and Evelyn were also suitably dressed for the weather and the long trip ahead.

"Thanks, mate," Mike said, as he shook the cabby's hand. "I don't know how you made it in such bad fog." Mike paid the fare and gave the driver a good tip. The platform was almost bare. The only people waiting were a few fellow travellers and the few people who had turned out in such weather to see them all off. Sandra scanned the faces and was sad to see that Grandma was not there. She walked over to Grandpa Evan, and he gave her a big hug. "Your mama sends her love, my duck, but she could not face seeing you leave."

"It's all right, Grandpa. I understand. Tell her how much I love her, and that she will never be out of my thoughts. Bless you for coming on such a horrible night." Sandra loved Evan without measure. Her grandparents meant the world to her and always would. Auntie Elsie and Uncle Joe were too emotional to go to the station, but sat at home feeling very bereft. Mattie and Alf were there, and Sandra walked over to them. For a brief moment, Sandra thought she saw her mother shed a tear. Her father pulled her towards him and gave her a big bear hug.

"I'll miss you, love, but I know Mike will take good care of you all until we see you again." Sandra was amazed as this was the second time in a month that her father had been emotional. For the past twenty three years she could not ever remember him showing her so much affection. He reached out to shake Mike's hand.

"Look after them both, Mike, and make sure they remember us all."

It wasn't a long wait before they heard the train whistle as it entered the station. It thundered through the fog in a haze of smoke and steam, coming to a screeching halt as the wheels came to a stop on the steel rails. A porter jumped off the train and began loading passengers immediately. The train was already behind schedule and there was no time to waste.

Mattie looked at the trio as they were about to step on the train, and suddenly saw her own life flash before her. Where had the time gone to, and how much of her daughter's life had she missed? She wanted desperately to hold on to her and to tell her she loved her. It was too late. They were already on the train and it was slowly pulling out of the station.

Mattie clung to Alf, and cried genuine tears of regret. Regret for all the years of lost time, when she had put personal pleasure over parenting. Regret for the last several months of strained relationship after her last visit to Leabrooks. *Damn that Lambert blood. Am I such a bad mother? I really do love her but somehow I never seem to be able to get it right,* Mattie thought as she hid her face in the rough tweed of Alf's jacket.

Alf was always there for her, and he put his arms around his wife and felt her relax in the warmth of his embrace. He was still the only man she truly loved and knew she could depend on. She would need him now more than ever.

Evan watched the train pull away, and the last sight of Sandra was of her fur hat being waved out the window as the train disappeared into the fog. "God keep them safe and please bring us together again soon," he whispered into the night.

Mike found an almost empty carriage for them all and stowed

their luggage before settling down for the journey to Southampton. Maurice wrapped his arm around Evelyn, who was wiping the tears from her eyes.

"I hate goodbyes," she cried.

"It's not goodbye, love. It's hello to a new life." Maurice was just as eager to leave the mines as Mike was.

Mike could see Sandra was close to tears as she wrapped Martin in a quilt and placed him on the empty seat beside them.

"Please let him sleep until we reach Southampton," Sandra whispered.

That comment got a smile out of Evelyn, as she knew what a handful he could be. "Now you really are asking for a miracle," she said, as she looked at Martin swaddled in the quilt. He had been a perfect angel that night and they were both hoping this was going to be carried on throughout the long ten day voyage. Sandra had Mike to lean on, both figuratively and literally. It was a huge step they were taking, and as she snuggled into his side, she knew that the two most important people in her world were with her to face whatever life in a new country might bring.

Since she was thirteen years old, Mike had been there for her, and never once had he let her down. Mike looked down at the girl he had worshipped since the first day he had seen her, and his thoughts mirrored her own. He knew that whatever it took, he would provide a good life for them all in Canada. "Cheer up, my love. There is a new life waiting for us. It's going to be all right. As long as we have each other, we have everything."

"I know." Sandra reached up to kiss him, and as their lips met, any feeling of trepidation vanished. "Here we come, Canada!" Sandra smiled.

Postscript

The journey would bring some unexpected trials and tribulations, but they eventually made it to Kamloops, B.C. on 5th November 1965. Within the next three years, Mattie and Alf, Belle and Alf, Susan and Gary, and Mama Polly and Grandpa Evan would all end up following Sandra, Mike and Martin to Kamloops. There were births, marriages, deaths and divorces, as new branches grew and old boughs broke or died. Mattie continued to have affairs. Alf loved her and stayed with her until the day he died prematurely at the age of sixty-seven. Mattie survived for another twenty-five years. Before her death, Mattie finally found comfort in her own skin, and became the mother Sandra had dreamed of. Sandra also learned to be more forgiving when, many years later, circumstances took her own life in a different direction.

If there is any moral to this story it is: Life is what you make it. Nothing happens by accident. And the most important of all is that family is forever.

The third book, tentatively titled *Fallen Leaves*, is still a work in progress. It will continue the life of the central characters, up to the time that, one by one, their leaves fall from the family tree. As old leaves fall, new shoots grow and the circle of life continues. The final book of the Twisted Tree series is written as a biography and not a book of fiction. It will be my life from 1965–1981, when again, I end the book at a new beginning.

I have been very fortunate in sharing my life with two incredible men. I have loved, and been loved by them both. Wildly different, but, as I said before, nothing happens by accident.

About the Author

Sandy Latka was born in a century-old stone cottage in Derbyshire, England. Her eclectic and interesting career spans both sides of the Atlantic Ocean. Extremely well-travelled throughout the world, she received culinary course certificates from the School of Cordon Bleu in Paris and a Villa in Tuscany. She worked in the fields of interior design, real estate, banking, regional sales, inspirational seminars and government, and is the past owner of a British restaurant and pub and an interior design company.

Sandy's first foray into the literary world was with the publication of an internal reference book for a major international credit bureau. This project allowed her to travel across Canada from coast to coast, conducting interviews with government officials and statisticians. For someone who loves to travel, enjoys interesting conversations, and the challenge of being "put on the spot," this was a dream project. *Branches* is her second novel, part of a trilogy of books based on the lives of two families joined together by fate and fortune.

A member of Penticton Writers and Publishers, Sandy currently splits her time between a cliff-top home in Seba Beach, Alberta, overlooking Lake Wabamun, and a condominium on the lakefront in Osoyoos, British Columbia. Both of these locations are perfect sanctuaries for her research and writing.

Made in the USA
San Bernardino, CA
25 June 2015